CUT DEAD

Mark Sennen was born in Epsom, Surrey and later spent his teenage years on a smallholding in Shropshire. He attended the University of Birmingham and read Cultural Studies at CCCS. Mark has had a number of occupations, being variously a farmer, drummer and programmer. Now his hi-tech web developer's suite, otherwise known as a shed in the garden, has been converted to a writer's den and he writes almost full-time.

Please visit www.marksennen.com for information on the DI Charlotte Savage series.

Also by Mark Sennen

Touch
Bad Blood

MARK SENNEN

Cut Dead

AVON

This novel is entirely a work of fiction.
The names, characters and incidents portrayed in it are
the work of the author's imagination. Any resemblance to
actual persons, living or dead, events or localities is
entirely coincidental.

AVON

A division of HarperCollins*Publishers*
77–85 Fulham Palace Road,
London W6 8JB

www.harpercollins.co.uk

A Paperback Original 2014

1

Copyright © Mark Sennen 2014

Mark Sennen asserts the moral right to
be identified as the author of this work

A catalogue record for this book is
available from the British Library

ISBN-13: 978-0-00-751819-7

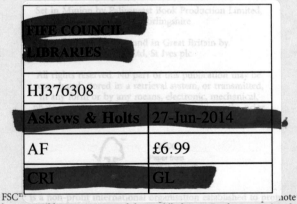

FSC™ is a non-profit international organisation established to promote
the responsible management of the world's forests. Products carrying the
FSC label are independently certified to assure consumers that they come
from forests that are managed to meet the social, economic and
ecological needs of present and future generations,
and other controlled sources.

Find out more about HarperCollins and the environment at
www.harpercollins.co.uk/green

Acknowledgements

It doesn't seem so long ago that I was writing the acknowledgements for the first DI Savage novel and now here we are at book three already. Thanks for getting this far must go to the following:

All at HarperCollins/Avon for continued faith in Charlotte. My editor, Lydia Vassar-Smith, offered oodles of helpful advice on Cut Dead (most of which I took). Keshini Naidoo provided flawless copy editing which went well past simply correcting my cringeworthy errors. The rest of the Avon team (the unsung heroes) did all the hard work which actually gets the book into your hands.

Thanks to Claire Roberts at Trident Media for excellent representation, advice and more.

A special shout-out to Neil Vogler and Bertel Martin for numerous pub conversations on all things literary, Plymouth, and beyond.

Thanks to my wife, Gitte, for ongoing life support and also to my daughters who now accept that their dad is an author - although they still don't understand why they are not allowed to read the books.

Finally, as always, the biggest debt of gratitude goes to you, the reader.

***

I'd like to highlight two organisations which are mentioned in Cut Dead. They would appreciate your support:
Dartmoor Rescue Group
Storybook Dads

To the real Charlotte Savage

Prologue

The song ends and Mummy and Daddy clap. The candles on the cake flicker in the draught and Mummy tells you to blow them out. You lean forward and purse your lips, your brother moving alongside you to help, and you both puff with all your might. One, two, three, four, five, six. All out. The room plunges into darkness and you feel a sudden fear.

'Lights on!' Mummy says and Daddy switches the light on and marches forward, the big knife in his hand, the blade shiny, sharp, ready for cutting.

The big knife lives in the kitchen, stuck to the wall above the cooker by magic. At least that's what Daddy calls it. The knife winks at you every time you pass by, a flash of light reflecting off the stainless steel, the glare mesmerising. You don't like being in the kitchen alone with the knife, especially not at night.

Because that's when the big knife talks to you.

'I am temptation,' it says. 'I am the explorer. I am the light.'

You've heard someone else speak like that too, in the cold of the church, but although the words are similar you don't think they can mean the same thing.

'OK, so who's going to have the first piece?' Daddy says and

1

for a moment you forget about the knife and instead concentrate on Daddy's words, knowing he is trying to trick you. You mustn't be greedy, must always be polite; if you aren't, you'll get hit. You point to your brother. He smiles and claps his hands.

'Can I, Daddy, can I?'

'Of course you can, here, let's see.'

Daddy takes the knife and rests it on the white icing, using his other hand to push the blade down into the cake. He cuts again and then slides the knife under the cake and withdraws the slice. He stops. Doesn't give the piece to your brother after all. Daddy frowns. The inside doesn't look right, the yellow sponge is soft and mushy, not cooked properly. Daddy doesn't like that. He turns to Mummy and sneers at her.

'What's this?' *Daddy's face reddens.* 'I'm out working all day and you can't prepare a cake on this, of all days. Our special day. What do you think, boys?'

'Naughty Mummy, bad Mummy, naughty Mummy, bad Mummy.' *You and your brother start the chant, the chant your Daddy has taught you. You hate singing the words, but if you don't there'll be trouble. There's been a lot of trouble in recent months because Daddy's changed in some way. You don't understand why, but you wonder if it's your fault, something you've done.*

'Yes, boys. Naughty Mummy.'

Daddy steps forwards and slaps Mummy in the face. She raises her hands, but it's too late. The blow catches her and knocks her sideways. Then Daddy has her by the hair. He is dragging her out of the room into the hall, pulling her up the stairs. Mummy is screaming and Daddy is shouting. They are upstairs now, the door to their bedroom slamming shut. You know what's going on up there because once you peeked through the keyhole. Daddy is doing something to Mummy and she doesn't like it. Afterwards Daddy will be sorry and Mummy will say everything is going to be alright, but this time you wonder if Mummy's words will come true because the big knife has gone. Daddy has taken it with him. You wonder how you will be able to cut the cake without it, but then you remember the cake is bad.

Your brother is crying and you tell him to pull himself together. You whisper the words Mummy says about everything being OK, but even as you say them you know they are lies. Parents lie to their children all the time. They tell them things called white lies. But there are other types of lies as well, other colours. You've learnt that.

'It's OK.' You repeat the words to your brother as you touch him on the shoulder, but you know something has changed today and nothing is ever going to be OK again.

Now

'Evening, Charlotte,' someone says as she climbs from the car. Another person nods. Not a greeting, just a simple recognition that she's here to share the load. The dirty work.

She walks across the field. Except it isn't a field, the mud more sludge than earth, pools of water in footprints showing her the way from the gate to the tent. Not a tent for camping. Not sleeping bags to slip into at night, snuggle down, cool air on face, stars above visible through the opening of the tent.

No, there are no stars tonight, only cloud from which rain tumbles in streams, as if from a million hosepipes. There are bags, yes, although these ones are black, the tent white, vertical sides flapping in the breeze, and inside, the light comes not from a weak torch but from halogens. The people here aren't on holiday, not smiling, not laughing apart from one joke about the weather, the incessant rain. Even then the laughter is nervous, not genuine, as if the banter which preceded the joke was merely to take minds off the task in hand, away from the hole in the ground which the tent covers. But words can't do that, can't take her thoughts away from the horror down in the pit where a pump thrums, slurping water up a hose to discharge it a few metres away. A generator chugs somewhere in the background and every now and then the halogens dim for a moment as the engine misses a beat.

She wonders who set this all up, who coordinated everything, who the hell is in charge of this nightmare. But really, those details don't matter at the moment. The only thing which matters is that she doesn't throw up, doesn't cry, that she keeps her mind on the job.

Job, what a laugh. They don't pay her enough for this; couldn't. Nothing is worth this. Staring down into the hole, seeing the pitiful sight within, smelling the decomposing flesh, thinking about her own little girl, dead years now. Thinking about her other children too, knowing she loves them more than anything. Knowing nothing can be worse than this for a mother, for a parent, for anyone with an ounce of humanity inside them.

And while the others are talking, making comments, offering suggestions, she's letting her mind go blank, allowing just one thought through: a promise to the three souls dissolving down there in the mud that she will find who did this. A promise she will do more than just find them.

Chapter One

Bere Ferrers, Devon. Saturday 14th June. 11.20 a.m.

Joanne Black had managed the farm for more than half a dozen years, ever since her husband had run off and left her for a younger model. At first it had been a real struggle, a steep learning curve for a woman who had never even liked gardening and who used to get squeamish if the cat brought in a mouse. Needs must, though, and within a couple of years she was looking after the five hundred acres as if she had been born to the task. Help had come from a neighbouring farmer and from her farmworker and if either had been sceptical at first, they'd never showed it.

Joanne had inherited the farm from an uncle who had no other relatives. At first the plan had been to sell the place and do something with the money, but somewhere down inside Joanne had felt that was wrong. As a child she'd often visited Uncle Johnny. She remembered one occasion when she helped him bottle feed an orphan lamb. 'He needs you, he does,' her uncle had said and Joanne felt a warmth in knowing that. Back home her mother said her eyes had sparkled when the lamb nuzzled the bottle and sucked down the milk. Somehow the uncle had seen that sparkle and years later, when writing his will, he'd taken a gamble. Right at

5

the moment she and William, her ex, had been going to consult the land agent about selling the farm, Joanne had changed her mind. Taken a gamble too. Uncle Johnny may have believed Joanne was a long shot, but hell, she was going to see to it his bet paid off.

William's view was that she'd gone mad. What did they know about farming? Wouldn't a couple of million in the bank be better than feeding lambs on a cold, frosty January morning?

No, it wouldn't.

Joanne chuckled to herself now as she opened the post. Bills, yes, but a letter from Tesco confirming a contract to supply them with organic lamb, and two bookings for the holiday cottages. There was also a large cardboard tube. Joanne pulled off the end-caps and extracted a roll of paper which turned out to be a poster. A note slipped out from the tube too and she recognised her brother's handwriting: 'Hope you like this, sis. Happy Birthday, love Hal.' Hal lived in the US and worked for a large software company. Joanne unrolled the poster and gasped when she realised it was an aerial photograph of the entire farm. She had looked at maps on the web where you could load up such an image, but this was much better quality and at poster-size the detail was amazing.

Spreading the picture out on the kitchen table, Joanne spent a good ten minutes examining every last nook and cranny on the farm. As she worked her way down one edge of the poster, where a corner of a field had been left to seed because the combine harvester couldn't turn in the odd little space, she spotted a strange marking on the ground. She remembered how archaeologists used aerial pictures to find and map the extent of prehistoric monuments and wondered if the markings could be something similar. If it had been in the middle of the field she would have been worried about preservation orders, but this lay in the centre of a useless patch of scrub.

Interesting.

She'd finish her coffee and then head out on the quad bike, see what the ground looked like up close. There might even be something worth finding down there, she thought. Something like buried gold.

Two hours later, and if gold *had* been buried in the field, then Joanne was wondering whether somebody had got to the treasure before her.

'Here, Joanne?'

Jody, her farmworker, was manoeuvring the little mini-excavator into position at one end of the patch of earth. The excavator had a bucket claw on the end of an arm, the machine most often in use for digging drainage channels, and now Jody placed the claw above an area of disturbed ground.

Earlier, Joanne had zoomed down to the corner of the field on the quad bike and found the spot easily enough. She was surprised she had never seen it before, since the outline of a rectangle showed where the dock and nettle and seedlings grew at a different density from the rest of the scrub. At one end of the rectangle the seedlings were this year's, the grass and weeds not so well established. Somebody had dug the muddy earth within the last twelve months or so. It was then she'd decided to get Jody down with the digger.

Joanne nodded at Jody and the mechanical arm creaked as the claw hit the ground, the digger lifting for a moment before the shiny steel blades penetrated the topsoil and Jody scooped up a bucketful of earth, swinging the digger round and dumping the spoil to one side.

Twenty minutes later the hole stood a metre deep and

about the same square, and still they could tell they hadn't reached the bottom of the disturbance. Joanne began to think the exercise was futile, not the best use of Jody's time nor hers. She looked at the heavy clouds: imminent rain. Time to give up and head for a cup of tea. Even as she thought it, little specks started to fall from the sky. 'Pittering' her uncle used to say. Next it would be pattering and then the heavens would open.

'Joanne?'

She turned to where Jody had deposited the last bucket of soil. Amongst the earth and stones a piece of fabric stood out, the shiny red incongruous against the grey-brown sludge. She moved over to the spoil heap and peered at the scrap of material. Roman? Viking? Saxon? Unlikely, she thought, not in nylon. And not with a Topshop label either.

Joanne looked back into the hole to see if there might be anything else down there.

The arm had pushed up through the mud, as if reaching out and upwards, trying to escape from entombment or perhaps trying to cling on to the piece of clothing, the last vestiges of their dignity. Slimy water sloshed around the limb and nearby the round curve of a breast stuck out like a white sandy island on an ocean of grey. Joanne stared into the abyss, for all of a sudden that's what the hole had become, at the same time groping in her coat pocket for her mobile. She dialled 999 and when a man with a calm voice answered, she was surprised to find she responded in the same manner.

'Police,' she said.

And then she began to scream.

DI Charlotte Savage carried yet another plastic crate from the car into the house and through to the kitchen where her husband, Pete, stood unpacking. She dumped the crate on the floor and he looked over at her and shook his head.

'One more and that's the lot,' Savage said, before turning and heading back outside.

The summer half-term holiday had turned sour after the weather had delivered nearly a week of blustery conditions. Sunshine and showers would have been OK had they remained at home, but instead they'd opted to have a week sailing. Their little boat was cosy with two, but cramped with four – and if you added in a good measure of rain, a moody teenage daughter and a bored six-year-old son the situation became more of an ordeal than anything approaching fun.

Pete had insisted on sailing east from Plymouth rather than begin the holiday with a beat into the wind, saying the weather was forecast to change, giving them an easy run home. They had stopped overnight at Salcombe and Dartmouth, ending their journey at Brixham. But the promised north-easterlies never developed. Instead the weather worsened as two lows in quick succession came from out of the west, the second developing into a nasty gale. Because of time constraints they'd set out from Brixham as soon as the second low passed, intending to do the journey back to Plymouth in one hop. Once they'd rounded Berry Head though the weather deteriorated further and they put into Dartmouth again. A phone call home and Stefan came out in their car and swapped places with Savage and the kids, the idea being that Pete and Stefan would bring the boat back, whatever the conditions, while she took the kids home. Stefan was the family's unofficial Swedish au pair and a semi-professional sailor. With Pete having been twenty years in the Royal Navy – the last five as commander of a frigate – the two of them thought nothing of bringing the boat back to Plymouth in a near gale.

At home she waited for hours until at last a call came through from Pete saying they were passing the breakwater at the edge of Plymouth Sound. Twenty minutes later Savage stood on the marina pontoon and took their lines, Samantha, her daughter, shouting to her dad that he didn't look so clever. Stefan was grinning.

'Remind me never to go to sea with him again.' Pete pointed at Stefan. 'He's crazy.'

'The trouble with you, you old softy,' Stefan said, 'is you're used to wearing your carpet slippers when you helm a boat.'

'The forecast said seven decreasing five or six,' Pete said, as he repositioned a fender. 'But it was a full gale force eight and the waves came up from the south out of nowhere.'

'They look a bit bigger when you're looking up at them instead of down, don't they?' Stefan said, still smiling as he threw Savage another rope.

The phone rang at around seven in the evening as she was clearing the last of an enormous spaghetti bolognese from her plate. The brusque tone of Detective Superintendent Conrad Hardin rumbled down the line, his voice breaking up as he tried to find a signal for his mobile.

'Three of them, Charlotte,' he said. 'Three. Understand? Never seen anything like . . . don't know how . . . need to try and . . .'

'Sir?'

'Bere Peninsula, Charlotte.' The signal strong for a moment, Hardin's voice clear. 'Tavy View Farm. Nesbit is there, John Layton too, a whole contingent descending on the place, media as well. Bloody nightmare. Meet you in an hour, OK?'

Savage eased the car down the lane past a BBC outside broadcast vehicle and a white van, nudged into a space behind the

10

familiar shape of John Layton's Volvo, and killed the engine. The car settled into the soft verge, the rain glittering in the headlights before she switched them off too. She sat still for a moment, a tingle of excitement creeping down her spine. Breathing slowly in and out, she let the memories of the past week with Pete and the kids slip away, clearing her thoughts for the task in hand. Her mind had to become a blank canvas, ready for the first wash of colour, the broad brush strokes, the intricate detailing.

A bang on the roof startled her, and she squinted through the window to see the bulky figure of DSupt Hardin standing alongside. He tapped on the glass and she lowered the window.

'Sorry for calling you out, Charlotte,' he said. 'But you know how it is. Thing like this needs quality officers on board. Can't afford to muck this one up, because the case is going to be something big. And I don't mean in a good way, get my drift?'

'Sir?' Savage felt her heart rate rise. Was this the case which would dispel the boredom of the last few months? She hoped so, because since early in the new year she'd been on what she classed as menial duties; Hardin's punishment for straying from the straight and narrow.

'Best see for yourself. Across the field. Hope you brought your wellies.'

Hardin stood and walked away, disappearing into the dark for a moment before he reached a circle of light where a uniformed officer in a yellow waterproof was arguing with a woman. Savage noted the little black on white letters on the woman's jacket: BBC. Seemed like even the Beeb didn't respect the right for privacy these days.

Savage got out of the car, put on waterproofs, a white coverall over the top. A pair of boots completed the outfit and she trudged down the lane to where the uniformed officer guarded the gate to a farmyard. Through the gate and Savage approached a police Transit, one of the rear doors of the van standing open. Inside, the interior resembled a mini-office and John Layton, their senior Crime Scene Investigator, sat at a desk with another officer. Layton's trademark Tilley hat was perched on his head and little globules of water glistened where they had beaded on the canvas material. Below the hat was a thin face with a Roman nose and intense eyes which took in everything. Right now those eyes were scanning the screen of a laptop which displayed a schematic drawing of some kind, overlaying a large-scale map of the area.

'Charlotte,' he said, noticing her for the first time. 'Go and take a look.'

'You sure?'

'Sure I'm sure. The place is a complete mess already, nothing left to preserve. Besides, we've established a safe entry route. The field is too wet for my stepping plates – stupid little things are sinking right down into the mud – but we nicked a load of pallets from up in the farmyard and laid them down. Looks bloody stupid, but it was all I could think of. Got some proper walkways coming later, if we need them, but doing any type of fingertip search in this quagmire is going to be nigh on impossible. Here, sign yourself in. You'll need this too.'

Layton handed her a torch and an electronic pad and she scrawled her name before turning away and walking past the van to another gateway. A second uniformed officer in bright waterproofs stood in the gateway, water running down off the peak of his hood and dripping onto his nose.

'Evening, ma'am,' he sniffed. 'One week until midsummer, so I heard. Reckon my calendar must have been printed wrong.'

Savage nodded and continued past, switching on the torch and following a line of tape leading into the darkness. Several sets of footprints had filled with water and the torchlight picked out their muddied surface. In the distance something glowed white, almost welcoming in the way it provided a beacon to aim for.

She squelched on until she came to Layton's makeshift stepping plates: a number of pallets laid in a line which curled away from the edge of the field and towards the white glow. Closer now, and Savage could see what she already knew: the glow came from a forensic shelter. White nylon with blue mudflaps at the base. The chug, chug, chug of a small generator didn't blot out the noise of rain on the shelter's fabric, nor the low hum of conversation coming from within the tent.

A figure in a white coverall stood at the entrance and Savage was pleased to see that the wisp of blonde hair coming from beneath the hood belonged to Detective Constable Jane Calter. Calter was always as keen as mustard and hadn't yet acquired the cynicism which afflicted longer-serving members of CID. When Savage reached the shelter she tapped the young detective on the shoulder. Calter turned.

'Hello, ma'am.' Calter pointed to the centre of the tent. 'Not my idea of a Saturday night out to be honest.'

Savage peered through the opening, shielding her eyes against the glare from the halogen lights within, painful after the darkness. You could only call the excavation a pit; 'hole' didn't do the yawning void justice. One of Layton's CSIs stood up to her neck in the pit, her protective suit splattered grey-brown with gunge. Savage moved closer, realising as she did so that somebody else was down there. A face looked up at her, mud caked thick on grey eyebrows above little round glasses.

'Charlotte.' Dr Andrew Nesbit, the pathologist, knelt at the bottom of the shaft. No jokes today. Face as grim as the weather. 'Never a nice time, but this . . .'

Savage stepped over to the edge of the hole, where scaffold

boards had been placed around the top to stop the edges giving way. Nesbit's arm gestured across the sludge and Savage breathed in hard at what she saw.

Three of them, Hardin had said. But 'them' implied something you could recognise as human. Whatever was down there in the mud looked a long, long way from that.

'Bodies only,' Nesbit said. 'No heads. And by the look of things on this first one, no genitals either.'

'Christ,' Savage heard herself mutter under her breath, not really knowing why. The reference to a higher being was futile. No God could exist in a world alongside this sort of horror. 'Male? Female?'

'All females I think and they're . . .'

'What?'

'Markings, I guess. On one of them at least.' Nesbit moved a hand down and wiped sludge away from one of the grey forms. 'Cut lines. All over.'

'Was that what killed them?'

'No idea, not here. We'll need to get them out to discover that, only . . .'

'Only what?'

'I think I've seen this before. Years ago.' Nesbit stood, shook his head and then moved to the aluminium ladder and began to clamber from the hole. 'I'm sure of one thing though.'

'Andrew?' Savage cursed Nesbit, hoped he wasn't playing games with her. 'What is it?'

Nesbit stared down into the mud, shook his head once more and then looked at Savage, something like desperation in his eyes. Then he seemed to get hold of himself. Smiled.

'I'm getting too old for this, Charlotte. Much too old.'

14

Chapter Two

In the early hours of Sunday Hardin had sent most of the team home. Not much they could do, he said. Better to take some time off while they could, because from now on they'd be working flat out. Plans for Sunday onward were to be shelved, all leave cancelled. Savage managed a few hours' broken sleep and then she was up, the morning passing in a blur of unpacking, cleaning and sorting. Jamie and Samantha were happy to be back from the trip; not so happy it was school the next day, the holiday gone, their precious time wasted in the rain-soaked ports of Brixham and Dartmouth.

By Sunday afternoon the bad weather had blown through and at three o'clock Savage left home. Passing a supermarket on the outskirts of town, she could see the car park was packed. With the forecast promising sun if not warmth, people were out shopping for food for their barbecues. Sausages, burgers, baps, cheap lager and warm white wine. Perhaps later, when the full news about what had been found at the farm broke, appetites would be tempered, fires doused, parties moved inside, excuses made so people might return home and lock their doors.

15

She drove through Plymouth and headed for the Bere Peninsula. The finger of land was almost encircled by the Tamar and Tavy rivers and where they met the confluence formed a 'V' shape pointing towards the city, with the village of Bere Ferrers stuck right down at the bottom. The rivers left the eight or so square miles of the peninsula all but cut off by water. This meant that although Tavy View Farm lay only a couple of miles north of the city, getting there involved a circuitous journey first to the north and then through a maze of country roads, the whole route putting a dozen miles on the clock. Isolated, Savage thought as she headed to the village. And maybe that was the point.

As she coasted down the lane to the farm, high clouds drifted above, their lower sections tinged with darkness, every now and then blotting out the sun. Various police vehicles occupied most of the farmyard so she parked in the lane. A train trundled out from Bere Ferrers as she walked through the gateway into the farmyard, the low rumble causing people to lift their heads and watch as it took the slow curve down to the railway bridge across the Tavy and disappeared into the woods on the far side. Just beyond the bridge, the smaller river joined the wide expanse of the Tamar and downstream towards Plymouth, Savage could see the span of the Tamar Bridge. Upstream, the banks closed in beyond Weir Quay and began a great 'S' curve, Amazon-like, before reaching Cotehele and Morwellam. Later, if the weather held, there'd be tourists and locals thronging the National Trust properties up there.

In the farmyard Savage found the incident room Transit van jammed between a stack of black-clad silage bales and a muck-spreader. Hardin and Detective Chief Inspector Mike Garrett sat inside, Hardin pouring coffee from a thermos into a plastic cup. Savage stepped up into the van and perched on one of the stools alongside Garrett, just touching distance to Hardin on the other side of the van. Garrett was an older detective, nearing retirement. His dress sense was as impeccable as his manners, his record as unblemished as his neat white hair. DSupt Hardin sat sideways to a desk, unable to get his bulk comfortable in the small space, his face reddened by the close atmosphere. On the desk sat two laptops and numerous files. One laptop showed the same large-scale map Layton had been looking at the previous night.

'Thank goodness the bloody rain stopped earlier,' Hardin said to Savage. 'The hole was becoming like a swimming pool.'

'Some swimming pool,' Savage said. 'Anything turn up overnight?'

'Not much.' Hardin took a slurp of his coffee, made a face and peered at some notes on one of the laptops. 'Now, preliminaries: enquiry teams to interview the villagers and residents in outlying properties; widen the forensic search to include areas of interest both on the farm and beyond; go over our records and see what the hell we missed last time around.'

Hardin stopped. Nodded with a wry smile at Savage.

'Yes, that's right,' he said, lowering his voice and reaching across and tapping the laptop screen. 'Which means this thing has the potential to go worldwide. Unless we're careful the investigation will balloon out of control and we'll no longer be able to set the agenda. That's why I want you, Mike, on the media side of things. They won't mess with you. You'll need kid gloves though. One wrong word and you'll see it repeated across a million copies of The *Sun*. You and Charlotte will share the deputy role with me as Senior Investigating Officer. Charlotte, you'll liaise with your old boss, ex-DCI Derek Walsh. He, of course, was the lead last time around.'

'Last time around. I'm guessing you're talking about the cuts on the body?'

'Yes. Nesbit's retreating a little now. Wants to get through the post-mortems first. Won't say one way or another. Me? – I think our notorious cold case just turned hot.'

He's back, Charlotte, he's back.

Savage recalled the pathologist's whisper to her as he bent his wiry frame into his car in the small hours of Sunday morning. He'd closed the door, and for a moment she'd seen a haunted look in his eyes before he started up and pulled away into the night.

'The Candle Cake Killer,' Savage said, for a second feeling an icy chill. 'I was on maternity leave and on my return I joined Vice for a while so I wasn't on Walsh's team. Of course I know all about the case.'

'Charlotte,' Hardin said, pointing an accusing finger at her. 'I do not, repeat *do not* want that moniker used again, understand? First, we don't know for sure if this is the same killer, and second, the name is too cheery by half. As if there was something to celebrate.'

Savage nodded, seeing the pit and the mud and the grey forms lying in the sludge, thinking Hardin was right, cheery wasn't it at all.

'Now, these bodies,' Hardin handed them each a checklist and then scratched an ear and grimaced. 'Three of them. I was hoping, *praying* even, they were all from way back. If this investigation remained a cold case we could simply assign a few officers to it. New evidence, fresh look, blah, blah, blah. Perhaps we might come up with a lead, perhaps not. No matter. Job done, public satisfied. However, from what I'm hearing from Nesbit, that's not the case. Two of the victims could be the missing women from the original case. They disappeared in 2007 and 2008. But Nesbit says even considering the favourable conditions, the third body wouldn't have survived so well-preserved. The corpse is much more recent. We'll have to wait for the post-mortem but it's likely been buried just a year or so ago.'

'Which means trouble,' Garrett said, looking across at Savage and smiling. 'Media-wise. They'll say he might have been killing all this time.'

'Unless he has been away somewhere,' Savage said. 'Prison, abroad.'

'Possible,' Hardin said. 'Let's hope so. Otherwise there are a whole load more bodies buried somewhere.'

'There's another problem with the media,' Garrett said. 'No escaping the issue either. A ticking time bomb.'

'Well?' Hardin's fingers drummed the table. 'Spit it out.'

'The date,' Savage said, spoiling Garrett's punchline. 'The killer takes his victims on the longest day of the year. There's just six days until the twenty-first of June. Meaning that's how much time we've got before he strikes again.'

Hardin looked down at the screen on his laptop, eyes moving to the bottom right-hand corner. He clicked. Stared at the date in the pop-up window. Shook his head, as if not quite believing he had missed something so blindingly obvious.

'Fuck,' he said.

A specialist recovery team had arrived at the farm along with the light on Sunday morning. They'd brought with them vanfuls of equipment and a temporary roadway to allow access across the now quagmire-like field. The twin strips of the aluminium track undulated their way over the ground, down to the dump site where a yellow JCB stood. The digger's bucket hung in the air, suspended over a new hole which ran parallel to one side of the crime scene tent. Savage clumped down the metal track to where Layton stood talking to one of his CSIs. Off to one side a large patch of concrete – the remnants of some old building – provided a convenient and mud-free storage area for several of Layton's crates and much forensic equipment.

'John?' Savage said pointing to the new hole. 'What's that?'

'Control trench,' Layton said. 'The ground's not been disturbed there, you can see the layering and the way the soil is compacted. There's also mature tree roots from the nearby hedge. The trench marks the boundary and we'll dig back in from there once the recovery crew have finished.'

'How long will they be?' Savage said, looking across at the tent, inside which several figures worked.

'Another hour or so. We've removed the first victim but the other two are in a very delicate condition. The crew are having to bring much of the mud along with the bodies. From what I've seen they're well-preserved but fragile. That deep, there were no worms or anything and they existed in an anaerobic state. With no air, there was little decay. They're the consistency of butter though.'

Savage walked forwards and peered through the entrance of the tent. Unlike Nesbit and the CSI team from last night, the recovery crew were taking no chances, and the two people down in the hole wore drysuits with breathing apparatus. They moved back and forth, sluicing, shovelling and wiping the mud from the two remaining corpses. Little by little they were exposing the bodies and inching a large stainless steel tray beneath each one. Once the bodies were atop the trays, they could be lifted and taken to the mortuary.

'You think you'll get much from there?' Savage said as she moved back to Layton. 'Forensics I mean.'

'When the bodies are out we'll begin to sift through the spoil and then dig out further in all directions. The first thing it would be nice to find would be the heads. If you're talking about something which might point to the killer we'll have to wait and see. The killer might be forensically aware but on the other hand why bother taking precautions here? I would have thought it was likely they assumed the dump site would never be found.'

Savage pondered Layton's point as she went back up to the farmyard. It was possible the killer chose the burial site because of the remoteness, but in Devon there were numerous places just as remote, if not more so. Most of them didn't involve having to trespass on private land, with all the risks that would bring. Which meant the choice of dump site was a decision the killer had made for other reasons; something, perhaps, to do with the farm. There was also the matter of the practicalities of burying the bodies. How were the victims buried over so many years, without the farmer knowing?

If she didn't know, that was.

Joanne Black had spent the night at a friend's house at the far end of the village. The constant noise and commotion had become too much. That, and the thought of the horrors in the field. She'd returned to the farm in the morning and shown willing, answering questions and attempting to provide teas and bacon butties for the never-ending stream of police and ancillary workers who continued to arrive.

By lunch time she was exhausted, so when Jody suggested they head up to Yelverton to the Rock Inn for a pub lunch she jumped at the chance. It was only after they'd finished their meal and Jody was on his second pint of Jail Ale that she posed the obvious question.

'Where the fuck did those bodies come from, Jody?'

'Hey?' Jody raised an eyebrow and turned his head to take in a nearby family with preschool children. They'd heard the profanity, if nothing else. He nodded over to an empty table tucked away in a far corner. 'Over there, Ms Black. Be better. Anonymous.'

Anonymous was not something she'd ever be again, Joanne thought. Infamous more like. Once the news filtered out. Tongues wagging, curtains twitching, rumours spreading like foot rot in a flock of sheep.

'So?' Joanne whispered once they'd relocated. 'What do you know?'

'Nothing, Joanne.'

'You've been at the farm, what? – twenty years?'

'Longer.' Jody smiled. Shook his head, as if not quite believing the passage of time. 'Twenty-five this August. Left school at sixteen and my dad said I had four weeks to find a job or else he'd find one for me. I was sweet on a girl up Calstock way so I spent the time chasing her instead of looking for work. First week in August Dad told me to come and see your uncle. Been here ever since.'

'Well, Jody, I couldn't have made the farm the success it is without your help.'

'It was nothing.' Jody smiled, winked and then took a sup of his beer. When he lowered the glass the jovial expression had gone. 'But if you're implying I know something about them people down in the hole then you're wrong.'

'Of course not.'

'Well then, what are you on about?'

Joanne stared at Jody for a moment. Held his eyes. Then she looked around. Dark wood, brass trinkets on the red walls, black and white photographs from pre-war Devon. Parts of the pub, she knew, even went back as far as Drake.

'History. My uncle. Things which happened at the farm

long before I took over.' Joanne picked up her glass and drained the remaining beer in one. 'That's what I'm on about.'

Savage didn't catch up with the farmer until mid-afternoon. As they walked down to the crime scene together, she made a visual assessment of Joanne Black. In her early fifties, she had hair matching her name. Dark in thick strands, streaks of grey in there, but glamorous with it. The Hunter boots and stretch jeans helped, as did a figure kept in shape by manual work. The woman's face wore the signs of days spent outside and under the sun but Savage thought the lines around her eyes showed far more character and beauty than the smooth glacial skin of a Photoshopped cover model ever would. She strode down the track, chatting to Savage about the farm. Casual and confident, but a hint of nervousness. Perhaps that was no more than to be expected.

A couple of paces behind them DC Patrick Enders puffed along, unwrapping and eating a Mars Bar as he walked. How the young detective managed to retain his boyish good looks on the diet he ate, Savage had no idea. Maybe his wife ensured he ate healthily at home. Then again, the lad had three young kids. Savage knew from her own experiences that burgers and chips would appear more frequently on the menu than three-bean salads.

As the three of them carried on down the track Joanne explained to Savage that the field had been used for silage, swedes and wheat over the past few years. However, the odd little corner formed by the river edge and the railway line as the embankment approached the bridge had always been left to scrub. The patch was not only tight to get the tractor in but there was also a spring which made the ground cut up something awful.

The spring explained the need for the pump, and as they

approached the tent the noise of the generator drifted across. They left the metal track, their feet sucking in the mud with every step until they reached the pallets. Joanne paused some way from the tent and turned to Savage.

'They're gone, right?' she said. 'I really don't want to see anything like that ever again.'

'Yes,' Savage said. 'The bodies were removed an hour or so ago.'

Two CSIs were poking around in the nearby hedge, but there was nobody in the tent as Savage pushed the flap to one side.

'We don't need to go in. I just wanted you to see how big a hole had to be dug. It will give you some idea of the disturbance that must have made when the bodies were buried.'

'Urgh, to think they've been there all the time.' Joanne shook her head as she glanced into the tent, then turned away and looked back up the field to where they had come from. A number of police vehicles clustered in the farmyard, alongside a big green John Deere tractor. 'But the distance. We'd never have heard anything at night and the scrub here would have shielded any digging from the eyes of whoever was working the field.'

'Even high up in the tractor?'

'With the mess you lot have made it's hard to imagine what the ground was like.' Joanne pointed over to the hedge. 'See there. The nettles and brambles are almost head height.'

'I guess it would also depend on the time of year, right?' Savage said. 'I mean, how often would you be driving past the corner?'

'This has been down to winter wheat the last two years. We drill in the autumn. Then we spray several times and spread fertiliser too. That would be up until May or June.

We harvest in August. But you're too focused on the job in hand to be looking around you.'

Savage did just that. Looked around. The hedge Joanne had pointed to was thorn, thick on the field side with brambles and nettles. Down at the bottom of the field the estuary mud came right up to the edge. At any other time than spring high tide access from the water would be near impossible. The fortnightly spring high tides in Plymouth occurred in the morning and evening. Meaning, Savage reckoned, that apart from in the depths of winter, it would be daylight at high tide. If the killer hadn't come through the farmyard then the only other way in was to carry the bodies along the railway line. It would have been hard work, but flat.

Savage nodded over at the track. Explained her thinking about the railway line to Enders.

'What, risk getting electrocuted, ma'am?' Enders said, the wrapper from his Mars Bar slipping from his hand. He bent to pick it up. 'Or run over by a train?'

'There are only a few a day,' Joanne said. 'None at night. And they're diesels.'

'So,' Savage said, 'someone could walk across the bridge or down from the village with no worries. They could have parked somewhere adjacent to the line and then climbed over the fence. After dark it would be unlikely they'd be spotted.'

'But why me? Why my farm?'

'There could be a reason, but maybe this just seemed like a good place.'

'Fantastic.' Joanne moved away from the tent and gazed across the field. 'How long are you going to be here? I've got people in the holiday cottages from the middle of the week.'

'You'll have to put them off, I'm afraid. Sorry.'

'Bugger.' Joanne shook her head. 'You must think me

heartless, thinking about my own financial worries after what's happened to those people.'

'Not at all. After all, none of this is your fault and it must be hard—'

'Being a woman? Would you say that if I was a man?'

'No,' Savage smiled, 'but then your life wouldn't be so hard, would it?'

'It's the attitude which gets me. I am not sure why a woman shouldn't be able to drive a tractor or worm a cow. I'll admit I leave banging in fence posts to Jody, but other than that I'm as good as the next.' Joanne turned to Enders. 'Dear Lord, listen to me, I sound like some ball-breaker from the last century.'

'Don't mind me.' Enders raised his hands. 'I'm only against feminists when they come armed with scissors.'

'I'm not that type. Although I might make an exception for blokes who drop litter . . .'

'Never again,' Enders said as he fumbled in his pocket to check he still had the wrapper. 'Promise.'

Chapter Three

Today the Big Knife is safe at home. You never take it with you on your reconnaissance missions. That would be much too dangerous. The knife has a mind of its own and can only be allowed to come out on one day a year. The Special Day. Not far off now. Not long to wait. There's just the small matter of selecting your victim. Truth be told though, this one, like the others, selected herself. Free will. A wonderful thing. But people should use it wisely, make their choices with care. And accept the consequences of their decisions.

You watch as she steps out of her house. A lovely young woman. Slim, slight even. Long brown hair tied back. A white blouse hiding small breasts. A grey skirt hiding dirty secrets. The blue gloss door swinging shut, closing on the life she led before. She turns to lock the deadlock. Click. Can't be too careful these days. Not that it makes any difference. She's yours – and nothing anyone can do or say will make any difference. She made the only decision which matters years ago. No going back now.

At the kerb she looks up the street and waves at a neighbour. Exchanges a greeting. An au revoir, she'd call it, being a French teacher. You'd call it a goodbye.

The little blue Toyota she gets into matches the colour of the front door. It's a Yaris. 1.2 sixteen valve. The colour match is a nice touch, intentional or not. It's little things like that which catch your attention. Simple things. Serendipity. Chance. These days so much else is too complicated to understand.

Like your dishwasher.

The thought comes to your mind even as you know you should be concentrating on the girl. Only you can't now. Not when you are considering the dishwasher problem.

This morning you came down to breakfast to find the machine had gone wrong. You took a screwdriver to the rear and pulled the cover off, expecting to find a few tubes and a motor, something easy to fix.

No.

Microchips. And wire. Little incy-wincy threads of blue and gold and red and black and green and yellow and purple weaving amongst plastic actuator switches and shut-off valves. Pumps and control units, fuses and God-knows-what.

Except God doesn't know. Not anymore. That's the problem.

Once he knew everything. Then man came along and took over God's throne, claimed to know everything. Now nobody knows everything.

You called the dishwasher repair guy out to take a look. He knows dishwashers. What about TVs?

You asked him as he worked on the machine and he said 'No, not TVs.'

His words worried you, but then you remembered you don't have a TV. You never liked the way the bits of the picture fly through the air into the set. That means pieces of people's bodies are passing through you. Not just their teeth and hair – the nice bits you see on the screen – but their shit and piss, their stomach contents. All of it has to come from the studio to your house and the thought of the stuff floating around your living room makes you gag.

'Fridges?' you said, swallowing a mouthful of spit.

'Yes, fridges. Can find my way around a fridge. At least to grab a tinny or two.'

The way he smiled and then laughed you weren't sure if he was joking or not. Hope not. You don't like jokes. At least, not ones like that.

'Microwave ovens? Specifically a Zanussi nine hundred watt with browning control. The turntable doesn't work.'

'Not really, no.'

'What about chainsaws? I've got a Stihl MS241. Eighteen-inch blade. Runs but there is a lack of power when cutting through anything thicker than your arm. Having to use my axe. And that's not half as much fun.'

The dishwasher man didn't answer, just gave you an odd look and put his tools away. Drew up an invoice which you paid in cash.

You looked at the invoice and noted the man's address in case the machine went wrong again. The man left the house and got in a white Citroën Berlingo van with the registration WL63 DMR. Drove off. As the van pulled away, the wheels slipping on the white gravel, you saw it was a 1.6 HDi. 90 hp. Nice. Useful to have a van like that if you need to move something heavy around.

The girl!

She's driving off too, the blue Toyota disappearing round the corner.

That's OK. Cars run on roads the way the electricity flows in wires inside the dishwasher. Each wire goes to the correct place and each road does too. The road you are interested in goes left at the end, then straight on through three sets of traffic lights. Third exit on the roundabout. First right, second left and pull up in the car park. Usually she takes the first bay next to the big metal bin, unless it's taken. Then she'll have a dilemma and might park in any one of the other fifty-seven spaces. But you really don't need to worry about that now.

No, you'll see her again in a few days. Up close. And personal. Very personal.

Chapter Four

No sign of yesterday's sun, the air cold, the drizzle getting heavier by the minute. Covert ops, DS Darius Riley thought, meant sitting in a car, dry, if not warm, with a newspaper to read and food and drink on tap. Not this. Not freezing your nuts off on a summer's day in wildest Devon.

To his immediate left DI Frank Maynard sat grinning at him. The DI pulled the hood on his Berghaus up. Mumbled something about 'the right equipment', something else about 'soft city boys'. The joke was wearing thin, but the fact Riley was both black and from London meant it was open season. In Maynard's eyes, if you hadn't grown up shagging sheep on Dartmoor then you were a 'bloody foreigner' and open to ridicule.

Riley adjusted his position in an effort to make himself more comfortable. Difficult since he knelt in what he could only describe as a ditch, although Maynard had assured him the pile of stone and earth topped with scrub was in fact known as a Devon hedge. Whatever. The only good thing about the barrier was the cover it provided. Twenty metres farther along the hedge DI Phil Davies stood with a pair of binoculars peering through a gap in the vegetation, his grey hair wet and plastered to the top of his head like sticky rice. His stance suggested to Riley he wasn't enjoying the outing much either. Chalk and cheese the pair of them, but Riley had to admit a certain grudging respect for Davies. Earlier in the year the DI had likely as not saved Riley's skin, and although the task involved some very dodgy dealing, Riley owed the man. Even if Davies usually moved in circles something akin to the mud squelching beneath Riley's knees – the murkiest depths of Plymouth's underworld, a place of backroom bars, wraps handed over in alleyways and girls standing under street lamps waiting for their next trick. But at least there you stayed dry.

Not here. Not on Operation *Cowbell.*

No. Operation *Cowbell* meant getting cold, wet and miserable while waiting for people to turn up and buy illegal red diesel from some farmer who was just trying to scrape a living from a few hundred acres of poor quality land. True, the farmer, a man by the name of Tim McGann, had some connection to organised crime over in Exeter, but Riley thought the whole investigation would have been better left to Customs and Excise.

A rustle came from Riley's left and he turned to see Maynard unwrapping a foil package containing ham sandwiches. Maynard took one out and munched on the wholemeal bread. He'd not be happy either, Riley reflected. It wasn't his idea to have Riley and Davies along; their assignment to the case was down to DSupt Hardin. Both Riley and Davies had been involved in a failed drugs operation and being shunted to the backwoods of *Cowbell* was punishment. Three months in and they'd identified a handful of farms selling diesel and recorded dozens of people buying. They'd trekked across muddy fields, staked out isolated barns, and visited parts of Devon and Cornwall so remote that to Riley's mind they seemed like the wilds of America. They'd witnessed illegal activity, certainly. But was it worth the hours the team had spent compiling the information?

Riley reached into his pocket for his own sustenance only to find the flapjack he'd brought along had got wet and crumbled into a thousand pieces. The mush now resembled porridge. In the back of Maynard's car there was a bag containing Riley's lunch – a triple cheese selection and a can of Coke purchased from the M&S close to the station – but the car was several fields away and he couldn't see Maynard letting him off just yet.

'How much longer, boss?' Riley said. They'd been in the ditch since six-thirty and the only vehicle to come along the winding lane to the farm had been Postman Pat's red van. 'We've been watching McGann's place for two days and not a snifter so far.'

'Patience,' Maynard said. 'Don't they teach you anything up at Hendon these days?'

Riley shrugged his shoulders and was about to risk suggesting that when lunch time came they should adjourn to a nearby pub – if there was a nearby pub – when he felt the buzzing of his mobile. He pulled out the phone and squinted at the message.

'Something's come up, sir.' Riley tried hard to suppress a smile as he read the text. 'Missing person on Dartmoor. DC Enders is on his way and he'll collect me from the bottom of the lane. Depending on how things work out I might not be back today.'

Maynard screwed up the tin foil, put it carefully in his pocket and reached for his flask.

'Pity,' he said, smiling. 'I was just about to pour you a cup of coffee.'

* * *

33

Savage had woken to the radio.

'*The Candle Cake Killer* . . .'

BBC Devon were already using the name, despite the lack of any official confirmation. Callers to the station got the date thing too.

'*Five days,*' one said, anguish in her voice. '*FIVE DAYS!*'

Somebody needed to put out a statement soon, Savage thought. Otherwise the media would be controlling the agenda from the get-go.

Down in the kitchen she continued listening as she prepared breakfast. The station was running a morning special on the history of the case. A chance for listeners to catch up over their cornflakes. Pete hustled Samantha and Jamie to the table and tucked Jamie in. Not cornflakes: toast and Cheerios, fresh orange juice, strong coffee for Savage.

'So?' Pete said, buttering a piece of toast and gesturing at the radio with the knife. 'This for real?'

'Officially, no,' Savage said. 'But as you well know from your line of work since when has "officially" got anything to do with the truth?'

Pete smiled. 'Well, official or not, be careful, OK?'

'Be careful?' Savage went across and kissed Pete and the kids. 'Makes a change that you're the one who's worrying.'

'If you'd seen the Naval cadets I'm teaching at the moment you'd still worry. Last week a crash-gybe nearly had me—'

Savage didn't hear the rest of the story; she'd already waved goodbye and headed out the door.

On the drive into the station the roads seemed quieter than usual first thing. Perhaps people were already being careful. They'd remember the last time, of course, memories which should have been consigned to history since the Candle Cake Killer case was dormant, the trail gone cold several years ago. Savage knew a statutory review took place annually, but the general consensus was that the killer was dead. It seemed the only explanation for the cessation of the crimes. At the time the story had been front page news, an unwelcome focus on Devon and Cornwall and one the tourist board wanted to erase all memory of.

It had been the cake, of course, which had given him his name: a Victoria sponge, sprinkled with icing sugar, a varying number of blue or pink candles on top, the candles lit and blown out. The candles and holders were obtainable from any of the large supermarkets, the sponge homemade, rich and moist, baked with duck eggs in a nine-inch tin. One slice of cake cut and removed, crumbs on the floor indicating the missing piece may have been eaten there and then.

Fifteen candles on the first cake, seven on the next, nineteen on the final one. Pink, blue, pink.

Whether the cake was intended to wish someone happy birthday, represented another type of anniversary, or was something completely different, the police had no idea.

The victims were females aged thirty-four, twenty-five and thirty-nine. Not known to each other and having no connections other than living in Devon.

And they had all gone missing on the longest day of the year.

Mandy Glastone had been the first. Thirty-four and recently married, no children, a nurse by profession, she had vanished on the twenty-first June 2006. Her husband had arrived home to find the cake on the kitchen table, along with his wife's handbag containing car keys, house keys and mobile phone. Nobody on Devon Road in Salcombe, quiet in a summer rainstorm, had seen or heard anything.

Phil Glastone had been the main suspect, a few years older than his wife and previously married to a woman who claimed she'd received more than the occasional beating from her husband. A claim the police saw no reason to disbelieve. Glastone was questioned, investigated, questioned again. He denied having anything to do with his wife's disappearance.

When some two weeks later a fisherman came across Mandy Glastone's headless and mutilated body in a river high on Dartmoor, Mr Glastone was arrested on suspicion of murder. Glastone's car was impounded and a forensic team went over every inch. Hairs from Mandy's head were found in the boot, but that didn't prove a thing.

DCI Derek Walsh, the SIO at the time, hadn't been entirely happy with the case, specifically the marks on the body. A criss-cross of cuts overlaid with spirals and other shapes. River creatures had been at the corpse, but the cuts hadn't been made by them. As far as the pathologist could tell the woman hadn't been beaten and cause of death couldn't be determined. Were the marks a sign of some kind of ritual killing? Was the date significant, the murder something to do with pagans, the summer solstice, mumbo-jumbo and witchcraft? Then there was the clay, a lump found down in her throat below the point at which her head had been severed, the purpose of the material not clear.

With no further evidence and the complications of the cake and the cuts, the CPS decided charging their suspect was a step too far. 'No evidence, no motive' they'd told the team and Phil Glastone had walked free.

Twelve months later, June the twenty-first again, a twenty-five-year-old woman disappeared after having spent the evening in her local pub. Single, employed as a manager in a shoe shop and living in a rented flat in Paignton, Sue Kendle was never seen again. When friends called round the next day to collect her for a prearranged outing they became worried when she didn't answer the door. Two police officers gained entry and found signs of a struggle: furniture tipped over, a picture frame smashed, the carpet in the hallway rucked up. And in the kitchen a Victoria sponge with seven candles on it, a slice missing, crumbs on the table.

Glastone was brought in once more. Under intense questioning he broke down and admitted beating Mandy, but denied killing her. The interrogation team pushed hard but it turned out that this time he had been away on business in Switzerland; his alibi appeared to be cast-iron. He was released without charge.

No body this time either and despite ongoing searches, Sue Kendle was never found. With no leads, the investigation went nowhere.

Twenty-first June 2008. Thirty-nine-year-old Heidi Luckmann lucked out. She had risen early and driven her car to Burrator Reservoir from her home in Horrabridge, a village between Plymouth and Tavistock. A couple in the car park at the eastern end of the reservoir remembered the rather tatty red Vauxhall Corsa and the attractive woman with the Border Collie. As they geared up for their walk – stout boots for the moor and waterproofs against the summer drizzle – the dog had bounded across for a chat, Heidi coming over and apologising, the couple not minding one bit.

When they returned four hours later they noticed the dog lying by the side of Heidi's car, waiting for his mistress.

The Dartmoor Rescue Group and a search helicopter scoured the surrounds of the reservoir and the nearby moor all that afternoon and well into the evening until the light faded from the sky sometime after ten p.m. They found nothing.

Police forced their way into her cottage in Horrabridge and in the kitchen they found the cake. Nineteen candles.

Missing slice. Crumbs. There was no sign of Heidi Luckmann and despite an exhaustive search over the following weeks she, like Sue Kendle, was never found.

The story broke then, someone leaking details about the cakes which previously had been kept from the press. The media lapped it up and trust the good old *Sun* to come up with the name which would stick: *The Candle Cake Killer*. Not good English but fantastic copy nevertheless.

For a while hell descended on Devon in the form of various TV companies from around the world and dozens of reporters, but with no more bodies, no leads, and never a word from whoever was responsible, the interest dried up.

The next year the police were ready. Early June and they put out measured warnings, trying not to alarm the public but appealing for vigilance on and around the twenty-first of June. The media became fired up again, hoping for another misper, praying the cycle would continue.

It didn't. Nobody went missing. Nobody was murdered. There was a brawl outside a pub, a boy racer killed himself and his girlfriend when their car overturned on the A38, a house fire claimed the life of a much-loved family pet in Plymstock. All good stuff, but hardly justifying the presence of television crews from across the globe. The TV vans packed up, the reporters paid their hotel bills and the police scratched their heads. Had the warnings worked? Or had the killer got scared and decided to give this year a miss?

A year later and again nothing happened. The media had lost all interest now, no TV crews and only an occasional feature appearing in the national press. There was nothing much more to say and for the police, nothing much more to go on. The case remained open, but in the absence of fresh leads it lay dormant. Waiting. Like Heidi Luckmann's dog.

*   *   *

Crownhill police station was on the north side of the city, situated in a tangle of arterial roads. The twin grey-brown concrete buildings at first sight resembled two upturned cardboard boxes. Rows of narrow slits had been cut in the side of the boxes to serve as windows, but Savage thought the place looked more like some sort of bunker than anywhere people might work. She slotted her car into one of only a few free spaces in the car park and went inside.

Up in the crime suite excitement was writ large. A huge sheet of paper on one wall was adorned with a giant '5', below, in smaller writing, 'days left'. Savage thought about the caller to the radio show. Tension, amongst the general public as well as within the investigation team, could only rise as the days ticked by.

A dozen officers and indexers sat at desks in the open plan room. Each person had a keyboard with two screens and a phone headset to hand. Steam rose from several cups of coffee, one officer passed around a bag of M&Ms, while another bit down on a bacon roll. Most focused on the screens in front of them, where a cascade of documents threatened to overwhelm the casual observer. Savage stood by the entrance for a moment. She felt a frisson of emotion. She knew most of these people well, they were her second family. Each had their good points as well as a whole host of foibles, but each understood that they would only succeed in their task if they worked together as a team. Savage respected all of them and liked most; for one or two she even had an affection approaching love.

She went across the room to speak to Gareth Collier, the office manager. He'd abandoned a fishing trip but was sanguine about having to come in even though he'd booked a few days' leave.

'Was supposed to be out at Eddystone today,' he said.

'After a few pollack. To be honest I'm not bothered. Sea's a bit lumpy and I had a couple too many last night.'

Savage couldn't imagine Collier having too many beers, nor could she see him being seasick. He was ex-military, with a severe haircut to match, discipline his middle name. She cocked her head on one side. Collier held his hands up.

'Alright. It's my brother-in-law. He's down for the week and this is better than spending eight hours stuck on a small boat with him.' Collier shook his head, embarrassed at the lie. 'Anyway, *Radial*. The name.'

'*Radial?*' Savage said. 'Where did you get that from?'

'Don't blame me. You know how it is. The computer spits out the name of the operation at random. Mind of its own.'

'You put that up?' Savage pointed to the countdown.

'Yes. It's called an incentive. Something to focus the mind.'

DC Calter raised her head from a nearby desk and glanced over.

'Something to scare us all shitless more like,' she said.

'That too.' Collier allowed a hint of a smile to show on his face. 'But knowing the date when the killer is likely to strike at least means we can organise our resources more effectively. We can also use the fact to lean on external agencies to pull their fingers out. If they don't we can blame them when things go tits up.'

'Let's hope it doesn't come to that,' Savage said. 'Now explain this to me.'

Collier had manoeuvred a number of whiteboards into the centre of the room. The middle one had 'POA' written in marker pen at the top.

Plan of Action.

The office manager began to outline his thinking. Confirming identification, he said, would be the key. Once established beyond doubt the bodies belonged to the missing women, they could proceed on the basis that this was the work of the Candle Cake Killer. Until then they could only assume.

'But we'll go with the assumption for now,' Collier said. 'Because we've sod all else.'

'And once we've confirmed ID?' Savage said.

'We move through my plan.'

Collier indicated a set of bullet points, lines leading away to boxouts where he'd scrawled instructions. Savage picked out an awful lot of uses of the word 'review': Review victim case history. Review connections between victims. Review family suspects. Review forensic evidence. She expressed her concerns to Collier. Didn't the word imply the previous investigation had missed something?

'Yes.' Collier reached up and scratched the stubble on the top of his head. 'Of course it does. And they did miss something. Else I'd be out on that bloody pollack boat with my brother-in-law.'

Collier moved on. Off to one side of the board he'd boxed out another area. Inside the box was the word 'profiling'. As he pointed the word out a smirk slid across his face.

'Dirty word, hey?' he said. 'Round here, anyway.'

The trek back to the lane for the rendezvous with Enders took Riley forty minutes. The route had to be circuitous to avoid any possibility of being seen and at two points he had to crawl on his hands and knees. By the time he reached Enders' car he was muddy, soaked and in a foul mood.

'Did you bring my stuff?' Riley said as the young DC's smile emerged from behind the steamed-up glass as the window slipped down.

Enders jerked a thumb towards a holdall sitting on the rear seat. Riley got in the back and as Enders started up he opened the holdall and began to change into the spare kit. The clothing was gym gear Riley used if he fancied running home from the station, but it was better than remaining wet.

Before long they reached the main road and headed north. Within half an hour they drummed across a cattle grid and onto Dartmoor. They left the jumble of little fields behind and the rugged moorland terrain opened out before them, the road sweeping its way north-west, climbing towards Princetown.

Riley had expected the weather on the moor to be dank and dreary, what with the earlier mist and rain. However, as they climbed upwards they emerged into sun and blue sky, leaving behind a bank of cloud hugging Plymouth and the lowlands. The rolling hills and granite tors appeared flat, washed of any contrast by the harsh light. Riley leant back in the warmth and wondered if Maynard and his foil-wrapped sandwiches had been just a bad dream.

Enders interrupted his thoughts by filling him in on the misper. He told him the bare facts as he knew them from the brief he'd been given: the man, Devlyn Corran, was a prison officer at HMP Dartmoor and he'd disappeared yesterday morning after he'd finished his night shift and left to cycle home. He never arrived and there'd been no word from him since. No sign of his bike either.

'Horrid place to work,' Riley said. 'On a good day it looks like Colditz Castle. Dread to think what the inmates are like.'

'You've been watching too many movies,' Enders said. 'Dartmoor is only one step above an open prison. If you were hoping for a load of baying psychos you're going to be disappointed.'

'Actually I'm tired and wet so what I really fancy is to get my head down for a few hours in a segregation cell. Do you think the Governor can fix that for me?'

Before Enders could answer they spotted a white Land Rover up ahead. The vehicle was crawling along on the wrong side of the road with its offside wheels bouncing on the rough verge. The words 'Mountain Rescue Ambulance' ran along the body of the Land Rover above a chequerboard of orange and white reflective squares.

'Dartmoor Rescue Group,' Enders said. 'They must be searching for Corran.'

To the front of the vehicle, about twenty metres away, a man and a woman were striding through the moorland heather parallel to the road. A Border Collie ran back and forth, sniffing the air as it covered the ground in great scampering bounds.

'Callum Campbell,' Enders said. 'He's one of the group's leaders. Met him last year when I went on that moorland hunt with DI Savage.'

Enders accelerated past the Land Rover, beeped the horn once, pulled over and they got out. Campbell raised an arm and walked across. He towered over them, a giant of a man with blond hair stuffed under a fleece hat, eyes the colour of the clear sky, a Scottish accent when he spoke.

'Nicer weather than last time,' Campbell said to Enders, before turning to Riley and shaking his hand.

Riley introduced himself and recalled Enders' trip across the moor had taken place during the night in appalling conditions. In sleet and snow the team had fought their way to a remote tor, only to discover a body which had lain there for weeks. Enders had told Riley the story at least half a dozen times.

'Any sign of Corran?' Riley asked.

'No. We were out all yesterday afternoon and evening, but I wanted to conduct a more detailed search this morning. We started at Dousland, where he lives.' Campbell looked back down the road the way they had come. 'The village is about three miles yonder and we've done the right-hand side only. Figured if he got knocked off his bike he'd be on this side, since he was heading home. I am pretty sure we didn't miss anything on the first pass, but I wanted to make sure.'

'He was definitely on his bike though?' Riley said.

'Yes. Apparently he cycled to and from work most days. It's about five miles from the prison to his house and mostly downhill, so he could have done the trip in fifteen minutes or so.'

'Not much time for something bad to happen,' Riley said. 'Assuming, that is, something bad did happen.'

'Well, if it didn't then where the hell is he?' Campbell spread his arms in an expansive fashion, sweeping them round to encompass the wide open panorama. Then he shrugged and plodded back onto the rough ground to continue the search.

Chapter Five

Collier's earlier allusion to issues with profiling took substance later in the morning as Savage overheard the beginnings of a call Hardin took on his mobile.

'But, sir, do we really need to—' the DSupt said before he stomped away, phone in hand, pushing through the doors of the crime suite and out into the corridor.

Five minutes later he was back, the phone thrust into a pocket in his jacket.

'This is total bollocks!' Hardin thumped a desk, causing a young DC sitting nearby to nearly wet herself. 'Mr Peter Wilson didn't have much success the last time did he? In fact he should have been done for wasting police time in my view. If I recall the only profiling he put any effort into was that of a certain blonde indexer who went by her squad nickname of Big Marge. I can't believe the Chief came up with this stupid idea.'

'Do you mean *Dr* Wilson, sir?' Savage said, trying to understand the gist of the conversation from having heard only a fragment of it. 'The psychologist?'

'Yes,' Hardin said. 'That was the Chief Constable. He wants us to consult Wilson. Apparently Wilson's been in touch with the Police Commissioner. The Commissioner's not supposed to dictate tactics, but he's been all over the media this morning arguing the case should be the force's number one priority and that we should explore all avenues. Including profiling. Local politicians are getting reports from hoteliers and B&B owners that cancellations are already beginning to come in. And as you know tourism is worth millions to the local economy. No tourists, no economy.'

'And we're approaching the busiest time of year.'

'Exactly. Which is why the Chief wants to throw everything at this one.'

The Chief was Simon Fox, known as Foxy to the rank and file. Like all leaders, he had a tendency to push down directives from on high. Any complaints would be met with a smile on his lamb-like face. Followed by a sting from his scorpion tail.

'That's good, isn't it?'

'Yes. I no longer have to worry about budgetary constraints. I'm doubling the number of people assigned to *Radial*. We'll have enough officers for comprehensive door-to-door enquiries, plenty of indexers and a team to staff the hotline number twenty-four-seven.'

'But Wilson?'

'That's not so good. I'm surprised Dr Wilson has the nerve. Considering.'

Considering.

Back when the Candle Cake Killer first surfaced Dr Wilson had, from what Savage had heard, been a walking disaster. Fox, recently arrived in Devon as the new Chief Constable, had insisted on bringing a psychologist on board, despite the resistance of the SIO, DCI Walsh. They had to show willing, Fox said, had to show they were trying everything, because if the media saw they'd given up they'd be holed below the waterline. After the disappearance of Heidi Luckmann confirmed they were looking for a serial offender, Wilson came up with his first profile. He said the killer would strike again, that they would escalate. The clay which had been found in Mandy Glastone's throat led Wilson to hypothesise that the killer worked in arts and crafts. He also said he drove some kind of van, had a history of mental illness and a severe problem in relating to women.

'Don't we all' was – according to office legend – what the recently divorced Walsh had said as he'd torn up the pages Wilson had prepared and asked the psychologist to leave the building and not bother coming back.

Simon Fox had got wind of the event and although Wilson had resigned in a huff and couldn't be persuaded to return, the Chief insisted on Walsh working the art angle. Every gallery, art shop, pottery and studio was marked down for a visit. Every artisan in Devon and Cornwall tracked down and interviewed. Lists were procured of people farther afield, their names ticked off against elements of Wilson's profile, those who merited further investigation interviewed by detectives travelling from Devon or by local forces.

Nothing.

After the killer had missed his midsummer appointment a year later, Walsh informed the team the investigation was being scaled back. And he got a cheer when he mentioned Wilson was being investigated for professional misconduct with a female patient and that Devon and Cornwall Police were seeing if they could recover any of the fees they'd paid.

'I would quite like to deliver a personal message to Wilson,' Hardin said, interrupting Savage's thoughts. 'F-off. He'd like that, being a psychologist. Unfortunately it looks as if we've got to get all cuddly with the man instead. Fox is adamant. We've got to "move with the times" apparently. Wilson failed before because he wasn't given enough assistance. I'm hearing words like "bygones", "hatchet" and "bury".'

'You're saying we're being forced to use him?'

'Not officially, not on the payroll, but yes. You might know that Wilson has worked with the FBI over in the States. According to the CC he's got the experience we need to crack the case. Personally I think he doesn't want to rock the boat. Profiling is good PR and Fox believes it would be better to have Wilson on board rather than having the man trying to capsize us with snide remarks in the media.'

'I haven't heard much good about Wilson,' Savage said, 'but it makes sense to at least talk to him, doesn't it?'

'No,' Hardin said. 'It bloody doesn't. And seeing as how close you were to DCI Walsh I'd have thought you were the last person who'd want to do that, but if you want to consult with Wilson then be my guest. I'll mark you down as his liaison officer. Apparently he's up in London on Home Office business. Back Tuesday evening. I'll pencil you in to meet with him Wednesday, shall I?'

Savage opened her mouth to say she hadn't meant for *her* to consult with Wilson, but Hardin had already pulled out his phone and a couple of swipes later the task was.

The improving weather had brought out a trickle of walkers, but otherwise nothing disturbed the empty streets of Princetown. The little settlement at the heart of the moor was not much more than a bunch of houses hugging a T-junction, the buildings clinging to the throughways as if letting go would mean they would vanish into the wilderness. With the incredible scenery right on the doorstep, the town should have been the South West's equivalent of Windermere. For some reason it wasn't and the place was one of the most deprived in Devon. Without the prison as a source of employment it was doubtful if there would be a reason for anyone to remain.

Enders turned off the road and into the prison car park, pulling up in an empty bay alongside a minibus.

'Grim,' Riley said. 'Can't say I would enjoy being banged up here, the place is a ghost town.'

'You wouldn't be worrying about nightlife, sir, and think of the views from your cell window.'

'Well, at least I would be looking out. From here the place looks like some northern mill.'

The grey granite buildings with their tall chimneys did resemble a factory from the nineteenth century. The sunshine washed the stone with a golden glow, but failed to warm the atmosphere. Riley could only imagine what kind of hell the place would be in bad weather, with mist and rain swirling round the satanic structures.

They got out of the car and walked to reception, where they introduced themselves to a prison officer who was all smiles. Riley wondered if he was as friendly to people who arrived in the back of a van.

'You here about Devlyn?' the officer said, taking a second glance at Riley's tracksuit as he prepared visitor's badges for them. 'We're all very worried. His wife is distraught. Nice man. Straight, honest, prisoners relate to him well.' He shook his head. 'Barry will take you up to see the Governor.'

A large man with a severe haircut appeared and he beckoned them along a corridor, unlocking the first of a number of gates which took them along more corridors to the Governor's office. The anteroom resembled a doctor's surgery with numerous health and wellbeing posters as well as information on prisoner rights. A secretary asked them if they would prefer coffee or tea and then the Governor emerged from his office.

'Keith Rose.' The man held out his hand and Riley introduced himself and Enders.

Rose was younger than Riley expected, maybe late thirties, with bushy uncontrollable blond hair which added to his youthful appearance. He wasn't at all the stereotype of the older, caring governor Riley had been expecting, nor did he look like one of the evil and vicious characters he had seen portrayed in numerous prison films.

They went into Rose's office. A formal area with a large desk and a computer monitor on it lay to one side, on the other a sofa and two armchairs clustered round a low table. Rose gestured to the sofa as the secretary came in with cups and a pot of coffee and put them on the table.

'First time here?' Rose said as he dismissed the secretary and poured the coffees himself. 'I'm glad you've come on a good day. Too often the weather only serves to confirm people's stereotypes of the moor and the prison.'

'I had my preconceptions,' Riley said, 'but once inside there is far more space than I would have imagined.'

'We try as hard as we can. Removal of liberty is the punishment, nothing beyond, despite the growing clamour from the public and some sections of the media. You know, we've got some good things going on here, people really trying to make a difference.'

'Storybook Dads?' Riley had seen a feature on the news the other week. Prisoners recording stories for their children to listen to at bedtime.

'Yes, a fantastic initiative which I can't take any credit for, but I am delighted the prison is associated with the work they do. There's been some great publicity and the scheme shows prisoners are simply human beings like the rest of us.'

'Devlyn Corran.'

'Ah, yes. To business.' Rose took a sip from his cup of

coffee before continuing. 'I can't tell you how concerned I am about Devlyn. I mean, how can he go missing on a Sunday morning when there is only open moorland between here and his home?'

'That's what we need to discover,' Riley said. 'But perhaps we could start with the basics.'

'Of course. What do you want to know?'

'Let's get the facts around Sunday morning down first. Mr Corran had been on a night shift, right?'

'Yes. He started at nine on Saturday and clocked off at eight the next morning. He cycles to work when the weather is fine and someone saw him unlocking his bike and leaving sometime soon after eight. You know it was his daughter's fifth birthday party Sunday afternoon? The previous evening he'd joked he needed a quiet shift because he'd only be able to grab a few hours of sleep before the party started.'

'And was it? A quiet shift, I mean.'

'Oh yes. Rarely anything other. You shouldn't believe everything you read or see. Prisons these days are about training and education, not rioting. Especially not here at Dartmoor.'

'You're Category C, correct?'

'Yes.'

'Meaning there aren't any dangerous prisoners here? Ones who might bear a grudge, who might be able to arrange for something nasty to happen to a prison officer?'

'I don't think that's likely.' Rose paused and then leant forwards, took the coffee pot and poured himself a top-up. 'But anyway Devlyn has only been here for a year or so. He transferred from somewhere up north, I believe. If you give me a moment I'll check.' Rose got up and went over to his desk where he sat down. He clicked the mouse a couple of times and then stared at the monitor screen for a few seconds. 'Full Sutton, Yorkshire.'

51

'Can you tell us anything about the reason for his transfer?'

'No, his record just says the move was due to personal circumstances. His time at Full Sutton was exemplary. He worked with long-term prisoners and sex offenders. Still does, as a matter of fact, few days a month over at the Vulnerable Offenders Unit at Channings Wood in Newton Abbot.'

'And the prison, Full Sutton? What's that like?'

'Nothing like here.' Rose stood and returned to the sofa. He picked up his cup, took a gulp of coffee and then ran his tongue over his teeth, as if trying to remove something unpleasant or bitter. 'HMP Full Sutton is a Category A prison and houses some of the most dangerous men in the system.'

After working through a number of administrative details with Hardin, Savage left the station and headed back to Tavy View Farm, intent on catching up with John Layton. In the lane outside the farm a Sky TV van straddled the verge, in front of the van a BBC outside broadcast car. Satellite dishes on their roofs pointed heavenward, ready to supply up-to-the-minute reporting.

She parked behind the Sky van, went into the farmyard past a watchful PC, and headed for the field. The temporary aluminium tracks remained in place but the big yellow digger had gone, a huge water bowser in its place. Nearby, the crime scene tent stood in an area of devastation, three new exploratory trenches carving through a landscape of mud and spoil heaps. The pump unit stood idle and the trenches had backfilled with a thin layer of grey sludge. Two CSIs, their white suits plastered with mud, were washing debris through sieves and the resulting discharge trickled down across the field. Savage tracked the stream to where it reached the boundary fence and the railway embankment. Then she went to find John Layton.

When Savage explained her intentions he wasn't happy. 'Your call, ma'am,' he said, 'but the DSupt won't like it.'

Layton shook his head and followed Savage down across the field. Two strands of slack barbed wire marked the edge, beyond a hedge in need of attention, the hawthorn trunks thick and ineffective as a barrier. She climbed over the barbed wire, slipped through a break in the hedge and pushed up through some scrub before stepping onto the railway line. The ballast was wide enough for two tracks but only one remained. To the right the track curved back towards the village and the station; to the left the lines of steel headed across the Tavy Bridge and seemed to converge in the distance, pointing almost, Savage thought.

'That way,' she said, 'and I'll take the rap for any Health and Safety issues.'

Savage knew DSupt Hardin would want things done by the book, in this case meaning getting permission from Network Rail before venturing onto the line. The result being half a dozen men in fluorescent vests tramping along the tracks with them, leaving her no room to think.

'Over the bridge?' Layton came through the scrub and then looked up the track away from the crossing. 'Not back towards Bere Ferrers station?'

'We're on a peninsula. It's a long way to get here from anywhere. Plus the village is tiny. A car parked in a lane would be noticed as being unusual. I reckon the killer came from the Plymouth side.'

'He dragged the bodies across the bridge?'

'There are no trains in the middle of the night and in darkness no chance of being spotted. The burial site is only a short way from the end of the bridge.'

Layton shrugged his shoulders and they started walking. The bridge began as a stone structure but after a couple of spans became steel, a series of seven columns forging their way through the rising water of the river Tavy. Halfway across, Layton paused and moved to one side. He peered down into the water at the swirling eddies caused by the incoming tide.

'We need to dive the area to be sure, but I guess any evidence, such as clothing or a weapon, will be long gone.'

'What about the heads?'

'You mean plop, plop, plop?' Layton looked down into the water again, bit his lip and then shook his head. 'I don't think so, Charlotte. Whoever removed the heads has most likely kept them as trophies.'

'Along with the genitals?'

'Yes.'

'Great. If we ever find this guy – assuming it is a guy – remind me to let you enter his property first.'

'It'll be a pleasure.' Layton turned from the edge of the bridge and grinned. 'But let's not get ahead of ourselves.'

They walked on and the bridge ended with another stone section, the line arriving at the far bank where woodland came down to the edge of the estuary mud. To the left of the track a chain-link fence hung loose from a set of concrete posts. A light push and you'd be able to hold the fence down while you climbed over it. Even if you were carrying a body. Beyond the fence a rough path wriggled past a number of mature trees and crossed an area filled with saplings. On the other side of the young trees a swathe of mud and gravel ran away from them parallel to the railway line.

'That track runs to Tamerton Lake,' Layton said. 'From there a lane goes to Tamerton Foliot where you're right on the edge of the city. If your hunch is correct then the killer is away in minutes. Anything goes wrong and he gets spotted burying a body on the peninsula we'd be setting up roadblocks and checking vehicles in totally the wrong place while he hotfoots it over here.'

'Clever,' Savage said, 'but I wonder if there's more to it than that.'

'Some connection to the village, you mean?'

'If he just wanted to dispose of a body there are many places more remote. We're going to need to trawl through all the Candle Cake Killer stuff.'

'I don't recall any of the physical evidence linking to this particular area, but I'll check.'

'John?' Savage stood at the fence and pointed to the top wire where several pieces of thread had snagged.

'Trying to do me out of a job?' Layton smiled and then came over, bent and examined the material. 'Looks like denim. I wouldn't mind betting this is a shortcut home for kids from the peninsula who've missed the last train or bus.'

'There.' Savage pointed at something half-hidden behind a tree. She clambered over the fence and stumbled through the undergrowth to a nearby medium-sized oak. A chain encompassed the trunk and then wrapped itself several times around the top tube of a bicycle. A padlock secured the two ends of the chain. Oldish but well-oiled, the bike a little rusty but the tyres inflated and in good condition. 'I think you're right, but it's not just kids. Someone is using the route regularly, maybe as a commute to work.'

'Crafty bugger.'

'Well, it would save them miles by going this way. A quick walk down to the bridge, across and then take the bike along that.' Savage looked through the trees to where the track snaked away from them. 'It's only a mile or so to the edge of the city.'

'Unlikely they would have seen anything.'

'Unlikely, but possible. They could have been doing the journey for years.'

Layton joined her at the tree for a moment before moving off towards the track.

'Get a four-by-four down here,' he said as he peered up and down the rutted surface. 'Not a car though, not without a risk of getting stuck. And an hour from here and you're anywhere in Devon.'

'So if my hypothesis is correct, the killer drives in from this end at night, takes the body over the bridge when it's quiet and there are no trains, and buries it in the field. That part of the farm is well away from the farmhouse so they've got several hours of darkness to do their work. The area is covered with scrub and small trees so the dump site is shielded from the field. As Joanne Black said, she or her farmworker could pass within a few metres and not see anything.'

'Jesus.' Layton pulled his phone out. 'We're going to have to do a fingertip search of the railway line and the whole of this area. Been a year ago or more, but given it's not a regular thoroughfare – Mr Shortcut excepted – we might get something.'

'The rail company? I was hoping to avoid them.'

'Not now, boss. Can't have my guys and girls on the line with trains coming back and forth. We're at least going to need some guidance on how to proceed. My guess is they'll send a crew down. Be some jobsworth in charge as well. Sorry.'

Layton shrugged and began to punch in a number as Savage strolled up the muddy track. The direct link into Plymouth crystallised the problems they were up against, she thought. 'Anywhere in Devon' Layton had said. Which meant *anyone* in Devon. And the population of the county was well over one million people.

Chapter Six

Back home after your trip to town and your mate Mikey holds up the Sun, grins an inane smirk and points to the headline.

'Scream Teas.'

You like it. Trust the nation's favourite rag to come up with something special for you. This isn't what it's about – the fame and glory – but you're flattered nonetheless. However, you know you mustn't believe your own press. You're not some preening celebrity or a politician bending to every whim.

Mikey points to the date on the paper's masthead and shrugs, making a mock, clown-like sad face. The poor mutt can't say much, doesn't really understand the Gregorian calendar, but he knows the Special Day is coming soon. He puts the paper down and slips one hand inside his trousers and you see him begin to move his hand rhythmically.

'Outside!' you say, pointing to the door and Mikey scampers from the room, his demeanour somewhere between a monkey and a stallion.

You shake your head. The boy is crazy, but he helps you run the place, provides the muscle power. His strength is frightening at times, but he's as good a guard dog as your Rottweiler, his blank staring eyes and gaping mouth usually enough to put off casual visitors even before they've opened the gate to the yard.

Yesterday it was a rep selling solar panels. Some rip-off scheme no doubt. From the kitchen window you watched the man get out of his Audi and move to the gate. Mikey was chopping logs in the shed, but he must have heard the car because out he came, scampering across the yard with the dog alongside, a big smile on his face.

The bunch of colourful brochures under the rep's arm slipped down and, caught by the breeze, they whisked themselves through the bars of the gate and landed in a large puddle. The man opened his mouth to say something as Mikey uttered one of his guttural wails and then thought better of it. He moved back to the car, jumped in and reversed along the track even as Mikey was picking up the soggy brochures and raising a thumb in appreciation of the glossy pictures.

Now, you shake your head as you watch Mikey cross the yard. The dog scampers out of its kennel and barks, wanting to play, but right now Mikey's not interested. He shouts at the dog and enters his little shiplap shed. He keeps his puzzle magazines and God-knows-what-else in there. The rep's brochures are probably in there too, although you doubt Mikey is going to look at them now.

Ten minutes later and he's in the yard again. On his pogo stick. Boing, boing, boing. That great grin of his, the lopsided face, tongue hanging out, his mind concentrating on staying upright. But upright doesn't last for long. He falls and smacks his head on the ground, the mark of the graze visible. The pogo stick gets flung to one side and Mikey scrabbles in a clump of dock. 'That's for nettles, you idiot,' you feel like shouting out the window, but maybe you're wrong and anyway, it will save on the cost of a plaster.

Mikey wipes a piece of dock leaf on his forehead and then looks over to the window. You tap the glass and point at the pile of white silica gravel sparkling at one side of the yard. 'Get on with your job,' you mouth. Mikey shrugs and goes back to moving the stones from one side of the yard to the other. He takes up his shovel and begins to load the wheelbarrow. You are not really sure why you asked him to move the stuff, but it gives him something to do.

Best not wear out your workhorse though, as you're going to need his help and you don't want him tired. Not with what's coming.

Chapter Seven

As Enders drove out of the prison car park and back through Princetown, Riley opened the file the Governor had given them and began to leaf through the bundle of paper.

'Not much more in here, Patrick. Nothing to suggest a reason for him going missing. Not on his kid's fifth birthday. I mean, even if you are having an affair or something you don't leave like that, do you?'

'Darius?' Enders jabbed a finger at the windscreen.

They had left Princetown and were heading westward across the moor. The road wound into the distance, climbing a low rise next to a stand of pines. A queue of cars snaked back towards them. At its head a patrol car was drawn across the road, blue light strobing. A Volvo estate had pulled onto the verge near the copse, the rear door up, a jumble of plastic containers and toolboxes in the back.

They approached the queue and overtook, coasting by on the right and ignoring the glares from inside the stationary cars. They stopped next to the patrol car and got out. There was no sign of Campbell and the rescue group, but it appeared as if they'd found something. The patrol officer inspected Riley's ID and pointed down the road. A series of

60

white lines had been spray-painted onto the tarmac and John Layton knelt next to one of them, tweezers in one hand, plastic container in the other. Riley walked down the road to the CSI officer. Layton glanced up as he neared, tipped his battered Tilley hat back with one finger and held up the tweezers.

'Good of you to come out, John,' Riley said. 'From what I hear you've got a lot on your plate.'

'Dog's dinner, mate, but I didn't have much choice. Got a call on my phone. Only the bloody CC. He was quite firm on the matter.' Layton's eagle-like eyes darted from Riley back to the tweezers as he held them over the container and dropped a glittering shard of plastic in. He screwed on a lid and shoved the container into one of the many deep pockets in his tan raincoat. 'Red and silver plastic. From a reflector. Some metallic blue paint on there. Could have come from a collision with a car.'

'Bit of a long shot, isn't it?' Riley said. 'It might be from anywhere.'

'There's some blood on the road surface too. Plus the rescue bods found a bicycle pump away from the road, down in a clump of heather, as if it had been thrown there.'

'Corran's?'

'A Bontrager Air Support pump. Distinctive, and according to his missus, Corran's bike had one.'

'No sign of the bike though?'

'Nothing.'

'So what do you think happened?'

'Well . . .' Layton spotted another piece of plastic on the road and bent and repeated his tweezer, container, pocket action of earlier before standing and pointing to a clump of heather encircled with blue and white tape. 'That's where the pump was found. Apart from the marks made by the person

61

who found the pump, nobody has walked the ground nearby in the last few days. My guess is Corran was knocked off his bike and whoever hit him picked up the bike and took it with them. Corran as well. The pump probably came dislodged from the bike and they flung the pump out there thinking no one would ever find the thing.'

'Or Corran did.'

'Sorry?'

'Corran knew what was happening,' Riley said. 'He flung the pump away thinking it might be the only thing marking the spot where he'd disappeared.'

'You're implying this wasn't an accident, not a hit and run?'

'Can you get some prints off the pump?'

'If there are any, yes. I've got a team coming from Plymouth. We'll do a search of two hundred metres of the road either side of the probable collision point. After that everything will go back to the lab and we'll see what we've got.'

'Thanks, John. Good work.'

'Don't thank me, thank Campbell. That bicycle pump. We're talking needles and haystacks. Bloody miracle.'

Riley stood still for a moment and then turned three-sixty, scanning the desolate moorland. Heather, rock, bog and a few trees, the road slicing through the middle of the wilderness, a tenuous link to civilisation. The black line of tarmac marking Corran's route back to his home and wife and kid. His route to somewhere else as well. Maybe somewhere he hadn't wanted to go.

Sometimes Paula Rowland wondered if she was cut out to be a teacher. Surely there were easier jobs? Jobs where people did what you told them to instead of giving you backchat and filthy looks. Jobs where the government wasn't constantly on your back telling you how useless your profession was. Jobs where the coffee machine worked.

Paula peered down at the paper cup beneath the dispenser nozzle. A brown slick rose from the bottom of the cup as water trickled in. She touched the side of the cup. Cold.

'Heater's packed up again,' a voice at her shoulder said. Cath. Her best mate. Best mate at the school, anyway. 'Here, have one of these.'

Cath held out a small carton of orange juice, part of her extensive packed lunch. Paula smiled and took the carton.

'Thank you,' she said. 'Been a tough morning. Year Ten girls.'

Cath nodded. Paula didn't need to say any more. The Year Ten girls were notorious. With knickers full of hormones, their antics left some of the more developed boys with their tongues hanging out. Controlling the two groups was akin to trying to keep a pack of dogs and bitches apart when the bitches were on heat.

'It's the language of love, miss,' Kelly Jones had said when Paula snapped at her. 'French kissing and all that.'

'French letters more like,' another girl blurted out.

Things got worse from there on in as the class tried to come up with as many names for condoms as they could. She'd smiled to herself; she hadn't known half of the slang names. Love glove? Well, at least it was better than the dirt the boys had come out with.

Paula slumped down on one of the sofas, Cath joining her, other teachers saying 'hello' to the pair and then carrying on with their conversation.

The topic, for once, didn't revolve around problems with specific children, government education policy or Ofsted. Over the weekend the news had broken that a sicko had abducted several women and dumped them at some farm out in the countryside. He was on the prowl. No woman was safe now the Candle Cake Killer was back.

The name rang a bell somewhere inside Paula's head but she couldn't remember the specifics.

'Can't remember?' There was astonishment from the other teachers. Paula smiled. Tried to explain that she had been a student up in Newcastle. She'd spent a year abroad in France and most of the rest of her degree course had been conducted in a drunken haze.

'But it was here,' Cath said. 'Plymouth. Your hometown!'

She dimly remembered her mother warning her to be careful when she'd returned home after her finals.

'Yes,' someone else said. 'The twenty-first of June. The longest day. This weekend.'

Well, she told them, her boyfriend was coming over on Saturday. He was a PE teacher. Worked out. He could handle anyone.

The rest of the lunch break descended into a string of 'ooohs' and 'aaahs' as her female colleagues begged to be introduced to any hunky mates her boyfriend might have, and Paula forgot all about the Candle Cake Killer until home time. It was when she was pulling out of the car park and joining the main road that she noticed a battered pickup truck. The truck had every right to be on the road, of course, and there was nothing particularly odd about it.

Except she'd seen the very same vehicle driving down her street when she left for school that morning.

Back at Major Crimes by mid-afternoon Savage took an unwanted call from Hardin. Due to technical issues at the hospital the first post-mortem had been delayed from the morning. He and Garrett had been due to attend, but the DCI had left to conduct a media briefing. Would she like to take his place?

Savage didn't think she had much choice in the matter so she said 'yes'.

'Of course, ma'am,' Calter said when Savage had hung up. 'I mean, you wouldn't want to be at home with your feet up with the newspaper and a glass of white in your hand, would you? Not when the alternative is watching a decomposing corpse being sliced and diced.'

Savage returned to her car and drove the short distance to Derriford. As was customary, when she arrived at the mortuary Nesbit greeted her with a joke.

'Ran out of coins for the meter,' he said, peering over the top of his glasses and giving a little smile. 'The result being the entire refrigeration system has ceased to function. We've been having to stuff ice bags into the drawers to keep everything sweet. My PM schedule has gone haywire. The best thing to happen is if people would stop dying.'

It appeared as if the pathologist was only half-joking, because to one side of the main anteroom several wall panels lay on the floor and two technicians fiddled with a bundle of multi-coloured wiring and circuit board. A cleaner mopped a puddle of brown liquid from around the base of one of the big body storage cabinets and Savage wondered if the odour assailing her nostrils wasn't even more acrid than usual. In Nesbit's office Hardin sat munching on a biscuit, oblivious to the smell, steam curling from a cup of coffee.

'Good to see you, Charlotte,' Hardin said as she entered. 'Long time since we've done one of these together, hey? Makes a nice change from paperwork.'

Lovely, Savage thought. Much better than wine and a newspaper.

Hardin wiped some crumbs from his mouth, took a final slurp from his cup and rose from his seat. The two of them returned to the anteroom where Nesbit was scrubbing up at a sink.

'What did you mean Saturday night,' Savage asked him, 'when you said you'd seen this sort of thing before?'

'Exactly that.' Nesbit dried his hands and then pulled on gloves. He looked at Savage. 'Mandy Glastone. Tangled in some unlucky fisherman's line, she's pulled up from the murky depths of a pool on the river Dart on Dartmoor. Those marks . . . we thought at first they'd been made by crayfish, although a biologist doubted it. Then I wondered if they could have been caused by a thin piece of monofilament moving back and forwards in motion with the river current. Once she was on the table though I could tell she'd been cut with a knife. A sharp knife.'

Nesbit gestured with an arm and the three of them walked through into the PM room proper. The cadaver was already in position, the waft of the fans failing to do much to take away the despair in the air. Savage regretted not bringing any mints with her, the feeling doubling when she approached the body.

'Remarkably well-preserved, isn't she?' Nesbit said. 'Considering she has probably been dead for a fair number of months.'

If this was well-preserved then Savage didn't think she wanted to see the other two bodies. She peered at the corpse on the table. The woman was partly still covered in sludge, the mud drying to a light grey. The angular shapes of the bones rose as the translucent skin sagged around them like papier-mâché on a wire frame. In places subcutaneous fat had slipped down and collected in weird globule-like formations. Cellulite for zombies.

'As long as a year?' Savage said, thinking of the date fast approaching.

'Possible. The anaerobic conditions have slowed the decomposition process. No air equals no bugs and no microbes. It's why the other two bodies are still more than just skeletons.' Nesbit paused, and noticing Savage swallowing a gulp, he smiled. 'Something to look forward to, hey?'

'Can't wait,' Savage said as she ran her eyes over the corpse again, thinking the dried mud resembled the war paint of some primitive aboriginal warrior about to go into battle. Except this woman wasn't going anywhere. Not without her head.

'Tricky to determine what exactly killed her,' Nesbit said as he began a preliminary examination, dictating a few notes as he worked his way around the body. 'Possibly the decapitation, but as with Mandy Glastone, the first victim, we can't know if that caused death or not.'

He indicated to one of the mortuary technicians to wash down the body and soon water was sluicing the mud away, revealing the odd cuts across the torso, some lines curving this way and that, some going straight across and meeting or bisecting each other. The other technician began to take pictures, the light from the flash sparkling in the flowing water.

'What do you think, Charlotte?' Hardin said, speaking for the first time. 'Dan bloody Brown?'

Savage had to concede the patterns were like nothing she'd seen before. For all she knew they could well be some ancient language, hieroglyphics written on skin instead of stone. Although that didn't make much sense.

'No,' she said. 'If you are leaving a message you don't bury it away six foot under.'

67

'Why do it then?' Hardin shook his head and moved closer. 'Unless you're a bloody loon.'

'I think with this killer that's a given, sir.' Savage turned to Nesbit. 'Do the older bodies have the cuts?'

'In places, yes,' the pathologist said. 'The skin is not intact so if the markings were ever as extensive as these ones they are gone now.'

'Then I think the act was the thing, not what resulted.'

'Interesting theory.' Hardin cocked his head, as if trying to view the markings from a different angle. 'So we'd be wasting our time trying to deduce anything from them. They're meaningless.'

'I didn't say that.'

'No, Charlotte, I know you didn't,' Hardin said. 'There'll be some photographs somewhere of Mandy Glastone, but if I remember rightly there were more cuts on her.'

'So this latest attack is less frenzied? Strange, as a serial killer develops he often goes further.'

'But these aren't frenzied, are they?' Nesbit said. He picked up a plastic spatula and traced one of the cuts. It curved from the side of the woman's left breast down to the belly button and around her waist in a sweeping, graceful arc. 'These are, I hate to say . . . artistic?'

'Done with care?' Savage said.

'No care for the victim, obviously, but care for the precision of the line, yes.' Nesbit looked up at Savage. 'We considered the cuts with the Glastone woman, wondered about the date, the summer solstice. Some sort of ritual. To be honest, back then I thought it was the stuff of fiction, but . . .'

'But what?'

'This girl. The two others. Could be something to ponder.'

'Was she . . .' Savage began to think on Nesbit's words. Had the girl been sacrificed? Perhaps tortured? 'Was she alive?'

'See there and there and there?' Nesbit indicated dark brown splodges on the abdomen. 'Blood has come from all the cuts but here it has flowed rather more freely and stained the skin. That couldn't have happened after death.'

'Shit,' Hardin said. 'I just remembered why I don't like attending these things. I'll need a couple of extra glasses of sherry this evening.'

'You'll be lucky to get home in time for drinks, Conrad. We've a few hours to go before I finish up.' Nesbit glanced at Hardin and then across to Savage. 'If it's any consolation she might not have been conscious when the cutting took place, but unless the killer tells us we'll never know.'

'We can hope though,' Savage said. 'Can't we?'

Nesbit didn't answer. Hope, Savage thought, probably didn't play much of a part in his professional life because invariably there was none for the people who appeared before him. Hope was an emotion for the living, those left behind, those praying for some sort of resolution.

Nesbit was poring over the cuts, making measurements and counting the number. The way he moved the spatula, the tape measure, was ordered, done with *care*. The killer had done the same, Savage realised. She was wrong earlier, Nesbit right as usual. There was no frenzy here, only purpose. The killer wasn't driven by a homicidal rage, they were driven by their *craft*. Was it possible the art angle which Dr Wilson, the psychologist, had suggested at the time of the earlier disappearances was correct? Unlike an artist though they didn't worry about whether anyone would see their endeavours. Their work displayed the pleasure they took in the task at hand, but to do it was all they needed.

Savage wondered what sort of person could kill in such a way? Maybe a better question was what sort of *thing*? Surely not anyone with a scrap of humanity. For a moment she looked heavenward, an almost involuntary action, and the harsh overhead lights made her blink. What had this woman and the other victims done which could merit such violence being done to them?

'Charlotte?' Nesbit walked across to her. 'We'll open her up now. See what else we can find. Are you OK?'

'Sure, Andrew,' Savage said, not feeling at all sure. 'Never been better.'

Towards the end of the PM Savage took a call from Calter. She muttered her apologies to Nesbit and headed from the room, glad of a breather. After the cool of the autopsy suite the heat of the summer evening outside the building hit her like a wave.

'Phil Glastone, ma'am,' Calter said. 'The first victim's husband. I've just spoken to him. To say he sounded aggrieved that we want to talk to him about the latest developments would be an understatement. He was bloody livid.'

'Abusive?' Savage said.

'Yes, although I've heard worse. The gist of it, once the swearing was over, is that he can see no reason to cooperate with us this time round. I told him he had no choice. Made an appointment for tomorrow morning, OK?'

Savage said it was fine, congratulated Calter on dealing with Glastone and hung up. She found a nearby bench and sat down. She'd go back in a bit, but the PM room, self-evidently, was a place of death. Out under the sky with the late sun on her skin and a gentle breeze flicking through the trees, she could think of nicer things for a few minutes.

Inevitably though, having been in the mortuary, her mind turned to Clarissa, Samantha's deceased twin. Clarissa had died as a result of a hit and run accident on Dartmoor. A dreamy summer picnic beside a stream had turned into a nightmare from which Savage and her husband had never fully recovered. Partly this was because the driver of the car which had killed Clarissa had never been traced. But earlier in the year, having done a favour for Kenny Fallon, Plymouth's crime boss, she'd received a promise. He'd get her a name, he'd said. A name, she thought, could change everything, bring closure. So far though, Fallon had been silent and other than a couple of texts to tell her he was still working on identifying the culprit, there'd been nothing.

Come on, Kenny, get your act together, she thought. Perhaps, when the first few frenetic days of the case had passed, she'd call him. A dangerous business considering Fallon's status, but she couldn't wait on him forever.

Half an hour later and she was back inside, but the body had gone, Hardin too, a mortuary technician sluicing away the only sign the woman had been there at all: grey sludge and body juices.

Nesbit came out of the mortuary office wielding a set of notes and shaking his head.

'I'll not be able to give a cause of death, but we can hypothesise it was from the torture. Either blood loss or maybe a heart attack. Not much else, I'm afraid. The body was remarkably well-preserved considering, but no way of knowing much about the weapon from the cuts. Not after this length of time. The head was removed with something like an axe. I can see the crushing of one of the vertebrae. In the woman's pelvic region a great deal of flesh has been cut away – genitals, everything. It's not much comfort but I believe the removal happened after death.'

'Any useful forensic?'

'Apart from the material at the base of her throat?' Nesbit reached for a plastic container. 'I'll wager it's the same as found in Mandy Glastone's oesophagus.'

Earlier Nesbit had cut up from the stomach – or what remained of it – and found a cylindrical lump of clay. He'd hypothesised the clay must have been forced down the throat of the victim before the head had been removed.

'Apart from the clay.'

'Yes, although I'm not sure it's relevant.' Nesbit smiled at Savage and then patted his stomach. 'She's had a baby, Charlotte.'

'What?' Savage was hearing Nesbit's words but not understanding.

'A child. Amongst all the cuts there's the faint sign of a Caesarean scar. At some point this woman has given birth. I expect there'll be medical records you can check should you be of a doubting nature.'

'No, Andrew,' Savage smiled. 'I'll take your word.'

'We'll be doing the other two tomorrow. They're in a bad way, but we'll try to tease out what we can.'

Savage thought of the grey forms which had lain in the bottom of the trench alongside the first body. Wondered what story they might be able to tell, the secrets they might give up, the secrets they would hold on to forever.

Chapter Eight

Savage got hold of her old boss first thing Tuesday; Walsh's soft burr as he answered her call hinting at a modicum of surprise. He was, as she expected, keen to be involved, keen to see the scene out at the farm. The experience, he admitted, would provide some sort of closure. He'd meet her there within the hour.

Savage was waiting in the farmyard when Walsh drove in and tucked his little Fiat between Layton's Volvo and the big tractor.

'Morning, sir,' she said as Walsh got out and retrieved a pair of wellies from the boot.

'You don't have to call me sir, remember?' Walsh pulled on the boots, steadying himself on the car. He was only in his early sixties, but with his hair long gone grey, if anything, he looked older. Retirement could be cruel to some people, Savage thought. Shorn of the excitement of the job ex-officers searched around for something to replace the adrenaline rush, but nothing could. A sort of mental deflation often followed. It was sad to think of Walsh going that way.

'Yes, sir,' she said, smiling to try and deflect her mood. 'I mean, of course. It's easy to forget.'

'You know, Charlotte?' Walsh made a half glance towards the edge of the farmyard where a white-suited figure struggled with a wheelbarrow, atop which sat two plastic boxes filled with mud. 'Sometimes I wish it was.'

'This time we'll get him.'

'We?' Walsh chuckled. 'Hands up, last time I failed, but this time catching the bastard isn't down to me, is it?'

'No.' Savage shook her head and they began to walk out of the farmyard, following the aluminium track down across the field. Away in the distance, up close to the boundary hedge, the white tent stood in the centre of the muddy patch, like some sad remnant of a festival. Only nobody had partied here.

'Odd,' Walsh said. 'The location, I mean. Far easier places to dispose of a body or three. Risky too. Does the farmer have dogs?'

'Yes, she does, but they're shut up at night. If they bark it's usually at foxes or cars in the lane.'

'She?'

'Women have got the vote, sir. In case you haven't noticed.'

'Only joking, Charlotte.' He jerked a thumb back over his shoulder. 'And does *she* have a gun?'

'Yes, a shotgun. The farmworker too. He occasionally goes out at night to shoot a few rabbits. He's seen nothing suspicious though.'

'This guy wouldn't want to take risks. You know his form. We believed, back then, that the victims had been targeted weeks in advance. He was careful not to be disturbed, not to leave fingerprints or anything else. The kidnappings had been planned to a T.'

'Dr Wilson? I've been reading his reports. I'm supposed to meet with him.'

'Fuck Wilson,' Walsh raised a hand and tapped his

74

forehead. 'This was common sense, nothing you couldn't work out with half a thimbleful of intelligence and a couple of true crime books as reference material.'

Common sense or not, Savage knew Wilson had identified the killer as a highly organised psychopath. Intelligent, educated, he was in control of the situation. Wilson had gone further: the lines on the body of Mandy Glastone were akin to the final brush strokes on a canvas, he'd said. Beforehand the artist had to prepare by deciding on the subject, gathering the materials, preparing the canvas, arranging the materials. Wilson stressed in this case his ideas were not metaphors; the killer actually *was* an artist of some type, he would view the killing as a project. The head and genitals of the victim he would keep as a trophy, part of the post-crime re-enactment cycle.

However, the actual evidence for the killer having any connection to the art world had been circumstantial: the cuts on Mandy Glastone *could* have been caused by a craft knife. Equally the PM report said they could have been made by any blade with a razor edge. The patterns themselves were interesting; whether one had to be an artist to create the swirling forms was a matter of conjecture. Finally there had been the material found in the victim's oesophagus, stuffed down her throat before the head had been removed. Clay. Could the killer be a potter or regularly work around potters, maybe in some communal studio somewhere?

'What about the arts and crafts theory?' Savage ventured. 'Was that common sense?'

'No,' Walsh said. 'Total lunacy. Where these guys get their ideas from I haven't a clue. I was against committing resources to that particular angle, but as you know the Chief Constable disagreed. Personally I think Wilson was leading us a merry dance. Down the garden path to a potter's shed.'

'You think he was deliberately misdirecting you?'

'Charlotte,' Walsh grabbed Savage's arm and stopped walking. 'When you get to meet Wilson you'll realise the guy is a charlatan. They all are, psychologists. Circus tricks to impress the common people. They make the stuff up as they go along and then couch it all in terms you and I can't understand. The longer the report, the more obtuse and difficult to fathom the better.'

'Leading to a bigger bill?'

'And a bigger ego.' Walsh stared to laugh and then carried on walking. 'You know I reckon all the pseudo-scientific garbage these people come out with is just something to cover up their inadequacies.'

They left the metal track and followed a row of scaffold boards which in turn led to some industrial-sized stepping plates which Layton had managed to procure to replace the pallets. Savage pointed out the railway line and told Walsh how she believed the killer had come across the bridge.

'Now that does make sense,' Walsh said. 'But we still need to work out why here?'

'"We", sir?'

'Ha! No, "you" and it's not sir.'

Walsh began to ponder the history of the farm. They'd need to find out about disgruntled farmworkers, neighbouring farmers, villagers who for some reason bore a grudge.

Savage explained about Joanne Black and her uncle. The farm had been an inheritance, before that the uncle had in turn inherited it from his parents. There didn't seem to be any other relations involved. If the killer had a connection to the farm it wasn't through his family.

'It's not exactly convenient though, is it?' Walsh said as they approached the tent. 'There has to be a reason.'

Savage gave a little cough to alert the two CSIs in the

tent and then introduced Walsh. Both nodded a greeting and then went back to trowelling through the layers of silt. Despite the fresh breeze blowing through the open ends of the tent, the stench was still appalling. A sweet, sickly odour which cloyed at the throat.

'Jesus!' Walsh said.

Walsh would have been to many crime scenes, so Savage guessed the reaction was to the size of the hole rather than the smell. Leaning forwards, Savage pointed out where the bodies had lain. The sides of the hole had been shored up with more scaffold boards and to the left a yardstick stood upright. Alongside, pinned to the boards at differing heights, little numbered labels marked the depths of various finds.

Noting her interest, one of the CSIs pointed to the lowest label, which was some thirty centimetres from the bottom of the pit.

'Reckon we've reached the limit now,' the CSI said. 'The last thing we found was a ring down the foot end of body number one. The Kendle woman apparently wore a ring on a toe. The thing has gone off for the poor next-of-kin verify.'

'Poor next-of-kin' wasn't a term you could apply to Phil Glastone, the first victim's husband. Glastone had been a suspect on account of his record of domestic abuse, he hardly deserved sympathy. Might he, Savage wondered aloud to Walsh, deserve a second look?

'Tosser,' Walsh said. 'Arrogant beyond belief Mr Glastone was. We had him pegged until he came up with an alibi for the day Sue Kendle went missing. We tried to disprove it but couldn't make headway.'

'What about the third? Heidi Luckmann?'

'No specific alibi for that day, but by then Wilson's theory had gained credence. Glastone's solicitor was canny and somehow the Chief Constable got to hear about the pressure

I was applying. Since Glastone was a programmer and hadn't been near a paintbrush since primary school, the Chief told me to steer clear.' Walsh nodded towards the far end of the pit. 'Glastone liked women. You know, *really* liked them. The type of guy who won't take "no" for an answer. He'll have found himself a new squeeze and if he's knocking bells out of her then maybe she'd be keen to spill a few beans. Of course just because he likes to get a bit heavy-handed doesn't make him a killer, but nevertheless it might be worth a word for this latest one.'

Walsh began to tell her some more about Glastone, how he'd been clocked more than once picking up toms in cities across the UK. His car registration had been recorded kerb-crawling in Bristol and Nottingham and he'd received a caution for an incident involving an escort in a travel tavern in Birmingham.

'This goes back, mind, but I doubt he'll have found God in the intervening years.'

'What about his alibi for the Kendle murder?'

'Brick wall that, Charlotte. Unless he had an accomplice.'

'Two of them?'

'Many hands.' Walsh turned away from the tent. 'Could explain how he was able to kidnap them so easily.'

'Did you think this before, back when you were SIO?'

'Toyed with the idea.' Walsh nodded down towards the railway line. 'But the bridge has got me thinking. It's a long way across and this hole is bloody deep. Having somebody to help makes a lot of sense.'

'Shit,' Savage said. 'If this is a double act Hardin won't want that to get out. We'll have a full-scale panic on our hands.'

'If the media reaction last time around is anything to go by, full-scale panic won't be the half of it.' Walsh began to walk away from the tent and up towards the farm. He stopped half a dozen stepping plates later and turned back to Savage with a smile on his face. 'As I said, Phil Glastone probably hasn't found God, but if you think praying might be a good idea then it's not too late for you.'

When Riley arrived at the crime suite on Tuesday morning he found Davies beaming from ear to ear.

'Big fan of the Chief Constable, Darius,' the DI shouted across the room. 'We're both off Maynard's bloody bird-watching excursion, thank fuck. Missing screws are apparently more important than a couple of litres of illicit diesel.'

When Riley came over Davies explained Hardin had no option but to pull them from Operation *Cowbell*. Simon Fox had requested a couple of experienced officers be permanently assigned to the Corran misper investigation as a personal favour to the Governor at HMP Dartmoor, and every other available detective seemed to be dealing with the Candle Cake Killer.

Davies took Riley's elbow and steered him to the corner of the room where the DI had set up a mini incident room. A small whiteboard rested against the wall. On it an aerial photograph showed Princetown and HMP Dartmoor, the buildings within the circular walls of the prison looking like spokes on a bicycle wheel. There was also a mugshot of Devlyn Corran in uniform and an array of Post-its, Davies' handwriting scrawling across them. The DI had obviously been hard at work.

'So,' Davies said. 'Fill me in. What did you discover yesterday?'

Riley recounted the facts as he saw them. He explained about the search team, told Davies about the prison governor's comments regarding Full Sutton and Channings Wood and outlined Layton's theories concerning the bike.

'He's dead though, isn't he?' Davies said, jabbing a finger up at the snap of Corran. 'This sort of thing is hard to fake so I don't think Corran's taken a dive. Stands to reason we're looking for a body.'

Riley nodded but didn't say anything. Davies would be desperate to make the Corran case turn into something juicy, something which would keep him from having to go back to Operation *Cowbell* for a good while. A misper inquiry might run for a couple of days, but if leads weren't forthcoming then the pair of them would be back in the soggy ditch with Maynard. Murder, on the other hand, was an entirely different ball game.

'So do you reckon it's down to some nonce then?' Davies said. 'Corran pissed somebody off or maybe found out something and they or associates of said pervert top him.'

'Difficult to say, boss. Needn't be a sex offender at Channings Wood or Full Sutton. Could be a prisoner at HMP Dartmoor.'

'Nah. Petty thieves, minor fraudsters, a few in for a bit of aggro. They're hardly going to get angry enough to risk a life stretch because Corran spat in their food tray.'

'I don't know where you get your ideas of prison from, sir. These days *Shawshank* it isn't. You know what they call the place dealing with sex offenders over at Channings Wood?' Davies shook his head. 'The Vulnerable Prisoners Unit.'

'Vulnerable? Bollocks. They'd be bloody vulnerable if I ever got to work there I can tell you.'

'What I'm saying, sir, is I think it's highly unlikely Corran was bashing someone around at any of the prisons he worked at.'

Riley sighed inwardly. Davies' ideas about policing and criminal justice came from either underworld Plymouth or from whichever bedside trash he was reading at the time.

To be fair to the DI, underworld Plymouth would have surprised a lot of people, but it didn't translate to much else. Certainly not to the red diesel inquiry. Maynard had found the whole thing amusing. Every time Davies started on another story Maynard would mumble, 'Quiet out here, isn't it,' and then point to some countryside feature which neither Riley nor Davies were the least bit interested in. The man drove Davies crazy.

'Well,' Davies said. 'If prison is a dead end, then what else?'

'Anything from a simple hit and run to gambling debts, marital problems, an affair, a family feud even. I've actioned getting hold of Corran's financial information.'

'Gambling debts, I could go with that one. Corran runs up a big debt, keeps on borrowing, gets to the point where he can't or won't pay and then—'

'I don't know, sir. How does knocking off Corran get them their money back? Better to threaten his wife and kid.'

'And if that doesn't work they have to whack him, right? Leave a message.'

'But what's the message? A few bits of broken bike lamp?'

'Corran will turn up and mark my words, he won't be looking pretty when he does.'

'Right.' Riley glanced down at the spread of printouts on the desk, grabbed a couple so as to look willing and then turned to leave. 'Going to read through these and then do some research on Corran's missus. The locals were in contact with her on Sunday and Monday, but I need to speak to her myself so when I'm done I'll be off to Dousland for an interview. I'll take DC Enders with me. Do you want to follow up your idea and go over to Channings Wood?'

'What, you mean get up close and friendly with those sickos?' Davies shook his head as if in distaste, but then grinned. 'Be my pleasure.'

As Riley reached the doors of the crime suite he remembered something. He shouted across to Davies.

'What about DI Maynard, sir? He's up on the moor again this morning. Shouldn't we let him know we're not going to be joining him?'

'Maynard?' Davies chuckled. 'Leave him. He's happy enough out there on his own getting a hard-on over some fucking chiffchaff. Be a shame to spoil his fun, wouldn't it?'

Savage returned to Crownhill and collected DC Calter at a little after eleven. They headed out of the city into the rolling countryside of the South Hams on their way to Salcombe and a meeting with Phil Glastone. Calter wasn't buying Walsh's theory about Glastone having an accomplice nor him being in the frame on account of his record of domestic violence.

'Don't get me wrong, ma'am,' Calter said. 'I'd like to live in a world where we could legally take a pair of garden shears to his bollocks, but hitting his wife doesn't make him a killer. Besides, even if he'd killed his wife, why would he go on to kill those other women and why the gap of all those years until this one? And I'm sorry, but Walsh's idea of him having an accomplice sounds like sour grapes because Glastone's alibi back then played out.'

Savage slowed as they came up behind a tractor winding its way into the village of Modbury. Calter didn't miss a trick and she was probably right. Walsh had had tunnel vision. Easy, Savage thought, to get fixated on one suspect and do everything to make the evidence fit. In the circumstances she could understand why that had happened. The pressure to get a result back then would have been enormous; the public outcry, the political pressure both locally and nationally, the feeling the inquiry was slipping away from them.

'Let's run with it for now,' Savage said. 'See what Mr Glastone has to say for himself.'

Twenty minutes later and Savage was parking on double yellow lines opposite Phil Glastone's place on Devon Road. No chance of finding a space nearby with the season beginning to take off.

'Impressive place,' Calter said, peering up at the property. 'For a wanker.'

The houses were on one side of the street only, sitting above triple garages. The door to Glastone's garage was open, inside a Volvo SUV and an Alfa Spider, beside the cars a smart RIB on a trailer, a huge outboard attached to the back of the boat. With nothing opposite but a wooded area which fell away steeply, the house had uninterrupted views. On the estuary far below a yacht glided by, heading seaward past another on the way in. The harbour master's boat was already on its way to intercept the newcomer, to collect fees and guide the boat to a buoy. On the far side of the estuary the beach at Millbay thronged with mums and pre-school children, busy on the golden sand. Salcombe itself was spread out below and to their left, a town of winding streets and overpriced boutiques, chock-full of tourists in the summer, but a ghost town of empty holiday properties in the winter.

On the first-floor balcony of Glastone's place a figure stirred from a sun-lounger, reached for a shirt and pulled it on over a bare torso. Then he waved down and disappeared inside French windows. Seconds later and the man came through the front door and pointed to a patio area to the left. His shirt was only buttoned halfway up, dark curls of hair on his broad chest matching the curls on his head. His biceps were pumped and there wasn't a shred of fat round his waist. He glared down at Savage. Didn't speak.

Savage and Calter climbed the steps and joined Glastone on the patio.

'Mr Glastone? DI Charlotte Savage and DC Jane Calter.'

Glastone nodded. Indicated the chairs around a teak table. Sat. Still said nothing.

'Just a few questions,' Savage said, pulling out a chair and sitting.

'Now you've found the bodies I guess an apology will be forthcoming,' Glastone said. 'Not that sorry is worth much after all this time. Mud sticks, and you clowns threw a lot of the stuff at me.'

'Last year, twenty-first of June,' Savage said, taking an instant dislike to the man. 'Can you account for your whereabouts around that time?'

'Account for my whereabouts?' Glastone laughed, but the laugh vanished into a sneer. 'What you mean is, did I fucking murder this latest one?'

'There's no need to get angry, Mr Glastone,' Calter said, scraping a chair out for herself. She pulled out her notepad and waited with pencil poised. 'Just tell us where you were.'

'As it happens I was here. Like most other days. I work at home, see?'

'You're a web designer, aren't you?' Calter said, looking at her pad. 'Bed and breakfasts, local shops, is that the sort of thing?'

'No I'm not a bloody web designer. I'm a database developer.'

'Databases?' Calter turned her head to take in Salcombe. 'Much call for that sort of thing around here?'

'What sort of Stone Age rock have you crawled out from under? I work remotely for a Swiss company. Occasional meetings in London or Zurich, a lot of time on Skype, millions of emails.'

'So no work colleagues to verify your story?' Savage said. 'A visitor to the house maybe?'

'Without checking my diary I can't tell you who I spoke to that day, but there'll have been emails I'm sure.'

'What about your wife, Mr Glastone?' Savage turned her head to peer in through the open door. 'Was she around back then?'

'My wife?' Glastone raised his hand to his mouth, a sure sign, Savage thought, of a lie or an indiscretion.

'Your *new* wife. I believe you remarried after Mandy's death?'

As if in answer there was a clatter of dishes from inside, something falling to the floor and breaking. Savage made to rise from the table and go and investigate but Glastone waved her to sit down.

'Carol?' Glastone raised his voice. 'What the hell's going on in there?'

A moment or two later and a figure ghosted out from the dark shadow and stood blinking at the door.

'I . . .' The woman paused at the sight of Savage and Calter. 'I dropped a plate. Clumsy me.'

A smile broke on the thin features of the woman's face but it lasted only a second. She moved forward and placed a hand on Glastone's shoulder, as if for support. She had mouse-brown hair and wore a bright summer dress with short sleeves. A shawl half-covered her arms which were slim and goosebumped, despite the warmth. Above the right elbow, a black and purple bruise encircled the arm. The woman drew the shawl across the bruise and looked at Glastone.

'Police, Carol,' Glastone said. 'They're still trying to fit me up for Mandy's death all this time later.'

'We are not trying to fit you up,' Savage said to Glastone before turning to Carol. 'If you can remember what you were

85

doing around the twenty-first of June last year it would be very helpful.'

'Last year? The twenty-first?' Carol looked to Glastone yet again, as if he should answer, but then spoke for herself. 'I'd have been at the school, I think. I help out most days as a teaching assistant. I'd be back here by four-ish and then I'd prepare the dinner.'

'But you don't know, you're just guessing?'

'No, I remember clearly now. We had some fresh fish I bought on the way home. We opened a bottle of Sancerre and I made a béarnaise sauce. I recall thinking it would be a lovely evening for eating on the balcony, knowing the light would be with us until late. The longest day, see?'

'Yes,' Savage said, thinking she had asked Carol to remember and the woman had remembered all too easily. 'Is that Salcombe Primary? Where you work?'

Carol muttered an assent and Savage and Calter got up.

'We're finished for the moment, Mr Glastone. If you could check your emails and send us a record of any you sent on the twentieth to the twenty-second of June, that would help. Any calls too.' Savage placed a business card down on the table and nodded to Carol, catching the woman's eyes and trying to appear friendly. 'And anything else you would care to share with us, Carol, just get in touch. Anything at all.'

As they walked down the steps to the road Calter leant close to Savage.

'The bruise, ma'am, did you see it?'

'Yes.' Savage glanced back up at the house, but Glastone and his wife had already retreated inside. 'Changed your opinion of Mr Glastone yet?'

'No, but I'm going to check in the boot. See if there isn't a pair of garden shears in there.'

86

'No easy alibi for last year and I thought Carol was a little too quick to remember what she was doing, right down to the sauce she poured over their fish. Would you be able to do that?'

'Easy for me, ma'am. It's always vinegar. But I still contend beating his wife doesn't make him a serial killer.'

'No, but we need to get over to the school and check Carol's story and if it doesn't pan out then I want to talk to her alone. See if we can get her to open up. Glastone's not off my radar just yet.'

Chapter Nine

Three beeps and then silence. The absence of noise makes you look up from your newspaper and you note that the dishwasher has run its cycle. You turn to the clock on the wall. Two hours and twenty-three minutes. So far so good, although on forty-five degrees eco mode the cycle should have gone on for another half an hour. You put the paper down and go and inspect the contents. The dishes are clean but there is a pool of dirty water in the bottom. You sigh and realise you will need to visit the repair man. He won't like it much, but then you don't like looking at the water with the scum floating on top. Why did he say he knew about dishwashers if he didn't? He lied and you find lying worse than rudeness.

The repair man will have to wait though. Other matters need to be attended to first. Your eyes flit back to the headline on the newspaper which lies on the table next to a half-eaten crumpet, the top brown with Marmite. Lovely, a crumpet with Marmite on. Nicer than strawberry jam. Perhaps not quite as nice as one with apricot but it's a close run thing.

Thinking about the crumpet toppings makes you realise you haven't checked your jars recently and the next ten minutes are taken up with a rummage through the walk-in pantry examining the jams and relishes you have in stock. You take your special pad and pencil and double check the best-before dates. There's a fine line you think, between everything turning out OK and it all going to pot. A few hours either way, the balance tilted, from delicious to total fucking crap.

Finished with the jams, you cast a glance at the back of the pantry where there are some bigger jars, huge Kilners, a few of them not far off the size of a small bucket. Usually they are for preserves, marmalades and the like. These jars don't contain anything sweet though, oh no. These jars contain things which were once far more dangerous. No longer though, not now you have neutralised them.

You leave the pantry and make a shopping list in the margin of the front page of the newspaper. List done, your eyes shift to the main story. The article says the police have found some bodies. Your bodies. With the Special Day so close the news is worrying. What will you do with the next girl? It's not right she can't lie with the others. The location means everything. Especially after what happened to you.

Geography. You respect it but other people don't. They attempt to transcend space with emails and text messages. Electricity moving down wires, electrons buzzing through the air. What's so wrong with a fucking letter?

But back to the location issue. You'll have to find somewhere else for her to go when you've finished. Not safe at the farm, not with all those police everywhere. Unless they're gone by then, but you don't think that's likely. They'll be watching. Expecting you to return because that's what it says in the manual. On those television programmes too. The ones with policemen in them. You don't watch that sort of thing. In fact you don't watch anything because you don't have a television. You guess that's in the manual too: keep a lookout for people who don't have a television. Likely as not they've committed a serious crime.

A serious crime.

Which brings your mind back to the girl.

Verdict: guilty.

Sentence: a trip to your place, a session with you and the Big Knife followed by some quality time with Mikey.

If she's lucky she'll be dead long before then.

Chapter Ten

Some sort of sports day was taking place at Salcombe Primary when Savage and Calter arrived. Children ran round the outside of a playing field practising for a relay race while teachers arranged chairs in a row at the edge. A voice croaked 'one-two, one-two' from a dodgy PA and a couple of parents arranged snacks on a trestle table. A handwritten sign gave prices: a cup of tea and a fairy cake for fifty pence.

In the school office the administrator seemed reluctant to give out any details about Mrs Glastone even after she had verified Savage's credentials by calling Crownhill station.

'Carol's had a rough time of it,' she said as she led them through to the next-door room. 'I think you'd better speak to Mrs Cartwright. Mind you she'll not have more than ten minutes. It's our Olympics today.'

Savage was thinking of Jamie's own sports day, coming up in a few weeks' time. She hoped she'd be able to attend. Missing her children's red letter days always pained her and, as she had told Pete many times when he'd been away from home, once they were gone they were gone.

Jenny Cartwright, a smart woman in her thirties who

91

looked like she should be running a quoted company rather than a school, introduced herself as the Head of Teaching and Learning.

'We're an academy, see? A number of small schools in a federation. We pool resources and expertise. Share our experiences. There's an executive head who runs everything across the federation.'

To Savage the set-up sounded like the sort of rubbish which could well find its way into the police force. But then again maybe it already had. The senior management were as removed from the day-to-day issues of policing as Jenny Cartwright's boss was from dealing with a six-year-old who'd stumbled in the playground.

'Carol Glastone,' Savage said. 'She's a teaching assistant here, correct?'

'Carol's great. Really involved. Treats the school like family. She should be here this afternoon, actually.' Jenny raised a hand to her mouth. 'Oh my God, has something happened to her?'

'No. We spoke to Carol this morning. We just wanted to confirm whether she was working last year around the twenty-first of June.'

'She's had quite a bit of time off recently. I'm sure we can check.'

Jenny got up from her desk and went through to the admin area. A couple of minutes later she was back with a large hardback record book.

'As I say, she was ill at the start of this year, fell down the stairs at home and broke an arm, but last year . . .' Jenny paused, fingers turning pages in the book. 'Of course! Yes, she was working all through that week.'

'You sure? There can be no mistake?'

'No.' Jenny closed the book. 'Might I know why you're asking? Is it for an alibi of some kind?'

'I'm sorry,' Savage said. 'I can't disclose that. What time does Carol usually work to . . . I mean, does she stay on at the end of the school day?'

'She might if there is a staff meeting or something. For instance today many of us will stay behind afterwards clearing up. Usually we'll be out of here by four.'

Savage nodded and turned to Calter. The DC made a mark in her notebook and then looked up at Savage as if to say 'I told you so.'

'OK, thank you, Jenny.' Savage stood up and offered a hand.

'But . . .' Jenny glanced at Calter and then back to Savage. 'I thought you might . . . perhaps . . .'

'Yes?'

'The husband. He . . . I don't know how to say it. Maybe I'm being silly, Carol's life is really none of my business, is it?'

'This kind of thing is all of our business. I can tell you we're aware of Carol's domestic issues, but we can't do anything until she makes a complaint.'

'So the alibi wasn't for Carol. It was for him.'

'We just wanted to know at what times Carol would have arrived home on the days concerned last year. You've answered that. She was here all day and would have left for home around four.'

'Home? No, you asked me whether she was working and then you went on to some more general point about what time we get out of school. Last year she and Mrs Williams took the Year Sixes down to St Ives for their residential. Carol wouldn't have been at home at all that week.'

As they walked back to their car Calter apologised to Savage. Maybe Glastone was back in the frame after all.

'But why if it's him,' Calter said, 'has he started killing again? He doesn't fit our profile of somebody who's been out of action for some reason. Mr Glastone has been living and working in Salcombe the whole time.'

'Carol Glastone?'

'Hey?'

'He got married to Carol Glastone two years ago. Maybe that has something to do with it.'

'I'll bear that in mind, ma'am, should I decide to get hitched. Another reason not to if married life is going to turn your husband into a serial killer.'

'So far, touch wood,' Savage said, opening the car door and climbing in, 'mine hasn't yet.'

Devlyn Corran's house lay on the edge of a lane about half a mile from the village of Dousland. The little cottage sat back from the road at the top of a steep, grassy bank. Riley and Enders parked alongside the bank behind a shiny new Mini and got out. Brick steps led up the bank to a plateau with a vegetable garden on one side and a small area of lawn on the other. A child's swing hung from the branch of an old tree and the yellow seat moved in the wind. A pink and silver helium balloon tugged at its string trying to free itself from where it had been tied to the side of the porch and Riley could see a banner hanging in a downstairs window, gold lettering which read 'Happy Fifth Birthday Emily'.

He pushed the gate open and reflected the day probably hadn't been happy at all. Riley didn't have kids so he had no idea if going ahead with the party would have been right or not. He wondered aloud to Enders what he would have done. Would he have continued with the celebration? Carried on as normal? Mrs Corran would have had a difficult time explaining to young Emily why Daddy wasn't coming home.

'Lies,' Enders said. 'When you've got kids you get used to making them. "TV's not working", "we can't afford it", "the sweet shop's closed". That's apart from the Father Christmas, Tooth Fairy sort of bollocks. She'd have thought of something.'

'Patrick?' Riley gestured at a bedroom window where a streak of blonde hair and a tear-stained face poked from behind a curtain. 'Must be the daughter.'

'Heartbreaking, Darius. Heartbreaking.'

Mrs Corran answered the door and she'd been crying too. Without the tears her face would have been attractive, with full lips, a perfect nose and blue eyes framed with a mass of flaxen hair, but compared to her head the woman's body seemed a little too slim and the black denim dress and black leggings she wore hung on her like clothes on a rail. She guided them into the front room where a large tropical fish tank and a big television jostled for primacy either side of a fireplace, the grate choked with soot and as cold as the atmosphere. The woman introduced herself as Cassie and gestured to the sofa. She asked the inevitable question, was there any news?

'No, Cassie, I am afraid not,' Riley said as he and Enders sat down.

'Still no sign of his bike then? I mean if it had been an accident . . .' Cassie went and stood by the fish tank. A vivid orange and white clownfish nosed against the glass and Cassie looked down, almost as if the fish would provide her with an answer.

'We would have found his bike.' Riley filled in the words, but didn't mention anything about hit and run drivers being a bit more wised-up these days. Even to the extent where someone might pick a body up from the road and move it away from the scene. 'I am keeping an open mind at the moment. This could be an accident, it could be something else.'

If the news provided any sort of comfort to Cassie it wasn't evident from the tears which welled in her eyes.

'You mean . . . he . . .' Cassie's voice trailed off again.

'I know you've told the story to the officers who came yesterday, but I'd like to go over one or two areas again and get some more background information.'

'OK.' Cassie sounded unsure. She moved from the fish tank and perched on the edge of an armchair. 'But I don't know what else I can tell you. Devlyn went to work as usual Saturday night and never turned up Sunday morning.'

'So there was nothing different you remember about Devlyn on Saturday? Nothing bothering him?'

'He was a bit withdrawn, tired perhaps, but he got up lunch time and went fishing in the afternoon. Down to Bigbury-on-Sea, I think he said. Then he helped me with some of the things for the party, played with Emily and went off to work.'

'And when did you realise he was missing?'

'His shift was supposed to end at eight a.m., but sometimes he'll stay on for a chat afterwards or maybe something will come up and he'll need to work an extra hour to cover for an absence. By ten I thought something wasn't quite right so I phoned the prison. They said he'd clocked off on time and someone had seen him getting on his bike. I gave it a little longer and then I put Emily in the car and we went looking for him. When I got back to the house an hour or so later I phoned you lot. Felt stupid at the time, as if I was causing a bother over nothing, but now . . .'

'Usually people turn up after a few hours. We simply don't have the resources to send officers out looking for everyone who goes missing. I understand the rescue group began their search late on Sunday afternoon?'

'Yes. The ironic thing is Devlyn wanted to be a member, but he didn't think he would be able to spare the time and being on call wouldn't fit in with his job.'

Cassie's eyes glazed and she turned her head towards the mantelpiece where a picture showed a figure in walking gear standing on a snow slope. The man's bright red cagoule and over-trousers stood out against the white and he held a snowball in his right hand, making to throw it at the camera.

'Is that Devlyn?' Riley said.

'Yes. In the Dales, Ingleborough. Before we had Emily. Years ago.' Cassie looked away from the picture and down at the floor where specks of multi-coloured confetti were dotted across the white carpet. It appeared as if Emily had had some sort of party after all.

'When Devlyn worked at Full Sutton?'

'Yes. We loved our life up there with the moors and York and everything.'

'So why did you leave?'

'I . . . Devlyn . . .' Cassie clasped her hands together, not in prayer but clenched in anger, the skin on the knuckles tightening to white over bone.

'Cassie?'

'Devlyn had an affair. Afterwards he was sorry about straying, they always are, aren't they? He said he would never be unfaithful again and suggested we leave the area and move away. Far away. So here we are.'

'So the reason was nothing to do with the prison or his work?'

'No.' Cassie paused for a moment and Riley thought she was going to say something else. Instead she leant forward and picked up some of the confetti from the floor. She stared at the pieces as they lay in her palm before raising her hand to her mouth and blowing hard. The confetti rose in the air and then fell to the floor in a flutter of pastel colours. 'Happy ever after, isn't that what they say? As long as you both shall live?'

Joanne Black and her farmworker, Jody, stood on the slab of concrete not far from the crime scene tent. A couple of CSIs were still working around the hole and when Joanne had come from the house she'd seen someone in the mobile incident room. Other than that most of the police had disappeared in search of lunch.

'What'll we say?' Jody had asked as they walked down the track into the field. 'I mean when they ask us why we're down here.'

'Farming, Jody,' Joanne replied. 'It's what we do, remember?'

Once at the slab Joanne had waved her arms around, talked loudly about crop rotation, drill depth and spraying cycles. She'd pointed out various areas of the field, sounding exasperated as she worried about how they were going to clear up all the mess. Looked to the hedge. Wandered around.

When the CSIs had stopped paying attention, one bent to a trowel, the other operating some sort of probe, she'd confronted Jody.

'It was here,' she said. 'A bungalow. I remember. Wood-panelled sides, asbestos roof, a little veranda.'

'Yes.' Jody peered down at his feet and pointed out a line of holes in the concrete. 'All these, they're from a shed we put up after the house was demolished. Lasted a couple of years but it got torn down in a storm. Cursed, your uncle said.'

'Pah.' Joanne paced along the edge of the slab. 'So tell me again, the bungalow, when did you take it down?'

'Be soon after I started working here.'

'Something like twenty-five years ago then?' Joanne looked

to Jody for confirmation and he nodded. 'And you don't know why?'

'It had got in a right state, beyond saving. When I asked your uncle, he said the place was haunted. Bad memories.'

'Double pah.'

'You don't believe it was haunted or you don't believe he said it?'

'I don't believe *he* believed the place was haunted.' Joanne reached one side of the slab. Toed the edge. Turned. 'Jody, I used to come down here when I was little. I played with a girl who lived here. She was older than me – I'd have been six or seven, she was early to mid-teens. Those days kids did that, played across age groups. Anyway, when I came back one summer after not having been to the farm for a year, my uncle said the family had moved away. I remember being disappointed my friend wasn't here but I never thought any more of it. Years later there was gossip about the girl, why she'd left. Gossip about my uncle.'

'That's villages for you, Joanne. A load of tittle-tattle. Houses might not be cheap round here, but talk is.'

'No smoke, Jody. *Something* went on.'

'But that was long before this.' Jody stared down to the white forensic shelter. 'Decades. What makes you think there's any kind of connection to the girl?'

'When did I inherit the farm, Jody?'

'Let's see . . . be around 2006. We had a dry start to the summer and I remember you wanted to invest in some irrigation equipment, you all keen but knowing nothing. I told you it were a waste of money. The rain came in July and we had a bumper harvest.'

'Yes. My uncle died that spring, the way old people seem to. Waited until the lambs were frolicking, the daffs in bloom, and then popped off.' Joanne pointed down to the shelter.

'Know when the Candle Cake Killer committed his first murder?'

'No, but I reckon you're going to tell me.'

'Same year.'

'A coincidence. Nothing more. Also, that first one, she was found on Dartmoor.'

'And I know why, Jody. It was because we had the caravan down here sat on the plinth. When William and I took over we renovated the house, didn't we? Lived in the caravan for three months when the floors were being renewed. The following year the caravan had gone and we were back in the house, well out of it.'

'So the next body goes in the hole?'

'Yes. The hole standing only a few paces from the bungalow. The bungalow where a girl and her family left one spring in a hurry to get away. The girl who had something to do with my uncle.'

'It's a stretch, Joanne,' Jody said. 'Anyway, who was she? I mean I'm from Yelverton, didn't come here as a kid. Your uncle never said either.'

'Laura or Lauren. A name like that. Someone in the village must remember who lived here.'

'You're talking well over forty years ago and the family may have been transient. The house was a tied bungalow. Farmworkers.'

'*Someone*, Jody. Even after all this time.'

'Ms Black?' Jody glanced over at the CSIs. 'You going to tell this lot?'

Joanne paused. Walked across to Jody, raised a finger and reached out and touched him on the lips. Smiled.

'No,' she said. 'Not just yet.'

Chapter Eleven

You sit in the car, Mikey alongside you. The glow from a street lamp washes the interior, turning the pages of Mikey's magazine yellow. Puzzles. Colouring-in, spot the difference, tic, tac, toe. Not crosswords or word games, anything with letters is much too complicated for Mikey. You glance over. He's working on a join the dots picture. It's a mess of spidery lines, each dot on the page joined to every other dot. Like the wires in the dishwasher, you think. Or the road. Any place in the world joined to you here, any time linked somehow through history. All you have to do is work out the route to where you want to go.

The girl.

You look over to the house. A glow at a downstairs window quickly fades to darkness. You count to ten. Raise your eyes to the top floor. A white light comes on, a figure silhouetted for a second as somebody reaches and draws the curtains across.

'Wait here,' you say to Mikey. 'Finish your drawing. I'm going round the back for a closer look.'

Mikey nods and you get out of the car and cross the street. The house is a little terrace, but there's a passage down the side, a tall gate which isn't locked.

Careless, you think.

You open the gate and step through, groping down through

101

the black in the passage until you emerge into a little garden. A patio, beyond a handkerchief-sized lawn. From somewhere close by there's a gurgle of water swirling round a drainpipe. Your eyes follow the pipe upwards to where a half-open window splays light into the night. She's up there in the bathroom. Taking a shower.

You shift sideways, move out onto the patio, stand on the tips of your toes. Now you can see her reflected in a mirror, although the image is blurring as the surface of the mirror clouds with condensation.

Never mind. You're not here for that.

You move across the patio to the back door. There are several plant pots to the right beneath a window. A couple of begonias – tuberhybrida if you're not mistaken – and three succulents. You lift the pot nearest the door and shake your head with disbelief as a glint of silver shines up from the paving slab beneath.

Two keys on a ring.

The back gate and now the keys. Beyond careless. More like an invitation.

You bend and pick up the keys, move to the door, try one of them in the lock.

Click. Click.

The lock is one of those double ones and you have to revolve the key twice. Then you push the handle down. Swing the door open. Step up into the kitchen.

Quiet and dark. Dim light through the door into the hallway coming down from upstairs. Air tinged with scent wafting down too. A fragrance. Shower gel? Shampoo?

She's up there in the bathroom. Water running over her body. Soft bubbles on her skin. You imagine your hands reaching out and grabbing her, the soap slippery under your fingertips, the girl struggling, screaming.

Stop!

Really, you shouldn't be thinking like this. You should be checking a couple of things and getting out of here. Taking the keys to one of those late-night places to get copies made and then returning the originals to their rightful place under the pot.

But where's the fun in that?

Ignoring your better judgement, you ease yourself out of the kitchen and into the hall. The stairs rise to your right, carpet deep and silent. So easy to glide down the hall and climb up towards the woman, towards heaven.

'Get guuurrlll!'

Mikey!

You spin around and there in the kitchen is the lad. He has a grin on his face and he points at the ceiling.

'Guuurrr—'

You bound towards him and place your hand over his mouth.

'Shhhhush,' you say. 'Not now. Out.'

You spin him round to face the door and give him a shove. Follow. Back on the patio you push the door shut and lock it. Glance up at the window. Still the noise of running water in the drainpipe. Steam coming from the window. A faint humming.

She didn't see you and she's quite safe.

For the moment.

Chapter Twelve

Paula Rowland came down to the sight of some mud and gravel on the floor in the kitchen, a strange musty smell lingering in the air.

Cats?

She'd left a window open a fraction a few weeks ago and a tom had squeezed in and urinated on her living room floor. Several applications of carpet cleaner had left the room smelling of chemicals. If the cat had sneaked in again somehow she'd kill the bloody animal.

The kitchen window was closed, as were all the other downstairs windows. She'd left the bathroom one ajar last night to clear the steam from her shower. Had the animal managed to get in that way? She opened the back door and stepped out onto the patio. The window was high above her. Unless a cat could climb a drainpipe there was no way in up there.

She went back inside and cleared up the mess, wondering where the clay and tiny white crystal-like gravel had come from. Maybe, she thought, she'd got some stuck to her feet somewhere and the gravel had fallen off in the kitchen. She washed her hands and made herself a bowl of cereal, switching the radio on and changing from BBC Devon to a non-stop music station when she realised the breakfast show was doing nothing else but talk about the Candle Cake Killer.

Paula was fed up with the over-the-top reporting of the last couple of days. On and on they went, almost as if they wanted something to happen. Even the children at school had picked up on the media response, the older and hardened kids all jokes and bravado, but one or two of the younger ones distressed. The headmaster had said he'd work something into Friday's assembly, make sure everyone went home for the weekend vigilant but reassured. 'I want them to know,' he'd told teachers at a staff meeting, 'that none of us needs to be worried.'

Paula switched the radio off as a One Direction song came on, the boys' crooning not suiting her mood any more than the rant of the news programme. She finished her breakfast with the head's little speech still in her head.

None of us needs to be worried.

Sensible words, Paula thought as she spotted something glittering on the floor. She bent to pick up the piece of gravel and then dropped it in the sink. She turned the cold tap on and the crystal swirled around with the water for a moment before disappearing down the plughole, out of sight and mind.

First thing Wednesday, Hardin called a meeting in briefing room A to discuss the strategy for the twenty-first of June, along with the current state of play. A dozen members of the team squeezed themselves round the big table, the rest sat on rows of chairs, a lucky few with a view out the window. Gareth Collier had reproduced his countdown chart, the number '3' scrawled on a piece of paper and stuck on the wall at the end of the room.

Savage pulled up a chair alongside DCI Garrett as Hardin rose from his seat and moved to a whiteboard sat on an easel.

'This,' Hardin said, 'is my plan for D-Day.'

Hardin had linked his laptop to a projector and the first slide glared white on the board, blank apart from a single line of text which read 'June 21st. Tactics.' Somebody down the far end of the table murmured 'pray' but Hardin didn't hear.

'The media.' Hardin keyed the laptop and revealed a series of bullet points. 'I've drawn up a series of releases which will be given to the newspapers and put on our website. Senior officers will take to the airwaves and TV screens to explain and answer questions. The key to everything will be to seek to reassure people and prevent panic. Public order and safety will be dealt with by uniforms and they've got their own briefs. However, Major Crimes has a role to play. We can use the media as a positive force to help further the investigation. What we don't want is anyone deciding to take the law into their own hands. We don't want trial by social media. I've tailored the texts we'll be using to be measured but at the same time stressing the importance of following our recommended precautions. The Chief Constable will mention the investigative strand in his announcement, but he wants to restrict himself to the one appearance for the moment. We need an air of normality and to avoid chaos at all costs.'

Hardin paused for breath and then began to outline his thinking on policing and detection. There was a balance to be struck, he said as the existing slide dissolved and was replaced by another set of bullet points, between reassuring the public, protecting them and catching the perpetrator. The three strands were essentially incompatible. Reassurance came from bobbies on the beat and patrol cars up and down every street. In the real world – a world unfettered by such political niceties – protecting the public depended on an efficient response. Units spread across the city and the county might look good, but responding to an incident would be a logistical nightmare. Finally, catching the killer required a breakthrough to be made before the twenty-first or the setting of some kind of trap which could be sprung on the day. Both methods would require huge resources which couldn't be spared from the other two objectives.

Hardin raised a hand to wipe his brow and reached for his glass of water.

'Thankfully the deployment issue is out of my hands. The Chief Constable will be making such decisions. All we have to do is get on with the job in hand. Which is catching the bastard. To which end; Charlotte, Mike?'

Thanks a bundle, Savage thought as she got to her feet.

'Phil Glastone. He's a database programmer. He lives over in Salcombe.'

'Guilty!' somebody shouted from the back of the room.

'Very probably,' Savage said. 'At least of having too much money. Apart from that you'll all know he was fingered for the killing of Mandy Glastone the first time around. He wasn't charged and had an alibi for the Sue Kendle disappearance.'

'Good?' an officer said.

'Yes. He doesn't have a plausible alibi for last year though so it's imperative we go back and see if we can find any new evidence which might disprove his original statements.'

'Shaky ground, Charlotte,' Garrett said. 'The CPS didn't want to proceed back then. I can't see them being very happy with us trying to disprove an old alibi. Then there's the intervening time gap. Why did he stop?'

'We don't know. I'm seeing the psychologist, Dr Wilson, later. I hope he'll shed some light on possible scenarios.'

Somebody groaned and a burst of muttering spread across the room. From the very back row came a noise like a duck quacking.

'OK,' Hardin said. 'I still think Glastone's worth keeping an eye on. Especially on the twenty-first. Next. Mike?'

As Savage sat down Garrett got to his feet. He began to detail his suspect, a sex offender who'd been five years inside. The dates didn't quite match the quiet period, but Savage had to admit the man was a more plausible suspect than Glastone.

After Garrett had finished there were two more presentations from other senior detectives, but neither seemed to Savage to be worthy of serious consideration. Hardin came across to her at the end.

'Dr Wilson. You're seeing him later, right?' Hardin put his head on one side. Savage nodded. 'Well let's hope he's got something more substantive than this lot. Else we're buggered.'

Savage glanced across at the far wall. Collier was removing the piece of paper with number three from the board. He folded it once and then dropped the paper in a nearby waste bin.

By Wednesday lunchtime Riley and Davies were scrabbling around for scraps. Davies' visit to HMP Channings Wood the previous day had resulted in a long list of prisoners Corran had worked with, but the man himself – dead or alive – was proving elusive. With the hell that was the Candle Cake Killer kicking off in Plymouth they'd been reduced to doing the door-to-door work themselves with just the members of the Tavistock Rural team to lend a hand. Bright and keen as they were to help, there were only three of them: two PCSOs and a PC. Operation *Radial* it wasn't. They managed to finish the last street in Princetown by one o'clock but their notebooks were as empty of substantive facts as the sky was of clouds.

'Dinner,' Davies said, meaning to Riley's way of thinking, lunch. Davies added 'not here' and they set off to drive over the moor to the Warren House Inn a few miles north-west of Princetown.

The only reason Davies appeared to have chosen the place seemed to be so he could show Riley the fire in the bar.

'Nice,' Riley said, not quite understanding the significance of the smouldering logs until Davies told him the fire had been burning continuously since 1845.

'About the time Operation *Cowbell* started,' Davies said. 'At least that's the way it feels to me.'

Now there was an uneasy silence between the two men as they sat and waited for their meals. Riley, not for the first time since they'd been working together, was trying to get a handle on the older detective. What made him tick, what kept him going, despite his unpopularity?

Davies looked across at Riley and chuckled. He shook his head. Stared down into his pint. Spoke.

'That business earlier in the year. Kenny Fallon. I wondered whether an explanation might be in order.'

'Sir?' Riley pulled his pint nearer, took a sip. Kenny Fallon was the kingpin in the Plymouth underworld. A man who'd worked his way up from the grim streets of the North Prospect area of the city to the point where he was now worth millions, half his businesses legit, the other half kept at arm's length. Riley had been part of a long-term drugs op which had aimed to catch Fallon as he smuggled several million pounds of coke in aboard a luxury motor yacht. The operation had, quite literally, sunk, Fallon escaping without charge.

'I know what you think. You and Savage.' Davies took a sip of his own pint, the foam from the Guinness painting a moustache for a moment before his tongue slipped out and wiped it away. 'Bent. Am I right?'

'You were in league with Fallon, feeding him information so he could get the gear in under our noses. That operation – *Sternway* – was years in the planning, months of work. It all went down the pan.'

'You were undercover, Darius, up in London?' Riley nodded. 'It's like that with me. I'm not undercover, but I'm down there with the scum, mixing it up, they know who I am. "Phil Davies? He's that dodgy copper. Don't worry about him." Without me, there'd be no little birdy telling us about some scrote selling smack outside the local school. No one would tip us a name when there's been a particularly unpleasant murder. We wouldn't know who's who in the organised crime network.'

'With respect, sir, that's complete bollocks.'

'Yeah, you think so?' Davies shook his head and chuckled. 'You've got a lot to learn about how things operate down this part of the world, Darius.'

'Like getting a wad of fifties in a brown envelope?'

'Allegedly.' Davies winked. 'Makes me legit in their eyes, doesn't it? Anyway, if it hadn't been for Kenny Fallon you'd have been mincemeat. Ricky Budgeon would have cut you up into little pieces.'

'If I remember correctly it was good detective work by DC Calter which saved me.'

'And if *I* remember correctly there was a large element of luck too. On the other hand Fallon led me and Savage right to you.'

There was that, Riley had to concede. Ricky Budgeon, a man Riley had crossed up in London when he had been undercover, had captured Riley. Intent on killing him, the cavalry had arrived in the nick of time.

Riley's phone rang. Nick of time again. He answered it and got up, stepping away from the table and making his way outside the pub. He spoke to the caller for a minute or two and then hung up.

'Corran,' Riley said, when he returned to the table. 'The financial stuff has come through. The wife's taken out a life insurance policy recently. On Devlyn.'

'Canny bird.' Davies took several gulps of his beer. 'How much?'

'Two fifty K.'

'Nice little earner.' Davies whistled and then considered the froth on the remains of his pint. 'So, there's several possibilities. One, the whole thing is a set-up and Corran isn't dead. He's holed up in some cheapo hotel watching daytime TV, waiting for a call from the Mrs. Being a PO he'll be canny, he'll have met cons on the inside who tried this kind of thing and failed.'

'Meaning?'

'They'll play it long. Very long. When she's got the cash she'll move away, back up North probably. It'll be in a year or two's time, but then they'll be able to collect.'

'Without a body?' Riley shook his head. 'That's not going to happen, boss. There'll have to be an inquest, evidence from us. We're back to the bike lamp again. Doesn't prove a thing.'

'OK,' Davies conceded, 'number two: Mrs C killed hubby. Somehow she's made it look like a hit and run. The body will turn up and she gets the dough.' Davies tipped the remainder of his beer down his throat and then banged the glass down on the table. 'Tell you what, I reckon we get back down there and press her. Take her into Crownhill and let her sweat.'

'I don't think so,' Riley shook his head. 'There's a little girl, the daughter. Distraught. No way the mother was acting, which means she didn't do it.'

'Which leaves number three. The two of them knew Corran was in danger, they were aware of the threat. The policy is just what it says on the tin. Insurance. In which case she knows, right?'

'Possibly.'

'There you go. My plan still holds. We question her hard. Use the child as a bargaining tool. Social services, child protection, the works. The mother will be squealing before too long. Promise.' Davies stared down at his empty glass and then nodded to where a waitress was bringing their food across. 'Now, I'll need something to wash this lot down, Sergeant. Your round I think.'

Savage's appointment with Dr Peter Wilson was for Wednesday afternoon, the psychologist back from London. 'Home Office business,' his secretary had said. 'Meetings.'

Wilson had a suite of rooms attached to a smart new private health centre in Plympton. The sign at the entrance announced various treatments and practitioners including an acupuncturist and a reflexologist. Wilson offered psychotherapy. The good folk of Plympton obviously had more money than sense, Savage reflected as she pushed through the entrance doors and made herself known to a receptionist.

Dr Wilson was a stick-like figure, made slighter by the huge mahogany desk he sat behind. When Savage entered he rose and extended a hand across the vast green leather top, bare apart from a rather smart Rolodex-type card index, a little flip calendar, and a pile of well-ordered papers. Savage couldn't help but think the desk was about status and not utility.

'DI Savage,' Wilson said. 'Pleased to meet you.'

The grasp of Wilson's palm felt bony, like shaking hands with a skeleton. His arm seemed to telescope out from the sleeve of his suit, the suit itself of high quality, but ill-fitting. Wilson had no presence, his neat but nondescript brown hair sitting on an angular face with little eyes which were unable to meet hers for more than an instant before flittering off in another direction. Perhaps for a moment even alighting on her breasts, waist and legs. Hell, Savage thought, this was Walsh's fault. Preconceptions were clouding her judgement.

'Call me Charlotte,' she said as way of reparation, before sitting in a high-backed chair set to one side of the desk.

'I hope,' Wilson said, 'I can be of more use to the investigation this time. I am certainly older and wiser.'

'Dr Wilson, you have to understand we're not officially involving you at this stage, but we would value your opinions on the case. Specifically how any new evidence might fit in with your previous analysis.'

'I see.' Wilson glanced over at a photograph on the wall. The picture showed Wilson shaking the hand of another man, the pair standing in front of some sort of crest. Wilson looked back at Savage. 'FBI. I spent some time over in the States. That's the Deputy Director thanking me for a paper I presented at a conference a few years back. Funnily enough, the paper was entitled "When the Killing Stops" but I guess you guys know everything there is to know about serial murder so perhaps we should call it a day and I'll get back to work.'

Savage sighed. 'You have to bear in mind the failure of the previous investigation still rankles. There was also a

113

personal matter concerning your behaviour with a member of staff. I don't know the ins and outs of what happened and maybe there were jealousies involving other people. Memories are long.'

'The woman . . . well, I was younger. To coin a phrase, I had a moment of madness. As a psychologist you may say I should have known better, but I'm human too. However, I've learnt from my errors. I'm now in private practice and I can't afford to make the same mistakes again. And as to the failure of the investigation, well that's why I want to help now. The inability to catch the killer infuriates me as much as it does you. Or, for that matter, DCI Walsh.'

'Ex-DCI Walsh. He's retired.'

'Has he really?' Wilson smiled. The question was rhetorical, Savage realised. The psychologist knew damn well Walsh was no longer with the force. 'Well, I can understand retirement must be tough for him. Knowing he's not going to be involved. Realising he didn't prevent the killer claiming yet more victims. Living with failure.'

'We're consulting him.' Savage waited to see the reaction – a slow intake of breath – before she continued. 'Just as I'm consulting you now.'

'The Deputy Director always used to comment on my methods of working.' Wilson reached out and touched the Rolodex. The thing was some sort of executive version, made of wood. Wilson thumbed through a few index cards. 'I brought this over to the US from the UK and the thing became a bit of an "in" joke. You see, I helped track down a killer by the name of Peeking Paul and I did it without the use of computers or technology.'

Wilson swivelled his chair and got up. He walked to the window and put his hand to his chin.

'Look, I've dealt extensively with serial offenders. Recently

114

I've been over at Channings Wood in Newton Abbot studying paedophiles and other sex offenders. I *know* these sort of people, know how they operate, what they are capable of. The killer could be out there right now. Passing by on the street, passing within a few feet of one of your officers. You'd never know. You might have had him in custody, he might be your next-door neighbour, he might be an anonymous worker at some factory on an industrial estate. You've no idea who he is because there are no witnesses and no forensic. If he doesn't make a mistake then last year's victim is destined to be the first of another set.'

Wilson turned back from the window and Savage nodded. Everything he said was true.

'The date.' Wilson returned to his desk and once seated he pointed at the little calendar next to the Rolodex. 'I assume the date has not escaped your attention?'

'Of course not. We're trying to formulate some sort of strategy, both investigative and preventative, but we haven't got long. Which is why we could do with your input.'

'That paper I mentioned a few minutes ago.' Wilson glanced across at the picture on the wall again and then turned back to Savage. 'I didn't do it to show off. The paper considered what happens when, literally, the killing stops. Often investigative forces can do little until another death. It's unpalatable but true. The good news, if it can be called that, is when the killing does start up after a long respite, it can be the beginning of the endgame for the killer. They go crazy, make mistakes. Sometimes it's almost as if they want to be caught, but that's the wrong way around. They come to believe they *can't* be caught. Which is why as soon as I heard the police had found the bodies of the missing women I got in touch.'

'So how do you think you can help us?'

115

'I'll need to see the burial site ASAP. This afternoon if possible. Obviously with the first corpse – Mandy Glastone – there was no burial, she was dumped in the river. Uncharacteristic. Analysis of a grave site can reveal a lot about a killer. It was what was missing from my report of the first killing and the missing persons. And it was what helped me catch Peeking Paul.' Wilson doodled on a piece of paper. 'The Candle Cake Killer is not going to get the better of us this time. This time we will catch him.'

Us. We. Wilson clearly believed he was back on the team. With what she'd heard, Savage could think of no reason he shouldn't be.

Apart, she reflected, from the issue of Walsh's feelings.

Davies had been a little too much mouth and not enough trousers when it came to pressing Corran's wife. After lunch they'd called in at the Dousland cottage, Cassie Corran as distraught as ever. Maybe Davies' softness was down to the fact that, unbeknown to Mrs Corran, they'd spotted her through the living room window as they arrived, tears flowing down her cheeks. Or maybe it was the little girl, Emily. While Riley and Davies were there she'd run in from outside. Cassie was still crying and Emily had produced a tissue from her pocket and told her mother not to cry. Daddy would, she promised, be back soon.

Riley had asked about the life insurance and for a moment the woman's expression had made him think they were on to something. But the look on her face was fleeting. When Riley went on to ask about people Corran might have been worried about she looked blank, didn't know. If the whole thing was an act then it was a very good one.

Back at the station there was a message from a junior CSI on Layton's team. The results from the analysis on the paint

116

sample Layton had found on the road had come through. Riley called him up.

'It's a blue paint,' the CSI said, 'but the lab couldn't get a match. Either from a re-spray or a much older vehicle. Not much help I'm afraid.'

'Result?' Davies said, coming over as Riley hung up.

'Sort of,' Riley said. 'If narrowing the vehicle down to about a quarter of the cars on the road is a result.'

'Any ideas?' Davies scratched his day-old stubble. 'I mean how we go about finding the driver?'

'No witnesses, sod all forensic evidence, no body to examine? No, sir, I don't.'

'I thought you fast-track boys had all the answers.' Davies shook his head. 'What's the problem, that university education wasted on you, was it?'

The DI tapped Riley on the back before walking away, Riley not sure if the gesture was an admonishment or a consoling pat.

Davies gone, Riley bent to his pad and began jotting random thoughts, then drawing circles within which he wrote single words: Corran; prison; criminals; road; accident; bicycle; wife; history.

History. Corran's history. That would need to be fully investigated, sure, but was there something simpler here, something his over-educated brain was missing?

There was.

Riley swivelled his chair and moved his hands to the keyboard of a nearby terminal, thinking about RTAs or rather RTCs as they were called these days, the implication being that no incident on the road was an accident. Soon a list of traffic offences committed on Dartmoor scrolled in front of him. There was a paucity of serious ones. Riley supposed that could be because the moor wasn't a place routinely patrolled. Just two incidents flagged themselves up as being of interest. Both had resulted in fatalities.

In the first incident, a couple of years ago, three teenagers had been killed when their souped-up Fiesta had taken the run down from Haytor towards Bovey Tracy at way over the forty limit. The driver had lost control and the car had rolled and collided with a stone wall.

In the second incident a girl of nine had been killed while cycling on a minor road in the depths of the moor. A hit and run driver had failed to stop. The family of the girl had been picnicking close by and had seen the car speed away, but the driver had never been traced.

Riley stared again at the report. Took in the girl's name. *Clarissa Savage.*

Not . . .? Riley leant back in his chair, put his hands behind his head and glanced round the room. Then he beckoned to one of the nearby indexers, a guy who'd been doing the job for years. Riley pointed to the screen and asked if his assumption was correct. It was, the man said. Tragic. The DI hadn't been the same since. But then that sort of thing would do that to you, wouldn't it? Make you sad, bitter, make you look at life in a different way?

It would, Riley conceded, thanking the man and then reading the report again. The log detailed a blue Subaru Impreza. Even if the colour was the same, that was all. The event was a coincidence which left Riley feeling saddened, but Savage's daughter's death was an accident. Tragic, as the indexer had said, but in no way comparable to the Corran case.

Chapter Thirteen

You sit in the little dinghy as it bob, bob, bobs. A queasy feeling bubbles up from somewhere in your abdomen. Boats do that to you. It's the way they float on the water when they shouldn't. The same way an aeroplane hangs in the air on tiny wings. Not nice. Not right. But at the moment you don't have a lot of choice in the matter. Not if you want to watch what's going on.

Up the slope from the estuary you can see the farm. Buildings cluster round in a square, fences run in lines bisecting fields, hedges crawl the perimeter marking out the boundary of the land where hell started for you all those years ago. You don't remember any of it of course. You were never actually there, but nevertheless here is where it started. Without this place you'd have been fine. Normal. You wouldn't have suffered. You wouldn't have had to embark on this sick crusade. Because that's what it is: a crusade. And right now there's a group of infidels trying to stop you.

You dip the oars and pull, trying to keep the dinghy moving in a straight line. You don't want the people up in the field to notice you, to think there's anything unusual about the lone oarsman down on the river. You're just someone out for an afternoon row. Enjoying the sun, the fresh air, the smell of death drifting down the slope.

You're trying to see exactly what's happening at the farm. You know they've found your hiding place. Taken the bodies away. Those people up there, the police, they're causing you problems. You can't complete your mission with them milling and mulling and messing around. How long will they stay? A day or two? Longer, and there will be real grief. Like with the first one. You couldn't bury her where you wanted. Had to dump her body on the moor. You don't want to have to do the same with the next one. Which means everyone has to leave. The men up there. The women too. You've seen the one who owns the farm. The black-haired whore who took over the place. By rights you think the farm should have been yours. But that's not why you do what you do. The fact is incidental.

There's another woman who's been hanging around too. She's got red hair like a beacon. She's a police officer and you wonder what she'd look like tied to the oak table with Mikey drooling over her and the Big Knife sweeping and swooping.

Good. That's how she'd look. Tasty.

At the moment she's not part of your plan and for her sake, you hope it stays that way. But for you? Well, if she becomes too much trouble then you'd go for it. Oak table, Mikey, Big Knife and all.

Chapter Fourteen

Bere Ferrers, Devon. Wednesday 18th June. 2.32 p.m.

Savage sat outside the health centre, trying to juggle a number of appointments for the afternoon. Wilson wanted to visit the scene as soon as possible and she'd need to be there with him.

'Meet you there,' he'd said. 'Clearing the diary for this one. Got a patient to see and then I'm all yours.'

The psychologist had smiled, Savage unsure whether the double entendre had been intentional. As she flicked through her 'to do' list on her phone she wondered about the details of the harassment case against Wilson. The man obviously had a problem relating to women and she certainly hadn't warmed to him. Then again, maybe that was what it took to get inside the minds of serial killers. The phone vibrated, John Layton's name flashing up.

'Your Mr Shortcut been proving elusive then?' Layton said. 'Because I might have something for you.'

At first Savage wasn't sure what the senior CSI was on about. Then she realised he meant the unknown person who'd been using the route across the railway bridge at Tavy View Farm. She'd emailed Layton earlier asking if there wasn't an easier way of tracking the man down because so far they were having no luck. A PC sent down to watch the bike for a couple of hours around five p.m. Tuesday had reported the chain hanging loose from the tree, no sign of bicycle or rider. He'd been ordered to wait but a burglary-in-progress report at nearby Tamerton Foliot saw him called away. Two suspects were apprehended and taken in for processing and another emergency intervened. His late shift ended and by the time a replacement officer was able to return to the bridge the surrounding woods were filled with birdsong, sunlight piercing the horizon. And the bike was safely locked to the tree.

They couldn't spare anybody to repeat the debacle. Hence the email to Layton.

'UV,' he explained to Savage as he gave her the address. 'And I'm not talking sunbeds.'

'Sorry?' Savage said.

'The bike was marked with the postcode of the owner. Under UV light it showed up. As you suspected, the address is in Bere Ferrers.'

'On my way, John.'

Convenient, Savage thought, since she had to return to the village to meet Wilson.

The PL20 postcode led her to a semi-detached house on Station Road, the door opening after several knocks to a man bleary with sleep.

Mr Shortcut turned out to be a man by the name of Adam Narr. He was in his sixties and had a round face with a bulbous nose like a washed new potato. Savage explained nothing beyond the fact that she wanted a word. Narr took her through the house to the back garden where there was a circular table with four chairs and then excused himself. The plot was small, down to grass with a little vegetable patch at the far end. Peas and runner beans twisted up an elaborate tepee of bamboo canes and through the greenery Savage could see a low fence and fields which swept down to the estuary. To the right lay Tavy View Farm and farther away the railway bridge.

When Narr returned it was with a mug of tea for himself, nothing for her. He gestured towards the farm.

'You'll have come about them bodies no doubt,' he said. 'Tavy View. Knew it weren't right having a woman there. Man's job, farming. Bound to be trouble.'

The logic of Narr's words was lost on Savage so she ignored them and instead asked him about his trips over the bridge.

'You see you didn't mention any of that when the enquiry teams interviewed you. In fact you denied going near Tavy View Farm.'

'Hey?' Narr tried it on for a moment but he didn't have a liar's face. 'I've done nothing.'

'Your bike, Mr Narr. We know you use the bridge to get into Plymouth, but you told us you hadn't been anywhere near the railway line.'

'Well I would, wouldn't I?' Narr picked up his mug and slurped a gulp of tea. 'I expect it's not legal taking the shortcut, but residents have been going that route for years. At least they used to before everyone had cars.'

'And you don't have a car?'

'I do, but this way saves me a fortune in petrol, not to mention the difficulty parking. It's less than four miles from the other side of the bridge. An easy cycle to where I work.'

'Which is?'

'Derriford. I'm a night porter. Mostly nights anyway. Sometimes a half shift.'

'You can forget about trespass, Mr Narr. We're not interested in how you get to work. What we are interested in is whether you've seen anything in your comings and goings. Specifically around this time last year midsummer but at other times too.'

'Seen anything?' Narr's head turned, his eyes wandering to the right and the bridge. 'What, you mean like the killer?'

'Anything suspicious, anyone else on the bridge. Cars parked on the other side. Perhaps a boat on the river.'

'Bloody hell.' Narr took another swig from his mug and then drummed the fingers of his left hand on the table. 'He came across the bridge. That's what you're telling me. I'm coming one way, him the other. Jesus, he could have had me. Fuck the petrol, I'm going by car from now on.'

'That might be the safest,' Savage said. 'Now, did you see anything?'

'I've had a close call. He could have stabbed me, run me over, thrown me into the estuary even.'

'Run you over? Why do you say that?'

'Hey?'

'You said the killer could have run you over.'

'Yes, I did. Don't know why.'

'Was there a car parked on the other side of the bridge in the lane?'

'Now you come to mention it, there might have been at some point. Probably was a year ago too. I remember a smart top-end model being there on a couple of nights when the weather was warm. An executive's car. Never saw anyone inside. I assumed it was some businessman type out for a session in the woods with his secretary. You think that was the killer?'

'Can you remember anything about the vehicle? For instance the make or the colour.'

'Dark. Black or a dark shade of blue. It was possibly a German car. A BMW, Audi, Mercedes kind of thing. When

124

I say "executive" I mean expensive. Come to think of it, the thing was more of an SUV. Not a true 4x4.'

'And that's the first time you've seen a car down there?'

'Yes. At that time of night anyway. I was doing a half shift and knocking off at midnight. I'd have been there around half an hour later after leaving work. I never saw anybody though.'

'Are you sure?' Savage said.

'Yes. I definitely didn't see anyone.' Narr picked up his mug of tea again. This time his hand shook, liquid spilling out onto his trousers. 'The thing is, you've got me worried now. Just because I didn't see him, it doesn't mean he didn't see me, does it?'

After finishing her interview with Adam Narr, Savage went back to the farm to meet Dr Wilson. An unseasonal mist had risen from the Tamar, hiding the river's surface from view and marooning the peninsula in a sea of ethereal white. The railway line floated above the mist, forging across to the mainland and Plymouth. In the farmyard, Wilson leant against the gate looking down towards the field and the estuary.

'This,' Wilson said, turning as Savage approached, 'is more like it.'

'Meaning?' Savage said.

'Last time there was nothing. Except for the body of Mandy Glastone.' Wilson offered a thin smile. 'And with all respect to the woman, she wasn't much use. The location did nothing to help us as it was obviously random. I need more than a single body to enable me to build a profile.'

Savage nodded, wondering about the cuts, the cake and the candles, the victims' homes, the date, the clay which had led to the notion of the suspect being an artist. More than enough to start with she thought.

'This art business you mentioned back then . . .'

'What of it? DCI Walsh wasn't very impressed with my theory. It took the intervention of the Chief Constable to get any progress.'

'But the theory didn't lead anywhere, did it? Hundreds of studios visited, artists questioned, nothing came of that line of investigation, not one suspect.'

'That I have to concede but it doesn't mean I'm not correct.'

'You may well be, because we've found some more clay.'

'*What?*' There was shock for a moment on Wilson's face and then a smile spread. 'I told you! Back then, I told you!'

Savage wondered if she'd made a mistake, added to the pool of arrogance which Wilson drew from. It could only fuel his overbearing manner.

'The latest body,' she said. 'The clay was in the woman's oesophagus and stomach. Dr Andrew Nesbit is performing the remaining PMs today as we speak, but he's not hopeful of getting much so we might not be able to find out whether the killer did the same with the other victims.'

'Interesting.' Wilson reached for the catch on the gate and swung it open. As they walked down the metal tracks, he began to elaborate. 'The killer is trying to silence the woman. Or should I say *women*. Shoving the clay in the victim's mouth would be a symbolic act. Using the materials of his trade he strives to deny the woman, all women, a voice. The victims speak to him, plead even, but he doesn't want to listen. Women are an abomination to him, he can only think of them with heads or limbs missing, bodies contorted, genitals deformed or absent. He wants to remove their lies, remove their identity, most of all, remove evidence of their womanhood. I'm telling you, clay is the answer, the clay. Find the clay and you'll find the killer. Do you understand?'

Jesus, Savage thought, thinking of the bodies in the trench.

No heads, no genitals, certainly no longer recognisable as women. Wilson was spot on. Perhaps the force had made a huge mistake when it had abandoned the investigation and put aside the psychologist's theories.

Wilson continued, getting into his stride, a stream of consciousness filled with words Savage didn't understand. She wanted to stop him and ask how much of this was new information, lessons he'd learnt in the US. The FBI had much more experience in such things and she knew the National Center for the Analysis of Violent Crime in Quantico, Virginia were experts in identifying the signature aspects in serial killings. Had Wilson picked this up there? Maybe even, as he'd suggested, contributed himself?

'. . . and will seek to achieve self-actualisation, the peak experiences needing to be more frequent to satiate his needs.' They were nearing the crime scene tent now and Wilson stopped and looked around. 'During all this you can be sure he'll be watching us. We need to be aware of that.'

Savage glanced around too, seeing the nearby hedges and beyond, only mist.

'Not here, surely?'

'Oh yes.' Wilson picked his way across the stepping plates to the tent. 'Killers return to the crime scene for many reasons. To have sex with the bodies or to retrieve trophies, to relive the moment of the murder, even more prosaically to clean up and ensure they've left no incriminating evidence.'

'So far we've found nothing.'

'And you won't.' Wilson lifted the flap of the tent. 'My goodness. Wonderful.'

'Really?' Savage's mind flitted back to the first time she'd seen the hole on Saturday. Shorn of the ghoulishness of the night the hole was just an excavation, the temporary resting place for three souls, yes, but nothing wonderful about it.

'Yes. Even my friends in the FBI would be impressed with this.' Wilson peered into the hole and then back at Savage. 'This might seem a strange request, but could I be permitted a few minutes on my own? I need a little space to work.'

'Sure.' Savage moved away from the tent and walked back to the metal tracks. The first night she too had needed space to focus. She'd had to blot everything from her mind. Today Wilson had the luxury of peace.

Savage looked around the field and thought about the psychologist's idea about the killer revisiting the scene. If the killer was going to return to the site he'd be conspicuous. So far there'd been some sort of police presence twenty-four-seven but it wouldn't continue for much longer. Savage wondered about posting some sort of watch. Decided it was worth asking Wilson about.

Back in the tent Wilson had a small camera out and was taking pictures, the flash firing in the low light. Fifty metres past the tent Savage could see Layton and two other CSIs working a new area of ground marked out with tape. Beyond them the mist had thinned and the river was now visible. A solitary rowing dinghy drifted on the Tavy, slipping beneath the columns of the bridge as the oars dipped and left circles on the water.

The noise startled Narr and he jerked awake, knocking the garden table and spilling his second cup of tea. He cursed. The policewoman had not long gone, leaving him in a bit of a state, and now he glanced around the garden, almost expecting the murderer to come at him with an axe.

After a moment he realised somebody was at the front door. He got up and went inside, surprised when he opened the door to see Joanne Black and her farmworker standing there.

'Joanne.' Narr smiled and then nodded at the man alongside. 'Jody. This isn't, I guess, a social call?'

'No, Adam.' Joanne shook her head. 'Can I have a word?'

Narr showed the two of them in, holding the door and admiring Joanne from the rear as she walked past. Not a bad arse, he thought. Wouldn't say no to rutting with her. Out the back, Jody slumped down on one of the garden chairs. Joanne stood gazing out over the fields.

'Rum do,' Narr said. 'Those bodies turning up on your land.'

'You could say that.' Joanne didn't move. 'But they didn't just turn up. Someone put them there.'

'And you know who did?' Narr glanced down at Jody, but the farmworker shook his head. Narr smiled at Jody and then went and stood beside Joanne. 'No, you don't have a clue. But you think I might.'

'You've lived in this house all your life, Adam.' Joanne glanced across and then back at the fields. 'You're as much part of this village as the church or the pub. I said as much to Jody. If anyone knows, you do.'

'I can tell you I don't know the killer. I've had the police come knocking twice. Told them the same. Who from round here would do such a thing? Can't say I'm much enamoured of most of the people in the village, but even I don't suspect any of them of murder.'

'But the farm, *my* farm. You know all about that, don't you?' Joanne waved her hand in the direction of the river. 'On my land there's a concrete plinth. There used to be a bungalow standing on the site, but Jody says he and my uncle demolished the building twenty-five years ago. Back when I visited the farm as a little girl I was looked after a few times by a young lass who lived in the bungalow. Her name was Laura or Lauren. Something like that.'

'Lara.' Narr grinned. 'She were my age. Fit. Every red-blooded male in the village and beyond was after her. She were like a young bitch coming into heat for the first time. We all had our tongues hanging out over her, but she wasn't interested. Gossip said she liked them older.'

'Really?' Joanne looked at Narr again. Held his gaze this time. 'When I returned to the farm one year she and her family had gone. My uncle didn't give a reason other than they'd moved away.'

'Moved away. That'd be it. Crafty old sod.'

'So there *was* more to the story then. I thought as much. What happened?'

'Your uncle was sweet on Lara. Very sweet. But he was twenty years older and she was young and flighty.'

'And she liked older men?'

'She may well have done, but not your uncle. Plus her parents weren't happy about it.'

'Are you saying . . .?'

'I'm saying when the bee comes after the honey you best keep the lid on the jar. The family upped sticks and left and I guess that were the reason.'

'My uncle wasn't married to my aunt back then?'

'No. Soon after Lara left he married a woman around his age – your aunt. As you know, she died a few years before your uncle. They never had any children.'

'Which is how I came to inherit the farm.'

'Yes.' Narr shook his head. 'Lucky bugger.'

'You might say that.' Joanne looked out over the fields again. 'But I'm not feeling so lucky now, am I?'

Chapter Fifteen

When Savage walked into the crime suite Thursday morning Gareth Collier's number countdown had reached '2'. Keyboards clattered in a frenzy as the indexers hunkered down at their workstations, Collier moving between desks like a lion circling his prey. Every now and then he'd pause at somebody's shoulder and raise an arm and scratch the stubble on top of his head. Then his arm would shoot down, a finger jabbing at a screen. The office manager knew all too well that this was where the murders might be solved, but a wrong entry or a piece of data misfiled could lead to disaster.

The big news evidence-wise was the SUV Adam Narr recalled seeing on the Plymouth side of the railway bridge. Phil Glastone owned two cars, one an Alfa Romeo 8C Spider, the other an SUV in the form of a Volvo XC60. On hearing the information, several members of the team had reacted as if Glastone was as good as convicted. Savage wasn't so sure. Narr had identified the type of car, not the make or model. And there was no way he could pin down the exact date he saw the car. She explained to the team that they needed to work at the alibi Glastone had given for the Sue Kendle murder. They also had to make sure the vehicle info was watertight. Finally they needed to understand his motive and why he took a break from the killing. Glastone had been living and working in Salcombe the whole time, so there had to be a reason for the hiatus.

After she'd finished her mini-briefing Collier came over to Savage.

'Knife edge, ma'am,' he said. 'If we take the vehicle picture book out to Narr and he says the car he saw was a Volvo XC60 then we're rocking. Anything like that could pin Glastone down and link him to the bridge. We build a case from there, bit by bit. Forensics, phone traces, additional witnesses. On the other hand, we get the wrong piece of information and he could be above suspicion.'

As if in response to Collier's statement a phone rang. Across the other side of the crime suite DC Calter reached for the handset and answered. She nodded, wrote something down on a pad and hung up.

'Confirmation that two of the victims are Sue Kendle and Heidi Luckmann,' she said to a room all of a sudden silent, every officer hanging on her words. 'And as for the third, well we've got an ID for her too.'

Body three turned out to be a woman by the name of Katherine Mallory. Samples collected by Nesbit at the PM had resulted in a DNA match relating to a missing person inquiry up in Bristol. The woman in question had been cautioned as regards a cannabis possession charge a couple of years ago and her DNA was still on file.

Following the ID Calter worked the phones for an hour and then briefed Savage.

'I've spoken to somebody from the Avon and Somerset force. The girl went missing last year. Twenty-first of June.'

'Shit,' Savage said. 'That confirms it then. Anything about a cake?'

'Not according to the material on the system.'

The inquiry hadn't been high priority, Calter said. The girl was over eighteen, not in any way thought to be vulnerable, and after an initial investigation the Bristol team concluded she went walkabout after a tiff with her lover. The file was still open, but the officer on the line had been keen to notch up another result once the formalities had been dealt with.

'They solve their misper and we get a murder,' Calter said. 'Hardly seems a fair exchange.'

'Not very fair on the girl either,' Savage said. 'Let's hope there's at least a few red faces up there.'

Savage took the sheaf of papers from Calter and began to read through the material. She headed out of the crime suite and up to Hardin's office, where a grunt like something from a wild boar greeted her knock at the door.

'The unidentified woman, sir,' Savage said as Hardin looked up from a copy of *The Sun* which sat beside a plate with a stack of chocolate cream biscuits. 'She went missing up in Bristol, but was originally from Dartmouth. Her name's Katherine Mallory. Katie to her friends, Kat to her lover.'

'And who is he, the lover?' Hardin said. 'Should he be on our radar as a person of interest?'

'She, sir. He is a she.'

'Oh.' Hardin glanced at his computer screen and reached for his mouse, possibly, Savage thought, for a directive on dealing with lesbian suspects or next-of-kin. After a couple of clicks, he continued. 'Well, you'll be having words, won't you? Don't think Mike Garrett would be up to the job.'

Savage outlined what else they knew about Katherine Mallory's disappearance, including the absence of the killer's motif: the cake.

'I'll be visiting her parents first and then going up to Bristol later this afternoon,' Savage said. 'To see if we can get to the bottom of it. I'll speak to the local force and Mallory's lover. The parents will have no idea, Katherine not being linked in any way to the Candle Cake Killer.'

'What I want to know,' Hardin said, picking up a chocolate cream and turning it over in his hand, 'is where *was* the bloody cake? I mean this girl goes missing, a victim we now know of our man, but there's no cake. Do you think the Somerset and Avon force could have made an almighty balls-up?'

'I can't see how they could have missed it, but you're right, if they did then someone's for the chop.'

'Chop?' Hardin said, pausing as if he was about to come up with a witty pun. Nothing doing he continued. 'Phil Glastone. I want you to find out if he's got connections to Bristol. Whether he could have possibly known the Mallory girl. You said she was originally from Dartmouth?'

'Close by, yes, Dittisham.'

'Nice.'

Savage could see from Hardin's expression that the thought of Katherine Mallory living in Dittisham was far from nice. He was probably trying to resolve the girl's sexuality with the picture-postcard image of the riverside village stuffed with million-pound houses.

'The local connection is possible,' Savage said, 'although Glastone is nearly twice the girl's age. Maybe he knew her through the parents. As to Bristol, well I wouldn't be surprised if Glastone visits the city to do with his job.'

'Remind me,' Hardin said.

'He's a database programmer. Freelance. Well paid. He lives in an expensive house, drives a new Alfa, takes several holidays abroad each year.'

'Right.' Hardin's face creased again. Well paid IT professionals

134

didn't appear to command any more respect than lesbians. 'Well, get up there and find something. Anything.'

'Yes, sir.'

'And remember, Charlotte, we need results.' Hardin turned to a calendar on the wall where June's picture showed a Dartmoor brook, several children playing in the water, the whole thing bathed in warm light. He jabbed his finger at the twenty-first. 'Within the next two days, got it?'

When Marion Mallory opened the front door and saw the two people on her step she knew something wasn't quite right. The woman, late thirties, with red hair tied back, looked hesitant. The man, a good deal younger and with a pleasant, open face, wore a smile which wasn't really a smile. Their expressions spoke volumes.

The pair were too neat to be selling anything, their suits – a grey knee-length skirt and a jacket for the woman, charcoal for the man – somehow too official for debt collectors, God-bods or political canvassers. It was as the woman reached into her jacket and extracted a card, the word 'Savage' jumping out, that Marion realised.

'Oh, you've found something then?' she heard herself say, the sentence phrased as if the pair were reporting the recovery of a stolen car.

Then she was stepping back into the house, a hand reaching out to the wall for support. Wishing her husband was home. And crying. The tears running down her face hot and angry and futile.

Savage had driven east in the early afternoon, accompanied by Calter and Luke Farrell, the family liaison officer she had brought with her as much for her own comfort and support as for Katherine Mallory's mother. Farrell came in his own car so Savage and Calter could continue on to Bristol and a meeting with Katherine's lover.

The village of Dittisham sat on a great curl of the river Dart a couple of miles above Dartmouth. Dittisham, pronounced 'Ditsum' by those in the know, wasn't so much a playground for the rich as a retirement complex for those affluent enough to be able to afford to live there. A mixture of thatched cottages, bungalows and huge detached houses clung to the slopes above the river and the Mallorys lived in one of the latter, halfway down Riverside Road. Savage had to admit the view was close to priceless. With the tide in, the Dart was as picturesque as ever with boats frittering this way and that. A ferry was making the crossing from Dittisham to the quay at Greenway House and Savage pointed out the place to Farrell as the two of them walked up to the front gate, Calter remaining in the car. Three was definitely a crowd in this situation.

'Know who used to live there, Luke?' Savage said. Farrell shook his head. 'Agatha Christie. We could probably do with her help now.'

'I don't think Miss Marple would help soften the blow, boss,' Farrell said. 'Stiff upper lip, cup of sweetened tea and all that crap.'

Farrell had been proved correct and Marion Mallory's initial matter-of-fact manner had vanished into tears and sobbing. The anguish had increased when Farrell broke the news that Katherine had likely been a victim of the Candle Cake Killer. Over the year Katherine had been missing Marion had obviously prepared herself for the worst, but the worst turned out to be nothing compared to the truth. In the last few days she'd seen the news, the TV pictures of Tavy View Farm, the endless recounting of events; she'd never imagined her daughter caught up in it all.

The tears, though, had come and gone with the tea and now there was only a bleak recounting of the events, the little snippets of information which Marion would remember long after she'd forgotten her daughter's smile.

They were in the living room which, size excepted, was no different from a million others. Television, sofa and armchairs, a coffee table with the morning's papers still spread out alongside a pile of post and three teacups, now drained of their contents. A clock on the mantelpiece and next to it a photograph of a girl. Not a girl, a young woman, twenty-seven, maybe a little younger in the picture, but frozen at that age forever now.

Savage sat in one of the armchairs, while Farrell perched on the sofa next to Marion. Farrell's unruly mess of hair and youthful demeanour contrasted with his sombre suit, the effect at once uplifting and reassuring. Whether intentional or not, Farrell's presence always seemed to make both victims and other officers more relaxed.

The details told, Marion confessed she'd known her daughter was dead from day one.

'You do, don't you?' she said. 'And yet, however much you wish it wouldn't, somehow the sliver of hope conspires to stick around. A cruel and unusual punishment is what I'd call it.'

Savage knew about that form of hell from when her daughter Clarissa had been in a coma after being knocked off her bike. Although at least in her own case, the hell hadn't lasted much more than a day. Not the weeks and months which Marion Mallory had had to endure. Savage saw the anguish written in the lines on her face, could sense the emptiness sitting in the woman's soul. That kind of void could eat you up little by little until nothing good remained. Savage had to prevent herself from clenching her fists in anger, instead making a silent promise that she'd get the bastard who had caused all this misery. She swallowed, aware of what she needed to say next.

'I hope this doesn't add to your distress, but the post-mortem has revealed that Katherine had given birth at some point. Did you know that?'

'Yes.'

'You didn't say anything at the time. There's nothing on the missing person report we have from Avon and Somerset police.'

'Isn't there? I guess it never crossed our minds. She had a child at fifteen, Inspector. A girl. Sadly Katherine had anorexia and other issues. There was no way she could keep the baby. I don't think she regretted her decision. It wasn't something we tried to keep secret, more we just didn't want to be reminded of it. The baby was adopted years ago. Do you think it could have a bearing on the case?'

'I doubt it, but we just need to cover all the bases. The child would be, what, twelve now? Is it possible Katherine tried to make contact?'

'I don't see why she would. She left that part of her life behind after she recovered from her problems.'

'And you never tried to get in touch with the child's adopted parents or your grandchild yourself?'

'Grand . . .' Marion reached out into the air, grasping at something invisible, before Farrell took her hand.

'Sorry, I didn't mean to—'

'To tell you the truth I desperately wanted to contact her when Katherine went missing, but my husband argued we should hold back because it would only cause the child confusion, maybe upset her. Katherine's own problems began as she became a teenager and . . . well, do you understand?'

'Yes. It was a noble decision. Perhaps when the child turns eighteen?'

'Ma'am?' Farrell glanced across at Savage and then back to Marion. 'It's a good idea, but the child has the final say in this situation. There will need to be checks.'

'Of course.'

'You don't think this could be something to do with that, do you?' Marion's hand tensed, gripping Farrell's for a moment before she let go and placed her hands in her lap.

'Unlikely. But let's say she *had* tried to contact her, perhaps she crossed paths with someone. A taxi driver, a neighbour of the adoptive parents perhaps. The person could be in our system, along with hundreds of others. If we could find a link between the victims we may be able to find Kathcrine's killer.'

'The Candle . . .' Marion couldn't complete the sentence, the tears coming again, before she wiped her eyes and composed herself. 'I don't understand how Kat got mixed up with this. I mean, she was living in Bristol. I thought the victims were from Devon. Anyway, it was years ago, wasn't it?'

Marion Mallory's words stayed with Savage after they'd concluded the interview and said their goodbyes.

Years ago.

The time interval was significant. Serial killers usually increased their rate of killing and only death or capture ended a spree once started. Rarely did the gap between killings lengthen or the killings stop and restart.

As Calter drove, Savage called up Dr Wilson and put the question to him.

'Gary Ridgeway,' Wilson said. 'Known as the Green River Killer. Killed dozens of women and then the murders almost completely stopped.'

'This is the States, right?' Savage said.

'Oh yes. They don't do things by halves over there.'

'And why did he stop killing?'

'He found the love of a good woman. Between 1982 and 1985 he killed over forty women. Then from '85 onward until 2001 when he was apprehended he only killed four more.'

'Only. Jesus.'

'Yes. Like I said, that's the US for you.'

'This woman . . .'

'Ridgeway met someone in 1985 and later married her. It was his third marriage but this time the relationship worked out. At least until he was arrested.'

'I've been thinking about prison or the killer being abroad as the reason for the gap in the killings; do you think instead it could be something like you just described?'

Wilson didn't answer and there was a long period of silence. Savage checked her phone to see she still had a signal.

'Dr Wilson?' she said. 'Are you there?'

'Yes, I'm thinking.' There was a further pause before Wilson continued. 'There are no women in the killer's life; he hates them, remember?'

'But if there was someone, could her presence explain the lull?' Savage stopped for a moment herself. Thought about Glastone. 'Or maybe even the reverse?'

'Sorry?'

'Could the presence of a woman in the killer's life where before there was none cause him to kill?'

Again silence. Wilson computing the question. Savage imagined him in his consulting room staring at his beloved picture of the Deputy Director of the FBI for inspiration. Some seconds later Wilson's voice came whispering through.

'Yes. I believe it could.'

Then the line went dead.

Chapter Sixteen

Clifton, Bristol. Thursday 19th June. 3.55 p.m.

The details of Katherine Mallory's ex had come from Avon and Somerset police, Calter managing to arrange an appointment to interview her for Thursday afternoon. The woman, Rachel Grenfield, lived in the Clifton area of Bristol on College Road. Savage let Calter drive, but even with the DC hitting the speed limit whenever she could the journey still took over two hours.

'Lucky to find a space round here, ma'am,' Calter said to Savage as they parked up right opposite the house. As they got out she gestured at the stone wall which ran along one side of the road. 'You know what's on the other side of this don't you?'

Savage confessed she didn't and Calter smiled. 'The zoo. Her flat is on the top floor, right? Bet she has a great view of the gorillas.'

Savage glanced across the road at the imposing stone terrace. The houses were four- and five-storey and the top floors almost certainly would offer a vista which took in the zoo.

They crossed the road and went up some steps. A moment after Calter had pressed the doorbell they were buzzed into a lobby and a voice shouted down for them to 'come on up'.

At the top of three flights of stairs the door to Rachel's flat stood open. Savage knocked and entered, turning to the right into the living area where a woman stood gazing out of a window. The flat was smart, clean and uncluttered; Rachel the same. She wore a suit, her brown hair just brushing the padded shoulders of a dark jacket.

Mourning? Savage thought, but when the woman turned from the window the expression was one of bewilderment rather than sorrow.

'Nice place,' Calter said as she came through and indicated the room and the view.

'I'm a solicitor,' Rachel said, as if that explained everything.

It did explain the neat sheaves of paper on the glass coffee table, the law books too. Maybe it explained the woman's manner as well. The officer at Bristol CID had mentioned Rachel did criminal defence work. She'd be used to dealing with the police. Used to putting them in their place.

'We're sorry about Katherine Mallory,' Savage said.

'Don't be.' Rachel dismissed the comment with a wave of a hand and then indicated they should sit.

Savage eased herself down into the low sofa while Calter opted for a steel and wooden contraption in a corner, pulling out her notebook as she tried to make herself comfortable.

'When I heard yesterday I shed a tear but Kat was just a fling. Ten or eleven weeks, no more.' Rachel moved across the room and through a doorway, the sound of running water coming a moment later and then the hiss of a kettle starting to heat. 'We had loads of sex, but that was about the extent of the relationship. Kat was immature. It was hardly a meeting of minds.'

Cups rattled and Savage and Calter said yes to the offer of tea. The kettle rumbled to a boil and Rachel brought out three mugs and a fancy glass tea pot, the steam condensing on the inside.

'Milk and sugar?'

'Just milk, thank you,' Savage said, thinking the woman herself was cold as the fridge. 'When she went missing, you weren't troubled?'

'Kat was flighty. She stayed round my place most nights, but she'd disappeared once before after we'd argued. Didn't turn up until two days later.'

'Which is why you didn't worry.'

'I'd been busy, but the next day I found her bag behind the sofa. Her purse and mobile were inside. She never went anywhere without them so I called the police. Told them I was concerned. They came round here and sent someone over to her old digs, but said there was little they could do. Kat wasn't a kid, she was mid-twenties, mind of her own.'

'And this time you'd also had an argument?'

'Yes, a silly one really, about me flirting with another girl. Well, as I said, the relationship was physical. For me it was going to be good while it lasted, but it wouldn't last. If you get my meaning.'

'So she wasn't your soulmate or anything,' Savage said. 'I can understand that. But she was your friend, right?'

'Yes. Obviously. I'm not heartless.'

'Did she confide in you, perhaps tell you secrets about her past life?'

'About lovers and stuff?' Rachel considered the question for a moment before answering. 'No, not really. I knew she came from a privileged background, that her parents were stinking rich and didn't care much about her.'

'Did you know Kat had a baby when she was fifteen? That she gave it up for adoption?'

'But . . .' Rachel's face bore a genuine look of astonishment which then slipped into understanding. 'You've thrown me, but it makes sense. Like I said, Kat was childlike herself. Clingy at times, aloof and moody at others. I thought it was the lack of love from her parents. I can see now it could have been to do with the baby.'

'Yes.' Savage got up and moved to the window. Calter was right about the zoo. Over the high wall Savage could see the gardens spread out, people wandering the paths, kids running ahead of their parents, eager to chalk up another animal to the day's tally. Close at hand there was some sort of enclosure with water, a series of interlinked pools with walkways between them. A dark shape came to the surface and the smooth black head of a seal emerged before sliding under again and leaving nothing but a ripple. Not much more than that for Kat Mallory. Savage turned back to Rachel. 'And apart from the argument there was nothing else amiss, nothing unusual?'

'What do you mean?'

'Any odd behaviour, something she may have said, something worrying her.'

'No. And to be honest the argument was over and she'd already apologised in her own way.'

'Sorry? I thought you said you didn't see her again.'

'I didn't. But she left me a present. After I realised she wasn't coming back I began to see it as a leaving present rather than a kiss and make up present. Now I don't know what to think.'

'Can we see it?' Calter said, looking up from her pad, shifting to let the steel frame dig into a different part of her back. 'The present?'

'No, of course not.' Rachel laughed, but all of a sudden Savage could see tears in her eyes as well, the recollection of the gift bringing forth memories of Kat. 'You don't keep something like that, do you?'

'I don't know, Rachel,' Savage said. 'Perhaps you'd better tell us what it was and what you did with it?'

'I ate it, of course.' Rachel shook her head, the tears gone in an instant, the contempt for the oh-so-stupid police back. 'What else would you do with a bloody cake?'

So far Thursday had, in Riley's opinion, been a waste of time. There was still no sign of Corran and no further developments. Leads were drying up.

'Like my throat,' Davies said at five o'clock. 'Fancy stopping off for one on the way home?'

Riley declined. He had something else in mind.

He found John Layton in the canteen enjoying a glass of orange juice and a light read. The light read being dozens of photographs of the bodies from Tavy View Farm.

'What's this?' Layton asked, nodding a 'thanks' when Riley placed a new glass of juice in front of him. 'Something about the Dartmoor hit and run?'

'Yes,' Riley said, 'but not the one the other day.'

Layton cocked his head, puzzled. He reached for the orange juice.

'Go on.'

'DI Savage. The RTC which killed her daughter.'

'Forget it.' Layton placed the glass back on the table. Looked like he was going to get up and walk away. 'The whole thing is done and dusted. We found nothing.'

'But it's not done and dusted, is it? Not for DI Savage.'

Layton sighed, shook his head and reached out and tidied the crime scene photographs into a neat pile. He gestured at Riley to sit down.

'Darius,' Layton said. 'Don't you think we tried? More than just about any other case, we tried. The poor woman. Her husband, Pete, away, her working all hours doing the job, having to look after three kids and then suddenly only two. I've got a daughter near the same age. Tugged at my heart, I can tell you.'

'From the start, John, if you please.'

For a moment Riley thought Layton was going to refuse. The frown on his face suggested some sort of inner conflict, as if he didn't want to go over the affair again. But then he took a deep breath. Exhaled.

'Yes. OK,' he said. He reached for the fresh glass of juice again and took a sip. Put the glass down and looked across at Riley. 'August. Charlotte is on Dartmoor with the three kids. It's a beautiful sunny day and the four of them are picnicking beside a stream.'

'Pete?'

'He's away. For the moment.' Layton took another sip of juice. 'The twins – that's Samantha and Clarissa – are nine. I can tell you that age they're a handful, think they know everything. Anyway, Clarissa is on her bike on the road. The lane's a very quiet one, not the sort of place you'd go speeding along.'

'But someone did?'

'Yup. Fifty to sixty miles an hour-plus, I reckoned from the damage to the bike. Clarissa is knocked off, she's unconscious and in a critical condition. An air ambulance arrives within fifteen minutes, but Charlotte can't go with the crew, she has to stay with her children. Eventually she gets to the hospital. Pete, by a stroke of luck, is on his frigate in Gibraltar. He's able to get a military flight back. The little girl is in a bad way, brain dead the doctors say. She never recovers consciousness and the life support is switched off a day later.'

Riley drew in a breath, closed his eyes for a second, seeking some sort of answer from somewhere. When he opened them he could see Layton staring forward into space, his own eyes focused on thin air.

146

'And you never traced the car?'

'Self-bloody-evident that, Darius,' Layton said. 'Believe me, no stone was left unturned. At least not on the scientific side of things. DI Savage didn't get the index but she'd clocked the make: a Subaru Impreza. From a scrap of paint on the bike we worked out the car was a second generation model constructed sometime between 2001 and 2007. There were fifty-seven matching cars registered in Devon and Cornwall. Another twenty-five in Somerset. All the owners were visited and their cars checked for damage. Four of the cars had evidence of nearside damage or repair. One had been damaged before the incident in a crash Traffic had attended, leaving three possible suspects. One had a cast-iron alibi and the other two were questioned, but in the end to no avail. It wasn't considered feasible or – get this – economically worthwhile, to extend the search beyond that. Still, there were people putting in dozens of extra hours unpaid. Detectives took it upon themselves to visit cars farther afield. One of my CSIs spent the next year tracing every V5C2s and 3s that flagged up on the DVLA system.'

'Sorry?'

'A transfer to a new owner or to a motor trader or dismantler. The lad followed up each form submitted countrywide and there were hundreds.'

'Nothing?'

'Nothing.' Layton shook his head. 'Same for the other investigative avenues. Was this some kind of revenge attack? Was it deliberate? In the end no one knew.'

'Still open then?'

Layton nodded. He reached for his drink and necked the remaining couple of inches in one go. Picked up his photographs. Stood.

'Your heart's in the right place, Darius, but I'd forget trying to resurrect the case. For one thing you'll be wasting your time. For another it will only cause Charlotte more agony. No way any of us want that, do we?'

No, Riley thought as Layton walked off. Of course not. But if he owed Davies for saving his life he owed Savage too, and somehow he was going to find a way to pay her back.

'Bloody hell,' Calter said as they got back into the car for the drive back to Devon. 'She never realised and nor did the police.'

'They didn't know about the candles,' Savage said. 'By the time they'd turned up she'd eaten half the cake and chucked the candles in the bin. She told them about the cake alright but they never questioned that it had been baked by Katherine. Why would they? Our case was five years ago in time and a hundred miles down the motorway away in distance. Katherine Mallory was just another person on the misper list. No reason to think she was connected with the Candle Cake Killer.'

'Those candles, ma'am, why eleven? Not, as Rachel suspected, the eleven weeks that they'd been together, obviously.'

'Fifteen, seven, nineteen and now eleven. I've no idea.'

'I heard this guy on the radio the other day, ma'am.' As Calter started the car and pulled out she nodded towards the zoo. 'He was talking about monkeys and typewriters. Enough of them working away one-fingered and you'd get a Shakespeare play. We get enough candles we'll be seeing patterns left, right and centre.'

Savage looked at Calter, thinking she had the wrong metaphor but the right idea. The numbers didn't mean anything together, the number of candles somehow related only to each individual woman. But the previous investigation had gone over everything: birth date, age, height, weight, address, telephone numbers and combinations of those and other numbers.

'Something is missing,' she said. 'Forget your monkeys and Shakespeare, we simply need more information.'

'Good,' Calter said. 'Myself? All that flouncing around and stupid language, always thought it was total crap.'

The week seemed interminable. Maybe it was coming back after the break, Paula thought, maybe it was the fact the rain and grey clouds of the half-term holiday had turned into beautiful blue skies. Nothing could make the school day drag like beach weather, the idea she could be somewhere else rather than stuck in a classroom with a bunch of rowdy teenagers.

At least she'd had the chance to sample some of the fine weather. After school on Thursday she and two other teachers made a beeline for the nearest pub with a garden and the single bottle of chilled white they ordered quickly became two. They stayed to eat and then Paula had the sense to move on to soft drinks because the evening didn't show any sign of ending.

By ten they began to say their goodbyes and by ten-thirty Paula was walking back across Central Park towards her house in Peverell. The sky above was still pale with the remnants of the day and a lazy moon slipped above the horizon in the east. A couple of late-evening runners padded by, one puffing hard, not much more than shuffling along. Call that good for you? Paula thought, putting the wine, the plate full of nachos draped with cheese and the fact it wasn't even the weekend out of her mind.

She paused to chat to an older man with a dog who lived around the corner from her and then she was onto the final stretch where the trees crowded in on the right before the path exited onto Trelawney Road near her place, just a few houses down from the end.

Until this evening she'd forgotten about the incident earlier in the week. Seeing the tow truck twice was probably a coincidence, her anxiety heightened by the gossip in the staffroom. But now, walking across the park, her mind began to wander. Somewhere out there the killer was waiting to claim another victim. She'd seen the papers in the corner shop, the salacious headlines, the countdown to the weekend, the lurid speculation as to what he might be thinking, what he might be planning.

Silly, Paula said to herself. You've nothing to worry about. Just a couple of minutes to home.

The lamps along the path edge glowed, but the light they cast only served to emphasise the shadows beneath the trees. She quickened her pace, aware of a rustle in the undergrowth. And then, in amongst the trunks and low shrubs, Paula saw someone – *something* – move. Possibly it was a dog, a large one, bounding along for a second in a wash from one of the lights before it disappeared, a shout from the owner calling the animal away.

Paula walked on, half-trotting, feeling the sensation of eyes upon her. As she reached the end of the path, near now to the road and safety, she looked over her shoulder. Fifty metres or so away, masked by the gloom, there *was* someone. A man stepped out of the shadows onto the path and stared at her. Then the figure turned and walked away, clicking his fingers as he did so. Paula backed up, but kept looking, seeing a shape come from the trees and bound across to the figure. Not a dog, but a human, half-running, half-scampering until it reached the man and the pair of them moved away along the path, two shadows, one tall and thin, the other stooped and shambling.

Back home, front door locked and the bolts drawn across top and bottom, Paula made herself a cup of coffee. Sipping the drink with her legs curled up under her on the sofa, she wondered what she had seen. Some sex game? Two gays cruising? A couple out dogging? The word drew a smile until she remembered the shape, the man or woman on all fours, moving like a cross between a baboon and a huge hound.

The coffee tasted bitter now and she got up, went into the kitchen and poured it away, staring at her reflection in the glass of the window behind the sink. A mirror image, part of her. For a moment the wine clouded in, fuzzing her head. Memories bubbled up. The woman in front of her became a girl. Another part of her. How old would she be now? Fourteen?

Paula shook her head. Alcohol. Fun to start with but in the end a depressant. In the last couple of years she'd had enough of being down. She'd tried to deal with the issues through therapy and talking things through, unburdening herself of the guilt, had helped. Now she had a good relationship with her parents and at last a boyfriend who cared about her.

She ran water into the sink to flush away the coffee. She took some in her hand and splashed her face. Sobered up. Thought again of what she'd seen in the park. She looked at the window once more, this time trying to see beyond her reflection and into the small area she called a garden. If there was someone or something out there she'd never know. The Candle Cake Killer could be watching her every move, dribbling spittle from a demented and twisted face, putting a hand down his trousers . . .

She pulled open the cutlery drawer, selected the biggest knife she could find and went and got ready for bed.

Chapter Seventeen

You've been watching her again and that's excited you. Shouldn't really, because it's not about sexual gratification. You can get that any time with a yard of kitchen roll and your right hand. Back home now, and you need something to take your mind off the girl. A little preparation might do it.

Schlaaack, schlaaack, schlaaack.

The Big Knife slides across the whetstone, glinting with approval as each pass shaves a few microns from the steel and hones the blade to a razor edge.

The knife has to be sharp. Sharp means the skin parts as the knife glides across the body, cutting as you move your hand back and forth. No effort needed, just the weight of the blade. Like a razor cut, there's no pain, only the sensation of warmth spreading across flesh, the poison oozing from within. You've seen the look on their faces as they realise what is happening. They begin to think then, think with absolute clarity. In the remaining minutes and hours of their existence, they come to understand the truth.

Schlaaack, schlaaack, schlaaack.

Mikey comes into the room. Stops when he sees what you are doing. Grins.

The boy's only got two modes: happy or sad. Nothing between. You guess that's because his limited IQ allows for only the basest of emotions. He's never been officially diagnosed but he's got learning difficulties, other sorts of difficulties too. It wouldn't be PC to say so, but he is basically a dimwit. For your purposes, that's perfect, because Mikey believes anything you say and will do just about anything you want him to.

Handy.

Mikey always does the girls with you. Loves it. Lends a hand. More than a hand if you are honest. Mikey likes his fun. He takes a long time and sometimes you wonder where he gets the energy from.

'Got it?' you say to him. Mikey nods and holds up a new roll of gaffer tape. He's been helping you prepare things in the dining room. Spreading out the big plastic sheet. It covers the carpet completely and goes all the way to the walls where you fold the edges up and stick them with the tape. Then there's a piece for the table. Again, taped into place. You move to the wall near the window and point down to a section which still needs fixing. 'Over there, Mikey. Make sure it goes up to at least waist height.'

The plastic comes from a big roll you keep in the barn. One thousand gauge. Or 0.254 millimetres thick. When you've finished you can bundle the sheet up and burn the whole thing

The plastic makes a crinkly sound as you walk back and forth, reminding you of the time when Mummy and Daddy decorated the house. Of course, that's where you got the idea for the plastic from.

'We don't want any mess, do we?' Mummy said. 'Otherwise Daddy might get angry.'

That's right. No mess.

If only Daddy had thought of that then he might not have ended his days in prison with a piece of electrical cord knotted round his neck.

You don't intend to make the same mistake.

153

Schlaaack, schlaaack, schlaaack.

Back to the sharpening. Five more minutes and then you stop and scrape the blade across the back of your hand where the edge removes hairs as well as your Bic. Didn't really need a sharpen, to be honest, but it's part of the preparation, the ritual.

For now the Big Knife needs to be put away, but not in the kitchen. Kitchens are for cooking and eating. The Big Knife doesn't do cooking, not now, not since the cake. The cake was the last piece of food it cut. Not the last thing it cut, but the last piece of food.

Now the knife does other things and lives somewhere else.

You say 'live' because that's what it does. Not like 'lives in the drawer' – that's just bad English. Nothing can live in a drawer because it's dark and there's no food. Living things need light and sustenance and sometimes they need a little bit of love too.

So you keep the knife in the dining room, where it sits in a wall-mounted glass display case. The knife looks a little out of place, almost like a surrealist piece of art. That's because of the plastic plants, the rocks at the base and the blue background which simulates a flowing stream. The case once held a large stuffed trout, a fish your Daddy caught years ago. On the edge of your memory you remember the creature, all slimy, flapping on the bank of the river. Daddy taking the knife and sliding the point into the underside of the trout, the mouth still gasping for air as the guts slipped out.

You always point out the knife to your guests. You tell them the story about the knife being used to gut the trout. You see them thinking then. It's the way you describe the gutting of the fish. Perhaps you use too much detail when you explain the way the blade slips into the soft belly because you can sense their fear. They don't know about your past or your family history and yet you can tell they're scared. They don't want to hear any more. They don't really want to understand, to empathise. In short, they don't care.

Too bad. Once you've started the story you don't like to stop, and if they were to ask you to that would be plain rude.

You don't like rude. Plain or otherwise.

So you carry on. You tell them all about the cake and the birthday. You go over the bit about the trout again and then you tell them how your Daddy used the knife to gut your mother too.

That's when they usually start to scream.

Chapter Eighteen

Central Plymouth. Friday 20th June. 4.07 a.m.

The call came before the light. Riley reached out for his mobile, knocking it to the floor. He rolled off the bed and scrabbled in the dark until he was able to grab the damn thing and silence it. His girlfriend, Julie, mumbled something as Riley left the room. He pressed the phone to his ear, Enders' voice dragging the last remnants of sleep from him as he padded naked down the hall to the kitchen.

The line was intermittent and Riley struggled to understand what Enders was saying between the slices of silence and the pounding from his headache.

Red wine. Last night. Too much. Him and Julie giggling in the early hours as they'd gone to bed and tried to make love. Failing, but having hysterics doing so, they'd curled up together and fallen asleep, Riley as happy as he'd ever been.

Now though, he was paying the price.

'Say again, Patrick,' he said. 'Slowly.'

Enders repeated the information and waited until Riley had repeated it back to him. Then he hung up.

Shit.

His day off gone. Just like that.

Along with every other officer, he was on duty on the

twenty-first, tomorrow. Today he'd been expecting a lie-in, spending the morning in bed with Julie, getting up at lunch time. Riley looked at the glow from the clock on the oven. Not at four a.m.

He grabbed a glass, filled it from the tap, and gulped the liquid down. Again. Then he scribbled a note on a Post-it and stuck the message to the side of the kettle. Ten minutes later and he was driving through the empty streets of Plymouth, wondering if he'd pass a breathalyser test. Thirty and he'd reached a remote spot high on Dartmoor a few miles to the east of Burrator Reservoir. He couldn't miss the rendezvous because several vehicles half blocked the road, Callum Campbell's white Land Rover amongst them, Enders' own Suzuki Jimny just behind.

Torch light picked out a huddle of bright clothing standing a couple of hundred metres from the road next to a mound of rocks, the group silhouetted against a lightening sky. Riley could see Enders up there on the mound next to the Dartmoor Rescue Group members. The lad would be soaking up the atmosphere, loving it. Riley killed the engine, pulled his own windcheater from the rear seat and got out of the car. A hint of dawn showed as an orange radiance to the east, but sunrise was half an hour away at least. Down in the city, Riley had clambered from his bed into a pre-dawn still warm and humid from the day before. Up here on the moor the air was fresher and he shivered, regretting he hadn't put on an extra layer.

He walked up to the tor, the moorland grass and heather grey beneath his feet, hunks of bare granite a darker shade. When he reached the pile of rocks Riley could see they marked some sort of hole in the ground. More of a shaft really. A set of ropes disappeared down into a blackness pierced every now and then by white light moving back and forth.

'Old mine working,' Enders said as Riley came over. 'Yesterday evening a couple of walkers reported a ewe circling the shaft and calling to her lamb. The animal had fallen in. The shepherd came out with a big torch and spotted Corran down there with the lamb. Called DRG.'

'Bit of luck for us.'

'Lucky for the lamb too.'

'Yes.' Riley leant forwards a little to see down the shaft. 'How far down?'

'Careful.' Someone touched him on the shoulder. Riley turned to see Callum Campbell. 'Don't need another one going over the edge.'

'Shit.' Riley's heart missed a beat and he stepped back. 'And is that what happened? An accident?'

'Not an accident, no.' Campbell paused, gestured at the rocks and boulders. 'His bike's down there with him. Don't think he was riding the thing at the time, not over this type of terrain. Besides, the bike's totalled. Front wheel buckled and the frame bent.'

'Hit and run then,' Riley said, feeling a slight disappointment come over him. 'A simple disposal of the evidence.'

'Simple enough, yes. No less criminal.'

No, Riley thought. Someone had killed Corran, probably through careless driving. They'd compounded the situation by attempting to conceal Corran's body. His wife and daughter were owed an explanation. And they'd want to see justice done too.

Riley and Enders moved away from the shaft as members of the rescue team began to set up an elaborate tripod over the hole. A rope and pulley system would be used to lower a stretcher down to retrieve the casualty. When the equipment was in place somebody shouted 'below' and the stretcher slipped down into the darkness.

'Be more forensic, Darius,' Enders said as the rope ran through the pulleys. 'On the bike or the body. You run somebody off the road, it's going to leave some evidence.'

Layton had already found a paint fragment and had failed to match it, but maybe Enders was right and they'd find something else. As in the case with Savage's daughter Clarissa, a match could lead to a list of car models and from there to a bunch of owners via the vehicle database. Find them, check their alibis, examine their cars for signs of damage or recent repair. Boring, painstaking work, but necessary. In the end they'd maybe have a couple of suspects they could bring in. If they got lucky, one might confess. If they didn't, it was going to be tricky. Even if somebody did own up they could claim Corran swerved out in front of them, that they'd panicked when they found he was dead. Serious business; obstructing police, concealing a body, but they'd be out in a couple of years at the most. Riley didn't think Corran's wife and daughter would call that justice.

'Steady!'

Riley turned to see the stretcher swivelling just beneath the top of the tripod. Hands reached out and pulled the gurney to safety, the hard plastic underbelly scraping on rock.

Corran.

He lay on the stretcher, arms by his side, legs straight, secured by a number of straps. Grass stains and mud smeared his clothing and his mouth hung open. His cycle helmet sat at an odd angle but was still on his head. There were numerous scrapes on his face, his nose gone black and bent to one side. Farther down and his right leg was a mess of pulp, muscle and bone.

Campbell took a big torch and played the beam across the body. The light made the surrounding moor disappear into a world of shadows, Corran's features now white like a ghoul's.

'Bloody hell.' Campbell held the beam steady on the left side of Corran's head.

Riley moved alongside and knelt, one hand shielding his eyes from the beam. Just forwards of the ear a circular patch of black with a red, fleshy centre. Not much blood. Some bruising.

'Not an accident then?' Campbell said.

'No.'

Riley stood and took in the expressions on the faces of the rescue team. They were used to dealing with dead bodies, but this was beyond their experience. From the look of Enders' face it was beyond his too.

Not beyond Riley's though. He'd seen this before, up in London. This was a gunshot wound. Point blank. Devlyn Corran had been executed.

A couple of hours later Riley stood in a bathroom at Derriford Hospital. He splashed water from the tap against his forehead, the cool liquid for a moment soothing the pain of a headache. Chemicals from the pathology lab he reckoned. Some sort of allergy. That, the hangover and the thought of having to tell Corran's wife her husband had been murdered. Assuming she didn't already know, of course.

He left the bathroom and headed out into the foyer of the hospital. He went through the front doors and searched for Davies. The DI stood next to a 'No Smoking' sign, fingering an unlit cigarette.

'Fucking hey, Darius,' he said. 'This is more like it!'

Riley had called Davies from up on the moor and he'd been waiting at the hospital when Riley arrived trailing the mortuary van. The full post-mortem would take place later, but for now Nesbit had made a preliminary examination. There'd been no point him coming out to the moor, much as Enders had joked about how he'd like to see the pathologist lowered into the abandoned mineshaft.

Davies was still ranting on. A gunshot wound. To the head. Point blank. All the hallmarks of a professional hit.

'You and me, Riley, we're back in business, right?'

Riley nodded and then flicked his phone on and called Hardin. The DSupt wasn't one for small talk, especially at this time of the morning, so Riley gave him the news straight.

'Murder, sir. Nesbit's initial thoughts are the broken bones and internal injuries were caused when he was knocked off his bike. However, it was the gunshot which killed him.'

'Not what I wanted to hear,' Hardin said. 'Any idea on the shooter?'

'Do you mean the gun or who pulled the trigger?'

'The gun.'

'Small calibre. We'll have to wait until the post-mortem to get the bullet.'

'Proper operation now, Darius,' Hardin said. 'Need an incident room and an SIO. DI Davies, I reckon. Bit short on officers. You'll be his deputy.'

'Yes, sir.' Riley began to walk towards the car park, following Davies, who'd by now lit his fag. 'You want us to come in and get things sorted?'

Hardin didn't. He'd get someone to see to all the details. They were to get back on the moor. Find something. Riley hung up and told Davies the news that he was to be SIO.

'Thank fucking Christ,' Davies said. He took a drag on the cigarette and flicked some ash away. 'It's good riddance to the stupid diesel investigation forever. We can leave Maynard to sulk behind his hedge while we get on with some proper police work.'

'Mrs Corran,' Riley said. 'We need to be the ones to tell her so we can gauge her reaction.'

'*You*, Darius, you.' Davies jabbed a finger at Riley. 'I'm going to go into town and lean on a couple of lads, find out if anyone knows anything about a gun. You can go to the station and pick up a family liquidation officer while you're there. Luke Farrell will do. The boy can charm the knickers off a nun.'

Sensitivity, Riley thought as he got into the car, had never been one of Davies' strong points.

Friday. Nearly a week since the discovery of the bodies at Tavy View Farm. Like several other members of the team, Savage had a few hours off. Saturday was the longest day and, Hardin had promised, would be an absolute nightmare.

Mid-morning Savage headed from home to nearby Plymstock to pick up some bread and milk from the Co-Op. She took her little sports car, putting the top down and enjoying the sun. She'd bought the classic MGB as a near-wreck on a whim years back and Pete was fond of reminding her that it was as old as she was. Although, he always added with a smile, not in as good condition.

The car swept up the hill away from the house and then she was on the coast road, the Sound coming into view below. The water reflected the sun, a million wavelets like diamonds in the breeze, yachts criss-crossing their way through the patterns. Sod's law, Savage thought, as soon as their sailing holiday had ended summer had arrived.

In Plymstock she pulled the car into the car park at the back of the Broadway, a sixties shopping centre with retail space surrounding an open air pedestrianised area. Savage walked into the centre. Outside the butcher's, a life-size plastic sheep grazed a patch of grass. Nearby, children clambered on a wooden giraffe. At a table in front of the baker's an elderly couple drank coffee and fussed over who should finish the remains of a custard slice. The tableaux seemed a long way from Operation *Radial*.

She went into the Co-Op, emerging a few minutes later with her shopping, but pausing at the entrance as the wail of a fire engine rose in volume. The siren stopped, to be replaced by the sound of the vehicle's engine roaring somewhere beyond the confines of the centre. At the far end of the precinct, heads turned as two PSCOs sprinted past startled shoppers. The officers ran down a side street which provided delivery access to the shops. Savage broke into a jog and trotted after them.

She rounded the corner and saw the fire engine trying to squeeze through a gap between a delivery lorry and a car parked on double yellows. The PCSOs were waving the fire engine down to where they stood at the bottom of a set of stairs which led up to a row of maisonettes sitting above the shops. At the top of the stairs smoke billowed from a broken window, yellow flames beginning to lick out too. The driver of the fire engine gave up on subtlety and nudged the obstruction out the way, the front of the car crumpling, the windscreen crazing. Seconds later and the fire crew were out of the cab, two of them up the stairs, axes in hand, the others readying hoses.

As the lead fireman crunched his axe into the front door of the property on fire, Savage approached the nearest PCSO, tapped him on the shoulder and showed her warrant card.

'What's going on?' she said.

'A mob. Set about some guy as he came out of the bank. They chased him back to his flat, but he managed to get inside. One of them put burning paper through the letterbox and it looks like it caught.'

Fire officers continued to mill around as they ran a hose up the steps. A couple of minutes later one came out of the flat and down the stairs. Savage went across, flashing her card again.

'Fire's out and we've got an ambulance on the way,' the fireman said. 'The guy's in a bit of a state. Broken arm, gashed head, a lot of bruising.'

'Can he talk?'

'No chance, he's collapsed from smoke inhalation and we've got him on oxygen. Lucky we arrived when we did.'

'Ma'am?' The second PCSO approached holding out a Co-Op bag. 'Found this back in the Broadway. A couple of eyewitnesses say the man dropped it when he was attacked.'

Savage looked in. Nestled between a copy of the *Daily Mail* and a loaf of white sliced bread sat a chocolate cake, a pack of pink candles and a set of plastic candle holders.

Riley drove to the station and picked up Luke Farrell, and half an hour afterwards the two of them were climbing the steps to the Corrans' little cottage in Dousland. Farrell, whose blond hair appeared particularly mussed-up in the moorland breeze, went first. At the front door he stopped and smiled at Riley.

'I know there's a point to this,' he said, 'but let's go easy, OK?'

Riley nodded and reached for the doorbell. Then there were footsteps down the hallway, the door opening, Cassie Corran's hand going to her mouth, her body slumping to the floor.

Not guilty then, Riley thought, as he and Farrell helped her into the living room. Riley left Farrell with Cassie while he went to the kitchen to make some tea. Out the back Emily was playing with an older woman – a grandparent maybe? – oblivious to the crisis taking place inside.

In the living room Cassie's tears came with great gulping sobs, Riley's over-sweetened tea gulped down too, her hand steadied by Farrell as she placed the cup on the low table.

'Knew it,' she kept saying over and over again. 'Knew it would lead to trouble.'

Riley didn't say anything but he moved his head a fraction and glanced at Farrell.

'Knew what, Cassie?' Farrell said, taking Riley's cue.

'Knew where this would all lead. The money.'

Riley eyed the big flat-screen, the nice carpet and sofa, remembered the new car out the front and the fancy two-storey wooden playhouse he'd just seen in the back garden. Money, of course. If you discounted blind rage and madness, murder in the end always came down to one of two things: sex or greed.

'What money, Cassie?' Riley said. 'Where from?'

'Devlyn. Clever-clever bloody Devlyn.' Cassie sniffed and dabbed her nose with a tissue. 'He called it a no-brainer. Only it's turned out that he was the one with no brains. Stupid idiot. I never should have listened to him. We should never have moved here.'

'OK, Cassie, let's take this one step at a time. How much money are we talking about?'

Silence, Cassie wiping snot from her nose and then shaking her head and staring down at the carpet.

'How much?' Riley tried again. 'Ten grand? Fifty? More?'

'It wasn't like that,' she said, looking up. 'It was a monthly thing. Ongoing. At first a grand a month, then two. The last couple of months the amount was five K.'

'Five thousand pounds a month?'

'Yup.' Cassie shook her head and started crying again.

Riley leant back in his chair and took a mouthful of tea. He knew where this was going. Obvious. Devlyn Corran was a prison officer. He came into contact with dozens of unsavoury characters, even at a low-grade nick like HMP Dartmoor. There were a couple of possibilities: The money could be a keep-schtum sweetener or a retainer for performing a task like smuggling drugs, phones or something else into prison. Alternatively – and this Riley reckoned was more likely, considering what had happened – Corran had been blackmailing somebody, using information he'd discovered in the course of his work. Bearing in mind the type of people Corran worked with, doing that was nigh-on suicidal.

'Who, exactly,' Riley said, 'was Devlyn involved with?'

'I don't know. He printed letters out. Sent them once a month.'

'We've searched through your documents,' Riley said, looking over to the corner of the living room where a monitor stood on a computer desk, cables trailing down to an empty space below, the machine taken a couple of days ago. 'We found nothing of interest.'

'That's the family's. Devlyn has another one. Upstairs.' Cassie took a fresh set of tissues and then got up and left the room. A couple of minutes later she was back with a laptop. 'There's a password, but I can't get in.'

'Cassie, we could have done with knowing about this days ago.' Riley took the laptop. Didn't bother firing it up and trying to log in. Hi-Tech Crimes would remove the disk and copy the contents. No point wasting time.

'I was scared. Anyway, it wouldn't have made any difference, would it?'

Riley conceded the point and then tried to delve deeper into what Corran was up to, but Cassie couldn't tell them much more. She said Corran hadn't wanted any records, so he'd handwritten the envelopes. He'd worn gloves and used his left hand. Posted the letters in town. Untraceable. So he said.

'But the money,' Riley said. 'How did he receive it?'

'Cash. He'd turn up with a wad of notes. I don't know where from.'

'Cassie?' A figure at the living room door. The woman from the garden. 'Emily wants some lunch.'

'OK, Mum. I think the police were just going.'

'Righto.' The woman turned and left.

'Fish fingers, chips and beans,' Cassie said as she rose from the sofa. 'Emily's favourite.'

'I'd like to stay, Cassie,' Farrell said, reaching out to touch Cassie's arm.

'No, love, thank you.' Cassie smiled. Patted Farrell's hand. 'Family is what Emily needs now. Me and her gran, the three of us, we'll be fine.'

As the front door closed the last thing Riley saw was the white of Cassie's face in the narrowing slit, the colour all gone from the skin and looking as pale as her husband had as he lay on the gurney in the mortuary.

Chapter Nineteen

Bere Ferrers, Devon. Friday 20th June. 12.14 p.m.

Jody was away all day, spraying the corn they had over Yelverton way. Joanne moped round, finishing some odd jobs, trying to do some admin. Jobs done, she made coffee, taking the cup out onto the front veranda. If she kept her eyes focused east she could avoid looking at the mess in the field.

Most of the police had gone, just a uniformed officer at the front gate to the farm, there to prevent the media getting a closer look. But Joanne was still feeling the effects of the grisly discovery. The publicity had led to ninety per cent of the summer visitors for the holiday cottages cancelling their bookings. The other ten per cent, she reckoned, hadn't cancelled because the news had so far escaped them. Quite how, she had no idea.

Not so lucky now.

Unless you could call the money various newspapers had offered her a windfall. The police media adviser had told her to ignore them.

'To put it bluntly, Ms Black,' he'd said looking her up and down, 'you're an attractive woman. They'll play on that. They're not happy about the last victim being a lesbian. No sympathy there. They'll want you in skimpy farm wear and there'll be innuendo about Aga sagas and single mature ladies and all sorts. Money or no money, I'd give them a miss.'

So she did, letting her three dogs have the run of the farmyard when the police weren't around. Last she'd looked, there were no press cars parked in the lane so it appeared as if they'd got the message.

Adam Narr had given her a surname for the girl: Bailey. Lara Bailey. From the sound of it Joanne's uncle had got a little too friendly with the girl and the family had upped sticks. Narr didn't know where they'd gone. 'Plymouth' he'd said, as if that single word described anything and everything which might have happened to them.

After finishing her coffee, Joanne returned to the computer. Distracted from her accounts, she searched the online phone directory. Bailey was a common name, far too common to even consider ringing round. Besides, it was likely the girl had got married and changed her name. She'd be in her sixties, the parents probably long since dead. Tracking her down would be impossible. And anyway, what could something which occurred decades ago have to do with the bodies in the field?

Joanne closed the browser window and concentrated on the cash flow spreadsheet where more than a few columns had turned to red.

With the victim of the fire taken away in an ambulance, Savage awaited the arrival of Hardin. When he turned up his face was like thunder. He peered into the plastic bag as Savage held it open. Shook his head at the sight of the cake and candles.

'The bloody internet,' Hardin said. 'The Chief Constable received the news via some social media channel. Myself and the commander of the Plymouth division have just been in an emergency teleconference with him. He's apoplectic. Says we're losing control. And there's still twenty-four hours to go. God knows what's going to happen tomorrow.'

Hardin strolled across to the steps which led to the maisonette. Close by, Layton was chatting to two members of his CSI team who stood leaning against their van.

'Update,' Hardin said. 'Were these vigilantes on to something or not?'

'I guess we'll soon find out.' Savage nodded up the steps to where a fire officer was taking photographs of the black soot stains around the door and window of the flat.

'Just waiting for them to finish,' Layton said as he came over. 'But we need to know before we go in. I can't go nosing around in the bedroom if I'm doing an investigation into the fire.'

'But whatever you found wouldn't be inadmissible, would it?' Savage said.

'This isn't America,' Hardin said. 'Not yet, thank God.'

'It depends what we found,' Layton continued. 'Murder weapon, things he might have collected from victims, anything directly linking him – that would be in. Circumstantial evidence we might have more of a problem with, especially if we need to rely on it in court.'

'Well, Charlotte?' Hardin again.

'One of the PCSOs told me an onlooker said the man is ex-military. That's nothing special, but if what they told the officer is true then the guy's been away on various tours for a number of years.'

'So if the dates of his tour of duty match we're quids in,' Hardin said.

'You're *quids* in, I *go* in, guns blazing.' Layton turned away and strolled across to the man and woman next to the van.

The two CSIs began unloading a couple of crates from the rear.

'That's positive thinking for you,' Hardin said. 'Must be that dance night he goes to. Jive rhythms or something, isn't it?'

'Five rhythms, sir,' Savage said.

'Whatever. Sounds like New Age claptrap to me, but maybe I should look into doing it myself.'

As Savage tried to stop herself smiling at the thought of Hardin doing any kind of dancing, her phone rang. One of the *Radial* team calling from the station with information on the victim.

'Graham Bunce, ma'am,' the DC said. 'Forty-one. He's got a prior for assault, but although serious it was the result of a bar brawl. Served in Afghanistan with Four Two Commando and left the marines shortly before they returned from active duty in 2009. He was also in Iraq. With a bit of jiggling his tour dates *can* be made to fit.'

Savage hung up and told Hardin, stressing the problem with the dates.

'Great,' Hardin said, seeming to overlook the point. He waved across at Layton. 'Let's get the CSI boys in there pronto. Who knows, we might even have something to give that lot before too long.'

Savage followed Hardin's gaze. Dan Phillips, the *Herald*'s crime reporter, stood on the other side of the road next to a BBC woman and a cameraman. Phillips could smell a story like a shark scenting blood from five miles off. Right now the Candle Cake Killer was the biggest thing he'd worked on. He'd be hoping it could be his passport to the big time. Phillips raised a hand, waved and then walked across.

'Shit,' Savage said and moved towards the reporter, putting on her best smile. 'Dan. As always, a real pleasure.'

'You reckon you've got him then?' Phillips said, gesturing

to the block of flats, his little eyes dithering back and forth. 'Must admit I'm a little disappointed. I was hoping for a house of horrors. An Ed Gein *Psycho* sort of place.'

'We've got nothing yet.'

'Name of Graham Bunce, I understand. Interesting.' Phillips smiled, the grin hiding something. 'Former member of the armed forces. Never would have thought it.'

'He's got a conviction for assault.'

'Yes, I know. He's also got a CGC.'

'CGC?' Savage struggled to resolve the letters into some kind of meaning. The police and criminal justice system was filled with so much jargon it was almost impossible to keep up with every new acronym. She gave up. 'What's that then?'

'The Conspicuous Gallantry Cross. Second only to the Victoria Cross in terms of decorations for bravery in the face of the enemy.'

Nothing to do with criminal justice then, Savage thought. It did though begin to help them build a picture of the man. She glanced over at the flat. Layton and the other CSIs were working at the front door, Layton dusting the letterbox while the other two quartered the landing area. They'd be inside soon. Checking the bedroom. She wondered whether she needed to have words before they got that far.

'Still,' Phillips said. 'It just goes to show you never can tell. Family man too. Divorced, but with four kids. One's got a heart condition. I'm a bit offended you don't know that, seeing as the *Herald* ran a campaign to raise money for the little boy. Bunce and a couple of other ex-marines did the South West Coast Path with full military kit. All six hundred miles of it. Did you know if you do the whole route the total height climbed is over four times that of Everest?'

Savage shook her head and began to move away. She definitely needed to have words with Layton.

'Parasite,' Hardin said as she returned. 'What's he waiting for, feeding time at the zoo?'

Hardin was mixing his metaphors, but Savage ignored him and went straight into the information Phillips had provided.

'Military honour?' Hardin said. 'Doesn't prove a thing. In fact somebody inclined to do something crazy in battle could be exactly the kind of person to do something crazy in civvy street. Anyway, let's just wait and see what Layton manages to turn up.'

'Yes, sir,' Savage said, putting a hand behind her back and crossing her fingers.

Come Friday morning, Paula Rowland had scolded herself. She'd woken to the gleam of the knife on the bedside table, light from a gap in the curtains reflecting off the shiny surface and into her eyes. She was still alive. Not, as feared, murdered by a sexual pervert during the night. She went downstairs and hurried the knife away into the kitchen drawer, dismissing the fact the little barbecue on the patio had tumbled over as the work of nothing more demonic than the pesky neighbourhood cat.

Later though, leaving the school for a crafty fag and strolling round nearby Penlee Gardens with her friend Cath, she was sure she saw a man staring at her from across the grass. She was about to point him out to Cath but when she tapped her friend on the shoulder he'd gone.

When, at four – no drink tonight – she walked home through Central Park, she saw him again, sure this time it was the same man as earlier, maybe as the night before. Once inside she dialled the non-emergency police number and explained what had happened, surprised to find a sympathetic ear on the end of the line and even more surprised by the knock at the door just thirty minutes later.

The two uniformed officers – one male, one female – tried to reassure her. There were extra patrols planned for the next few days to deal with the threat from the Candle Cake Killer. They'd call round a couple of times, reroute a car to pass by in the night. Then they checked her door and window locks and gave her an attack alarm.

'Anything at all,' the male officer said as they left, 'any hint of him, you call triple nine. I'd try not to worry yourself though, love.'

Easier said than done, Paula thought, as she closed the door, bolted it, then went to retrieve the knife from the kitchen.

Back at Crownhill late afternoon Savage waited on Layton's search of the flat. She told Enders to do some more research into Graham Bunce in the expectation of a result from the CSI.

'No car, ma'am,' Enders said after he'd made a couple of phone calls and spent a few minutes logged into the Police National Computer. 'At least, not registered to him. Does make it difficult to see how he could have accomplished the abductions.'

'He could have borrowed one,' Savage said. 'And maybe he did have a car back at the time of the first killings.'

'Possible. I'm also trying to get his service record, but the Navy are being a bit cagey about the whole thing.'

'Did you tell them why you want it?'

'No. Thought I'd better not. Might make them even more reticent.' Enders glanced up at Savage for a moment and then tapped the screen. Bunce's address sat dead centre. 'Going back to the car problem, ma'am. Even if he did have the use of one, where did he take the women? Can't see him killing them in his maisonette. For a start he'd have a job getting them inside without anyone seeing.'

174

'Good point. I'll get the local enquiry teams to consider that when they do the door-to-doors. We'll need to get the lowdown on his friends, places he visited, hobbies which might take him to specific locations. Hiking, fishing, sailing. Maybe, like Glastone, he has a boat.'

'He lives in a poxy maisonette above a shop, ma'am. Can't see him owning a gin palace.'

'Not a gin palace, no. Perhaps a little workboat, something he could go upriver in. Maybe to Tavy View farm.'

Savage looked over to the map on the whiteboard. The railway line theory was all very well but the wide expanse of blue on the map which ran down from the Bere Peninsula suggested other possibilities. The estuary linked the peninsula with Plymouth and a boat moored in a dozen places around the Sound could reach the farm in half an hour or so. There was the issue of the tide times – access over the mud at low tide would be near impossible – but perhaps they needed to do more work on it. She went to a nearby terminal and brought up some tide tables, but before she'd got very far DC Calter entered the crime suite, her bag in hand, about to wrap up for the day. She came across and peered over Enders' shoulder.

'Graham Bunce,' she said. 'What's your interest?'

'Interest?' Enders said. 'Haven't you heard, he's up for the Candle Cake Killings.'

'*What?*' Calter appeared shocked for a moment and then burst out laughing. 'I'm assuming this is some kind of gag or wind-up. I ran the half marathon alongside him a couple of years ago.'

'And that makes him innocent, does it?' Enders said.

Calter shook her head and tried to suppress a giggle.

'Jane?' Savage said. 'This isn't a laughing matter, so please enlighten us as to what's so funny. Graham Bunce is a

175

suspect, but if you know a reason why he shouldn't be then out with it.'

'Why he shouldn't be?' Calter said. 'Couldn't be, more like.'

'And?'

'Here.' Calter moved to Enders' terminal and leant over in front of him. She brought up a browser and did a search. 'That's the reason.'

Savage peered at the screen. Calter had selected a page from the *Herald*'s website. It was the piece Phillips had been talking about, the six-hundred-mile walk around the coast path. There was a picture of Bunce flanked by his two colleagues. Enders read the introduction.

'Graham Bunce today completed his marathon walk around the coasts of Somerset, Devon and Cornwall, raising upwards of fifty thousand pounds for heart charities. Graham served in Afghanistan until he was wounded in action. *Registered blind*, he completed the walk with the help of two friends from Four Two Commando . . .'

'Shit,' Savage said. 'Bloody Dan Phillips. He knew this all along and never said anything to me.'

'Sorry, ma'am,' Enders said. 'What I don't understand is, if he's blind, how come the thugs went after him?'

'He's actually partially sighted,' Calter said. 'Very limited vision, but you wouldn't necessarily know from watching him.'

'What were the candles for then?' Enders said. 'He had a chocolate cake and the candles in his carrier bag.'

'He's got four kids,' Calter said. 'It's not beyond the realms of possibility one of them has a birthday coming up, is it?'

'No, no, no,' Savage said, feeling nauseous as she moved across the room to a phone. 'The DSupt is going to go through the roof.'

'Ma'am?' Calter nodded towards the door. 'Too late.'

Hardin stood at the entrance to the crime suite, red-faced, holding a sheet of paper.

'You know the source I have at the *Herald*?' he said, holding up the sheet. 'Well, he just sent me this.'

Savage wanted to hold her head in her hands, to dissolve into the ground, anything but look at the headline. She forced herself to read it.

Blind Man's Bluff the text said. Below the headline, the subheading didn't help much either: *Police Finger Sightless War Hero For Cake Killings.*

'This is not what I'd call bloody good policing,' Hardin said. 'More like a farce. We're in danger of losing the entire city. The media strategy's blown. Who's going to listen to our advice when this is the rubbish we come up with? Dan Phillips has made us a laughing stock.' Hardin contemplated the sheet of paper for a moment and then crumpled it up. 'I'm off home to get a few hours' rest, because tomorrow is going to be a long day.'

With that, Hardin turned and left.

'The longest day,' Savage said. 'God help us.'

Chapter Twenty

Everything is planned and ready. Every last detail taken care of. The plastic is down, some in the back of the car as well. Then there is the extra food you've got in because you don't need to be worrying about popping out for a pint of milk or a loaf of bread. Not when there is work to do.

And there'll be plenty of that. Not to mention the cleaning up afterwards.

Strewth.

Scrape, lift, sling. Scrape, lift, sling.

You've put Mikey back on the gravel job and he's going at it like crazy out there, filling a barrow every few minutes and ferrying the heavy load across the yard where he dumps it. The pile on the left gets ever smaller, the one on the right bigger. The other day you were worried about him getting worn out, but the energy the lad has is frightening. Ten minutes doing this will curb some of his unhealthy exuberance. You can just stand here and watch. You've been doing that for years. Like a disembodied spirit you've been looking down on your life, interested only in the journey, never the destination.

Mummy got sliced up near the beginning and Daddy killed himself in prison soon after.

Which was when you figured the rest of the route wasn't going to be on any fucking satnav. Not that the demonic things had been invented back then. And even if you'd had a map showing you the way you doubt it would have kept you out of trouble, out of the nick.

Fifteen years.

You were supposed to rehabilitate in there. Learn your lesson. Get help. All you ended up doing was brooding. Working out who the hell was to blame. Pretty bloody obvious that.

'Prison is like being inside the womb,' you said to a probation officer soon after release. 'When you're in there you're just waiting until the day you are kicked out, naked, screaming and unable to care for yourself. Unable to control yourself.'

The man nodded and you continued.

'Sometimes I think it would be better if I went back inside.'

The man nodded again, said something about you losing your parents. Difficult to come to terms with.

Difficult to come to terms with? Daddy slicing up Mummy with the Big Knife and then killing himself? You don't know anything about the problems of the man's other clients but if they are worse than yours you'd sure like to hear of them.

Fifteen minutes into the session and you get up and leave, the soles of your shoes clicking on the polished floor, the sound echoing through the room like a slow handclap.

Worth every penny, these fucking do-gooders.

Scrape, lift, sling. Scrape, lift, sling.

You tap on the window and make a sign of forking something into your mouth. Mikey turns and nods, holds his thumbs up and then returns to his job.

Scrape, lift, sling. Scrape, lift, sling.

You go to the kitchen and grab a couple of tins of beans from the pantry, open them, pour them into a dish and place them in the microwave.

The Zanussi nine hundred watt with the dodgy turntable. The one the dishwasher man didn't know how to repair.

179

Why is it, you think, as you pop a couple of pieces of bread in the toaster, that nobody knows anything about stuff these days?

The thought makes you feel physically sick. The complexity of everything. It's what did for Mummy. Not a microwave oven of course, but a conventional one. She dialled up one hundred and eighty degrees centigrade and set the timer for twenty-five minutes, as she must have done countless times before. Only she hadn't reckoned on you and your brother. You watched her blow up balloons for the celebration in the dining room for a while, but then the pair of you returned to the kitchen and peered through the glass at the cake. Bored of the slow motion miracle taking place within you began to fiddle with the controls on the oven. You rotated the dials and pressed the buttons.

Beeeeeep.

'Done already?'

In came Mummy. The cake looked perfect, but Mummy forgot to check inside. She should have used a knife, then Daddy wouldn't have had to.

You shiver as you set the timer on the microwave for sixty seconds. Every time you use an electrical device it's a pact with the devil himself.

Back at the dining room window while you wait for the beans to heat and the toast to pop things are simpler.

Scrape, lift, sling. Scrape, lift, sling.

You stare at the pile of gravel in the yard. Wonder if you might just get Mikey to move it all back again tomorrow.

But no, you think as you return to the kitchen. Tomorrow you're going to be busy. Very busy. Tomorrow's the Special Day.

Chapter Twenty-One

Bovisand, Plymouth. Saturday 21st June. 7.35 a.m.

The longest day dawned still, hot and humid. The sea beyond the cliffs at the bottom of Savage's garden spread like a huge mirror, stretching all the way across Plymouth Sound to Cornwall. Boats glided through the still water, leaving 'V' trails behind them. Was it her imagination or were there more craft than usual for a Saturday in June? Were people heading out to sea in search of a better life? A life beyond the reach of the Candle Cake Killer?

Down in the kitchen Savage turned on the radio. BBC Devon was wall-to-wall. A phone-in filled with people panicking, berating the police, threatening to kill anybody who crossed their thresholds. The presenter was doing his best to raise the temperature to boiling point and beyond, while at the same time trying to display a BBC-style tone of reassurance. The leader of the council came on and issued a 'keep calm and carry on' message only to be followed by a contradictory statement from the deputy leader, her old enemy Alec Jackman.

'Anybody comes through the door of my house today and they are as good as dead.'

'You don't mean that, Mr Jackman?' the presenter said.

'Yes I do. I've got a baseball bat and an old speargun ready and waiting and I urge every other citizen to similarly prepare themselves. Let's reclaim the streets and make sure this city stays safe.'

'That's quite a—'

The phone rang and Savage turned the volume down and answered.

'You listening, Charlotte? To the radio?' Hardin. From the sound of him, like a bear who'd not slept a wink. 'That man is a bloody disgrace. I've a good mind to send a couple of officers round to arrest him for incitement.'

'Jackman?'

'Idiot.'

'You can't blame anyone for wanting to defend themselves.'

'Trouble we don't need, Charlotte. Mark my words. You saw what happened when those thugs mistook Graham Bunce for the killer. The chap's lucky to be alive. If the general public take Councillor Jackman's advice the day will be taken up with us running from one 999 call to another. It'll be war. Now, on another matter, Glastone. You're over there today, right? Keeping an eye on him?'

Savage said she was. Two detectives from Dartmouth had done the early morning session and she'd be relieving them later.

'Good,' Hardin said. 'Stick to him like a limpet. Wherever he goes you go, but give him space, OK? Enough rope to hang himself, if you get my drift.'

'How am I—' The line went dead and Savage shook her head. Limpet? Enough rope? The two tactics were incompatible.

She took the MG into work, thinking that once again it was definitely a hood-down, wind in the hair kind of day. As she drove the coast road she could see that out in the Sound there were more boats than ever, the anchorages at

182

Mount Edgcumbe and Cawsand Bay rammed with yachts and motorboats. She hadn't been imagining it earlier. And from the traffic she experienced on the way to Crownhill, the exodus wasn't confined to the water either. The routes out of the city were nose-to-tail with cars and the danger of a road-rage incident, fuelled by the heat and the tension, was rising.

When she got to the station the place was close to deserted. All leave had been cancelled, every extra officer drafted in to help, and yet apart from a handful of junior detectives there was no one to be seen.

Calter lounged at a terminal in the crime suite, feet up on a desk.

'On standby, ma'am,' Calter said, nodding at the DCs on the far side of the room. 'In case anything turns up and we need some quick info. Everyone else is out. Oh, and would you believe it? – Darius and Patrick have managed to find us a fresh body. As if we need anything else on our plates.'

'A body?' For a moment Savage was confused. Riley had been working on some fraud case with DI Maynard and DI Davies. Had they inadvertently stumbled upon one of the Candle Cake Killer's victims? 'Where?'

'No need to worry, ma'am. It's a misper ending in a hit and run incident on Dartmoor. We could have done without the hassle though.'

A hit and run on Dartmoor. Clarissa.

Savage shot Calter a glance, but the DC was already gathering her things.

'Are we off, ma'am?' Calter said, unaware of the effect the words had had on Savage. 'Glastone, remember?'

'I hadn't forgotten,' Savage said. 'Let's go.'

*   *   *

Fifty minutes later, having struggled through the traffic in Plymouth, they arrived in Salcombe. They relieved the on-duty surveillance team and parked a hundred metres down from Glastone's place behind a large people carrier. Unless Glastone came strolling past he was unlikely to see them. Even if he did spot the car, he probably wouldn't associate the MG with the police.

The car had a black soft top, but although the roof attracted the heat they could hardly leave it down. There was no aircon either.

'Dripping,' Calter said, flapping the bottom of her shirt. 'Like a waterfall.'

'Thanks for that, Jane,' Savage said, passing across the bottle of water, just dregs in the bottom. 'Much more of this and they'll have to peel me off the seat too.'

An hour later and Savage took a stroll to the nearest corner shop. The place sold overpriced cans to tourists, but Savage bought half a dozen Cokes anyway. At least they were ice-cold.

She arrived back at the car to see Calter waving at her.

'He's just opened the garage doors, ma'am. He's off somewhere.'

'Maybe he's just getting some—'

'No. There!'

Sure enough Glastone's Alfa was reversing out, the soft top retracting automatically. Glastone wore shades and a bright white shirt, buttons down the front undone as if he was God's gift.

'All dressed up,' Savage said. 'With somewhere to go.'

She reached for the ignition and turned the key. Glastone was already out of sight as they pulled away but there was only one way out of Salcombe. Savage put her foot down and shot along Devon Road. She took the turn onto the main road without stopping, Calter grasping the sides of her seat.

They caught up with the Alfa as they reached the open countryside. The road was windy and now Savage hung back, trying to keep a bend between them so Glastone wouldn't see them in his mirrors.

Glastone headed north and then west, following the A379 back towards Plymouth. This time of year there was plenty of tourist traffic and Glastone relished overtaking at every opportunity. His Alfa could accelerate far faster than Savage's car and she had to take a risk every now and then to keep up. As they crested a hill Glastone passed a large motorhome. Savage pulled out too, but had to duck back in again as a stream of cars came the other way. It was half a mile before another opportunity presented itself.

'Now, ma'am,' Calter said, peering down the nearside of the motorhome. 'Clear!'

Savage pressed the accelerator to the floor and the MG lurched forwards. A dozen car lengths ahead the road swept down left and then right in a switchback, beyond a blind bend. The motorhome speeded up as they went down the hill and the MG seemed to inch past. Then a van appeared round the bend and Savage dived in front of the motorhome as the driver slammed on his brakes and leant on the horn.

'Jesus, ma'am!' Calter said. 'I've always fancied Jenson Button as my next beau but I think I may have changed my mind.'

As they wound into the village of Modbury they saw Glastone stuck behind a slow-moving lorry. So much for risking their lives, Savage thought. They went through Modbury and then the villages of Yealmpton and Brixton. At the outskirts of Plymouth they arrived at a roundabout; Glastone shot across in front of a bus. Savage had to wait as the bus lurched round and several other cars followed.

'Lost him, ma'am,' Calter said.

Savage shook her head and put her foot down, undertaking

the cars and the bus by using a cycle lane. Up ahead, Glastone slowed for a speed camera and again they closed to within a few car lengths. Now Savage held back, keeping her distance. Soon they were onto the Laira Bridge and into two lanes of slow-moving heavy traffic. They were several cars back when Glastone changed lanes. He looked over his shoulder, Savage unsure whether he'd spotted them. Then he shot forwards and jumped a set of traffic lights as they turned red. The MG was boxed in, no way through.

'Shit!' Savage said. 'He's gone.'

Calter wrenched the door of the car open and leapt out. A horn blared and she held up her hand as she moved across the road to the pavement and began to run after Glastone. Some hope, Savage thought. It looked as though the traffic had cleared up ahead. Glastone would be long gone.

Savage took her phone and called in, requesting all units to keep a lookout for the Alfa. As she hung up she spotted Calter jogging back. The DC crossed the road and jumped in the car. Savage reached onto the back seat, grabbed a can of Coke and handed it to Calter.

'No chance,' Calter said, pressing the can to her forehead. 'What do we do now?'

'Pray,' Savage said.

Saturday. Another week gone, the last couple of days Paula wondering if she was going a little crazy. Maybe like every other woman in the city. Never mind. Her boyfriend was coming over today. He lived in Exeter, occasionally stayed during the week, mostly at the weekend. He'd arrive late afternoon. Way before it got dark.

Rather than mope around at home, Paula decided on a spot of retail therapy. Out amongst the crowds in the heart of the town she'd feel safer. Only when she got to the Drake

Circus shopping centre she found the crowds much diminished. She wandered the cool of the mall and went into a few stores, trying on a few things, buying nothing.

On the way home she detoured to the Morrisons on Outland Road. She filled a trolley with things for later. Swordfish steaks, charcoal and lighter fluid for the barbie, white wine to go in the fridge, strawberries and cream for a treat. She paid, loaded the car and headed back.

As she turned into her road she passed a group of men on the corner. She recalled there'd been something on the radio in the morning about vigilantes taking to the streets. Fine by her. She drove down looking for a parking space, flicking a look in her mirror, still nervous about the other day. Silly really. In town there'd been nobody following her.

She got out of the car, grabbed the carriers of shopping and strolled down the pavement to her gate. Up the path and the key was in the lock, door opening, Paula darting in and shutting the door behind her. She went through to the kitchen and put the shopping on the table. She opened the back door and took the bag of charcoal and the lighter fluid out the back and filled the barbecue. A squirt of fluid, Paula unable to suppress a giggle at the way the white cream looked on the black charcoal, and then a flick of a match. Good. Should be going well by the time her boyfriend arrived. She went back inside, this time an earthy scent hitting her as she stepped into the kitchen.

The cat smell again. She obviously hadn't cleaned up properly the other day. She'd have to have another go later. She clicked the door shut behind her and went to the table to begin unpacking.

And saw the cake.

It sat in the centre of the kitchen table on a plain white plate. A sponge cake, white icing sugar dusting the top and fourteen candles arranged in a circle.

Fourteen.

She knew, then, what the police didn't. Everything clear. The reason for the abductions, the killings, the reason for the number of candles on the cake. But how on earth had . . .?

'Guuurrrlll!'

Paula whirled round to see a man appear from the hallway. A patch of hair sat above a round face, a mouth gaping, a bulbous tongue hanging out. She backed up and stumbled into the kitchen table. The man's pudgy hands reached out and grabbed her around the waist, spinning her so she had her back to him. One hand moved to her mouth, stifling the scream. She bit hard, tasting salt, but felt the hand push harder, a finger forcing itself in and hooking her cheek like a gaff on a fish. She bit down again, feeling calluses against her tongue.

'Quiet guuurrrlll!' The arm round her waist tightened. 'Got her!'

'I'm here, Mikey. No need to shout.'

Someone else came through from the hall and into the kitchen. The man wore a beard on a bony face with little eyes flitting back and forth, scraggly brown hair above, gangly limbs spidering out of ill-fitting clothing. The weirdo from the park.

'Hello, Paula,' the man said. 'Did you know today is the Special Day? And right now we are going to sing a little song together, so when Mikey takes his finger from your mouth you won't scream. Promise?'

The man pulled something silver from a pocket. He flicked his thumb down and a flame appeared. Moving to the table he lit each candle on the cake and then stepped back.

'Now then, you know the words so join in, OK?'

Paula nodded, breathing hard as the man began to sing Happy Birthday.

Chapter Twenty-Two

Plymouth. Saturday 21st June. 12.51 p.m.

After they'd reported Glastone missing, Savage continued into town. Before they reached the centre Calter took a call on her mobile from DC Enders. She listened for ten seconds, swore and hung up.

'All units, ma'am. Tothill Avenue, opposite Beaumont Park. Two minutes away!'

'Shit!' Savage swung the car out into the oncoming traffic, the tyres protesting with a squeal. She shouted above the noise of the over-revving engine. 'Tell me, Jane!'

'Somebody spotted a birthday cake through a neighbour's rear window. Heard some sort of bang like a gun and then screaming. She went out the front of her house and saw the neighbour's door was ajar. Then she called us. Response are on their way.'

Savage slowed and nosed the car forward. The little MG was narrow enough to pass right down the middle of the two lanes of traffic, but around them horns blared, drivers screaming at them. Up ahead a marked police car shot across a junction, blues and twos, vehicles moving to the side, pedestrians turning their heads. Savage floored the accelerator and followed, slipping into the moving space behind the patrol car.

They raced onto Tothill Avenue almost as one and then the patrol car braked hard, turning to block the road. Savage and Calter were out before the uniformed officers, Calter beating Savage to the front gate.

The neighbour had been right. The door stood open. And then there was a popping like a small-calibre weapon. Three bangs, followed by a scream.

'Jesus, ma'am,' Calter said. 'We've got to wait for an ARV.'

The officers from the patrol car had joined them, and one of them shrugged his shoulders.

'Not us, ma'am, but armed response are on the way.'

'Round the back you two,' Savage said, gesturing to the officers. 'We'll go in the front.'

'Ma'am!' Calter said. 'We're unarmed. It's suicide.'

'I don't think so.' Savage moved through the front gate and up the little path to the door. She pushed the door open and a yellow balloon wafted out from the hallway, bouncing once on the step before swirling past Calter.

'Anyone home?' Savage called down the passage, dark after the bright sunlight outside, before stepping in. She heard Calter mutter something and then the DC was right behind her.

'Careful, ma'am.'

Savage moved forward, a floorboard creaking underfoot. To the left the door to a living room stood open. She glimpsed something strewn across the floor, pink ribbon, a piece of wrapping paper. On a table beside the television a card, a big pink '7' on the front.

Then there was a crashing sound from up ahead and a scream echoed down the corridor.

Savage ran towards the door at the end and kicked it open to reveal a kitchen, glass scattered across the floor, one of

190

the uniformed officers at the back door, hand reaching in through the shattered pane to open it. To one side the cake stood on the table, seven candles, an older woman next to the table with her arms wrapped around a young girl, the screams turning to sobs, the officer at the door stepping back to let Savage deal with the situation.

Considering the circumstances the woman had been surprisingly calm. 'Better safe than sorry,' she'd said, adding, much to Hardin's relief, that there would be 'no solicitors'.

The little girl – Lily – got some stickers from one of the uniforms and a ride round the block in the patrol car. 'The best birthday present I've ever had,' she said. It transpired the woman in the house was Lily's aunt. She was looking after the girl because Lily's mum was working a Saturday shift up at the hospital where she was a midwife. Lily and the aunt had blown up a dozen balloons, popped them, opened the aunt's present and then blown up some more balloons and popped them too.

The mother turned up after an hour, flustered at being late because of an emergency C-section, in a state when she saw the three patrol cars, camera crew and photographers, not to mention the crowd of people gawping.

Right now Hardin and Savage stood with the girl and her mother and aunt, Hardin trying to turn his grimace into something resembling a smile for the photographer from the *Herald*. Once the pictures had been taken Dan Phillips walked forwards and held out his hand to Hardin.

'Nice one, Conrad. Always a pleasure. You and your lads must be worth a couple of dozen column inches a week. Makes my job so much easier.'

'Why don't you just f—' Savage nudged Hardin and stared at the little girl. Hardin coughed. 'F . . . F . . . find a birthday present for young Lily here. She's the one you need to thank. Without her there's no story.'

'My pleasure,' Phillips said, adding a wink and a smile. 'And I'll slip you a couple of fifties too. Like last time, hey?'

'If you don't—' Hardin moved down the garden path and Phillips backed off, pulling the photographer after him, the two of them chuckling away.

A couple of hours later and Savage was back at the station standing in the corridor outside the crime suite, Hardin trying to explain why he'd lost his temper.

'Media management,' the DSupt said. 'You go on these courses, think it's all about dealing with some terrorist alert or an innocent civilian shot by mistake. They don't tell you what to do in this situation. That reporter . . .'

'Dan's alright,' Savage said. 'Much as he annoys me sometimes, he's only doing his job.'

'His so-called *job* appears to be trying to put the fear of God into people. He's in training for a position on one of the tabloids and I for one won't be sorry to see him go. Did you see the paper this morning? Sensationalist rubbish.'

Hardin huffed a couple of times and then asked about Phil Glastone. Was there any sign of him?

'No,' Savage said. 'I sent the Salcombe beat officer round to his house, but Glastone hasn't returned.'

'So he's still on the prowl then.'

'I think he knew we were following him. If he's the killer he'd be stupid to do anything.'

'But that's what these maniacs are, Charlotte. Stupid. Keep at it, OK? Find the man.'

With the order still hanging in the air Hardin turned and was off to his office. Savage pushed through the double doors into the crime suite, finding most of the team inside. Legs were on desks, coffee cups scattered around, a smell of fish and chips drifting from one side where Enders was unpacking several portions from a carrier bag.

'Plaice, chips, curry sauce and peas?'

'Mine,' Riley said.

'Might have guessed,' Enders said. 'Fussy London-type that you are.'

'It's called having a sophisticated palate,' Riley said, getting up and taking the carton from Enders. 'Although, had there been one round the corner, I would have preferred a Lebanese.'

'Sod off!' Enders picked a can of Coke from a second carrier and lobbed the can across to Riley. 'And this will have to do instead of a bottle of vintage Blue Nun.'

'How did you know my favourite tipple?'

'With your "sophisticated palate" it was either the frigid mother superior or Mateus Rosé.'

Savage smiled at the banter and then moved across the room towards where Calter had just answered a trilling phone. The DC bent to the receiver, the pen in her hand moving at speed across a jotter pad.

'Ma'am?' Calter glanced up, the tone of her voice low but insistent. 'This time it's for real.'

By the time Savage and Calter pulled up on Trelawney Road in Peverell, John Layton had managed to seal the front garden and fifty metres of pavement either side of the house. White-suited figures crawled in the gutter bagging every cigarette butt, crisp packet and sweet wrapper.

'Ms Paula Rowland,' Layton said, handing Savage a photograph. 'Got this sent through from the school where she works.'

Savage looked down at the picture which showed a young woman in her early thirties. Slim. Long brown hair tied back. A pretty face.

'Witnesses?' Savage said.

'Some twitching curtains,' Layton said, pointing to a property a couple of doors up. 'A neighbour spotted a car moving off at speed around four o'clock. Paula had apparently only just returned.'

'Any idea who was driving?'

'No, but the neighbour says the vehicle was an old thing, a van or a tow truck of some kind.'

'And Paula was inside?'

'Couldn't say beyond there was at least one other person. An alert has gone out but it's more in hope than anticipation. The bad news is that the locals had spoken to the woman Friday afternoon. She reported a possible stalker.'

'And?'

'And nothing. A patrol car came down the street a couple of times last night. That's it. The alert was made by the woman's fiancé. He arrived from Exeter, where he lives. Found the front door not latched properly, went inside and saw signs of a struggle and the cake. Called it in. He's pretty shaken up from the sound of things.'

'Shit.' Savage nodded across to the front door. 'Inside?'

'Can't let you in yet. You can either take a look at the video we've shot or scoot round the back and peer in the rear window.'

Layton nodded and then pointed to a passage down one side of the house. Savage and Calter went down the passage and turned left at the end onto a gravel patio. A number of plastic crates and toolboxes sat on the gravel and the back door was open, a white-suited figure visible inside.

The woman looked up as Savage's feet crunched on the gravel. A blue gloved hand came up to form a stop sign and then she gestured to the large window.

Savage and Calter went across and peered through.

'Ma'am. The cake.' Calter tapped the glass and then moved her hand down to her stomach. 'Don't think I am going to be able to look at a slice in quite the same way again. Do wonders for my training regime.'

The sponge sat on the table, a dusting of icing sugar. A slice missing. Pink candles.

'Fourteen,' Savage said, as she counted. 'We're still no nearer to understanding the meaning of the numbers.'

'Beats me, ma'am. But then maths never was my strong point.'

'And the colours. Victim number two had blue candles, all the others pink.'

'Pink – blue, girl – boy isn't it?'

'We're missing something here.'

'Are we, ma'am? Couldn't this just be some sort of ruse, something to throw us as a curve ball? I mean the person who did this is a madman. Grade one. I doubt we could fathom him even if we catch him.'

'*When*, Jane. Not if, when.' Savage snapped the words out but she wasn't sure she believed them. They'd known the killer had been going to strike on the twenty-first – Paula Rowland had even tipped them off – but still he'd evaded them. For a moment a wash of abject failure came over her. Savage thought about the misery the Candle Cake Killer had already caused and the knowledge that there was still more to come angered and depressed her. Was this how DCI Walsh had felt each year when yet another woman went missing? She shook her head, cursed and reminded herself there was only one person to blame. And moping wouldn't catch them.

She moved over to the door and called out to the CSI. Was there anything else? The CSI reached for a clear plastic container and passed it across. Inside several slivers of dried mud lay cushioned in cotton wool. One piece was in a 'V' shape.

'Left behind from a boot. There's a chance we can get the size and possibly the brand. Analysis of the soil *might* pin down the area it has come from. There's bits of white gravel in there. Like something from a fish tank.'

The way the woman said 'might' didn't lend much hope. Savage thanked her and turned to the garden. Calter had plonked herself down in a wrought-iron chair – one of four clustered round a little table which stood on a circle of grey paving stones.

'How long,' Calter said, looking up at the first-floor windows, 'before Mr High and Mighty Layton allows us to get in and have a nose around?'

Long enough, it turned out, for Hardin to arrive, the DSupt stomping round the back and peering through the window, glass misting as he huffed at the sight of the cake.

'Shit luck,' he said, stepping back. 'For us and the girl. Layton told me there's a boyfriend. Can we see him doing this? Copycat?'

'No, sir,' Savage said. 'The locals have spoken to him. He lives over in Exeter. He's a PE teacher and he'd taken an under-twelve football team to Torquay this morning. He was with a fellow teacher when he came to the house. Alibi's solid. And you're not going to like this, but the local lads had already been out here to visit Ms Rowland. Apparently she called 101 to report she'd been followed. Advice was given, but no other action taken other than a patrol car swinging by last night.'

'Fuck.' Hardin moved farther away from the window and joined Savage at the edge of the patio. The little area was a suntrap, warmth washing up from the slabs beneath them.

Hardin stood and gazed into the distance. 'Evening like this, the young lass should be out here with a glass of wine, maybe using that barbecue over there to cook a couple of sausages for her tea. Friends round. You know the sort of thing?'

Savage looked across at the barbecue. It appeared as if Hardin's hunch might have been correct because a wisp of smoke rose from beneath the grill. Savage stepped over and saw the white of burnt charcoal, felt the radiant heat.

'There's . . .' On the wire frame something remained of Paula's meal, overcooked, the food blackened round the edges. Savage reached for a pair of tongs which lay to one side. She picked them up and prodded the meat. Only it wasn't meat. It was something a couple of inches long, almost like a sausage in the way the skin had burst in one place. But it wasn't a sausage, not with the little arms and legs and the head with tiny black holes where the eyes had once been.

Layton used a pair of forceps rather than the tongs to move the object on the grill. Then he touched the meat with the back of his gloved hand.

'Hot,' he said, gently closing the forceps, picking the thing up and popping it into a polygrip bag. The heat from the meat caused steam to condense on the inside of the polythene as he held the bag up and examined the creature within. 'Not what you were thinking.'

'Not an embryo?' Savage said. The sheer horror had gone, but looking again brought back the disgust.

'No.' Layton turned the bag around. 'My guess is the animal is a baby rabbit. A few days old at the most. They're naked and hairless when born. All burnt up like this, you can be forgiven for jumping to conclusions.'

'I'm glad I was wrong.' Savage looked back at the barbecue. The charcoal had gone white and ashy. 'From the look of it

197

the barbie has been going for a couple of hours. Paula probably lit it when she got home in anticipation of her boyfriend arriving. Can we get a time for when the rabbit was put on the grill?'

'Hmm.' Layton removed a glove from one hand and then held it over the grill. He waited several seconds before pulling it back. 'The coals are still pretty hot.'

'Meaning?'

'Hang on.' Layton walked away to where he'd left a large toolbox on the other side of the patio. He removed something the size of a small phone and then returned and pointed the device at the grill. 'One twenty. Hottish, but cooling. Without doing some kind of experiment it's a guess, but I'd say the rabbit has been on there for an hour and a half, perhaps a little longer. The flesh is overcooked, but it's not completely burnt because the grill was well above the coals.'

'Which matches with the time the next-door neighbour saw Paula leave.'

'Yes.' Layton held up the bag again.

'Well?' Hardin spoke for the first time. He stood several metres away, as if getting closer might mean he had to join Layton in prodding the bag. 'Um, bad news, yes? Cooking things like this.'

'The kidnapper put this on the barbecue. Unless,' Layton said, waggling the bag in Hardin's direction, 'Paula Rowland was partial to baby rabbit fritters.'

Hardin turned his head away. 'John, that isn't even remotely funny. Charlotte?'

'A whole new ball game,' Savage said. 'Suggests a change in the pattern.'

'Something for Dr Wilson to get his teeth into then?'

Savage looked again at the bag, visions of Wilson's pearlers munching down on the little rabbit, juice oozing from between his lips as he went on about his value to the FBI.

'Yes, I guess so.'

'Talk to him. Now.'

'Wilson?'

'This is way beyond what I'm used to dealing with, Charlotte. What any of us are used to dealing with. Dr Wilson's been there. He's studied serial killers, both in the States and here. Do you know he published a paper on an American killer who ate fifteen people? The killer used to fry the kidneys with a couple of eggs for his breakfast. Wilson interviewed the man apparently. Other nutters too.' Hardin stopped. Stared across at the bag containing the rabbit. Swallowed. 'This is awful, but he's worked on cases in the US which, quite frankly, are in a different league from the Candle Cake Killer. Whatever happened at the time of the first investigation we've got to put aside. We're all older and wiser now. He's in. Officially.'

'But DCI Walsh said—'

'I don't care what Walsh said. If we don't bring Wilson in then the Home Office will foist somebody upon us.'

'Better the devil you know?'

'Something like that. Call him.'

Savage glanced across at Layton. He shrugged.

'We're out of our depth,' Layton said. 'Love him or loathe him, Wilson knows his stuff.'

Savage nodded and then stepped away, pulling her gloves off and reaching for her phone. Wilson answered in seconds, the hum of a crowd in the background, somebody shouting a drinks order.

'There's been a development,' Savage said. 'A possible kidnapping. The DSupt would like you on board as part of the team.'

'About time,' Wilson said. 'I'm not glad to be proved right, but I guessed another killing was coming.'

When Savage told him what had happened and about the discovery they'd made round the back of the house he was nonplussed.

'A rabbit?' he said. 'You mean a pet one?'

'No,' Savage said. 'A baby one. Could have been a pet or a wild rabbit. I thought the animal looked like an embryo. I don't know if that was the intention. If it was then I'm putting the birthday cake and the embryo together and wondering if this isn't something to do with abortions. Possibly the work of a pro-life fanatic.'

'Choose your words carefully, DI Savage. Just because somebody holds particular views it doesn't make them a nutter. Slavery was once legal, now the practice is abhorrent.'

'Yes, but—'

'Have you any evidence Paula Rowland had an abortion? Or any of the other women?'

'We're working on it. Getting medical records is, as you probably know, difficult.'

'Quite rightly in my opinion. I think you'll find the line of enquiry a waste of time in this case. Dead end.'

'OK,' Savage said, exasperated. 'So tell me, why would the killer go to the trouble of toasting a rabbit on Paula's barbecue?'

'I'll do some work on it. See what I can come up with.'

'You do that. And make it quick. The girl's missing and you might be her only hope.'

God help her, Savage thought as she hung up. Wilson would take days to produce anything and then his report would probably consist of page after page of psychobabble.

She stared at the barbecue where two CSIs were examining the ground around the base and then went round to the front of the house where a DS was coordinating the door-to-door teams. So far, apart from the next-door neighbour, they'd found no one with anything useful to say.

'Most people were home, but with windows closed and doors bolted,' the DS said. 'From what I can gather folks were as scared of those guys.'

The DS pointed up the street to where a huddle of men stood on the corner. The impromptu vigilante group had already been questioned. At first they'd been reluctant to talk and it had taken the threat of a trip down the station to loosen tongues.

'Turns out the plonkers had got a little fed up with the heat.' The DS wiped his brow. 'They did what I'd like to do now and went for a breather just round the corner. The Fortescue. Came out when they heard the sirens. So much for reclaiming the streets.'

An hour later and Savage was in the pub herself. Hardin had come over all generous and put a fifty behind the bar so the door-to-door teams could grab a drink. 'Shandies only,' the barman said to Savage and nodded over to a corner where Hardin sat with half a bitter talking to the DtoD coordinator.

'Wilson any good?' Hardin said, as she came over, the other officer nodding a 'hello'.

'What do you think, sir?'

'Charlotte, I don't like the guy, but you can't expect him to provide us with a postcode. His analysis is only guidance.'

'Well, sir, to use your analogy, his guidance is about as useful as trying to give someone directions to your house in Plymouth using a London tube map.'

Hardin shook his head but didn't say anything. The DSupt was all quick-fix, instant solution, got-it-in-one. His mental inbox remained resolutely empty because he dealt with anything as it happened. If there *was* a quick-fix solution to finding Paula Rowland, that would be great, Savage thought, but she didn't think they'd come across one brooding in the pub.

'This rabbit thing,' she said. 'It's a new development, obviously. The cake is the killer's main motif, but for some reason he's decided to add to it.'

'What are you getting at?'

'The cake is a message, but back when the first killings occurred we never worked out what the cake meant. With Kat Mallory we've got no closer.'

'So?'

'So the killer's message was lost in translation. We didn't get it. We *couldn't* get it. Impossible when we hadn't found the bodies. Now he's giving us additional clues to decode that message.'

'He *wants* us to work out what he's up to?'

'Yes,' Savage said. 'There's no escalation in the conventional sense. There's nothing to suggest Kat Mallory's killing was any worse than the previous ones and he's sticking to the same pattern of one a year. For some reason he doesn't want to break that. Wilson told me killers get careless because they think they're invincible, but the cake and the rabbit aren't carelessness, they're very deliberate messages. We just don't know the meaning yet.'

'Well why doesn't he just come out and bloody well tell us?' Hardin said, necking the remains of his beer and then standing up to leave. 'It would save everyone an awful lot of grief, hey?'

As Hardin strode off Savage looked across at the coordinator, expecting some sympathy, perhaps a joke. The man shrugged. Said nothing.

Chapter Twenty-Three

Crownhill Police Station, Plymouth. Sunday 22nd June.
7.45 a.m.

Savage was at the station by seven-thirty the next morning.
She wanted to clear some of the endless admin work before
the nine a.m. briefing. Earlier, as she'd climbed out of bed,
Pete had moaned about yet another weekend without her
around. Could she, by any chance, remember the names of
her children?

Coming from him Savage had thought the jibe unfair.
Who was it who had been away on his ship for half the kids'
lives? Besides, work had been slack recently and she *had* been
around. Anyway, a week ago, staring down into the hole at
Tavy View Farm, she'd made a promise to the bodies lying
in the sludge. Family or no family, she intended to fulfil it.

In her office, she'd read halfway through one email when
a knock at the door brought Calter in.

'Phil Glastone, ma'am. The DSupt says we're to go and
question him again.'

'Really?' Savage said, thinking Hardin must have been
lying awake brooding half the night. 'Glastone knew we were
on to him, I'm sure of it. I can't see him committing a crime
when he was aware he was being tailed. Also, the car the

witness spotted bears no resemblance to his Alfa. The fact a kidnapping took place yesterday almost confirms he isn't the Candle Cake Killer.'

'Hardin's adamant, ma'am. He wants something for the media. They're asking about previous suspects and he's worried it won't be long before they doorstep Glastone.'

'Right.' Questioning Glastone would at least put him from the frame once and for all, Savage thought. TIE. Trace, interview, eliminate. Repeat a million and a half times across Devon and Cornwall and they'd be left with the killer. 'But at least let's take a pool car today. I need aircon.'

Calter drove the Focus while Savage pondered the possibility that Glastone could have anything to do with the disappearance of Paula Rowland.

'If he did do it then he'll have an alibi,' she said. 'If we can't get round that then there's not much we can do.'

'Might be like the other time, ma'am. The wife. If she's scared of him she'll say or do anything.'

'She can say what she likes, but her story will need to hold water. Phil Glastone can't get out of this with mere fairy tales.'

'So if she doesn't come up with something substantial we'll bring him in?'

'Let's see.'

Savage stared out at the countryside as they crawled out of Plymouth. Traffic snaked from the city and onto the country roads as people looked to take advantage of the hot weather. Locals heading for the beaches at Bigbury-on-Sea and Bantham, tourists intent on reaching Kingsbridge, Salcombe or Dartmouth for lunch. She wondered if people now felt safe knowing the killer had taken his victim. Safe, at least, until next year.

They pulled up on Devon Road a little after nine, Calter

slotting the car in behind Glastone's Alfa. As they got out of the car a shout echoed down from the house. The sound of something breaking too. Then more shouting and a scream. Calter beat Savage up the front steps and then she was round and in through the patio doors. Savage arrived a moment later.

Phil Glastone stood to one side of the living room next to a glass-fronted cabinet. The glass had disintegrated and lay in shards at his feet, along with several ornaments and a couple of photo frames.

'A stupid accident,' Glastone said, turning to Savage and Calter. 'Nothing to get excited about.'

'No, Mr Glastone?' Savage said. 'Where's your wife?'

'Upstairs. She cut herself. Silly bitch.'

'Go and see if she's alright, Jane.' Savage nodded at Calter. 'And Mr Glastone, please don't use language like that again or I might decide to continue this interview back in Plymouth.'

'OK.' Glastone held his hands up. 'Sorry. Heat of the moment.'

'Where were you yesterday afternoon and evening?'

'Oh, come on.' Glastone shook his head. 'Not that rubbish again. Are you seriously thinking I had something to do with the abduction yesterday?'

'News travels fast.'

'All anyone's been doing for the last few days is watching the TV. Me included.'

'You haven't answered the question.'

'Right.' Glastone moved away from the cabinet and went over to the sofa. He sat down. Making time, Savage thought. Glastone was trying to compose himself, rid himself of the anger and calm down so he could prepare an alibi.

'Well?'

'I was here, enjoying the sun. Did a bit of work. Had dinner. Usual stuff.'

'And was Carol here too?'

'Yes. All the time.'

'What did you have for dinner? Did you watch television? If so, what programmes? What time did you go to bed?'

'Hey?' Glastone shook his head, realising what Savage was up to. 'Don't mind if I get myself a drink, do you? Bit parched.' Glastone got up from the sofa and sauntered across the room and through into the kitchen. Savage heard the suck of the fridge as the door came open, the fizz of a bottle being opened, the rustle of a newspaper.

'Needed to remind yourself what was on TV?' Savage said as Glastone returned holding a glass of cola. 'Check the leftovers in the fridge perhaps?'

'You are so wide of the mark. We didn't watch television last night and we had pasta to eat. Read a bit down here. Then we went to bed and made love, OK?'

'Really?'

'Yes. Really. Sex. You should try it sometime. You might even enjoy it.' Glastone held his gaze on Savage. Didn't blink for ten seconds. Then he gulped some cola and went back to the sofa. 'Anyway, don't take my word for it, ask her.'

Glastone gestured to the doorway to the hall where Calter stood alongside Carol. A large plaster adorned the woman's right hand and a red welt on one side of her face was beginning to darken.

'Another accident, Carol?' Savage said.

'Something like that,' Carol said. 'I fell into the cabinet.'

'Fell, or was pushed?'

'Fucking hell!' Glastone said, back on his feet. 'You come in here expecting to fit me up for this bloody Candle Cake stuff and then because that doesn't work you make me out to be a wife-beater. Well you can get out of my house now. Go on, out!'

'Carol,' Savage said, ignoring Glastone. 'Can I ask what you ate for dinner last night? What you watched on television and what happened afterwards?'

'Last night?' Carol glanced across at Glastone. 'Sure. We had a pasta salad for dinner, we read a little, didn't watch television, but then we hardly ever do. Except if it's sport. Phil likes sport. Football especially. He always wants to watch that, don't you darling?'

'Yes. I do.'

'And your husband was here all the time? All afternoon and evening?'

'Not all the time, no.'

'Carol?' Glastone said. 'You know that's wrong. I was outside enjoying the sun and doing some work, wasn't I? Then we had dinner and then we went to bed and made love.'

'Oh,' Carol said, 'is that what you call it? If I recall you were away all afternoon and evening and didn't get back until the early hours.'

'You bloody bitch!' Glastone began to move across the room until Calter stepped in front of Carol. 'She's lying, Inspector. Making it up. I was here all the time. Check my laptop, you'll see emails I sent in the evening.'

'Emails can be faked, Mr Glastone,' Savage said. 'I'm much more interested in witness testimony. Carol, any idea of the time your husband returned?'

'Two-ish, I think. I heard him come in and spend a long time in the shower. He put his clothes in the washing machine too. Then he came to bed and, in his words we "made love". To be honest I didn't think there was much love about it.'

'What would you call it?'

'He raped me, Inspector. I didn't want sex but he forced me. He held me down and then had me anally.'

'You cow!' Glastone moved forwards but Calter intervened. Glastone raised a fist, but in a split second Calter pulled one of her Jujitsu moves and tripped and spun him to the floor, one arm pushed up in the small of his back.

'Are you prepared to make a statement, Carol? Down the station?' Savage said.

'You bet I fucking am,' Carol said. 'He's a bloody animal. From almost the day we married he's been at me. Right now I've had enough.'

'Phil Glastone,' Savage said, walking over to where Calter knelt on Glastone. 'I'm arresting you on suspicion of the rape and assault of your wife and on suspicion of the abduction of Paula Rowland. You don't have to say anything, but it may harm your defence if you don't mention something which you later rely on in court. Anything you say may be given in evidence.'

Savage stood for a moment. Wondered whether she'd get away with kicking Glastone in the face. Decided she probably wouldn't.

'Well?' she said.

'Tell her to get off,' Glastone said, his face squashed on the floor, Calter's knee in his back. His eyes flicked up to plead at Savage. 'She's really hurting my arm. I think she might have broken something.'

'Good,' Savage said.

Mid-morning Sunday, and Riley headed for Derriford Hospital for Devlyn Corran's post-mortem. There were still technical issues at the mortuary, bodies stacking up, some having to be taken elsewhere, but the gunshot wound meant Corran got bumped up the schedule.

208

'Lucky guy,' Davies said as he and Riley paced around outside the mortuary. 'Bet he can't wait to watch his entrails come out. I know I can't.'

Riley ignored the DI and checked his watch again. He was about to suggest they went for a coffee when Nesbit's assistant poked her head round the door.

'We're ready for you now,' she said.

'Great,' Davies said. 'Think I'd prefer to have my teeth filled.'

Inside, Nesbit had gowned up. He waited while the detectives did the same.

'Not seen you in here for a while, Phil,' he said to Davies. 'Plymouth's slimy underbelly taking a break from the mayhem?'

'Wouldn't know. Last few months I've been away chasing sheep.'

'Really?' Nesbit raised an eyebrow, but Davies didn't elaborate.

'Diesel fraud,' Riley said, feeling he needed to explain on behalf of Davies. 'We've been spending a lot of time stuck in ditches watching people filling up with red gold. It's never going to be on primetime TV, but someone's got to do it.'

'Yeah,' Davies said. 'But why the hell does it have to be me?'

The answer to Davies' question, Riley knew, lay back in events at the start of the year when Davies and DI Savage had almost stepped over the line which Hardin considered every copper should try to stay on one side of. Riley, quite unfairly he believed, had been implicated alongside them. Result was he'd had the joy of partnering Maynard and Davies on the three-month-long dodgy diesel investigation. Savage, until *Radial*, had been variously involved with minor cases, including one which led to the arrest of a gang of bicycle thieves responsible for the theft of over three hundred bikes. The oldest of the perpetrators was just fifteen.

'Well,' Nesbit said, 'let's see if we can pull you two out of your mundane lives shall we?'

Inside the post-mortem room Corran lay on the stainless steel table. His clothes had already been cut off and sat in a number of bags ready for the lab.

'John Layton will be able to tell you more than I can,' Nesbit said, indicating the bags, 'but there's scuffing on the right arm of the coat consistent with a friction slide on tarmac.'

'So it was an RTC then?' Riley said. 'At least initially.'

'Could be.' Nesbit moved over to the body. 'I've done a preliminary examination and there are numerous external injuries. They are certainly consistent with a severe collision with something.'

'Car,' Davies said. 'Don't need a university education to tell you that. Bike was mangled and we found parts of his lamp set.'

Nesbit nodded and pointed up to the head. He took a plastic spatula and prodded the nose.

'Broken. His chin came into contact with the ground as well. Major abrasions across part of his cheek too.'

The face was a mass of black, blue and red and Riley flinched at the thought of the skin scraping over the rough road. Corran had gone over the handlebars. Faceplant.

'He was wearing cycling gloves. When we took them off I noticed pieces of grit in both palms. However, falling off was the least of his worries.' Nesbit moved from the head and moved down to the legs. The right leg was a mush of flesh and bone. He lifted the leg at the calf and the knee joint flexed the wrong way. 'Smashed. I would imagine the vehicle ran over his leg.'

'And if that wasn't enough then they shot him.'

'I was, of course, coming to the head wound.' Nesbit looked up at Riley. 'I'll extract the bullet later, but there's no doubt he was shot at point blank range.'

'Silly question,' Riley said, 'but was he already dead?'

'Not silly at all. We've no way of knowing, but from the way the leg looks and the relative lack of blood on his trousers, the gunshot wound came soon after the other injuries.'

'He was on the ground,' Davies said. 'And they just performed the coup de grâce. What's bugging me though, is why did they bother? They could have simply run him over a couple more times.'

'Forensic,' Riley said. 'More mess on the ground and more chance of bits of Corran getting stuck to the car. Plus he could have been making one hell of a racket. The road isn't the busiest but if they had the means then why risk someone coming as they were going back and forth over him?'

'Indeed.' Nesbit nodded and moved to Corran's head where he poked at the hole with the spatula. 'If I can find the bullet then your ballistics experts will be able to confirm my guess that it was fired from a small-calibre weapon, probably a pistol. Totally illegal.'

'This was planned,' Riley said. 'Corran's routine was pretty predictable. They got tooled up. Waited until Corran left the prison and then ran him down and shot him. One question though. After Corran had been knocked off his bike but before he was shot would he have been able to throw something a few metres?'

'Like what?' Nesbit said.

'His bike pump. We found it ten metres from the road. I think he chucked it deliberately to try and mark the spot where he was hit and maybe to indicate he knew his attacker.'

'Hard to say. There are battleground tales of soldiers doing the most incredible things with half their bodies blown away. Who knows what's possible when you're in that state?'

God knew maybe, Riley thought. If you believed in some higher being. If you didn't, then you wouldn't bother wasting your final breaths praying. You'd do everything you could to try and protect the people you were leaving behind. Despite having been mangled – like his bike – Corran had managed to think clearly. He'd thrown the pump into the heather and his attacker hadn't wanted to waste time looking for it. Moments later Corran had been gone, but maybe in the last few seconds of his life he'd found a crumb of comfort.

But then again, maybe he hadn't.

Savage discovered Hardin in the crime suite, weaving between desks and checking on the latest reports which had come in from members of the public. A hand raised to scratch his chin as she approached suggested he wasn't altogether happy with developments regarding Phil Glastone.

'Just the one question, Charlotte,' he said. 'Where the bloody hell is Paula Rowland?'

'We'll find out shortly, sir,' Savage said. 'DC Calter and DC Enders are about to interview Glastone. That's top of their agenda.'

'And what happens if he keeps his mouth shut?'

'John Layton is round Glastone's place now. His car's being given a going over too. Carol Glastone's at the Sexual Assault Referral Centre at the moment having a medical examination and talking to a specialist officer. I'm going to be speaking to her later to see if she has any idea where Glastone might have gone. Hopefully we'll get some indication as to where Paula is.'

'Do you think there's a chance she's alive?'

'You want my honest opinion?' Hardin nodded. 'No, sir, I don't.'

'He couldn't have taken them somewhere, kept them for a bit?'

'We've got no idea what happened to the previous victims after they were abducted, but I wouldn't hold your breath if you were hoping for good news.'

'Bugger.' Hardin looked around the room, as if searching for something. His eyes alighted on the whiteboard with the aerial picture of Tavy View Farm. 'The killer's got to have some connection with the farm.'

'I've always thought so, but perhaps the place is just a body dump. No special reason except for its seclusion.'

'You'll need Dr Wilson to take a look at Glastone,' Hardin said looking back at Savage. 'Get his opinion on the man and see if anything matches the profile.'

'I've already checked the profile. Glastone's a database programmer. He's a bit of a nerd and very bright, but high intelligence is about the only thing specific. Glastone's got nothing to do with art though.'

'Get Wilson down here anyway. He should be listening in on the interviews.'

'Yes, sir,' Savage said.

Sixty minutes later and she was all cosy with the psychologist in a windowless room at Charles Cross custody centre. Two monitors showed a video feed from the interview suite, Calter and Enders on one screen and Glastone and his solicitor on the other.

'No,' Wilson said as he pulled up a chair and sat in front of the monitors. 'Not him.'

'Hang on,' Savage said. 'You haven't even heard him speak yet. How can you be so sure?'

'I've seen Glastone before, remember? He was a suspect for the murders years ago but he didn't fit the profile back then and he doesn't now.' Wilson sighed and tapped the monitor. 'Look at his body language, the way he's biting his lip, glancing around the room, constantly touching his face. This man is nervous. He may well have done something wrong, but he's not the Candle Cake Killer.'

'I don't get it.'

'The killer would be supremely confident in this situation. He's eluded you lot for years, he wouldn't see this as the end game at all.'

'We've got him in custody. I don't see how this *isn't* the end game.'

'Then you've got a lot to learn, Inspector. When I was at—'

'Please. No more of your Quantico stories. Let's just listen for a while.'

Savage concentrated on the screen where Enders was trying to elicit some sort of response from Glastone as to whether the man knew Paula Rowland. Glastone kept shaking his head and turning to his solicitor for support. Savage had to admit he did appear nervous. But then couldn't it be part of the act?

'Where were you yesterday, Phil?' Calter had taken over. 'Afternoon and evening.'

'I told you.'

'Look,' Calter leaned forward and lowered her voice. Flicked a lock of hair away from her face. Smiled. Classic interview technique, Savage thought. 'It would be far simpler if you admitted you were away from the house yesterday afternoon and evening. Who do you think we're going to believe, you or your wife?'

'I hope,' the solicitor said, 'that you are going to base any case on evidence. Not on one disturbed woman's voice against my client's testimony.'

'Phil?' Calter said, ignoring the solicitor. 'How about if I

214

told you we *know* you went out. With a little more work we'll get the full picture. Eyewitnesses, cameras, mobile phone records. It won't be long before we have comprehensive proof you weren't in Salcombe for a large part of the twenty-first of June.'

Glastone looked at his solicitor again and then put his hands down on the table.

'OK. I wasn't at home. I did go out.'

'Good. Now we're making progress.'

'Where, Mr Glastone?' Enders. No Phil from him, Savage noted.

'I drove into Plymouth to get some parts for the engine on my boat. But I was back home by late afternoon. I suppose I was only gone for a few hours.'

'Phil, Phil, Phil,' Calter said. 'Just when I was beginning to think you and I were getting on.'

The solicitor bent to Glastone's ear and whispered something. Glastone nodded and then spoke.

'Receipts. They'll be in my wallet. You've got that. Took it off me when I was booked in.'

Savage saw Calter and Enders exchange a glance and then Enders wound the interview up, saying aloud for the benefit of the recording that they were taking a short break. Enders reached for the controls of the audio and video equipment and the screens in front of Savage and Wilson went blank.

'Well?' Savage said. 'Changed your mind?'

'No,' Wilson pointed to the blank screen. 'I haven't. I can guarantee you Phil Glastone is not the killer. Nothing fits. Not his demeanour or anything about him.'

'He's clever, organised and, from what we've seen of his wife, prone to violence.'

'If those three things make you a serial killer then you'll need to bring in half the male population of the West

215

Country. If Mrs Glastone is telling the truth, *if* mind you, then Glastone is at worst a rapist in his own house. A violent rapist, yes, but don't go all politically correct on me and pretend that's as bad as someone who commits multiple homicide.'

'It's bad enough.'

'Yes, I agree. However, raping his wife doesn't make him the Candle Cake Killer, does it?'

'We'll see. We're gathering evidence right now.'

'Looked to me as if Glastone was furnishing his own evidence and I don't blame him one bit.'

'What's that supposed to mean?'

'The first time, you lot tried to fit him up. If the killer hadn't struck again you'd have had Glastone locked away. An innocent man.'

'We don't—'

'Yes we do!' Wilson raised his voice, his face contorted for a second. 'That man down there is not the killer. He's not clever enough for a start. There's no motive either. Nothing.'

'He's a programmer. Earns a packet, enough to buy a nice house in Salcombe and run an expensive motorboat anyway.'

'Motive, Inspector, motive.' Wilson paused and then nodded and lowered his voice. 'Sorry for shouting. I just don't want to see the wrong person banged up. Worse, I don't want the killer to be the one on the outside running around and murdering at will.'

'Well, we're on the same side then.'

There was a moment's embarrassing silence and then a knock on the door broke the spell. Enders' face peered round, his usual beaming expression absent.

'Gaelforce, ma'am,' he said, holding out a piece of paper. 'They're a commercial chandlers down on the dock at Sutton harbour. This receipt is dated twenty-one June. Yesterday.

216

One thirty-seven p.m. Telling the truth about where he went after you lost him at least, isn't he?'

Wilson smiled as Savage shook her head.

'Doesn't prove a thing. He could have taken Paula afterwards. Get on to Hi-Tech Crimes, Patrick, and tell them to prioritise getting the data from Glastone's mobile phone. When we've got the information we'll know for sure.'

'Yes,' Wilson said, smiling again. 'We will.'

Joanne Black spent Sunday morning on the tractor de-heading thistles on the three big pastures she owned up Bere Alston way. The rotary cutter on the back of the tractor whined and hissed as she sped around the field seeking out clumps of the purple flowers, lazy sheep watching her activities with bemused faces. By lunch time she'd finished and for a moment, as she stood by the gate and surveyed her work, the events at the farm were almost forgotten. Normality would return, she thought. It might be weeks or months in coming, but life carried on whether you fretted about your troubles or not.

Back home for lunch a police officer in the farmyard broke the news to her: the Candle Cake Killer had struck again. Joanne shook her head. The return of normality, it appeared, had been postponed. She turned on the radio as she made a couple of sandwiches. BBC Devon were trying their best to be sensationalist in a non-sensationalist way but failing miserably, the glee in the reporter's voice evident as she interviewed people on the streets of Plymouth. The questions were as dumb as the answers. Small talent meeting big story. Joanne re-tuned to 5Live where inevitably the failure of the police to prevent the kidnapping of the latest victim was being turned into a debate about funding. It wasn't until the top of the hour that she got the full story.

Radio off, she pondered developments for a moment and then went across to the phone. On the wall behind was a pinboard where she'd stuck a business card given to her by one of the young detectives. She removed the card and held it in her hand for a moment. Jody was probably right about her fears. The girl, the bungalow and her uncle were history, nothing to do with the Candle Cake Killer. Still, if there was any kind of link the police would be in a better position to find it than she would. Joanne reached for the phone.

Chapter Twenty-Four

The sheet rustles as the girl moves and for a moment she looks confused.

'Plastic,' you say to her. '0.254 millimetres. We like to keep things nice and tidy, don't we, Mikey? Saves a mess.'

'Yuuuhhhh. Mess. Fucking mess. Awwwfuuul.'

'Awful. That's right, Mikey,' you say. 'Awful.'

'Help!' the girl yells at the top of her voice. 'For God's sake let me go!'

Let her go? What is she on about? There can be no going back now. Not after the choices she's made.

'We can't do that, can we? You've been so naughty, see? Done things which need . . . how can I say this . . . punishing?'

'Pose her, Ronnie, pose her,' Mikey says, tongue hanging out. 'When we gunna pose her?'

'Expose, Mikey,' you say. 'The word is expose. And we'll be exposing her soon, don't worry.'

You move away from the table, reach for the Big Knife. You hold it out in front of you, the steel glinting in the light, the thing like some giant phallus. You return to the table and place the knife down near to the girl's waist, slide it in under her blouse and slice upwards. The material rips, threads parting with hardly a sound.

'This is my favourite toy, Paula,' you say. 'And its purpose is to explore, reveal and expose.'

The blade flashes again and again, Mikey moving close and pulling away the blouse, then reaching for her bra, dirty fingers scrabbling at her breasts.

'Leave her alone, Mikey,' you say. 'You'll get your turn later.'

'Aaawww!' Mikey snorts and then jumps down towards the girl's feet. You cut through her skirt, Mikey paws again and in seconds she's lying there in nothing but her panties. You slip the point of the blade in at the side and flick it up, Mikey grabbing and pulling until away they come.

'Lovely,' you say. 'Beautiful. As naked as the day you were born.'

Mikey sniffs the air, wrinkles his nose. Looks the girl up and down. You pause for a moment, examine the point of the blade, test the sharpness on the back of a fingernail.

And then you begin.

Chapter Twenty-Five

After Corran's post-mortem Riley and Davies returned to Crownhill. The station, usually quiet on a Sunday, was packed to overflowing. A press conference with the parents of the Candle Cake Killer's latest victim was due to take place later and the Chief Constable was in attendance. His visit had brought on a bout of presenteeism not seen since a minor royal had toured the station a few years back. Riley and Davies snuck in under the radar, their case overlooked in all the excitement. As they tucked into a late lunch in the canteen Riley put his thoughts to Davies.

'Despite initial appearances – the shot to the head – I don't believe this was a professional hit.'

'Been thinking along the same lines myself, Darius.' Davies cut into his pie and shovelled a forkful into his mouth, chewing the bits of steak and onion while waving the knife at Riley. 'Too messy, too risky, too bloody crazy.'

'Agreed,' Riley said. 'Which tends to suggest Corran wasn't blackmailing some big crimo. If he had, the hit would have been carried out by a pro.'

'So it was someone else then. Who?'

221

'I was wondering about white-collar. Plenty of them in HMP Dartmoor. Corran got wind of some scam or fraud and wanted in. It all works out to start with and then the victim gets shirty at Corran's increasing demands. He cracks and goes after Corran. Whoever the blackmailer was Corran wasn't expecting trouble. Otherwise he'd have taken more precautions.'

'All well and good,' Davies said, attacking his pie again. 'But what about the gun?'

'That's where you come in. Once we know the calibre you'll have to ask around and see what might have changed hands recently. Your casual killer doesn't tend to have a weapon lying around at home and they may well have drawn attention to themselves when trying to buy one.'

'Right.' Davies brought his fork down on a piece of potato. 'The business end of all this, the money. Still don't know about that. How he picked the cash up.'

'We're waiting on Hi-Tech Crimes. Hopefully they can get something from the laptop. But I reckon Corran was working some kind of clever drop and pickup which on the final occasion went wrong.' Riley stared at Davies' plate where the DI had mashed the potato and mixed it with a whirl of tomato sauce. 'Very wrong.'

The second interview session with Glastone didn't prove any more productive than the first. Again, the double act was Calter and Enders, the two of them trying to home in on the little slivers of information which Glastone provided. Again, nothing he said was of much use. He claimed that after he'd visited the chandlers he'd driven around a bit and was home by eight o'clock. Enders put it to him that Carol said he didn't get back until the early hours of the next morning. Even if they took the eight p.m. time as gospel there were several hours to account for. Glastone shrugged, continued to deny he was the Candle Cake Killer and said he didn't know who Paula Rowland was.

'He's hiding something, ma'am,' Enders said to Savage when the interview was over. 'What did Wilson think this time around?'

'Nothing,' Savage said. 'He wasn't listening in. Said there was no need, so he went home.'

'He's bloody confident Glastone isn't the killer then?'

'Too confident.'

Which, Savage thought, wasn't something they could afford to be. Paula Rowland was out there somewhere. She was probably dead, but they had to cling to the possibility she was still alive. Either way, they needed to find her. John Layton had put a team into Glastone's house but with no news so far there was only one alternative: they needed to press Glastone harder in the third session.

Savage began to go through the interview strategy with Calter and Enders when Doug Hamill from the Hi-Tech Crimes Unit called. The unit didn't usually do Sundays but Hamill had come in as soon as he got word they'd arrested Glastone. He knew the man's background and figured there'd be a lot of data crunching to do. A clue to the whereabouts of Paula Rowland might well be hidden on one of the four computers Glastone owned. Then there was the information on Glastone's mobile phone to deal with too.

'So do you have anything for me, Doug?' Savage said.

'Only where he's been, Charlotte,' Hamill said. 'All day Saturday. Salcombe, Plymouth, Noss Mayo, Salcombe.'

'Noss Mayo?'

'Noss Mayo. We didn't need the mobile data from the company. There's location history on Glastone's phone. Pretty little lines all over the map. Shows he went to Plymouth and then to the Ship Inn in the village of Noss. He must have switched his phone off for a while because we get a jump to a place about half a mile outside the village. After that the data show him returning to Salcombe.'

'Any idea of times?'

'Yup. He was only in the chandlers for around ten minutes. The time correlates with the receipt. Drove to the pub, got there some time before three and stayed until four-fifteen. Then we have the gap when his phone was off but the track resumes at around seven-thirty. He was back home at eight.'

'*Eight?*'

'Yes, 'fraid so.' Hamill was silent for a moment. 'Of course this only proves the location of Glastone's phone, but I can't see our good friends in the CPS wanting to build a case on Glastone's phone doing walkabouts and then somehow miraculously reuniting itself with him. Then there's the fact Glastone is a programmer. His phone is pretty high-end, but he'd surely know all about its capabilities. He'd turn off the location features if he was worried about being caught or at least clear the history.'

'Wilson said the killer is arrogant. He wouldn't believe he was *going* to get caught. Also, the phone *was* off for a while, wasn't it?'

'For around three hours, yes. When he was outside the village. On the map the place he went to looks like a cottage or small house.'

'OK, so he could have gone there to prepare, then returned to kidnap Paula Rowland. He brings her back and then goes off home.'

'Theoretically, yes.' Hamill paused again. 'It doesn't leave much time to . . . you know, do the things these sort of nutters do.'

'Which tends to suggest to me he hasn't done those things yet.'

'You mean . . .?'

'Give me the address, Doug, I'm on my way.'

The twin villages of Newton Ferrers and Noss Mayo sat on either side of a winding estuary. The estuary was a haven for visiting yachties and in summer every available mooring was taken and the Ship Inn packed with sailors from opening until closing. The data on Glastone's phone showed he'd left the inn and driven about half a mile south of Noss, ending up at a twee cottage set back from a tiny lane. Savage took Enders, leaving Calter to put Layton and the others on standby, ready to move if she found anything.

'The place is a semi, ma'am,' Enders said as they drew up alongside. 'Doesn't look much like the lair of one of the most notorious serial killers this country has ever known.'

Savage peered out of the car. The two cottages were mirror images of each other, right down to the white doors and honeysuckle curling over the porches. Both front gardens were laid to lawn, the grass grown a little long.

'Holiday homes,' Savage said. 'It's all too neat and sterile. Look at the curtains. They match.'

'Which one did Glastone go to?' Enders looked down at the printout he'd brought with him. 'The location data isn't accurate enough to show.'

'You take the right and I'll do the left,' Savage said.

They opened the identical iron gates set into the stone boundary wall and walked up the identical paths. Enders peered into the front window of his property.

'Kids toys, ma'am. A whole load of them.'

'No cars parked in the lane though. Whoever is staying has gone out for the day.'

Savage moved across to a window and held her hands up to her eyes to cut out the reflection in the glass. Inside the contents of the room backed up her hunch that this was a holiday home: dated furniture, a small bookshelf with a limited selection of books, a spread of *Devon Life* magazines and the brochures of a number of nearby attractions on a coffee table, a print of Dartmouth hanging above the fireplace. Draped across the arm of the sofa was a red nightdress.

'It's this one,' Savage said. 'Got to be.'

Enders clambered over the low wall which divided the gardens and squashed his face up against the glass.

'Ma'am? You reckon he's dressing her up to play with her? Like a doll?'

'Did you get that rubbish from Wilson? Because it doesn't fit the MOs of the others. Whatever, she's in there.'

'But what about Mr and Mrs Young Couple next door? Could Glastone get Paula in here in broad daylight while they were playing in the front room with the kiddie?'

'Maybe he got lucky and they were out. Do the honours could you, Patrick?' Savage pointed at the door. Enders hesitated for a moment. 'She could be in there, still alive.'

Enders shrugged, stepped back and then shouldered the door. The door shuddered, but didn't budge. He tried again and this time there was a splintering, the door banging open as the Yale lock gave way.

'Police!' Savage shouted. She ran into the house and gestured for Enders to check the ground floor. She stomped up the stairs where there was a bathroom and two bedrooms off a tiny landing. Both were empty, although one showed signs of occupancy, the duvet on the double bed ruffled and a skimpy top folded on a chair. Savage spotted a suitcase pushed under the bed and a recent paperback on the side table.

Enders came up the stairs.

'Nothing down there, ma'am. There's food and milk in

226

the fridge and today's *Telegraph* on the kitchen table. The dishwasher's half open, dirty plates and cutlery inside.' Enders looked around the bedroom. 'I don't get it. Where's Paula?'

'He must have gone somewhere else. Maybe he *was* being clever. Drove up here deliberately and then turned his phone off when he arrived. Went away and did the business and then came back here and turned the phone on again.'

'We should've questioned him before we came.'

'Maybe, but I wanted to wrong foot him. Anyway, I thought the girl might have been here.' Savage turned and began to go down the stairs. 'We'd better call John Layton out and see if he can come up with anything.'

As they reached the front door a car pulled up in the lane. The door opened and an attractive woman got out. Mid-thirties, long dark hair, dressed in a tracksuit, a kit bag in her hand. The woman stared up at the front door and then pulled out a phone. As Savage came out the door and down the path the woman was making a call.

'I'm warning you, I'm phoning the police!'

'DI Savage,' Savage said, taking out her warrant card.

The woman looked puzzled, but lowered the phone.

'Has there been a break-in or something? I've only been gone for an hour or so. Just went for a run along the coast.'

The woman closed the door of the car and came up the path.

'Kirsty Longworth,' she said. 'Did they take anything? Not that I've got much here.'

'Do you know a Mr Glastone, Kirsty?' Savage said.

'Phil? Of course. He's the owner of these cottages. We . . . I mean . . .'

'Sorry?'

'I'm on holiday here. Just for a couple of days. I live over in Exeter.'

227

'Not far to come for a holiday, is it?'

'No, I suppose not. But Phil and I . . . well, we had a few things to sort out.'

'You know Phil personally? You're not just renting the house off him?'

'No, I'm not renting the house at all. Phil's letting me stay here for free.' The woman sighed. Shrugged her shoulders. Gave an embarrassed smile. 'OK, we're lovers. Or rather, *were* lovers. Cheating on our partners, if you want to put it in such sordid terms.'

'Were?'

'It's over. I told him yesterday I didn't want to see him anymore. The affair was getting too complicated and anyway, I'm moving away. My husband's got a job up North so we have to relocate. I'm going to see if I can make it work with him.'

'And how did Phil feel about that?'

'He wasn't happy, but we parted on good terms. I think. He didn't rant and rave, if that's what you mean. In fact, we made love before he left.' Kirsty paused and put her head on one side. She pointed up at the smashed lock. 'Look, what's this about? You broke that, didn't you? Not burglars.'

'How long was Phil with you yesterday?'

'We had a very late lunch at the Ship and got back here about four-ish. We went to bed and I guess he went off at about seven. Maybe a little later.'

'He's out of the frame, ma'am,' Enders said. 'She was taken late afternoon.'

'Who was taken?' Kirsty said. She glanced at Enders and then back at Savage. 'You're talking about the girl on the news, aren't you? You're crazy, Phil can't have had anything to do with that. He was here with me and then he went home to his wife.'

228

'Yes, we know.' Savage turned to Enders. 'Patrick, get on the phone and call someone out to deal with the broken lock. Then we'll get back and charge Mr Glastone with what we've got. Which from what we saw of Carol Glastone is quite enough.'

'Charge Phil,' Kirsty said. 'What with for God's sake?'

'Assaulting his wife,' Savage said. 'If you could give Patrick your contact details because we might have a few more questions for you. Enjoy the rest of your holiday.'

Back at the station from her jaunt in the countryside, Savage found herself cornered by Hardin. She told him about Glastone being out of the picture. He wasn't happy.

'Good news would have been handy,' Hardin said. 'Because there's a press conference in twenty minutes with the parents. The Chief Constable has deigned us with his presence and he wants a good showing of senior officers.'

Savage followed Hardin down to the media room, the place already packed with reporters. Paula Rowland's parents sat alongside Simon Fox, the harsh lights from the TV crews probing every small facet of their faces. Not that there was much probing to do. Distraught was the only word to do justice to their expressions. Fox too wore a grimace as the hacks moved closer to get their pictures. They were hardened to this sort of thing, had seen it all before: the appeals for the missing person to come home, for whoever who was holding her to release their little baby. A family friend or relative would run through a short bio. She was a lovely girl, always laughing, many friends, caring. She was thoughtful, giving, looking out for others. Please come home.

Savage felt heartless and cynical for a moment as she wondered if there was any other type of victim. Were people involved in tragedies always angels at school, friends with everyone, the life and soul of the party with so much to look forward to?

Cameras flashed and the journalists started to ask questions. Fact was, they already knew the answers from covering similar cases whose victims had become immortalised in the public's psyche. History was composed of events like this and you revealed your age by how far back you could remember. Was it the searches on the moors, the prostitutes who weren't missed in Halifax and Leeds, the runaways who vanished into the hell which was Cromwell Street or two little girls missing in Soham?

The story each time differed, but the ending was always the same, predestined. While Mr and Mrs Rowland might be clinging to any little scrap of hope, looking for any chink of light in an otherwise black night, everyone else in the room knew the truth. Paula Rowland was dead. Brutally murdered. Probably raped first. Maybe tortured. The CC and the other police in the room would hope not. The journalists expected and hoped for the worst. The more gruesome the tale, the more column inches they could write and the bigger their expense accounts. In a few months one or two might bring out books. The Candle Cake Killer was a cash machine and every new victim meant a bunch of crispy notes spewing forth.

Savage was brought back to reality by the Chief Constable wrapping the conference. The Rowlands were being ushered to one side by their solicitor and a family liaison officer. Simon Fox came the other way and he approached Hardin and Savage.

'Jesus, Conrad,' he said, loosening the top button on his uniform. 'This is a bloody nightmare. Do you know the Police and Crime Commissioner is beginning to make noises about leadership?'

'Positioning, sir,' Hardin said. 'Elections later this year.'

'All the effort we've made to keep everyone onside. Policing by consent. Public cooperation. The plan's going down the pan. The Commissioner's been talking to his chums up in London. The Home Secretary is apparently concerned. Looking to take a personal interest. Total meltdown.'

'Sir?' Savage said. 'It's the councillors on the Crime Panel. Alec Jackman, amongst others. They're ramping things up and putting the Commissioner under pressure.'

'Well he should be able to take it. Not wilt at the first piece of heat. Pathetic. Typical of a politician. To be honest the whole concept was flawed from the start.'

Fox wiped the back of his hand across his brow where perspiration glistened in the white light. Savage had always thought the man a cool cookie, but now she wondered what had got into him. The Rowlands? Over the other side of the room Mrs Rowland had broken down. She hadn't been able to make it from the room and had collapsed on one of the plastic chairs which had been put out for the press. The situation was distressing, yes, but Savage thought Fox would have been able to deal with it. Perhaps it was the way things had run out of control. They had prepared for the worst before D-Day but had been unable to prevent the killer striking again. The impotence would hurt.

'Where's DS Riley?' Fox said. Savage shook her head, not understanding. 'I want a word with him. This prison officer death. I hear the man was murdered. As if we haven't got enough on our plate.'

'He'll be in the crime suite,' Savage said. 'I'll take you up there myself.'

'No,' Fox said. 'Not necessary. I can find my own way.'

Fox moved off and headed for the door. Hardin shook his head.

'When the skipper looks like he's about to abandon ship then it's time for the rats to get jumpy too, hey Charlotte?'

Savage nodded, but didn't say anything.

Riley was about to leave for home so he could get back and make up to Julie for missing most of the weekend when Simon Fox strode into the crime suite. Heads went down over keyboards, hands went to pens and scribbled on pads. Fox ignored everyone and walked over to Riley's corner. The CC wanted to know how the investigation into Corran's murder was going. Terrible turn of events, he said. Riley stood and apologised for the absence of DI Davies.

'He's working on tracing the gun, sir. Contacts.'

'Right.' Fox nodded.

Davies' contacts were notorious, stretching the gamut from small-time drug hustlers and street toms right to the very top of the Plymouth underworld. If the gun had been obtained in the city Davies would find out. Killing a prison officer was way out of line. Business would be affected. Unnecessary heat would rain down. Bad form.

'The thing is,' Fox said, 'if you get a likely suspect then if at all possible I'd like to know before any arrest is made.'

'Sir?' Riley didn't like the way the conversation was going so he played dumb. 'I don't understand.'

'Rumours, Sergeant, rumours.' Fox glanced around and lowered his voice. 'Corran dealt with sex offenders, I understand.'

'Yes. I believe he did a couple of courses up at Full Sutton and has worked over at Channings Wood. Vulnerable offenders.'

'Vulnerable offenders?' Fox cracked a smile. 'There's a certain stupidity about the label wouldn't you say? It's a contradiction in terms lost on the leftie do-good brigade.'

'Yes, sir.' Riley held his tongue. He wasn't about to get drawn into a political debate with the CC.

'All I'm saying is should a person of interest come onto your radar and the person is also, how shall I say it . . . a VIP? Then I want, if possible, to know of it first. Understood?'

'A VIP? How will I know?'

'You'll know. Possibly they might not even be a suspect, not related to the Corran investigation in any way, just somebody you come across in the course of your investigations. And if and when you *do* find such a person you're to come to me, not Davies.' Fox smiled and then pointed at the photo of Corran on the whiteboard. 'See, there's just a possibility this hit and run incident could be, ah, how shall I say it? – career changing?'

'Sir?'

'Promotion. Demotion. That sort of thing. Get my drift?'

Riley nodded, but Fox had already turned away and was walking towards the door, his message delivered.

Chapter Twenty-Six

You don't do it all in one go. What would be the point of that? You like to take a break now and then. Give your victims time to think. At some point in the day you make yourself lunch. Cheese on toast. Four minutes and fifty-one seconds under the grill. A little Tabasco. Ground pepper. A sprinkle of oregano. A few hours later, it's a snack. Those crumpets again. Marmite for you, jam for Mikey. A cup of tea. You sit in the kitchen and munch and slurp. Not long to go now, you think, sad that it will be over so soon.

Five minutes later and you're back in the dining room and hard at work, the plastic sheeting swimming in blood and other fluids, the flash of the knife as you move it back and forth once more. Beside you, Mikey is grinning. It's the grin of a man whose brain is barely more complicated than a cabbage, but the emotion behind the smile is pure.

As it would be.

Mikey doesn't have the wit or intelligence to understand exactly the reasons you do what you do, but he enjoys the process nevertheless. Like you, he can see the beauty, the justice and the meaning in the patterns the knife weaves as it caresses and opens the skin. He understands the process is about pain, because he's experienced his share too. He knows these few hours may stretch to a day or two, maybe even three with the strong ones, but they must stand in for years of misery, compressing all the horror into such a short space.

When the process is over, you never feel it is enough, but it has to do. Until the next time.

She's done screaming now, done doing anything much except for the occasional gurgle or cough. She'll be dead soon, but for now the blood still flows, oozing from the cuts, seeping from the wounds. The way you slipped from your mother's own wound and found life. Or rather, life found you.

Mikey wouldn't understand the symbolism. The only sort of symbol he understands is the stupid Apple logo on his phone which promises him mindless entertainment as he slides his fingers across the screen. He never gets bored, never tires of the games.

And neither do you.

The knife slits open another long gash, blood appearing moments later as if the blade is some sort of brush with a five - second delay. And really the knife is like a brush, you like an artist, the woman like a canvas. Only nobody gets to see your work except for Mikey, and he gets excited by a potato stamp painting.

You guess that must make you a true artist, not worried about the fame and fortune, not falling for the rubbish you see espoused in the papers by those egos who can serve up a plate of dog turds or a rotting fish and sell it for thousands. Your art must exist only in your own mind and, for a short while, in the mind of your victims.

Ephemeral. From the Greek. Meaning to last only one day. Like this woman.

She's dead now, Mikey's grin changing to a frown, his eyes turning to you as a dog looks to his master.

'Oh God,' you say, moving to slump in a plastic-covered chair, aware of Mikey pawing at the body, aware he is clambering onto the table. 'Awful. This is awful.'

But you know this is far, far worse than awful. It's sickening, the scene an abomination, the whole process degrading, inhumane, beyond any sort of comprehension.

'Clay, Mikey,' you say, trying to focus. 'We forgot the clay.'

Mikey's not listening. He's otherwise engaged.

You shake your head. You'll shove some clay in later when Mikey's had his fun, but for now you're exhausted. Emotionally and physically. You wipe the knife on your trousers and get up and place the blade back in the display case. You'll finish up tomorrow and for the next part of the job you need something a little less subtle than the knife.

Your felling axe should do.

Chapter Twenty-Seven

Monday. No news. As Savage made herself breakfast, the TV showed pictures of yesterday's developments in the continuing hunt for Paula Rowland: soldiers yomping over Dartmoor checking bogs and mine workings; coastguard rescue teams walking the coastal path; house-to-house searches in parts of Plymouth; helicopters with thermal imaging equipment buzzing isolated villages; a group of vigilantes intent on carrying out unofficial investigations of their own.

'Nutters,' Pete said. 'Why can't they just let you do your job?'

'The trouble is,' Savage said, 'we're not doing it very well.'

'Like us as parents.' Pete pointed to the kitchen table where a mess of Cheerios and milk and half-eaten toast had been left by Samantha and Jamie. 'A certain lack of discipline, methinks.'

Savage grabbed a dishcloth from the sink. Wondered if Pete was casting aspersions on her specifically. He seemed to read her mind, because he held up his hands.

'I know, I know,' he said. 'Takes two to tango. You were left holding the babies. But that's par for the course when you fall for an incredibly good-looking, high-flying naval officer.'

Savage bundled the cloth and threw it across the room at Pete, just as Samantha came in from the hallway.

'Mum! Dad!' she said. 'Are you fighting again?'

Again? Savage half-laughed, reassured Samantha everything was OK, and then told her to go and call Jamie so they could get off to school.

After she'd dropped off first Jamie and then Samantha, she drove out to Bere Ferrers. When the bad news about Phil Glastone had come through Hardin had insisted on a return to the farm. He'd spoken to a PolSA, the search adviser agreeing to set up a new sweep of the Bere Peninsula. Alongside the search there'd be a door-to-door blitz, repeating the one which had been done before Paula went missing.

When she arrived at the village the enquiry teams were just getting started and several officers stood in a group at one end of the main street, a DS allocating properties to be visited. Savage pulled up outside the farm where Enders stood at the gate, talking to another detective.

As she was getting out of her car she took a call from the officer who'd been interviewing Carol Glastone over at the Referral Centre. The medical evidence was strong, the officer said, and the statement Carol had given backed up the assault charges. Glastone had battered Carol and then raped her. Far from the first time it had happened. They'd be able to see him go down for that at least. At least? Savage wanted to know more.

'The rest of the stuff,' the woman said, 'is, I'm afraid, total fiction. You remember Carol said her husband arrived home in the early hours, washed his clothes, acted suspicious? Well she's retracted that part of her statement.'

Savage hung up. The conversation only served to confirm what they knew regarding Phil Glastone's movements on the day Paula had gone missing. She walked across to Enders and told him.

'She lied to you, ma'am,' he said. 'All the material we were going to use is gone.'

'She partly lied,' Savage said. 'He *did* rape her. Kirsty Longworth had ended her affair with Glastone. She said they parted on good terms. Evidently not, because when he returned home he was in a foul mood. He beat Carol and assaulted her.'

'You believe that?'

'Yes. And I can understand why she lied as well. She wanted to dump her husband in it. She was probably worried her evidence alone wouldn't see him put away. It will though, we'll see to that. It's just a shame she didn't realise, because we've wasted time on this when we could have been trying to find Paula Rowland.'

'So where do we go from here?'

'God knows. This place, the farm, isn't just a body dump. There are far more convenient places. I'm convinced there must be a reason the killer used the location. Something historical which could link in with Tavy View Farm.'

'And Dr Wilson?'

'Haven't put it to him yet. We've got to hope the door-to-door teams come good.'

As it turned out hope was not enough. Come lunch time, with the search of the peninsula still taking place, it was apparent the DtoDs had produced nothing new. Back in the farmyard the PolSA talked about widening the parameters of the sweep but it was obvious the man wasn't keen. The river was a natural boundary, he said, people over the border in Cornwall hardly knew of the existence of the village. Waste of resources.

'Crap,' Hardin said to Savage as the search adviser stepped

away. 'Eight teams, two up each one, scouring the peninsula and they don't come up with anything. Quality officers, Charlotte. That's what the force is lacking. You know I have to account for their time? And return on investment so far is zero.'

Savage wasn't quite sure what Hardin had expected the local enquiry teams to produce, but then again she was as surprised as him that nothing of any value had turned up.

'You can't blame them, sir,' Savage said. 'If we don't find anything then we can't make things up.'

'Sometimes, Charlotte, life would be a darn sight easier if we could.' Hardin huffed to himself and shook his head. 'We're coming under a lot of pressure. The Chief Constable rang me this morning. Had the effrontery to ask if we needed any help.'

'Additional resources?'

'That would be fine, but no. What he was talking about was sending down some clowns from the Met. Can you imagine a load of city-boys out here?' Hardin took his car keys out of his pocket. He turned to the farmyard gate. 'First time they lost their mobile internet or they couldn't find a latte within fifty metres they'd be panicking.'

Savage smiled to herself as Hardin strolled away, not at the image the DSupt had brought up, but rather the thought of a group of Met detectives slipping and sliding their way across the muddy fields of Tavy View Farm.

Riley arrived back at his flat a little after one. He'd done an early shift and now he was looking forward to an afternoon off. The Corran investigation was getting nowhere, Davies so far failing to turn up any information on the gun. Riley had been concentrating on finding more about Corran's past life in York, but detective work by telephone was proving difficult. He'd try and get hold of the Governor at HMP Full Sutton, but if nothing came of that then it was looking as if someone was going to have to take a trip to the North East.

Julie was staying over and she was kissing him before he'd closed the front door. Then she was waving him into the living room as she ran to the kitchen.

The summer had arrived with a vengeance and the room was hot, just the hint of a breeze coming in through the doors to the balcony. Riley discarded his jacket, unbuttoned the top couple of buttons on his shirt and went out there, picking up a pad and pencil from the coffee table as he did so. Last night he'd been mulling over a few things to do with Corran's hit and run when his mind had wandered again to the incident involving Clarissa Savage. Now Riley lowered himself into one of the recliners and with barely a glance out at the view, took up where he'd left off.

If, Riley thought, the official investigation into the death of Savage's kid had failed to turn up anything, there were only two reasons. First, it was possible the evidence simply wasn't there. Layton said the team had worked their butts off and yet they'd still found nothing. If that reason held then Riley would be able to do no better. Which meant he had to bank on the second reason: the evidence *was* there but the team hadn't managed to unearth it. Riley drew a line on his pad and split it into a Y shape. The left-hand branch suggested evidence which was buried beyond the reach of the police. To get to that he'd need to explore avenues of dubious legality. Davies was the obvious answer. Down in the ditch. The right-hand branch, on the other hand, was more worrying. It represented evidence which *had* been found but which had been covered up.

Riley dropped his pencil down and leant back in his

chair. Shook his head. Conspiracy theories weren't really his thing. He closed his eyes and felt the sun hot on his face. There was a low hum of traffic noise, people down at street level talking, somewhere far off a helicopter chopping through the thick air. He opened his eyes, aware of how strong the sun was, aware too he needed to change out of his work clothes. He got up and went inside. The living room was dark, but Julie had flicked the TV on. *Spotlight* were showing the clip of Simon Fox at Sunday's press conference.

We're keeping calm, making rational decisions, we'll get the killer in the end.

Except in the case of Clarissa Savage they hadn't.

A chink-chink came from the kitchen. Julie preparing a jug of something. Water, rum, chunks of fresh pineapple, lemons. Ice cold. Unlike Simon Fox's hand when he'd approached Riley in the crime suite after the conference.

All I'm saying is should a person of interest come onto your radar and that person is also, how shall I say it . . . a VIP? Then I want, if possible, to know of it first. Understood?

Riley shook his head. He was making the same mistakes a novice investigator would. He was linking two situations which had similar appearances but with entirely different contexts.

Julie came through from the kitchen with two tall glasses on a tray. She'd discarded her dress and now wore a bikini, a sheen of moisture from suntan lotion on her skin. Riley looked at her. Realised how much he adored this woman, with her smile, her curves, her easy manner.

'I've got a question,' she said, smiling at Riley. 'Balcony or bedroom?'

'You need to ask?' he said and reached forward and switched the television off.

* * *

After checking on the progress of the door-to-door teams again Savage returned to the farm to find Calter sitting in Joanne Black's cosy kitchen, a coffee aroma in the air, drop-scones cooking on the Aga hotplate. Joanne flipped a scone over and asked Savage if she wanted coffee. Savage said she would and then turned to Calter.

'It's work, ma'am. Honestly.' Calter pushed away an empty plate and pointed to her laptop. 'And I think we're on to something.'

Joanne, Calter explained, had phoned in yesterday about a possible lead. A story to do with the farm. There'd been a family who lived at the farm once. Or rather, not at the farm, but down in a bungalow which used to be on the concrete slab next to the dump site.

'And?' Savage looked across at Joanne. 'You think this could have something to do with the killings?'

'It sounded silly when I told DC Calter,' Joanne said, 'but yes.'

'There was a teenage girl,' Calter said. 'Apparently Joanne's uncle fancied this girl but she was having none of it and the family moved away. I'm thinking harassment, assault, maybe just bad feelings. Goes way back, so the whole thing could've been a bit of a long shot, but I thought I'd look into it.'

'And have you?'

'Yes, ma'am. Joanne's information about the girl pans out. I've had collaboration from one of the door-to-door teams. An old lady down the far end of the village remembers the story.'

'OK. So tell me.'

'Well there *was* a family with a young girl in the bungalow back in the late sixties. The girl was called Lara Bailey. Joanne would have been six or so, this girl a teenager.'

'I used to play with her,' Joanne said. 'One time I turned up to find the family had moved away. My uncle offered no explanation as to why. I'd grown quite fond of Lara and I remember being upset she'd left.'

'Now we're getting to the gist of it,' Calter said, turning to her laptop for a moment. 'Turns out Joanne's uncle wasn't quite telling the whole story. He probably wanted to spare her feelings. The girl and the family did move away, true, but there was a reason for the move. According to the old lady interviewed by the DtoDs Lara got herself pregnant by someone in the village. Even post the swinging-sixties, that was a big taboo. Especially in a rural area like this.'

'The uncle?'

'Not sure, but it was what happened after the family moved away which flagged the thing up for me.'

'And?'

'I've been chasing old records online and I've discovered that later on Lara Bailey drifted into prostitution. Received various convictions for soliciting and petty theft over the years. Did a two-year stretch for assault back in the nineties. A decade later in 2005 she was found in the front room of a derelict house on Caroline Place with her head bashed in. This was back when the Stonehouse area was crawling with working girls.'

'She died?'

'Yes. She'd been working the streets again and it looked as if she'd been done in by a client. No one was ever charged with the offence.'

'Shook me, that did,' Joanne said. She carried a plate of drop-scones to the table and then returned to the cooker for a pot of coffee. 'The way Lara's life turned out, a woman in her fifties selling herself, dying in such an awful manner.'

'Tragic I agree,' Savage said. 'And an unfortunate

coincidence she was murdered, but I don't see what it could have to do with our case. I can see what you're trying to do, Jane – and it's a commendable effort – but I can't see a connection with the Candle Cake Killer.'

'Neither could I, ma'am. Until, that is, I noticed the date of the woman's murder.' Calter lowered her head and peered at the screen of the laptop. She placed a finger on the touchpad and brought up a new window. 'Here's the crime report.'

Savage looked down. She ran through the text, trying to find the relevant details.

'There.' Calter's finger splodged on the screen top right. 'Twenty-first June 2005, ma'am. The longest day – and the year before Mandy Glastone was murdered. Another unfortunate coincidence?'

Savage drove away from the scene, intent on returning to Crownhill to consult with Gareth Collier, the office manager. DC Calter had come up with something, but quite how the information could be jigsawed into the existing investigative strands she had no idea. As she headed up the hill away from the village she slowed for somebody walking in the narrow lane. A mum carrying a baby in a sling. She thought about the words Pete had used earlier that morning:

Holding the baby.

There were babies in this case. The one presumably born to the young girl at Tavy View Farm. Kat Mallory's child given up for adoption. The tiny rabbit left on Paula Rowland's barbecue. Coincidence? Could be, but then again she sniffed the start of a possible trail. She filed the thought for later.

Back at the station Savage found Collier in the crime suite perusing a copy of the previous day's *Herald*, the headline *Why No Handle On The Candle Cake Killer?* He looked up as she approached.

'Easy for them to say.' Collier shook his head and pointed down to the text of the article. 'But they're right about the reasons. One, no motive. Two, nothing linking the victims together. Three, the time gap between the first lot of killings and the second. Four, the lack of any forensic evidence.'

'Look,' Savage said. 'I've got an idea. Don't dismiss it out of hand, OK?' Collier nodded. Savage went on: 'DC Calter's discovered some information about a bungalow which sat on the concrete plinth near the dump site. A young girl lived there with her parents decades ago. She fell pregnant as a teenager and moved away. Years later she's found murdered on the twenty-first of June.'

'Right.' Collier moved to one of the whiteboards. Picked up a marker pen. 'Name?'

'Lara Bailey.' Savage waited while Collier scribbled on the board. 'I'll say it again: murdered on the twenty-first.'

'I get the date, ma'am. One in three hundred and sixty-five. Long odds, I'll admit, but you know the birthday problem?' Savage shook her head. 'If you've got twenty-three people in a room there's a fifty per cent chance two of them will share the same birthday. Same, I guess, applies to murders.'

'Yes, of course the timing could be a coincidence. But there's two things which make me think not. First the murder took place in 2005, the year before Mandy Glastone was killed. Second, what about if we add in the fact that Kat Mallory also became pregnant as a teenager?'

'And was murdered on . . .' Collier began to draw a line on the board. He stopped. 'The others have children?'

'As far as we know, no, but I'm also thinking about the baby rabbit I found on the barbecue at Paula Rowland's place. I thought it was an embryo, figured some right-wing anti-abortion angle to the killings.'

'Interesting. Suggested actions?'

'We need to find out whether the information about children is correct. There must be birth records at the Registry Office. I should imagine it's hard to obtain and I doubt we can just go digging around. No special favours just because we're the police. However, Kat Mallory's death puts a different gloss on the right to privacy. The child she gave up for adoption is at risk, and as you know "risk" is a word which gets people to sit up and take notice.'

'Too right. "Risk" means the buck stops with you if you fail to do something which later turns out to be negligent.'

'Exactly.'

'So . . .' Collier drew a circle on the board with his pen. Put a big question mark inside. Raised an eyebrow. 'What's the motive? Preventing teenage kids from having sex?'

'Doesn't make sense. The killer buried the bodies and expected they'd never be found. No deterrent effect there.'

'He's the one who got the victims pregnant?'

'Can't see that either. Not if Lara Bailey is our first victim. Anyway, why would you kill them *after* the babies had been born?'

'OK.' Collier scribbled on the board again. 'We go with what we've got already. I'll pull together some actions on the Bailey family – tracking down relatives and the child Lara had. Then I'll contact the Registry Office and find the parents who adopted Kat Mallory's baby. Interview everyone concerned and eliminate.'

'Or not.'

Collier had added a little stick-figure baby beneath the picture of Kat Mallory and now he drew a line from the baby to the top of the board, where the word 'killer' sat in a circle.

'Yes,' he said. 'Or not.'

* * *

247

After making love with Julie, Riley had prepared a meal. He'd raided the fridge and magicked up a Greek salad. Crusty bread with olive oil drizzled on top and a light white wine. The whole lot taken out onto the balcony, from which they could watch the procession of yachts heading back to their marina berths. They'd whiled away the rest of the afternoon chatting, Julie doing some paperwork, Riley dozing and reading.

'Popping out for a run,' Riley said to Julie around five. 'An hour, no more.'

'Make sure it isn't,' Julie said, brushing her lips against his cheek. 'Because I've got plans for a special dessert for you. Very sweet, but it won't keep for long.'

Riley grinned to himself as he rode the lift down and emerged out onto street level, knowing exactly what Julie had in mind. The thought kept him motivated for the first ten minutes and for the next five he slowed a little, not wanting to arrive too sweaty and out of breath. Padding across the grass of Victoria Park he tried to get his bearings. There, on the north edge, was St Barnabas Terrace, and halfway along he could see a familiar car tucked into a disabled parking bay.

Riley jogged across the park, crossed the road and paused at the car. There was a disabled badge in the windscreen. Riley shook his head, not getting it, and then opened the front gate and walked up the concrete ramp to the porch.

A couple of raps on the door and a shadowy figure appeared behind the glass.

'What the fuck?' Davies said, swinging the door open and eyeing Riley up and down. 'Don't tell me Hardin's had you run over here to pester me out of hours?'

'No, boss,' Riley said. 'But you don't look too pleased to see me either way. Can I come in?'

'Thrilled. And yes, come in off the street. You plus that hoody, lowering the tone of the neighbourhood.'

Riley stepped into the hallway, dark after the bright sun. The passage went to the back of the house and Riley followed Davies through, aware as he did so of grab rails on the walls, some sort of lift on the stairs.

Davies paused in the kitchen, grabbed a couple of bottles of beer from the fridge, and then continued through to the garden.

Out back a small area of lawn ran just a few metres to a wooden shed and a boundary wall. Beyond the wall a strange grey building loomed, arched windows in a gable end.

'St Barnabas?' Riley said before noticing a woman in a wheelchair clipping a shrub to one side of the lawn.

'My wife,' Davies said.

The woman looked up. Dark brown hair tumbled across her face as she moved. She shook her head to flick the hair aside. Smiled.

'You must be Darius,' she said, placing the secateurs in her lap and swinging the wheelchair round. 'I've heard all about you from Phil. I'm Eva.'

Riley stepped forward and took her hand. Eva, he thought, was gorgeous. A vivacity radiated from her and for a moment he wondered if he'd misheard Davies. Was this woman his *wife*? Eva smiled again, almost as if she could read his mind, and then she was asking him about police work, life in London, his move to Devon. Ten minutes later and she made her excuses and wheeled herself inside, leaving Riley still wondering how she'd ended up with Davies.

'Is she . . .?' Riley found himself stumbling. He was never good at dealing with stuff like this. Felt stupid for asking.

'No. Not going to get better if that's what you mean. She fell off a horse years ago. Suffered serious spinal injuries.

Paralysed from the waist down. As you can see we've had the house adapted and there's a carer who comes in to help four days a week, nights if I'm on a late one.'

'Still tough though,' Riley said.

'Tough. Yeah. That'll be it, Darius. Not that you'd know anything about it.'

'Boss, I . . .'

'Don't judge. Not until you've assembled all the evidence, right?'

'It doesn't make the stuff with Fallon right, but I guess I understand.'

'Sergeant, I wasn't looking for your approval, but thanks anyway.' Davies raised his bottle and touched it against Riley's. 'Now, remind me again why you've disturbed my afternoon?'

Chapter Twenty-Eight

Thuck.

You give an experimental swing and the axe hisses through the air and embeds itself in the block of wood next to which the body of Paula Rowland lies. Her eyes are open, staring. Whichever side of her you move they seem to follow you. You walk across the yard, lean on the gate, glance back. She's still looking, the stare unblinking, accusing. The eyes unsettle you, make you wonder about the propriety of all this. But then you think about what the bitch did, the potential misery she might have caused, and you know you are right.

You walk back to Paula and heave the body sideways, lifting it so the girl's neck is on the wooden block, a graceful arch, the throat exposed.

You adjust your stance, like a golfer readying yourself for the swing.

Thuck.

The axe falls, hitting Paula's neck and embedding itself in the block. Her head breaks loose, the spine severed but for some strands of skin and muscle holding the skull. A lump of clay oozes, sausage-like, from the oesophagus. Like the cake, the clay is part of your signature, although its use with Mandy Glastone was entirely functional. You stuffed her mouth full of the stuff to stop her screaming.

The clay slips to the ground as the head moves backwards and forwards a couple of times, odd in the way the flap of skin holding the head to the body resembles some kind of hinge. Paula is very much unhinged now. But then she must have been when she was alive. To do what she did. To a child.

Unhinged.

Like your mother. Not your mummy. You use the word mother as a purely biological term. The woman from whose womb you emerged all those decades ago. A seed spat out and then cast onto foul ground. Picked up and loved, cared for and nurtured by Mummy. Until Daddy used the Big Knife on her.

Years later, not long after you'd been released, you exacted revenge on Mother and really that should have been the end of it. But you began to wonder about the other children. Hundreds of them. Every one put in the same situation as you. Discarded as if some piece of worthless rubbish. Of course, not everybody suffered in the same way as you, but the perpetrators didn't know that, did they? They didn't know how things would turn out. They were reckless. Any reasonable person would conclude they'd done wrong.

A reasonable person?

You know the phrase is a legal term, but legally these people have been getting off scot-free for years.

One night, soon after killing Mother, you're outside for a cigarette under a chilled night sky. Stars up there. Millions of them. So many you can't count the specks of light. Worrying, stars not being counted, crimes not being accounted for. You voice your concerns to the universe. What if these bitches didn't get off scot-free? What if they were brought to book? What if they all fucking paid? Two wrongs don't make a right, but in this case they might. Yes, God willing, they just might.

But how to find them?

In the end, of course, they came to you.

252

The list. A new name and address on it each year. Mandy Glastone, Sue Kendle, Heidi Luckmann. Then a stay of execution, enforced. Five years when no new name appeared, all the time you wanting so much to continue the killing but a voice inside imploring you not to:

You're not crazy, are you? Not an animal? You need to control your urges. Stop letting the past determine the future.

Week after week, the same voice nagging:

Concentrate on your work. Look after Mikey. Forget about what happened. Mummy and Daddy are history. Live your own life.

Nagging, nagging, fucking nagging:

It's too risky. Anything goes wrong and you'll be caught. You don't want to go back inside, do you?

You listened and, although you were tempted many times, you obeyed. Until the voice had a sudden change of heart:

I think this year we might start over.

Which was when Katherine Mallory skipped along. Black ink on white paper. The ink you were unsure about, but the paper definitely ninety GSM. And now Paula Rowland, things moving along nicely once again. Shame you have to wait a whole twelve months until the next one.

You sigh and adjust your grip. Tiger Woods. No, maybe not him all things considered. Rory McIlroy, a good boy. Then you swing the axe again.

Thuck.

The flap of skin is cut through and Paula's head thuds as the skull falls and hits the ground, rolling over a couple of times until it faces upwards, the eyes still staring at you as if you've done something terribly, terribly wrong.

Chapter Twenty-Nine

Crownhill Police Station, Plymouth. Tuesday 24th June.
9.55 a.m.

After a meeting with Hardin first thing Tuesday, Savage went to the crime suite. A few minutes later an ebullient Collier came in, waving a couple of sheets of paper in the air.

'Only got two confirmations so far,' the office manager said. 'But it could be you're right with your theory. Mandy Glastone, née Fullsome. She had a nervous breakdown in 1991, long before she met and married Phil Glastone. Pregnant at the time, she couldn't deal with the baby after the birth. The father did a runner and the baby was taken into care and later adopted. Fifteen years later, when she was murdered, the information about the baby never came out.'

'Say that again,' Savage said. 'How many years later?'

'Hey?' Collier narrowed his eyes. Looked at Savage. 'Fifteen.'

'We've cracked it. Well done, Gareth. Fantastic,' Savage said, tapping Collier on the back. 'What's he called, the killer?'

'Sorry, I don't—'

'Jesus, ma'am!' Calter jumped up from her desk. 'The *Candle* Cake Killer.'

'Fifteen,' Savage said. 'Fifteen candles on the cake left at Glastone's house.'

'But . . .' Calter shook her head. 'Doesn't work. There were only eleven candles on the cake Katherine Mallory's girlfriend found and the child is twelve now.'

'Yes,' Savage said. 'Eleven candles, but that was last year. Plus one and you've got twelve. What about the other victims, Gareth?'

'Got an FLO round with Paula Rowland's parents now,' Collier said. 'It's a sensitive issue, but they've said Paula did give up a baby for adoption. Heidi Luckmann and Sue Kendle were both born out of county and I'm still chasing their records. At least now I know when they might have given birth.'

'Well done, Gareth,' Savage said. 'Even without confirmation for the others this is a brilliant result. I really feel we're making progress.'

'We are?' Collier said, shuffling the sheets of paper around. 'There might be a link between victims, but how does it help us identify the killer?'

'He's somebody who doesn't like the fact that the women gave away their children.'

'That's the motive?' Collier shook his head and then he turned to the whiteboard. 'I don't understand.'

'Neither do I, but for some reason the killer finds the thought of adoption so abhorrent he or she is prepared to torture and kill. Perhaps they were adopted themselves, but we can't assume so. The killer might simply be following some perverse moral or religious code.'

'There are plenty of crazies out there, ma'am,' Calter said. 'And as you always say, all we can do is find 'em and bang 'em up.'

'To which end we have a whole new investigative avenue. One which will require a great deal of sensitivity.'

'Narrows the victim down though. If you didn't give up a baby for adoption you're safe. We might even be able to provide protection for the others.'

'I wouldn't be so sure. Killers aren't rational thinkers. We might have got hold of the wrong end of his warped stick, but we're beginning to get somewhere. We need to get the information on Sue Kendle and Heidi Luckmann. If they both have some connection with adoption then we can proceed, with caution, in that direction.'

'I can see a problem, ma'am,' Collier said. He moved across to a free terminal and sat down. 'Look.'

Collier's fingers blurred over the keyboard. A couple of websites flashed on the screen. Then Collier was bringing up a calculator and inputting some figures.

'As I suspected,' he said. 'The number of adoptions under the age of one each year is tiny. There's hundreds of thousands of births so only a very small percentage of those children will end up being adopted. How's the killer going to find these people? As far as I can tell they can't just trawl through birth certificates looking for matches for their demented plan. They need to request individual certificates by supplying certain information such as the name and birth date of the adoptee. Coming across one by random would be highly unlikely.'

'Which means,' Savage said, 'the individual has some sort of privileged access or can gain it.'

'Glastone, ma'am,' Calter said. 'He's into databases, remember?'

'We're done with him, Jane,' Savage said. 'I hope.'

Mid-morning, and Riley managed to get through to the Deputy Governor of HMP Full Sutton, a man by the name of Greg Adamson.

'Good officer,' Adamson said after giving Riley some background on Corran's work at the prison. 'Developed a rapport with the prisoners. Essential that. Especially here, where many of them have no future beyond prison.'

Riley asked about Corran's contact with particular prisoners, his personal life, any problems he had either at home or inside, the reason for the transfer.

'Played away from home,' Adamson said. 'A bit on the side, allegedly. Easy to do when you've got changing shift patterns and irregular overtime. The Governor didn't want to see Corran's marriage break down, not when he had a little kiddie, so he agreed the best thing would be for him to leave the area.'

'And there was no other reason for the move? Nothing to do with the prisoners?'

'Far from it. As I said, he had a good rapport.' Adamson paused for a moment. 'Sometimes almost too good.'

'What do you mean by that?'

'Sorry?'

'You said Corran got too close to the prisoners.'

'Did I? Well, I meant one needs to keep a certain distance. Like I mentioned Full Sutton is different from your run-of-the-mill prison. Many prisoners with problems. Corran did a lot of work with serious offenders. Got right inside their heads. Maybe got a little too friendly. I should think Dartmoor would suit him far better.'

More dead air, Riley thinking it sounded like Corran being three hundred miles away from Full Sutton suited Adamson too. He wondered if the personal problems Corran had were mixed up with Adamson's own life. Did Adamson have a wife who might be someone's bit on the side, or was the man himself part of some sex triangle involving Corran?

'I hope Corran turns up.' Adamson was speaking again.

'Mind you, I doubt you can spare the resources to look for him, what with all that's going on down there.'

'No,' Riley said. 'We're pushed.'

Adamson hung up and Riley kicked back in his chair. The conversation had been a waste of time. Adamson had confirmed what Mrs Corran had said about her husband's affair, but that was it. Riley reached for the phone again to call Davies but it rang before he'd dialled.

'Doug Hamill,' the voice said. 'Hi-Tech Crimes Unit.'

Hamill explained he'd extracted the material from Corran's laptop. If Riley wanted to he could pop up and take a look.

Five minutes later and Riley was sitting alongside Hamill in the lab as the technician talked through what he'd found and then brought a document up on the big monitor. Riley leant forward and looked at the huge letters written across the screen.

I know who you are.

'Who?' Riley asked, thinking aloud. 'Who does he know?'

'No idea,' said Hamill. 'Not my job. Now look at this.'

Hamill closed the first document and opened another one. Riley read the words.

There's a plastic container under a flat rock at 50.2847 North 03.8977 West. Put £5000 cash in it by Friday.

'This was created at the end of May,' Hamill said. 'All the files I'm showing you were in a folder named "Revenue".'

'GPS coordinates,' Riley said, thinking he could have done with Enders who was into geocaching big time. 'Where is this?'

'I checked the location and it's on Burgh Island over at Bigbury-on-Sea.'

'Bigbury? That figures. Corran's wife said he went fishing there on the day he went missing. He might have taken his tackle with him as cover but the note tends to suggest he had a much more lucrative reason for going there.'

'There's other documents with coordinates in too,' Hamill said, pointing out the icons in a window on the screen. 'Lower amounts of money. The first one was created in January this year. The way I'm thinking is that your man wasn't known to the person he was blackmailing. Hence this rather convoluted way of doing things. I'm guessing, from what you've told me, this guy would send out the letter and then wait a few weeks to go and collect the money. No way anyone could stand and watch the drop-off spot for that long.'

But they had, Riley thought. Corran had played a very dangerous game. If you were going to blackmail someone it was better to do it all in one go, not give the victim a chance to ponder each time a new demand came. And Corran's demands were getting bigger all the time. Greed had literally been the death of him.

Savage was back home by six-thirty Tuesday evening, the investigation now at the stage where things were beginning to fall into place. Paula Rowland's parents had confirmed she'd had a baby when she was eighteen and the child had been adopted. With three out of the five victims known to have given up children the motive, if nothing else, had been established. Savage's team had spent the whole day chasing information: on Glastone and whether there was any possibility he might have gained access to adoption records through his work; trying to find the whereabouts of Lara Bailey's relatives – specifically her parents and any child she may have had; accessing the medical and social records on the other victims. Hardin's team concentrated on the search for Paula Rowland while Garrett did several media briefings.

Dr Wilson called her soon after she'd got in, her mobile vibrating on the tiled worktop in the kitchen as she buttered a slice of toast for Jamie. White bread with chocolate spread. Good parenting intentions had gone out the window once Jamie had reached the age where he could argue.

'This history stuff you've been researching,' Wilson said as Savage tried to scrape the remnants of spread, one handed, from the near-empty jar. 'I'm not sure you're on the right track.'

'No?'

'No. But I've got another idea or two.'

'Go on.'

'It's to do with the burial site and the placement of the bodies. Best if I met you there.'

Savage peered through the kitchen window. Throughout the day the cloud and humidity had been building and now the rain had come. Banks of white tumbled in from the other side of the Sound, squalls whipping the surface of the sea.

'Can't it wait until tomorrow?' she said.

'Prefer to do it now. And for Paula Rowland's sake the sooner the better.'

'Fine. Eight o'clock OK?'

Wilson said it was and hung up. Savage finished preparing Jamie's snack, took it upstairs and remonstrated with him about eating all his dinner. Along the corridor Samantha was Skyping with a friend who lived not a quarter of a mile up the lane.

'Out again, Mum?' Samantha said when Savage told her she had to go to work. 'Hope he's as good-looking as Dad.'

'Don't be cheeky,' Savage said. 'There's no one quite like your dad.'

'You can say that again.'

Savage found Pete in the living room, charts of the coast of Brittany spread over the floor.

'The summer holidays. Guernsey, Jersey, St-Malo and then

work our way westwards,' Pete said without looking up. 'If the weather's suitable, the Îles Chausey before St-Malo. What do you think?'

The trip looked like too much work for Savage, especially considering it was only a week or so since they'd scuttled back from Brixham. She guessed for Pete the hard work was the point. A busman's holiday for a bus driver who no longer drove a bus. Savage touched him on the shoulder affectionately and explained she needed to go out. Pete nodded, but he was already engrossed in a Channel Islands pilot book as she left the room.

An hour and a half later and she drove into the farmyard at Tavy View Farm and parked next to the green tractor. Joanne Black opened the front door and shouted through the rain, asking if she wanted a cup of coffee. Savage said she'd call in on her way back.

There was no sign of Wilson, but then Savage remembered he had a 4x4. Maybe he'd driven down the metal track.

She pulled on her waterproof coat, stuck a torch in one pocket and grabbed her wellies from the boot. Then she set off on the trek to the scene.

The clouds had lowered even farther since she left home, dark shapes scudding in. Although sunset wasn't for another hour and a half, the lights down in Plymouth were visible across the water, twinkling in the rain. She trudged down the track and across the field. The white forensic shelter stood down the far end, sheltering the hole, but no light emanated from within. There was no sign of Wilson's car either. By the time she reached the tent the rain had begun to get heavier, the sky darker.

She peeled back the door of the tent and secured the tie. The generator, pump and lights had been removed and inside, water lapped the sides of the hole a metre or so from the top edge. Without the pump to remove the runoff from the rain the hole had half-filled, the water brown and opaque.

Layton had said something about keeping the area protected for a few days in case they needed to do any more analysis, but Savage couldn't see what else might be gleaned from the mess. The ground penetrating radar and additional aerial shots suggested they'd pretty much got the excavation right; there were no more bodies.

She turned from the tent and looked down to the estuary and Plymouth again. The lights glowed brighter now, presaging an early dusk. Where the hell was Wilson? She took out her phone, but saw there was no signal. She tapped in a text message, pressed 'send' and held the phone in the air. There was a beep as the message found a stray carrier and zipped off into the ether. A minute or so later her phone vibrated. Savage peered at the screen. A reply from Wilson.

Emergency consultation with patient. Have to cancel. Tried to phone. Sorry.

Damn.

Savage shoved the phone in her pocket and gazed around at the tent and its surroundings. Wondered if she could do anything useful here. Now she was alone perhaps she could take a moment to get into the mindset of the killer. Night was coming. This could be just the sort of time of day the killer would have carried the bodies over the railway bridge and put them in the hole.

Layton's stepping plates had been removed after an extensive fingertip search had taken place, and a thick gloop of mud surrounded the scene. The CSIs had walked everywhere but as Savage moved around the outside of the tent she saw a distinct set of footprints leading down towards the railway line. They appeared recent, the rain only just beginning to fill the imprints with water. Savage moved closer and now she could see there were *two* sets of prints: one coming and one going.

She crouched next to one. The print was large and from the simple pattern looked like a wellington boot. The footprints led up and into the tent.

A nosey parker walking on the railway line?

Savage went back to the tent. The prints went right to the edge of the hole. Somebody had stood there. Could that person conceivably be the killer returning to the crime scene? Wilson had hinted at such a scenario. Had he been correct?

The light had begun to leach from the sky and now the line of trees marking the railway stood black against the background of the city. Savage took out her torch and flicked it on. The weak beam flashed around the inside of the tent as she checked to see if anything had been disturbed. No. Whoever had been this way recently had done no more than stand and stare.

She flashed the light down into the hole. The white light from the torch made the water resemble insipid tea. She swung the beam around, absently playing it back and forth across the surface. In the water something twinkled in the beam. She held the torch steady. Something metal-like, shiny. Something the person had dropped.

Thinking the object might be an item as innocent as a piece of silver foil – wrapping from a sweet or the innards of a cigarette packet perhaps – she looked around for something to hook it out with. Propped in one corner of the tent were a number of plastic measuring poles which had been used to demarcate areas of the search and provide sightings for the surveying equipment Layton had used. She grabbed a pole and lowered it down to the water. She wouldn't be able to hook the item out, but moving the pole around might reveal what the thing was and whether it was worthy of further investigation. Holding the pole with one hand and the torch with the other didn't make for a very accurate touch and as she pushed, the shiny object sank beneath the water.

Sod it.

Savage knelt in the mud, her knees sinking into the soggy ground. She placed the torch to one side, aiming the beam across the hole. With both hands she lowered the pole once again and stirred the water. The pole met resistance and she applied leverage, moving something beneath the water.

There. A twinkle in the torchlight. She leant forward for a better look, aware she could topple over. Not a piece of foil; something sparkling, much more precious than a discarded wrapper. A ring. On a finger, attached to a hand, the arm disappearing into the sludge.

Fuck!

Savage rolled back from the edge, sliding over in the mud and scrabbling for the torch. She grasped at the side of the tent, hauling herself upright and then leaning forward again, aiming the torch down into the water.

Did she imagine that? Were the situation and darkness playing tricks on her mind?

No. The torchlight picked out the fingers of the hand, white against the brown water. A left hand. A silver ring on the third finger, the sparkle of diamonds announcing a wedding which would never take place.

Paula Rowland.

Savage pushed herself to her feet and plunged out of the tent into the murk, aware of a rumble from down the field. Lights coming across the bridge. A train. Catterly-dum, catterly-dum, catterly-dum. The train reached her side of the bridge and slowed as the lead carriage hit the curve and the climb up to Bere Ferrers station. The noise had at first reassured her, something ordinary to bring her out of the nightmare. But as the carriages rumbled past in front of her, the interiors lit up, she saw there was nobody on board, like the thing was some demonic ghost train on a journey to hell.

She shivered, aware of the mud and wet creeping through her clothes. She needed to go back to the farm and call for help. The area had to be secured as soon as possible and that included stopping trains from going across the bridge. As she turned away, the last carriage passed below her. She saw a figure at the trackside, the shape silhouetted against the white of a window. Somebody standing, facing her way.

Watching.

The scene flicked off as the lights from the train passed by and the figure was lost against the dark embankment.

Savage began to move down towards the railway line but then stopped, sense taking hold. She turned and began to run up to the farm.

'Déjà vu,' Layton said as he climbed out of his Volvo, looked around the farmyard and then glanced at the sky. 'It's even bloody raining again.'

'Sorry to do this to you, John. Tonight's your dance night, isn't it?'

'Yes.' Layton shrugged, turned towards the back of the car, almost as if he was embarrassed to be caught enjoying himself. He opened the tailgate and pulled out a white suit. 'Back to earth with a bump, but nights like this make you realise there's always some bugger worse off than yourself.'

Paula Rowland was very much worse off. It was unlikely, given the circumstances, that they'd have found her alive, but while there was no body a tiny piece of hope remained. The hand rising from the sludge, the diamonds mocking mortality as they continued to sparkle, put paid to that.

'How are we going to get her out?' Savage asked.

'D Section. Inspector Frey's sending a couple of lads. Should be here in a few minutes.'

In fact it was thirty minutes before D Section's van arrived. Another twenty for two men to get into their drysuits and squelch down to the scene along with Layton, Savage and three more CSIs.

They opened the door on the far side of the tent so as to preserve what was left of the trail. Layton hung a powerful lantern from one of the roof poles and then he edged round the hole and covered a couple of the footprints at the other entrance with little cloche-like domes to protect them.

'Make sure you get the right ones,' Savage said.

'Not much chance of me getting it wrong,' Layton said. 'Dunlop size twelve. I reckon they're the same ones which shed those dried bits of mud we found on Paula Rowland's floor. Clunkers, anyway.'

'Clunkers?' Savage said.

'Big feet. Big load too, the way the prints have such deep indentations.'

'Somebody carrying the body then.'

'Yes. Huge compared to your dainty little things.'

Savage looked down at her feet, which she didn't exactly consider dainty, and then asked Layton about possible forensic from the mystery man.

'Difficult to get up here from the railway line without getting filthy,' he said, looking down at his own wellingtons where mud had worked its way past the tops and up the legs of his white suit. 'Especially if you're carrying a body. The man's clothing will be filthy and he'll carry the dirt into his car. If he drove down the track on the other side of the bridge there'll be mud on the tyres as well, gunge under the wheel arches.'

One of the men from D Section lowered a small aluminium ladder down into the hole and clambered down, dropping into the water which came up to his waist. There was no sign of the girl, but Savage pointed across to the far side.

'The body's over there.'

The diver waded through the water, hands outstretched, feeling beneath the surface.

'Here she is,' he said, lifting a pale arm from the water, the diamonds glittering again.

The other diver jumped down into the hole, sending water splashing up. Savage looked at Layton, wondering if they should be a bit more careful.

'No worries,' Layton said. 'She was dumped here. Literally. The sooner we get the body out of the water the more chance of preserving any evidence on her. We'll get something from the footprints, maybe down on the railway line.'

'A squad car blocked the end of the track soon after I called in, but they saw nothing.'

'I'll get over there later and see about tyre impressions. For now let's concentrate on this.'

The two divers lifted the corpse until the body floated on the water, gently cradling the girl, almost like some sort of baptism. Only you couldn't sprinkle water on Paula's forehead because her head was missing, just a couple of inches of vertebrae poking from the pulp of the neck. Like the other bodies, cut lines criss-crossed the torso, but this time there was a vivid contrast between the pale skin and the flesh below. The girl had been alive only a day or so ago.

The men hoisted the body to shoulder height and rolled her up onto the edge of the pit where the CSIs had laid out a body bag. Layton moved across and prodded the skin with a blue-gloved finger.

'She's not been in the water for more than an hour or so.'

He turned to Savage. 'I guess you're a witness. Whoever was down on the railway line dumped the body. Congratulations, you've seen the Candle Cake Killer.'

Savage had known that already, but Layton's words chilled her. Not only had she seen the killer, he'd seen her too.

Dr Wilson arrived at the farm as the clock was pushing up to midnight.

'Unbelievable,' he said, fiddling with his coat as he tried to loosen the zip in the fuggy warmth of the incident room van. 'To return to the scene, even though there was a chance of being caught. I only wish I had been there with you. Maybe we could have given chase.'

The phrase sounded antiquated to Savage, like something Sherlock Holmes would have said as he charged over Dartmoor after the hound. Wilson's take on the Candle Cake Killer seemed to be that the investigation was a game. She wondered if he inhabited some sort of fantasy world – possibly gleaned from his time in America – where the profiler was at the centre of things, the rest of the team hanging on his every word.

The three of them – Savage, Hardin and Wilson – sat in the van listening to the rain drum on the roof. Hardin had summoned the psychologist to the scene, wanting Wilson to see the recent developments ASAP. He also wanted to know where the hell Wilson's report was. 'The bloody fucking profile' as he put it. Events, Wilson said, had delayed his analysis. The baby rabbit on the barbecue and now the killer's return to the farm to dump a body meant a re-evaluation. He'd work something up, he promised. Anything, Hardin said, anything to help.

Which was where they were now.

'Unbelievable,' Wilson said again. 'Classic serial killer behaviour is to revisit the scene, maybe use the same dumping ground over and over. But I've never heard of one doing so after the site has been compromised. The fact he has suggests an audacity beyond anything I have seen, here or in my time at Quantico.'

Hardin shook his head. Savage knew his love of the States extended about a mile west of Land's End. US policing he thought abysmal. Quantico, he'd joked to Savage some days before, sounded like a cut-price supermarket, and was about as useful to British detective work.

'This is Devon, Dr Wilson,' Hardin said, tapping the van window where streaks of rain ran down the glass. 'This is not the country of Ted Bundy or the BTK Killer. This is not the country with the highest homicide rate in the developed world. For God's sake leave your preconceptions Stateside and give us something relevant to work with.'

'I—' Wilson stuttered and then reached into his jacket and pulled out a pad and pencil. He stared down at the pad.

'And?' Hardin bent his head to one side and gave one of his disconcerting sneers.

'I mentioned to DI Savage the other day that serial killer behaviour sometimes gives the impression the perpetrator wants to be caught. I said this is a mistaken viewpoint: the killer becomes convinced he is invincible, that they *can't* be caught. They do incredibly risky things and are amazed they still evade capture. They are laughing at the police, mocking them almost. In this case even going so far as to let an officer see them in the act of dumping the body.'

'Mocking us?' Hardin's face began to flush. 'He won't be mocking us when we get hold of him, he'll—'

'It's no good getting angry, Superintendent. That's just what he wants.' Wilson put his pad down on his lap and leant forwards, smiling as he put his hands out and brought them together in a slow motion hand clap. 'He's this close, touching us almost. He'll be watching, trying to get in amongst us, following our every move. This is the thrill the killer seeks, the sense he can move at will and we are powerless to stop him.'

'Powerless to . . .? For God's sake, keep that thought to yourself. Can you imagine what the media would make of such a comment? There'd be outright panic on the streets.'

'Don't worry.' Wilson tapped the side of his nose. 'Client confidentiality. Anyway you and the residents of Devon and Cornwall have nothing to worry about for the following twelve months. The cycle has ended. He'll be dormant now until next June. You've just got to catch him before then.'

Savage noted Wilson had changed from an inclusive 'we' to an accusative 'you', excluding himself from the responsibility of solving the crime. Hardin hadn't noticed. In fact the unexpected arrival of a twelve months' grace period seemed to have cheered him.

'Now then,' Wilson said. 'I need to get to bed. Tomorrow morning I've arranged to drive down to the Plymouth side of the railway bridge with your senior CSI. Apparently there's been a fingertip search, but I'd like to walk across and see the route the killer took for myself. Afterwards I'll work on the profile. Have something for you by the evening.'

Wilson stood and clambered out of the van. Hardin clucked to himself for a few seconds.

'Twelve months hey, Charlotte?'

'That's the pattern, sir. We knew it before. Wilson saying so doesn't change anything.'

'You still don't like him, do you?'

'Too many words, sir. But I'll eat them all with cold gravy and brussel sprouts if he manages to help us catch the killer.'

270

Chapter Thirty

You've got the big Kilner jars out from the back of the cupboard. Sat on the table their contents brood, suspended in the fluid, floating like some kind of revolting amoebas or creatures from the depths of the deepest ocean. Just now Mikey came bounding in. When he saw the jars he squealed and scampered away. You understand his sentiment. The things inside revolt you.

They've gone all white and colourless in the formalin and without the pink tinge of blood you wonder if for a moment they've lost their potency, if, perhaps, they are not quite so dangerous. But of course you'd be mistaken. These things have caused untold misery in pursuit of selfish pleasures for their former owners. 'Lock and key', you say to yourself as you check the seals round the top of the jars. They're quite intact, thank goodness.

You push them to one side of the table and fetch two clean jars from the back of the cupboard. One small, one enormous. You decant formalin from the big container in the shed into both the jars. Then you look at the plastic wrapped around something squidgy and nasty on the draining board. A casual glance would suggest the things inside were pieces of meat for dinner. But no, they're not for eating. Quite revolting. A horrible sight which brings back memories. And that isn't good.

You reach under the sink for the big rubber gloves. Pull them

*on. Take a deep breath. Begin to unwrap the parcel. You gag,
not from the formalin, but from the sheer thought of the power
of the flesh.*

*'No!' you say, picking the pieces of flesh up and holding
them at arm's length. 'You won't do that again. Not to me. Not
to anyone.'*

Plop.

*Down they go into the clear liquid, spiralling towards the
bottom of the jar. You flip the lid over, engaging the catch and
flicking it down.*

Thank God!

*You push the jar across the table to join the others. Paula,
Kat, Heidi, Sue, Mandy. The array of awfulness is almost too
much for you.*

*But stop! Enough reminiscing. Paula. You've forgotten some-
thing. The big jar's full of formalin, waiting. You look down
at the bucket on the floor. Something round in there. Round
with squidgy bits, hair, ears, bits of flesh hanging off where
you severed the neck. You reach down and lift Paula's head
from the bucket. Heavier than you'd have thought. The eyes
stare out. You wonder for a second if you should kiss her on
the lips. Decide not. You lower the head into the formalin,
Paula's face sinking down as liquid rises out of the jar and
spills onto the table. The Archimedes principle. Eureka. Pure
fucking madness.*

Chapter Thirty-One

Crownhill Police Station, Plymouth. Wednesday 25th June.
9.22 a.m.

Savage realised trouble was brewing when she arrived at the station and spotted the big car and its uniformed driver in the car park: Simon Fox, the Chief Constable, chauffeured over from Exeter first thing. He wanted the latest; wanted too, to give the team a roasting.

Briefing room A. Everybody in there, from Hardin down to the lowliest indexer. Fox stood at the top of the table in place of Hardin and he didn't waste much time on formalities. No beating about the bush. He thumped a bundle of newspapers down in front of him and fanned them out.

'This is appalling. Awful.' Fox stood, head bowed, staring at the headlines, the same lead on every front page. The same photograph of Paula Rowland too. 'Beforehand there was a glimmer, just a glimmer of hope. Gone now, isn't it?'

Fox looked up and scanned the room, starting with the senior officers. Hardin, Garrett, Savage, the other DIs, Layton, Collier. Then the detectives with specialised roles on the inquiry: the receiver, the action manager, the document reader, the exhibits officer, the disclosure officer, the house-to-house coordinator. Next, the mass of junior detectives, followed by the police support staff: the indexers, the researchers, the PR team. Finally Fox's gaze alighted on Dr Wilson, sitting snug right alongside Savage.

'Failure is a bitter, bitter pill,' Fox said, eyes remaining on Wilson before flitting off in Hardin's direction. 'But we have to swallow it. All of us.'

The eyes went round the room again, faster this time.

'I was sitting with the parents of Paula Rowland on Sunday at the press conference. Now I have to go and meet with them again. This time with an apology in hand. What else can I tell them? Can I honestly say we tried our best? Even if we did our efforts fell woefully short of what the public – what Mr and Mrs Rowland – should expect.'

The lecture went on and on, the atmosphere in the room souring with every minute. By the end nobody could be under any illusion as to the message Fox intended: catch the killer soon or else. Responsibility lay with each and every operational officer.

Operational officer.

Savage thought the term was a neat way for Fox to exclude himself from the equation, the buck-passing already in full swing. The police commissioner would do the same thing, leaving the troops on the ground to wonder what exactly the guys at the top did for their pay packets.

Fox was leaving now, his PA alongside muttering something about a few words for a press release as they hurried into the corridor. Savage was curious to know what the CC would say to the media. That the team were a bunch of incompetents?

Hardin was hot on Fox's tail, but he paused to speak to Savage and Wilson.

'Charlotte,' he said. 'We need something by tonight, understand?'

Savage nodded and was about to ask when the post-mortem would be taking place when Hardin turned to Wilson.

'And you.' Hardin jabbed a finger at the psychologist. 'Get me the bloody report by tomorrow or you're fucking history, OK?'

With that Hardin was off, lumbering down the corridor after Fox. Wilson shook his head.

'Charming,' he said.

Riley regretted asking Enders if he knew what he was doing as soon as the words left his mouth.

'Look, city boy,' Enders said as he glanced down at the screen on the handheld GPS. 'You're the one who doesn't know what you're talking about. This is my new baby. She's accurate down to a metre or so on a good day.'

'Your girlfriend, does she have a name?' Riley laughed and bent to turn over another rock. When he saw there was nothing underneath he let the rock down with a clatter. 'Nothing doing, Patrick. We'll keep trying for another ten minutes and call it a day.'

There's a plastic container under a flat rock at 50.2847 North 03.8977 West. Put £5000 cash in it by Friday.

Riley shook his head and wondered if the coordinates in the document on Corran's laptop were bogus. Perhaps some sort of misdirection. They'd been searching for half an hour already, working their way into a ravine on the west side of Burgh Island. The narrow cove had a little beach, the top end of which was littered with large stones. Riley reckoned he must have turned over almost all of them. Enders hadn't done so many. Mostly he'd just stood holding his precious GPS and pointed.

When they'd arrived they'd parked the car at Bigbury-on-Sea

and stood and looked across the strip of sand which joined the island to the mainland. Hundreds, probably thousands, of holidaymakers packed the beach and to the left of the island the water thronged with surfers. Every now and then one managed to stand on their board for a few seconds, but even Riley could tell the waves weren't up to much today. The island itself was a few acres of rough grassland sat atop steep cliffs. On the east side the white of the art deco hotel glared in the sun, the place a popular venue for weddings. Riley couldn't quite understand why, for a stream of tourists snaked their way past the hotel, gawping as they climbed to the top of the island. True, when the tide was high enough the island was cut off from the mainland with the only access on a weird sea-tractor, but even then the privacy lasted for an hour or two at most. To Riley's eyes, a more inviting option was the Pilchard Inn sat right on the shoreline. Riley glanced at his watch. Not long until opening time.

'Gold!' Enders said, face all grin. 'Told you this baby would find the goods.'

Riley shook his head and then clambered across the rocks and patted Enders on the back. At Enders' feet lay a translucent Tupperware box with a green lid. As the DC reached for the box Riley caught his arm.

'Prints,' Riley said. He pulled a pair of latex gloves from his pocket and stretched them onto each hand. He lifted the box and peered through the side. There didn't seem to be much inside, certainly not five thousand pounds.

'You going to open it?'

'Tell me, Patrick,' Riley said turning the box over and checking it. 'When you go geocaching with the kids, what do you find inside?'

'Trinkets, mostly. Key-rings, little plastic toys, similar things.

That's not the point though, it's finding the hiding place which is the big thrill.'

'Strange nobody found this then.' Riley began to lever off the top, working his fingers around the edge. 'All these people.'

'Not really. They didn't know where to look. We did and it still took us a while. Plus this cove is relatively inaccessible. Private land.'

'True.' Riley snapped off the lid. Inside was a single piece of paper, folded in half. Riley took the paper out, unfolded it and read the single word written in large bold sweeps of black marker pen.

'What does it say, Darius?'

'Not funny,' Riley said as he held out the paper for Enders to see. 'But the joke's backfired. This is as good as a confession from the person Corran was blackmailing that they killed him.'

Riley found Davies in the crime suite hunched over a stack of Corran's bank statements. He showed the DI the find from Burgh Island.

'"Bang"?' Davies said, staring down at the plastic evidence bag. 'Is that all?'

'All that was in the box. Just a single piece of paper.' Riley pointed at the bag. 'No prints on the paper. Some on the box, but they're Corran's.'

'You sure there was nothing else in there?' Davies turned his head and gave a little sneer. 'Not five Ks you and Enders decided to divvy up? A new three-piece for his wife, a smart set of new rags for yourself? Bung me a monkey and nobody will be any the wiser.'

Riley wasn't sure if Davies was joking or not but he didn't deign to answer. He just picked up the bag and moved it over to another one containing the box the paper had come in.

'I don't understand,' Davies said. 'The note I mean. Why was it still there?'

'Corran must have left it. The message probably unnerved him, we know he was a little withdrawn Saturday afternoon. Cassie Corran said he'd been off fishing. We can guess his trip to the sea didn't revolve around piscatorial pursuits.'

'Hey?'

'He went to Burgh Island and found the note. He must have realised he was in trouble, but he probably didn't think his cover had been blown.'

'You think somebody was watching?'

'As Doug Hamill told me, it's hard to know how. Corran had posted the letter several weeks before.' Riley thought about the hours he'd spent in various ditches on the diesel investigation. 'Even with a full team we'd have a job keeping up a surveillance op like that. On your own you'd have to be some sort of obsessive. It would be mind-numbing.'

'Must have been some other way then.' Davies itched his chin. 'The question is "how?" And, as Hardin keeps asking me, "who?"'

'The wife,' Riley said. 'Are we going to tell her? Maybe when she sees it in black and white like this she'll come to her senses and tell us what she knows.'

'Yeah,' Davies said rising from his chair. 'Let's get up to Dousland and do just that.'

Late morning, and Savage took a call from Wilson. After the meeting with Simon Fox he'd visited the railway bridge with John Layton. Last night's events, together with the trip that morning had crystallised his thoughts. Plus they'd never had a chance to discuss his new theory concerning the burial site and the placement of the bodies. She had to come and see what he was talking about.

Wilson gave her the directions to a rendezvous and ended the conversation, saying he wouldn't stand her up this time. Savage went in search of the DSupt but when she found him he wasn't enthusiastic to join her.

'Dartmoor?' Hardin's eyes roved to his cup of tea on his desk. Alongside, a fan of chocolate digestives lay across a plate. 'Not my thing to be honest. Besides, I'm working flat out on a brief for the CC. If you don't mind I'll give it a miss.'

Thirty minutes later Savage parked up on the moor at a pull-in off the main Princeton road. The moor fell away on all sides except one where a grassy slope rose to a distant tor, the green changing to grey near the top. There was one other car in the layby – a Mercedes SUV – but out on the moor a group of walkers trudged the path up to the summit.

Next to the pull-in a tiny lake, more a puddle, reflected a big sky. Ripples ran across the water distorting the scene, splintering the light into a thousand pieces. Savage looked towards the tor where a wisp of mist curled around the rocks before being dragged away by the wind. Thicker clumps of cloud marched in a procession from the west, building on the horizon. Sunshine and showers, the forecast said, no mention of which would be in the ascendancy.

She got out of the car and called Wilson. There was a gargled answer.

'Where are you?' she said into the dead air of her phone. She pulled it away from her ear and looked at the signal indicator. One bar. None. One again.

'Bloody hell.'

Then the phone rang. Wilson back on the line.

'I'm on the top. Sharpitor. I can see you. It's only about half a mile or so.'

Savage turned from her car and peered across the moor to a craggy outcrop. There *was* somebody up there in amongst the mist. Red waterproof. Arms waving. The figure disappeared as another finger of cloud caressed the top.

'What the . . . OK. I'm on my way.'

Savage slammed the door of her car and retrieved her walking boots and her own waterproof. Back end of the year just gone, she'd learnt the hard way that you needed the right equipment out on Dartmoor. Things could go wrong quickly up here. Even a short distance from the road. Even in summer.

She shut the boot, bleeped the locks and set off after the walkers, soon realising the group were fitter than her. They'd reached the top and disappeared from view before she'd got halfway up.

Minutes later, waterproof now loosened and flapping in the wind, she arrived at the clump of rocks. Granite boulders spilt down from the tor and speckled the grass with grey.

Dr Wilson sat on top of the rocks looking to the south-west. He shouted to her without turning his head.

'The Bere Peninsula. About eight miles that way.' His hand shot out and pointed. 'You can make out Tavy View Farm in the V of the river.'

Savage looked in the direction Wilson was pointing. Close by, around a mile distant but way below, the blue of Burrator Reservoir. Further off, the village of Yelverton and south of that along the A386, the outskirts of Plymouth. Beyond Plymouth, the river. Follow the grey-blue swathe back north and Wilson was right; the farm lay between the short stub of the Tavy Estuary and the Tamar. The railway bridge cut a black line across the river Tavy and then drew a smooth curve around the edge of the farm.

'Point being?' Savage clambered across the final few

boulders and sat next to Wilson. 'Assuming you didn't drag me up here just for the view.'

'Just for the view?' Wilson crooked his head round at her. Then looked back west. 'This is not just a view. This is *spectacular*. A spectacle which encapsulates everything the killer sees, everything which is on his stage. The farm with the body dump, the railway line the killer walks along, representing some kind of journey. We can see Plymouth, the city of bright lights and the home of the victims. Our killer works down there, but lives away from the light, out in the countryside. He wouldn't like being near other people. He values his solitude. He'll have a big house in a posh village. You see, Charlotte, how from up here, given the right clues, we can determine everything. A bit like God really. Or, continuing my metaphor, the audience. Pure theatre.'

'A map?' Savage said, trying to bring Wilson down from his flight of fancy. Wondering if Walsh's observations about all psychologists being not right in the head wasn't far short of the mark.

'Yes. Geographical profiling. The killer is not spatially aware but that doesn't mean he doesn't affect and in turn be affected by the space. What happened down there moulded our killer. You said something about babies to me. Could be, but there's more. The killer enjoys what he does, enjoys the torture and the suffering. Cutting those girls, mutilating them. Stripping them naked to expose them. But the enjoyment is forced onto him, he has to do what he does. *Has to*. Understand me?'

Wilson spat the last few sentences out and then picked up a small stone and lobbed it a few feet. The stone clattered onto a boulder and bounced away. Savage wondered what had got into Wilson. She knew profilers sometimes worked in strange ways, a kind of method acting where they would try to reproduce the offender's emotional state so they could get inside the killer's mindset. Was he doing so now? Or was he just bonkers?

Wilson took up a bigger rock. A piece of stone the size of a house brick.

'Granite,' he said. 'Hydrothermal activity causes the granite to decompose. That or other processes lead to the formation of clay. Funny how we're back to clay again, isn't it? The way the killer silences his victims, stops them protesting their innocence.'

Savage nodded, wondering what on earth Wilson was on about.

'Do you think we're close?' Wilson whispered.

'Sorry?' Savage said. 'Do you mean personally?'

'No, Inspector Savage.' Wilson laughed. 'I didn't mean close *sexually*.'

'What then?' The word 'sexually' had come out of Wilson's mouth with a slither. Like a snake. 'Close in what way?'

'Close to solving the case. Close to catching the killer.' Wilson weighed the rock in one hand and shifted, pushing himself up with the other and standing above Savage. 'You see, I don't think we are. Not close at all.'

Calter scrunched her eyes up and then released them, hoping the tension would dissipate. One too many beers last night when she should have been getting some shut-eye. The names and offences on the screen in front of her had long since blurred and become bastardised: James Cock-Out-In-The-Bushes Williams, Frederick Fondled-A-School-Girl Jenkins, Graham Two-Rapes-But-Out-In-Four Cansome.

She shook her head. None of these people were credible suspects. No matter how many times she worked the list nothing changed. The victims didn't match the profiles, the methods didn't match the offenders' behaviour and too many of them had full or partial alibis.

Calter kicked back her chair. Stood. The other people in the suite were heads down, fingers clattering over keyboards or voices talking into phones.

Enders was away with DS Riley on some other job. Whatever, she missed him and his humour, his apparent stupidity, the latter, she had come to realise, an affectation.

DI Savage was up on the moor somewhere and DCI Garrett had been summoned to Hardin's office.

'Coffee?' she called out to nobody in particular. A couple of hands went up and she acknowledged them and pushed through the double doors and headed for the canteen.

In the corridor outside John Layton scurried towards her, Tilley hat askew, a clear plastic evidence bag in each hand.

'DI Savage about?' he said, holding out the bags. 'Got these for her.'

Calter stared at the bags for a moment. A handful of brown-grey mud smeared the insides. She looked down the corridor and then at Layton's feet. His walking boots had left a trail of similar coloured mud on the floor.

'That's not like you, John. What's up?'

'Charlotte? Where is she?'

'She's gone off to meet Dr Wilson. Another one of his crazy theories.'

'*Wilson?*' Layton bit his lip and then shook his head. 'Here, come with me.'

Layton shouldered through the doors and into the crime suite. He went to the nearest desk, put both of the bags down and beckoned Calter over. He pushed a finger onto the surface of one bag, squashing the contents to reveal a claggy soil with streaks of brown.

'This sample,' he said, 'comes from the track on the far

side of the railway bridge. The place we suspect the killer parked up before carrying the bodies across the bridge and dumping them at the farm.'

Calter nodded and Layton moved his finger to the other bag. He pressed down again until a lump of the mud broke away revealing the same colour brown.

'They're the same?' Calter said.

'I haven't done a proper analysis yet, but they look pretty much identical to me.'

'So? I don't understand . . .'

'I obtained the first sample this morning when I accompanied Dr Wilson down to the Plymouth side of the bridge. He picked me up and we drove down there, walked across and he spun a few ideas. The second sample came from under the front nearside wheel arch on Wilson's car.'

'So you're saying whoever drove down there last night to dump the body would have accumulated mud on their car?'

'Yes, but that's not the point.' Layton prodded the bag once again. 'I didn't return with Wilson. He went back across the bridge while I got a lift with one of my CSIs who was at the farm. When we got back to the car park here at Crownhill I noticed the lump of mud in the bay where Wilson had parked earlier. When he came by to pick me up first thing.'

'I'm lost. Your mind is—'

'Wilson's car collected the mud *before* we went down the track. It must have fallen from his car while he was waiting for me to emerge from the station first thing this morning. From the freshness of the sample – the consistency – the mud attached itself to the car recently. Wilson had already been down the track in the previous day or so.'

'And he didn't say anything to you?'

'No. When we drove down there and explored the bridge, crossed over, it all appeared new to him.'

'Wait-wait-wait. Slow down.' Calter shook her head, the hangover still fuzzing her thinking. 'Can't there be a rational explanation for this? Could the mud have come from some-where else?'

'Look.' Layton prodded the second sample again, moved his finger back and forth until he revealed a crushed pale yellow flower. '*Melampyrum pratense* or cow wheat. There's a stand of willow at the end of the track. Cow wheat is a parasitical plant which attaches itself to the roots—'

'Stop!' Calter held out her hands. 'Chase. Cut to. You're saying this plant grows down there. There's one in the sample from Wilson's car. Combined with the mud it means Wilson had been down the track recently and lied about it.'

'Pretty much, yes.'

'So he's the killer?'

'I didn't say that, but . . .' Layton looked down at his finger and the yellow flower smeared with mud. 'Where's Charlotte?'

'DI Savage is with Wilson at this moment. Up on the moor. Alone.'

'Call her,' Layton said moving his finger from the bag and thrusting it towards a nearby phone. 'Now.'

'Let's walk a little. Over there.' Wilson pointed to another tor a few hundred metres off. 'It's a little remote but there's something I want to show you.'

Savage slid off the boulder she was on, the rough surface grazing her shin. Stepped back. Wilson still had the piece of granite and now he held the rock out in front of him. He smiled.

'The good thing about being a psychologist is you get to

285

be nosey. You find out all sorts of interesting things about people. Must be the same being a detective I guess.'

Savage nodded, stepped away across a patch of grass and headed for the tor. Something wasn't quite right with Wilson, she thought. On every occasion they'd met previously she'd wondered if he wasn't on the verge of some kind of psychosis but each time she'd put his strange behaviour down to the way he liked to work. Now she wasn't so sure.

'The thing is,' Wilson continued, 'you also learn about the lies people tell. Again, must be similar when you're a police officer. Lies are things we tell when we are too embarrassed to admit to the truth.'

'Dr Wilson, is this relevant?'

'Oh yes. Not to the case, but to us, yes.'

'*Us?*' Savage half-turned towards the psychologist.

'Yes, us,' Wilson said, his face burning with an intense expression. 'I . . . I . . . I was wondering if you would like to have dinner with me tonight. We could talk about something other than the Candle Cake Killer. Let our hair down. Get to know each other better. Perhaps afterwards . . . Well . . . You could come over to my place.'

'Sorry, no,' Savage said, beginning to regret having agreed to meet in such a deserted spot. 'I'm married. Happily. I'm not looking for anything else.'

'Really?' Wilson shook his head. Smiled. 'Don't try to hide your feelings. Don't bottle up your desires. You see I think we *are* close. Sexually. I've fancied you from the first day you walked into my office. I know you've felt the same. The coy, offhand way you speak to me, trying to act aloof. Your behaviour is all an act, a lie. Admit it, tell the truth. I for one am not ashamed of anything. I feel a burning desire for you. I want you. I want you now.'

Wilson moved towards Savage.

286

'No, Dr Wilson, you're wrong.' Savage moved across to another nearby boulder and stepped up. 'If you've misread me then I'm sorry, but I'm not interested in you. Come on, let's head back. We can forget this ever happened.'

'Forget?' Wilson looked up at her, the lump of granite still in his hand. 'I've been trying to forget for most of my life. Women like you remind me all too often.'

'Look, you've made a mistake,' Savage said. 'Don't make the same error you made on the last investigation.'

'A mistake? There's no mistake, I think I'm in love with you!'

Wilson stepped forwards and Savage leapt down, the boulder now between them. Wilson's smile became a sneer and he darted to the left, intending to come round the side. Savage moved in the opposite direction, keeping the boulder as an obstacle.

'Come on, Charlotte!' Wilson spat her name out. 'Let your hair down for once. Turn off the freezer. Deep down you're aching for me.'

'I can assure you I'm not.' Savage spun round and ran away from Wilson. A tumble of rockfall surrounding the tor a hundred metres away was her target.

'I want you and I mean to have you!' Wilson yelled and came after her, arms lunging forwards. He lobbed the rock and it crunched into the ground just beside her.

Savage ran on, but Wilson's long legs carried him over the rough ground faster. She felt a hand brush her shoulder as he caught her up. She made an extra effort and sprinted, but as she reached the rockfall she dropped to the ground in a ball. Wilson was right behind and he careered into her, falling over the top and rolling onto the sharp granite.

'You bitch!' Wilson shouted out as he lay on the ground. He scrabbled around for a rock, but the pieces were all too large. He panted and rubbed his arm where the sleeve had scuffed up, a patch of grazed flesh visible. 'You're a feisty number. Must be that red hair. Red for danger. No matter, I like a challenge.'

'Forget it!' Savage said. 'You haven't got a chance.'

She stood and moved away. As she did so there was a trilling and a vibration in her pocket.

The sound caused Wilson to put his head to one side, as if he couldn't work out what the strange noise was. Savage pulled out her phone and trotted back the way she had come.

'DI Savage,' she said.

'DC Calter, ma'am. Where are you?'

'Dartmoor. With Dr Wilson.'

'Not good, ma'am. Not good at all. Dr Wilson is now a suspect.'

'*What?* Are you serious?' Savage turned back towards Wilson. He was picking himself up, limping in her direction. And he'd managed to find another large rock. 'On the other hand, it could make a lot of sense.'

'You OK, ma'am? Do you need backup?'

'Um, might be a good idea. Can you see to it? Discreetly.'

'You'll need to tell me where you are.'

'Yes, of course.' Savage looked across at Wilson. He was closing. 'We're up on Sharpitor. Amazing views. You should come up here sometime.'

She scampered back to the original chunk of rock. Clambered up on top again.

'You're in luck, ma'am, there's somebody in the area. Can you see the road from where you are?'

Savage turned away from Wilson for a moment. A line of black snaked up from Yelverton to where she had parked and then dropped away again, before rising once more towards Princetown. A car, driving at what seemed an impossible speed, shot into view about a mile to the south. Not exactly discreet.

'Yes.'

'Guardian angels, ma'am. You keep talking to me, OK?'

'Sure thing.'

Wilson moved closer, but he'd seen the car too. His frenzy seemed to have diminished. 'Problems?'

'Not at all,' Savage said. 'New evidence. A suspect. Let's get down there and see what it's all about.'

'I'm sorry about just now. Can we forget it happened? Just like you said.'

'Sure,' Savage said, resisting the temptation to tell Wilson to get fucked. 'No worries.'

Wilson shrugged. He stared down at the rock in his hand. Weighed it. Then he flung it away. The rock bounced a couple of times, little chips of granite flying off, and then thudded into the ground. The psychologist lowered his shoulders, gone limp.

Savage went ahead, bouncing down the slope and keeping a good distance between herself and Wilson. When she reached the bottom Riley and Davies were standing beside their car.

'Thought I'd return the favour from earlier in the year,' Riley said, nodding over Savage's shoulder at Wilson who was still fifty metres away. 'Nick of time and all that.'

'We're here to arrest Wilson,' Davies said. 'Suspicion of.'

'For real?' Savage said.

'On the instructions of Hardin. He said you'd want to do the honours. Correct?'

'Too bloody right.'

Wilson reached the car park and stumbled across to his 4x4. The lights flashed as he unlocked the doors.

'You'll need to give those keys to me, sir,' Riley said,

stepping forward. 'We'll send somebody to come and pick your vehicle up.'

'What are you talking about?' Wilson turned away from the car and glared over at Savage. 'Can you tell me what's going on?'

'Peter Wilson,' she said. 'I'm arresting you on suspicion of the murder of Paula Rowland. You don't have to say anything, but it may harm your defence if you don't mention something which you later rely on in court. Anything you say may be given in evidence.'

Wilson stumbled away from the car and began to run back along the path to the tor. Seconds later Riley collided with him and Wilson went down in a heap with Riley on top.

'Now, sir,' Riley said, pulling himself up. 'Come along with me and try not to upset DI Savage. You wouldn't like her when she gets angry.'

Chapter Thirty-Two

Crownhill Police Station, Plymouth. Wednesday 25th June. 2.12 p.m.

Dr Peter Henry Wilson was booked into the custody centre at Charles Cross at a little after one-thirty. Back at Crownhill the atmosphere was of near-jubilation.

'In the good old days,' Davies said from one side of the room where he and Riley were back to working on their own investigation, 'we'd have been in the pub by now. All of us.'

A few minutes later Layton turned up with the evidence which had led to Wilson's arrest.

'Mud, John?' Savage said to the CSI as he plonked the two bags of soil samples down on a desk. 'That was enough to arrest him?'

'No. Not alone. The mud was enough for me to confirm my suspicions. I should have told you but I had an inkling. Yesterday I took a look at a hair I found snagged on the door at Paula Rowland's place. As you'll know I have samples from officers working on the case which I use for elimination purposes. It's almost impossible to prevent some kind of contamination what with all the people going back and forth at a crime scene. When Wilson came on board he had to provide fingerprints and a sample of hair. His sample matches the one from the house.'

'So?'

'Dr Wilson never went to Rowland's place. I thought he'd have gone to the scene to check it out, but turns out he didn't. I checked the log.'

'You're sure on this?' Savage glanced at Layton. 'Scrub that. Of course you are.'

'I've had the hair fast-tracked overnight. Should get the DNA analysis through within the next hour or so. Incontrovertible.'

'That he was in the house, yes. Not incontrovertible he's the murderer.'

'Nesbit's doing the post-mortem on Paula Rowland today and I wouldn't mind betting we'll get semen from inside her. And you're forgetting the mud.'

'There could be an explanation to that too. This needs to be watertight.'

'There'll be more. We can blitz his car and we're getting a warrant for his house as well. You know my motto.'

Layton didn't say anything else, just turned and went to find Hardin and chase the warrant.

With Layton gone Savage went through an interview strategy with Calter and Enders. Junior officers would be conducting the formal interviews with Wilson. He was a man who considered himself important, somebody who'd had the ear of the Deputy Director of the FBI. He didn't need his ego inflating any more. In fact, the opposite technique would work best. While the preliminary interviews were taking place, other detectives would be trying to get background information on Wilson. They'd be speaking to people in his professional and personal circles and trying to get a handle on the psychologist's life.

Savage arrived at the custody centre an hour later with the two young DCs in tow. With the evidence from Layton looking solid, Savage was obliged to disclose it. There didn't seem much point in waiting for the DNA confirmation so she went along to speak to Wilson and his solicitor before the formal interview began.

'This is utterly ridiculous,' Wilson said, standing up as Savage entered the room. 'I would be laughing if the situation wasn't so serious. Do you realise what you're doing to my reputation?'

'Your reputation,' Savage said, waving Wilson back to his seat, 'is the least of your worries.'

Sitting beside the psychologist was his brief, Amanda Bradley, a solicitor well-known to Savage. She doodled on a legal pad, fingers clutching the pencil, her red nails like talons. Bradley's style was verging on the ridiculous and the tight blouse and short pinstripe skirt she wore wouldn't have been out of place in an office-set porn movie. She reached across and touched Wilson on the arm and then turned and smiled at Savage, showing her perfect teeth.

'I am sure, Inspector,' Bradley said, 'that this will all turn out to be a big misunderstanding. If we can expedite the interview process with regard to the harm the uncertainty over my client's position is causing to his professional—'

'There's no uncertainty,' Savage said. 'We've found hair matching that taken from samples provided by him in Paula Rowland's house. The material is being DNA-tested right now. We fully expect a match.'

'Is that true?' Bradley removed her hand from Wilson's arm and shifted in her seat. Her clients ranged from low-life pond scum to super-rich criminals, but Savage knew the solicitor drew her own line of morality somewhere between bad and evil. 'Can there be some mistake? Cross-contamination?'

'Fit-up,' Wilson said. 'Ask them about DCI Walsh. *Ex*-DCI Walsh. He's behind this. It's professional jealousy. Because

Walsh cocked things up the first time around, he wants to ensure nobody else gets the glory.'

'Jealousy?' Bradley looked across at Wilson, her face askance, bright red lips pouting as if she could never imagine possessing an ounce of the stuff. 'How so?'

'Walsh is a washed-out has-been in a regional force. I've been lauded by the Deputy Director of the FBI. If I had been retained in the original investigation the case may well have been solved by now. Deaths would have been prevented. When I get out of here I'm going to draft a report and I'll see to it the press get a copy. I wouldn't be surprised if legal action is taken by the families.' Wilson smiled at Bradley. 'You might even see if your firm could represent them.'

'I see.' Bradley reached for her pencil. 'I assume you refute these allegations, DI Savage?'

'Entirely. Now I expect you'll want to consult with your client before we continue. In light of the developments.'

The clock had just ticked up to four when John Layton came crashing through the double doors into the major crimes suite.

'Bang to!' he said, flapping a piece of paper in his hand and waving it over his head as if he'd just found a winning lottery ticket. 'DNA's come in and Wilson's name is there in black and white stripes.'

'Barcoded!' someone shouted from the back of the room and there was a chorus of 'fucking got him' too.

Savage got up from where she was sitting and went over to Layton. Held out her hand.

'Superb work, John. This is one hundred per cent down to you.'

'Bloody good policing,' Enders said in a passable imitation of DSupt Hardin. 'Suck on one of my liquorice sticks.'

'Over to you now.' Layton handed Savage the piece of paper. 'He was at Paula Rowland's place, he was at the railway bridge too. You just need to get him to come clean.'

'Be my pleasure.'

'Hopefully I'll have more later. Off to Wilson's house right now.' Layton paused. 'You know where he lives don't you?'

'No. Enlighten me.'

'Crapstone. Near Yelverton, but not a million miles from the Bere Peninsula either. Sort of places doctors and the like live so it could be a coincidence, but I think not. Too close to the farm for that.'

'When we were on the moor Wilson talked about where the killer lived. He said it would be in a big house in a posh village. It's almost like he was directing me.'

'Perhaps he was. Anyway, as soon as the warrant arrives we'll go in. You'll be there, I take it?'

'Of course. After I've checked on the progress of the interviews.'

An hour later and Savage was back at the custody centre with Hardin. They sat at a desk watching Calter and Enders interview Wilson on a small monitor. Non-specific questions received a polite answer. Questions having any bearing on the murder of Paula Rowland met with a 'no comment'. Bradley fiddled, wiggling a pencil between her fingers so it appeared to be made of rubber.

Calter and Enders had begun by outlining the murders and establishing the parameters for the interview. Wilson was providing no alibis for any of the crimes, either the recent ones or the historical ones. Forensic evidence would show he'd been at Paula Rowland's house and crossed the bridge to the farm. He had a history of sexual harassment. The latest incident being his odd behaviour towards DI Savage.

'We're sure on this one, Charlotte?' Hardin said, tapping the screen with a fingernail. 'I mean the man is not without influence.'

'Are you scared a load of G-men are going to tip up at the station, guns blazing?'

'No. Not the FBI. I'm thinking of the Chief Constable. He's been on the phone with congratulations, but he wasn't exactly gushing. Remember, Fox was the one who insisted we recruit Wilson in the first place.'

'DNA, sir. We've got a strand of hair, remember?'

'Follicles?'

'Yes. It's nuclear DNA. There's no way he can wheedle his way out of this.'

'And the contamination issue? After all, he has been around the investigation. He could claim his hair has somehow been passed across to the crime scene.'

'With respect, sir, you know that wouldn't happen with John Layton in charge. Besides the strands were found at head-height, caught on the edge of the kitchen door. A rough spot must have snagged them.'

'He'll say they were planted.'

'He can say what he wants, but it's his word against ours.'

'That, Charlotte, is what I am hoping to avoid.'

Hardin turned his attention back to the monitor where Wilson was repeating the same answer over and over again: 'no comment'.

'We need more, Charlotte. If we're going to crack him open we need much more. What about the adoption angle – anything on that yet?'

'Working on it. Nothing so far, but interestingly we're having trouble locating Wilson's next-of-kin. He knows nothing of the developments we've been making on motive and for the moment I want to keep it that way. Later we'll have the results from the post-mortem too. Match anything Nesbit finds and it's all over for Wilson.'

'Understood. When this session is finished I want you at Wilson's house with Layton. Let's pray you can find something.'

Thirty minutes later and Enders came out and met Savage in the corridor.

'Did you hear the last bit, ma'am?' Enders said. Savage shook her head. 'Cool as a cucumber in a deep freeze. "You're making a big mistake," Dr Wilson says. "And you'll find out when the killer strikes again. Which, my ignorant little plodder, will be very soon indeed."'

'That's not going to happen,' Savage said, even as she felt a lump of fear rise in her throat. 'Not on my watch.'

Riley had to scamper to finish up at the station in time. The arrest of Wilson had curtailed the interview with Mrs Corran. The woman hadn't shown much sign of being able to add anything to their knowledge, but there was still paperwork to be done. It was only because Davies knew what was going on that Riley was able to slip away, the senior detective covering for him.

Round Davies' house the other evening Riley had posed his question about Clarissa Savage. How come, he'd said, nothing had ever been found? Sure, there'd been leads, but each one dead-ended. Brick wall stuff. No offence, mate, Riley said, but there was only one person he could think of who might be able to find a way through.

Davies had raised his eyebrows at Riley's use of mate, but then he'd nodded. Dropped a name. Which was the cue for Riley in turn to raise his eyebrows. According to Davies, the guy he'd named was already on the case and had been looking into the circumstances surrounding Clarissa Savage's death for months. He was, the DI assured Riley, close to getting a result. He reckoned the man would be only too happy to have a chat.

Riley chose Chandlers Bar at the Queen Anne's Battery marina for the meeting, reasoning he was unlikely to bump into anyone he knew there. He tucked himself away in a corner with a view of the door. At the bar a trio of sailors jabbered on about some race while to his right a couple ate a meal. Whispers of the couple's conversation drifted over and Riley got the gist of it: where were they going to charter this year? The Whitsundays again or Thailand?

The sailors at the bar turned to the entrance.

Two men entered; Kenny Fallon, Plymouth's numero uno crime boss, with a beefed-up heavy beside him.

They approached the bar and Fallon turned to the corner and eyeballed Riley. He raised his hand in a cup motion and tipped it back and forth. Riley held up his bottle of Becks and pointed to the label.

Minutes later, drinks bought, and the heavy had installed himself at a table out in the sun, pulled on some shades like he was a special agent protecting a president. Fallon strolled over and held out a hand.

'Kenny,' he said. 'But I expect you know my name already.'

'Darius,' Riley said. 'Darius Riley.'

Kenny Fallon was pushing fifty, but lean and wiry. Long grey hair and a little goatee beard. He wore a neat jacket, but replace the jacket with a grimy leather, Riley thought, and the man would resemble an ageing biker.

They played verbal tennis for a few minutes, batting the events of a few months ago back and forward. Fallon had been the target of an operation which Riley had been involved with and the police had almost managed to nab him red-handed in possession of several million pounds worth of cocaine. It was only down to the involvement of another gangster, keen to pay back Fallon for shafting him years previously, that everything had gone tits up and Fallon had escaped.

'In the end, Darius,' Fallon said, 'from what I heard, you would have been toast had it not been for me.'

'I think I have DI Savage to thank for that. And from what *I* heard, you do too.'

'Well, that's what we're here for. Savage.'

'Charlotte.'

'Yes. Charlotte.'

Fallon leant in over the table, but subterfuge was unnecessary; the raised voices at the nearby table suggested the couple were otherwise preoccupied. Holiday plans were up in the air, the woman now plumping for a holiday in the south of France, *sans* boat, hubby disagreeing.

'This car,' Riley said. 'The Impreza.'

'The one you lot couldn't trace.'

'The one *you* haven't been able to trace.' Riley paused as Fallon scowled and then he held up his hands. 'Look, truce, OK? Otherwise we're going to get nowhere.'

'Sure.' Fallon nodded.

'Any ideas?'

'You lot,' Fallon said. 'You got the wrong end of the stick.'

'How do you mean?'

'It's taken me a while too, I'll admit, but I worked it out. Your guys were looking for a car with front-end damage. But that's not the way it works. If it had been me I'd have either scrapped the car or, better, I'd have made sure I got a new panel sharpish. A rush job.'

'And?'

'Where do you go for one of them?' Fallon smiled as Riley shook his head. 'A breakers yard. Now, did you know I am in the scrap metal business? Got in a few years ago when commodity prices began to rise. Saw an opportunity. Bought into a little place out Torpoint way. Couple of lads with a truck collect stuff from farms and some of the smaller breakers yards.'

'So?'

'So I call up my boys and ask about Subarus. Where would I get a blue front wing panel for a pre-2007 Impreza? They tell me they can find out and off they go. Now cash is king at these places so there are no records of buyers, but Bill Hegg, who runs ReKlame Autos in Plympton, one-time mate of mine, has got a nifty computerised system for tracking his stock. He sends stuff all over the UK – he's a bit of a Subaru specialist you see – but it turns out that a customer visited in person and picked up a nearside front wing panel for a blue Impreza on the Saturday of the August holiday weekend.'

'One day after the accident.'

'Yeah. One day after the accident. Of course it could be a coincidence.' Fallon ran a hand over the smooth gloss of the table. 'In the right light and from a distance you'd probably see the panel didn't quite match, but in someone's garage . . .'

'Even if you thought to look, you'd never spot it.'

'Correct. So you're looking for somebody who owns or once owned an Impreza and stored it in a garage. Could well be one of the vehicles you already checked, especially if the viewing was conducted in poor-ish light.'

'Dozens of them,' Riley said.

'Hey?'

'Eighty-two local vehicles had no damage and thus their owners had no case to answer.'

'Evidence,' Fallon said. 'Funny me, of all people, bringing that up, but that's what you need, isn't it?'

'And?'

'Hegg will see you clear. I'll let him know you're coming.'

'DI Savage is to know nothing of this,' Riley said. 'When we've got the name we'll decide how to proceed, until then schtum, OK?'

'Fine.' Fallon picked up the menu card from its holder. 'Now, I'm going to plump for the classic New Yorker American burger. What'll it be?'

As Devon village names went, Crapstone was not one of the more attractive. In local dialect 'crap' meant 'crop' but that didn't help much if you were on the phone to someone sitting in a call centre halfway across the country.

'Did you know, ma'am,' Calter said as she and Savage drove past the sign indicating the village outskirts, 'that Enders' grandmother comes from Muff? It's in County Donegal. He's told me half a dozen times. Pathetic.'

'Boys will be boys,' Savage said.

'That's why I've always preferred men.'

'Talking of which, there's another fine specimen.' Savage pulled the car over and pointed up the road. John Layton stood next to his Volvo picking trail mix from a bag. He'd discarded his white suit and stood in shorts and sandals, the Tilley hat on his head tilted to one side as usual. A thermos flask stood on the bonnet of the car, a cup steaming nearby. Savage guessed the drink would be some herbal concoction.

'Hmm, you're right there, ma'am. Quite a catch if you're into muesli.'

'If you'd seen his wife you wouldn't be quite so mocking. She's gorgeous. Even with a child on the hip and one at the breast.'

'Earth mother?'

'And domestic goddess. There's an older child too. That makes three. Come on, let's get inside.'

As they approached Layton he swallowed a final mouthful of drink and then swilled the dregs around in his cup and flicked them into the hedge.

'Camomile?' Savage asked.

'Nettle,' Layton said. 'But one of my lads has a car kettle and some Gold Blend if you'd prefer.'

'Anything in the house?'

'No skulls on the sideboard, if that's what you mean. Forensically there's nothing out of the ordinary. We've collected a load of samples, but that doesn't mean a thing. However, if he did the butchery here we'll find something. No way you could carve someone up and chop their head off without making one hell of a mess.'

'And non-forensically?'

'There's hundreds of books on serial killers, but then there would be, given what Wilson does. Loads of documents, an old computer, a gun, a—'

'A gun?'

'Yes.' Layton moved to the rear door of the car and opened it. From a crate he retrieved a clear plastic bag. 'Don't get too excited, it's a Walther GSP, a target handgun. Point two-two.'

Savage looked at the weapon. Dark metal and with a wooden handle. Strange and angular. Long enough to be difficult to conceal.

'Could it be used to kill someone?' she said.

'Kill?' Layton stared at Savage. 'Of course it could kill. It might be a small-calibre weapon, but a head shot or a shot in a major organ and you're gone.'

'There were no bullet wounds on the victims.'

'No heads either.' Layton placed the gun back in the car. 'However, before we get carried away, in Wilson's favour I found some pictures of him when he was younger at various shooting competitions. He represented Devon. There's one of the whole team. Against him is the fact that owning this type of gun has been illegal since 1997. Plus the weapon has been fired recently.'

'You sure?'

'You can smell it.'

'Ammunition?'

'Several thousand rounds. I guess he was hoarding the stuff, but it wasn't exactly hidden away. Both the gun and the ammo boxes were in a cupboard in the living room. Amongst the pictures of Wilson there's also a couple of him with a CZ 452 bolt-action rifle. Takes the same ammo as the pistol. Wilson had a licence for it up until he went to the US. No sign of the weapon though.'

Inside one of the CSIs pointed out the cupboard with the ammunition, the bottom part of a pair of built-in bookshelves either side of the fireplace. The bookshelves contained medical volumes as well as dozens of popular true crime accounts of various notorious murderers: Ted Bundy, Jeffrey Dahmer, John Wayne Gacy.

'Bit of light reading, ma'am?' Calter held a book in her hand and opened the pages at the centre where an array of pictures showed dead bodies in various stages of mutilation. 'Tempting to take one or two of these as a morbid souvenir. Something to get out to show friends after dinner: "I got this from the house of the Candle Cake Killer." To be honest though I can't quite fathom why people want to sit down with a cup of tea and a choccy biscuit and read this stuff. I prefer a good Sophie Kinsella myself.'

'Never!'

'No, ma'am. Never.' Calter put the book back. 'Is there any evidence to show killers are interested in other killers?'

'Not that I know of. They tend to be self-centred if anything. Anyway, this material is part of Wilson's work. Even the sensationalist stuff. We need to find some more background information on him. Family, lovers, friends, that kind of thing.'

'Lovers? From the way he approached you I doubt he's had many.'

Savage moved to a pair of French windows, half open. Peered out. The back garden was huge, fifty metres to a hedge. Fields beyond. To the left she could see the next-door property, a lawn encircling a large pond. Voices.

'The neighbours,' Savage said. 'Let's try them.'

No answer came from several tries of the doorbell so Savage and Calter wandered round the back. The garden sloped away in a swathe of bright green down to a levelled area with a tennis court on which two teenage girls swatted a ball back and forth. On a terraced patio a couple sat lounging with papers, a large jug of a brown liquid which looked suspiciously like Pimms on a table.

'Excuse me?' The woman stood, the voice clear and authoritative. 'Can I help you?'

Savage reached for her identification and introduced herself and Calter. Explained that Dr Wilson was helping police with enquiries.

'Barry?' the woman said. 'These officers want to know about Dr Wilson. More your department, darling, don't you think?'

'What?' The man snorted and then folded his newspaper and placed it on the table next to the jug of Pimms. 'Don't suppose . . .?'

'No thank you.' Savage waved the man's offer away. 'What did your wife mean "your department"?'

'Nothing much. Just I was the one he talked to. Over the hedge. Once or twice I shared a beer with him down the local.'

'And what did you talk about?'

'This and that. Science mostly. I teach at Plymouth University. Geology. Dr Wilson is remarkably well-informed on the subject. But then, there's not much he doesn't know about.'

'Dr Wilson talked about geology?'

'Yes. Especially mining and quarrying. Local history. He is particularly interested in clay mining. Clay and tin mining have played a big part in the local area, forming the landscape and shaping the economy, clay in particular. Without—'

'Barry!' The woman waved an arm. 'I don't think the police want to hear all this.'

'That's not a problem,' Savage said. 'Do you know what Dr Wilson actually did?'

'Serial killers,' Barry said. 'He told us when he arrived here. He's worked with the FBI you know?'

'Yes. Did he ever talk about his family?'

'No, he—' the woman said.

'He did.' Barry interrupted his wife. 'Once. Down the pub. I asked him about his parents and he told me they were dead. Except he said it in a rather strange way. The exact phrase was "Yes, all of them." I only remember because he was usually so precise with his words. I put it down to the drink.'

Savage nodded and went on to ask some more questions, finishing by asking how long Wilson had been in the area.

'Well,' the woman said. 'He's Devon born and bred, but in this house only a year or so. He was in America you know. For five years.'

Savage wrapped up the interview and they left.

'Five years,' Calter said as they returned to Wilson's house.

'The gap between the old killings and Kat Mallory's disappearance.'

'I'm interested in his parents,' Savage said. 'All of them. Whatever that means.'

Chapter Thirty-Three

Crownhill Police Station, Plymouth. Thursday 26th June. 9.02 a.m.

First thing Thursday, and Savage was in a meeting with Hardin. He leant across his desk, eager for news on Wilson's house. Wanted to get the full lowdown. The juicy morsels. Was there anything useful, had they unearthed information on Wilson's past, about his family, his parents? Savage confessed the search teams had so far found nothing of substance aside from the target pistol. Hardin appeared bemused. Serial killers, he'd assumed, had cupboards full of trophies. Not silverware. Body parts.

'The gun,' Hardin said. 'A possible for the murder weapon?'

'Layton says it's been fired recently, but to be honest in the grand scheme of things the gun's existence is circumstantial. You were at Katherine Mallory's PM. Nesbit concluded the cut marks were made when she was alive. Whether Dr Wilson shot his victims at the end or not doesn't much matter.'

'It's called building a case, Charlotte. The little details.'

'But unless we can find a shell at the farm or even better, the victims' heads, the gun has no evidential value.'

'The heads . . .' Hardin bit his lip and leant back. 'I was

307

at Paula Rowland's PM yesterday and Nesbit reckons an axe was used again. And this time the knife marks were easy to see. The strange whirling patterns were still there but we might have been wrong about dozens of cuts. The woman had only fourteen.'

'The number of candles on the cake.'

'Yes,' Hardin said. He drew a figure 'S' on the desk with a finger. 'He cuts them once for each year, is that it?'

A knock at the door came before Savage had a chance to answer. Hardin growled out a 'come in' and DC Calter's face peered round.

'Sir. Ma'am. Sorry to be the bearer of possible bad news but there's a problem.'

'And?' Hardin said. 'Out with it.'

'Someone down at the front desk claims to have an alibi for Dr Wilson. A Professor Keith Robson.'

'*What*?' Hardin glared at Calter, face askance, then turned to Savage. 'Know anything about this?'

'Nothing, sir. I'll go and see.'

'Yes, DI Savage. You do that.'

Down at reception a tall, grey man stood perusing the posters on the walls.

'Professor Robson?' Savage approached the man, who turned and smiled. 'DI Charlotte Savage.'

'Don't you have nightmares?' he said. 'All this stuff is enough to give you them.'

'A few sensible precautions can cut crime dramatically. These posters make people realise how vulnerable they and their property are.'

'My point exactly. Fear of God, I shouldn't wonder.'

'That's not the intention. You told my colleague you had some information about Dr Wilson?'

'Indeed. I'm a professor of criminology. I'm visiting

Plymouth University to give a talk on the law and migrant workers and . . . Well, to cut a long story short, I attempted to contact Dr Wilson and discovered to my horror he'd been arrested for these cake killings.'

'And you have some additional evidence which might help us?'

'Not quite. Dr Wilson and I are associates. He's lectured a number of times at Manchester, giving talks on his work with the FBI.'

'That's all well and good but—'

'Dr Wilson could not have taken part in the latest killing. I checked on the web and the girl went missing at the weekend, Saturday, yes?' Savage nodded. 'On Saturday Dr Wilson was at a conference in Manchester. He attended a number of meetings and sat on two seminar panels. At three o'clock he gave a lecture to over three hundred people. Afterwards there was a buffet reception which lasted for some two hours.'

'So he could have returned to Devon after that?'

'No. A group of us then proceeded to the staff bar where we stayed until after midnight. Dr Wilson was with us. The next morning I picked him up from his hotel – the Radisson – took him to the airport and saw him onto a flight to Exeter. You have quite the wrong man, Inspector.'

As Savage expected, Hardin didn't take the news well. He summoned Layton and Savage to the briefing room, his face reddening from a hint of pink to a fiery tomato as Savage went through the alibi again. Then he exploded.

'How the hell could you let this happen, John?' Hardin banged the table and Layton flinched. 'And you, Charlotte? I warned you about cross-contamination. You get close and cuddly with Wilson during the week and then on Saturday you look round the crime scene. It doesn't take a genius to work out what happened. Heavens knows what a half-decent defence lawyer could do with it.'

'It didn't happen, sir,' Layton said. 'I told you the hair came from near the top of a door, caught under a sliver of wood. I'll stake my reputation that there's no way it could have got there accidentally.'

'John,' Hardin said with a sneer, 'it's not *your* reputation which is on the line.'

'The hair was left by Wilson.' Layton sat back and folded his arms. 'End of.'

'Unless somebody planted the evidence.' Hardin's gaze turned to Savage. 'Someone who wanted to get Wilson removed from the case, discredit him at least.'

'Sir, I—' Savage didn't manage to get any more out because Hardin thumped the table again.

'Ex-DCI Walsh. You and him are like that, aren't you?' Hardin held out his hand, first two fingers crossed. 'Walsh never liked Wilson, saw him as a jumped-up quack. He bitterly resented the fact the Chief Constable insisted Wilson be retained last time. I can't imagine how he was thinking when he discovered Wilson was to be used in the current investigation.'

'Sir, Walsh hasn't been near Paula Rowland's house. Check the scene log.'

'Precisely. Which can only mean somebody planted the hair for him.' Hardin leant forwards and smiled. Looked at Layton again. 'Right?'

Layton unfolded his arms and moved a hand up to his brow as if searching for his hat.

'You can't be suggesting Charlotte . . .?'

'Sir,' Savage said. 'I'd never be involved in anything dodgy. There's no way I'd plant evidence against Dr Wilson.'

'Is that so?' Hardin's tongue crept out and slid across his lower lip as if tasting the air for the truth. 'Because the way I see it, considering events at the start of the year, bending the rules a little is exactly the sort of thing you might do.'

'I resent that, sir. Wilson must have returned here somehow.'

'Some time after midnight until he was picked up from his hotel in the morning.' Hardin tapped the right forefinger of his hand on the table several times. 'Not long. What's the minimum journey time back from Manchester? No planes or trains that time of night so by road it must be. Four hours by car? Three hours if you've got your foot to the floor. But in that case you'd be triggering every speed camera en route and any patrols you passed would be on to you. And anyway, you're forgetting one thing. Paula went missing some time around four o'clock. Wilson was at a reception up in Manchester, probably trying to get into the knickers of some young student drunk on fizz by regaling them with tales of his FBI heroics. Whatever, he was surrounded by dozens of people and has a perfect alibi. He's out of the frame. To put it in your words, John: end of.'

Savage made the journey back to the custody centre, using the time stuck in traffic to work out what the hell had gone wrong. Had Layton really messed up? The CSI was so painstaking in the way he dealt with crime scenes, but had he for once let emotion get the better of him and not followed procedure?

Inside Charles Cross the custody officer nodded and led her down the corridor. No smile, but in the interview room Bradley's grin stretched from ear to ear. Wilson sat impassive, arms folded, feet up on the table.

'Reason and logic,' Wilson said. 'They always win out in the end.'

311

'Why,' Savage said, 'didn't you tell us you were in Manchester on the evening of Paula Rowland's disappearance?'

'I told you I didn't do it, Inspector. Was my word not good enough?'

'You were playing with us. You could have been out of here but you let us go round in circles.'

'But you had the DNA.' Wilson smiled, raised the pitch of his voice. 'Incontrovertible evidence. Do you know I thought I must be losing my mind, that you must be right all along? A split personality. The nice Dr Wilson and – growl – the evil monster. Of course, I am relieved to discover otherwise.'

'There'll likely be a compensation claim,' Bradley said through her grin as she shuffled some papers on the desk and slipped them into her briefcase. 'I understand Dr Wilson's garden has been damaged during a search. There's also a matter of an apology. We'll work on the wording for that.'

Wilson swung his legs off the table and stood.

'No hard feelings, Charlotte.' Wilson held out his hand. Savage kept hers by her side and moved to let him past. 'And tell DCI Walsh – ex-DCI Walsh – how close you were to catching the killer. Sadly, in the same way as he dismissed my advice, you have too. Now the killer will kill again. Pity.'

Wilson glided through the door to where the custody sergeant waited to book him out. Bradley stopped next to Savage. Looked her up and down.

'You need a break, love,' Bradley said. 'Some new clothes, a little time to pamper yourself. Because it's all beginning to slip away. Such a shame.'

She turned and followed her client down the corridor.

'There'll still be charges,' Savage shouted after her. 'Assaulting a police officer. Possession of an illegal weapon. Wasting police time.'

Bradley raised an arm in acknowledgement but didn't look back.

'Bitch,' Savage said.

It wasn't until the weekend that Riley had a chance to continue his unofficial investigation. Thursday and Friday he'd spent with his head down working hard on the Corran investigation as the flak over the arrest and release of Dr Wilson flew around the crime suite. Come Saturday morning he left Julie sleeping in, a note on the kitchen table promising lunch at a country pub, maybe a stroll somewhere. Later, an evening out with friends. Nothing on the note about where he was going.

Riley wondered, as he drove through Plymouth, if the deceit was a bad sign, something akin to cheating. Cross with himself for even going down that route, he flicked the radio on in search of distraction. The callers on the local BBC morning show were having kittens. Wilson's release meant the Candle Cake Killer was still at large. *What were the police playing at?* seemed to be the general consensus. Ten days ago, at the outset, Riley had been annoyed not to be on the case. Now he could see benefits, one of which was some spare time to do some more digging into the circumstances surrounding Clarissa Savage's death.

ReKlame Autos.

Kenny Fallon had told him the breakers had supplied a panel for a blue Subaru Impreza one day after the accident in which Clarissa was killed. As a coincidence it seemed improbable.

Riley found the yard at the unloved end of an industrial estate on the outskirts of the suburb of Plympton. Stacks of cars, six or seven high, sat to one side of the front lot, looking for all the world like a cross between an art installation and the set of a post-apocalyptic movie. He pulled his own car in alongside a classic Jag showing more rust than paint and got out.

High double doors to the warehouse stood wide, inside, rows of steel shelving reaching to the ceiling, each shelf stacked with car parts: alternators, shock absorbers, carburettors, brake hubs, cylinder heads. To the right of the main entrance a small door led to an office. Riley opened the door and went inside. Behind the counter a balding man of about fifty looked up from the girlie magazine he was reading. Next to the magazine a ledger book was also open, a pile of receipts to one side. The man nodded when Riley asked him if he was William Hegg.

'You must be Riley,' Hegg said. 'Kenny Fallon mentioned you'd be round. Don't get many of your type in here as a rule.'

'Meaning?'

'Detectives.' Hegg grinned, flicking the page on the magazine and eyeing the mature blonde sprawled diagonally top to bottom. 'Just look at her. Full bush, nice rack. Stunning.'

'I'm more interested in the racks out there,' Riley said, jerking a thumb in the direction of the warehouse. 'Specifically something you sold a while back.'

'Hey?' Hegg closed the magazine. 'Oh, wit. Very good.'

'I'm trying to trace a customer of yours who bought a front wing panel a few years ago.'

'Blue Impreza.' Hegg nodded, and reached for the ledger book. 'Kenny gave me the details. I told him I'd look into it. Well, now I've looked into it.'

'And?'

'Nothing doing, nothing found. Even if I'd found something, my customers value their privacy.'

'But Fallon said—'

'I don't care what Kenny said. In case you lot didn't realise he's not quite the big gun he used to be. We're mates, sure, but I'm not a monkey doing tricks on his say-so. Now if you don't mind I've got to get on with my accounts.'

'I see.' Riley turned away from the counter and made to leave. 'How would your precious customers feel if they turned up to see a squad car parked outside your front gate? Extended lunch break. Every day. From now until whenever. Bet their presence would quieten things down a bit so you'd have time to do your accounts.'

'Look,' Hegg flipped his book shut and the waft of air lifted a couple of receipts and blew them from the desk. 'I don't want any trouble.'

'There's not going to be any trouble if you just tell me who you sold the panel to.'

Hegg peered past Riley through the door to the warehouse and shook his head. He bent for the receipts and then stuffed them and the ledger book into a drawer beneath the counter.

'Tim Hamilton. Runs a panel shop over Okehampton way.' Hegg pulled a sliver of white card from the drawer and slid it shut. 'He was nothing to do with your problem, he's a mechanic. Just fixing up a car for someone.'

The card snapped down on the counter

'Thanks,' Riley reached for the card. 'I won't forget you helped me.'

'I'd prefer you did.' Hegg flicked open his girlie magazine again. Two brunettes were getting friendly head-to-toe. 'Now, as I said, I've got work to do, so I'd be grateful if you'd bugger off.'

Chapter Thirty-Four

Close. Very close. The police finding the hair. Need to think about that in the future. You don't want any more silly mistakes, else you'll end up back inside. And this time there'll be no getting out, no rebirth. It'll be a whole life term.

A slice of luck how things turned out though. The Manchester alibi. If only your good fortune extended to the state of your dishwasher. Right now you don't want to be worrying about such things, but it's gone wrong again and when you called up the repair man he refused to come out.

'Tricky, driving all the way out there,' the fuckhead said. 'You living in the countryside, see? One of the downsides. Not worth my while.'

Really?

You'll show him what is and isn't worth his while. His job is repairing washing machines, not making philosophical judge-ments on the country–city dichotomy. His attitude makes your blood . . .

Steady.

You don't need any more trouble. Which means you simply have to make a decision: Dixons, Currys or Amazon?

There's enough wire and electricity and electrons and shit swirling around in a new machine to make you sick. Better not add to the sum by buying from Amazon. Besides, they'll take cash in one of the stores and you might get to speak to a girl in a smart uniform. If you can avoid the slimy male sales assistants with their false bonhomie.

Alright, sir? How can I help you?

They could help by fucking off and leaving you alone for five minutes. You're sure that was the problem the last time. You'd decided on a basic model – quite adequate for your needs – when spotty boy comes across and talks you into buying a much more expensive unit.

Which six years, three months and five days later went wrong.

Six years, three months and five days? Is that how long things are expected to last in the twenty-first century?

Call that progress?

No, you don't.

You sigh and glance out the window.

The dog is going crazy. Barking, growling, straining at the limits of its chain, wanting to play with Mikey. The lad is out there with his football trying some step-overs. Only these are more like trip-overs, Mikey falling in the mud, face down. You shake your head, wondering not for the first time why you took him in. But the boy was alone on the streets. Homeless. He needed somebody. And after all these years you've grown rather fond of him.

Splat.

You've got to admire his perseverance because over he goes again. And again. And again.

Not much progress there either, Mikey about as close to emulating Cristiano Ronaldo as the police are to catching you.

Chapter Thirty-Five

Crownhill Police Station, Plymouth. Monday 30th June.
9.07 a.m.

Savage spent Saturday at home with Pete and the kids, Sunday afternoon out on their boat tootling around the Sound. Fish and chips collected on the way home, the kids in bed early, worn out from being on the water. There'd been little wind, their colourful spinnaker barely filling in the light air, the boat wallowing in the swell; a welcome change from the last trip. When they'd left the boat though, Pete had doubled up the ropes and added a few extra fenders.

'Summer storm,' he said. 'Coming in tomorrow. Best be on the safe side.'

The safe side had been Hardin's call too. Play it cautious. He'd stood down the majority of the team for the weekend. A few detectives worked over, but the DSupt had wanted to cool everyone down. The last thing they needed, he said, was a spot of red card rage, an over-zealous officer going hell for leather after a fresh suspect or someone trying to pin something on Wilson.

Monday morning, and Pete's forecast was correct. The weather was brewing, trees beginning to bend and swirl in a strengthening breeze, the sun more often than not hidden

318

behind clouds. Over the weekend the media had cooked up their own storm, keen to ratchet up the tension. There was fresh talk about whether the police could cope. In a Sunday morning TV interview a Home Office minister had expressed her 'utmost confidence' in Simon Fox and the Devon and Cornwall force; shorthand for 'Get your fingers out, or else.'

At Crownhill Savage headed to the crime suite, almost bumping into Layton on a corner.

'Sorry, ma'am,' Layton said. 'Busy, busy, busy.'

The CSI held a small ziplock bag in one hand, in the other hand a gun. Grey metal and wood. The target pistol recovered from Dr Wilson's house.

'Where are you going with that?' Savage said.

Layton didn't answer. Instead he smiled and jerked his head to the side as if to hint she should follow. He set off at a trot, almost collided with an officer with a steaming cup of something, and barged into the crime suite. Savage caught the double doors before they could close and followed him in.

'Well, well, well.' Davies looked up from a desk. 'If it isn't the Fairy Godmother and Cinderella. Brought us an invite to the ball, have you? Only there's a rumour going around that your magic's all used up.'

Riley stood at Davies' side and he shook his head and shrugged. 'John. Ma'am.'

'Well the rumour is wrong,' Layton said. He walked into the room and placed the gun on a desk. 'This is the gun I found in Dr Wilson's house. Not concealed but it had been recently fired.'

'Wonderful,' Davies said.

'And this is a bullet fired from the same gun.' He placed the plastic bag alongside the pistol. 'It came from a point two-two LR rimfire cartridge.'

'Fantastic.' Davies feigned disinterest and looked at his screen. 'Do you mind telling me what this has to do with our operation?'

'The bullet was extracted from the brain of Devlyn Corran. I believe you and DS Riley were there when Nesbit performed the PM?'

'*What*?' Davies snapped round and stared down at the bullet. 'Bloody hell! You *are* joking me?'

'Jokes are for comedians,' Layton said, a smile showing he was beginning to enjoy himself. 'Conjecture for fools. This is fact. I've fired the gun and the test bullets match.'

'So Wilson killed Corran?' Savage said.

'I've no idea who fired the gun, but it was used to murder Corran.' Layton looked away from the desk and turned to Savage. 'I gather you met him at his office on the Wednesday after the initial discovery of the bodies at the farm.'

'Yes,' Savage said. 'But what's that got to do with anything?'

'Wilson couldn't meet you earlier?'

'No, he was . . . Shit! Wilson was up in London. Something to do with the Home Office.'

'Another alibi,' Layton said. 'I dare say as unbreakable as the first.'

'John, you're taking us round in circles. You've brought us a new theory but now you say Wilson couldn't have killed Corran in the same way as he couldn't have abducted Paula Rowland.'

'Evidence, ma'am.' Layton pointed to the bags on the desk. 'I'm like Dr Nesbit in that way. I provide the facts but it's up to you guys to do the interpretation.'

'Ma'am?' Riley pointed to a sheet of paper on Davies' little whiteboard: *I know who you are.* 'Corran sent this message to the person he was blackmailing. Now John tells us Corran's been popped with a gun owned by Wilson, already a suspect

320

for the Candle Cake killings. Whatever the veracity of Dr Wilson's two alibis, the coincidence is too much.'

'But how did Corran know about Wilson?' Savage said.

'Thinking on my feet, ma'am,' Riley said. 'Corran worked at HMP Full Sutton before transferring down to Dartmoor. I spoke to the Deputy Governor up there. Corran specialised in the care, management and security of dangerous prisoners. According to the Governor of HMP Dartmoor Corran did some similar sessions at Channings Wood. There's a sex offender unit over there. I believe Wilson has been to the unit too. It's not beyond the bounds of possibility Corran and Wilson met.'

'Yeah,' Davies said. 'But how does Corran meeting Wilson mean he gets the lowdown on the identity of the Candle Cake Killer? Unless Corran came across Wilson sitting in a cell with some pervert saying "Look here, mate, I know exactly where you're coming from, I'm a bit of a serial killer myself." I don't want to rain on your parade, but that's fucking . . . how did you put it, John . . . *conjecture*?'

'Maybe,' Savage said, waving her hands apart. 'And the alibis need some serious work, but we go with what we know. Corran, bullet, gun. We can build the rest from there.'

'You know, Savage?' Davies stood and pulled his jacket from the back of the chair. 'That's the first sensible thing you've said in a long time. I'll bring Wilson in.'

'Hang on,' Savage said. 'We don't want a repeat of the other day. We need to be sure and we need to use this to see if we can't work the Candle Cake Killer stuff too.'

'OK, I'm hearing you. Let's go and find the DSupt and see what he thinks.'

He surged from the room without waiting for a reply. Riley followed but he stopped at the door and offered another shrug by way of an apology.

'Typical,' Layton said. 'Not a word of thanks. No "well done", "good work" or anything.'

'Well done, John. And good work,' Savage said, moving to follow Davies and Riley. 'Now if you could just get some more evidence which might break those alibis, that would be great.'

Dr Peter Wilson stood looking out on his garden. The green lawn was dotted with piles of soil where the police had dug holes in the expectation of finding more bodies. Wilson shook his head. Fools. What would be the point of burying the women here?

The sight of the lawn distressed him. It had taken time to get the grass looking so lush, to remove every last trace of moss, to even out all the bumps. He thought the lawn could do with a cut, but manoeuvring around the holes would be tricky and there probably wasn't enough time to finish the job. Pity. He enjoyed the cutting, the way the lawn looked after he'd zipped up and down with the mower, the neat alternating stripes of green. Caring for the garden was an effort, but then caring for anything was an effort. You got what you put into something though and the garden's appearance in the summer was reward enough for all the work.

The police had been working hard too. And not just in the garden. A few minutes earlier Wilson had taken a call from the woman detective, Charlotte. She was on her way out to see him. Things to discuss, she'd said.

Things to discuss.

For a moment when he'd heard her voice Wilson wondered if she'd changed her mind about him. Was she coming over to make amends, admit she fancied him? No, of course not. The bitch was like all the rest. Selfish. The real reason for her visit was because the game was up. She hadn't said so but he knew all the same.

Wilson turned back to the living room and walked in through the French windows. The room was a mess. Boxes of books, the furniture stacked in a corner, cupboards open.

The gun . . .

He'd kept the weapon in one of the cupboards along with some ammunition. The police had found it all too easily. A silly, silly mistake. So far they'd been idiots, but the phone call suggested they'd finally put two and two together. They knew the prison officer had been shot and now they had the weapon which shot him.

For a moment Wilson considered fleeing, but really that wasn't an option now. Running away would solve nothing. If he wanted to protect those he loved the most there was only one thing to do.

Wilson glanced at his watch. She'd be here soon. He needed to prepare. Get ready. It was time for the final act.

Hardin hadn't thought much of the bullet evidence. Layton, he'd muttered, was getting sloppy. Not to be trusted. And when he'd said the word 'trusted' he'd looked at Savage, shaken his head. Nodded at Davies too. It was then Savage had come up with a suggestion. She'd call the psychologist and suggest a meeting. He knew nothing of the latest development so she could use the new evidence to trap him, possibly solving both cases at the same time.

Now, as Savage turned her car in off the lane and coasted into Wilson's driveway, she was beginning to regret having opened her mouth.

'Can you hear me?' she said, trying not to move her lips.

'Yes.' Riley's voice came through static into her earpiece.

Savage pulled up on the driveway and looked towards the front door. It stood ajar.

'The door's open, but no sign of Wilson,' Savage said. 'I'm going in.'

'Oh so slowly, ma'am. And be careful. Any sign of anything amiss and you shout. We're one minute away.'

One minute was round a corner at the end of the lane in a car with the engine running. Davies at the wheel, Riley and Enders with their fingers on the door handles.

'Roger that.'

Savage climbed out of the car and moved over the drive. Grandmother's footsteps, each step making a crunching noise sure to wake Granny up. She reached the door and pushed.

'Dr Wilson? Peter?'

Her voice echoed in the bare hallway. A rug had been rolled up and leant against one wall. Several plastic boxes stood in a haphazard stack next to the stairs. A life packed away for investigation. Savage entered the house. Across the hall a door revealed the living room, inside the French windows stood open, a breeze wafting in and moving the curtains. She moved across the hallway, her steps clicking on the parquet floor. In the living room the sofa and armchairs had no covers on and had been moved to a corner. Another pile of plastic boxes contained all Wilson's books and papers. What had Wilson been doing all weekend? It didn't appear that he'd made any effort to unpack or tidy up. Savage shook her head and crossed the room to the patio doors.

Outside a number of holes dotted the lawn. 'Exploratory' Layton had called them, but his team had found nothing. Savage wondered what would happen to the property. Even if Wilson wasn't the Candle Cake Killer the house had now acquired a notoriety, the horrors of the killings forever associated with the place.

She called Wilson's name again and then came in from the garden and returned to the hall. Doors led to the kitchen, dining room, a study and of course there was the upstairs to check too. She moved towards the study. The small room had wall-to-ceiling bookcases on two walls and a large leather-topped desk with a matching armchair. In the centre of the green leather a white envelope had been propped against an upturned tumbler. Savage moved closer. A single line of writing spidered across the face of the envelope:

For the attention of DI Savage.

She reached out for the envelope and then stopped, aware of a noise behind her. She spun round, half-expecting Wilson to jump from behind the door, but there was no one.

'No sign of him anywhere,' she whispered, unsure if Riley could hear her, and then walked out into the hallway once again.

The first thing she noticed was that the front door had closed. Swung shut in the breeze or . . . No. The safety chain hung in a little loop. Then she saw Wilson. He stood atop the stack of crates, the pile creaking as he shifted his weight.

'What are you . . .' Savage had a moment to take in the rope which went from Wilson up to the chandelier and then made a sharp angle as it led across to the banister rail on the upstairs landing. For a second she thought Wilson was about to attempt some kind of Tarzan swing. But no, he wasn't like Tarzan because he wasn't holding on to the rope. It was tied round his neck.

'Charlotte,' Wilson said, trying to balance. 'I've decided it's better this way. Wraps things up. No more killing. No more tears. Lord knows there's been enough of them down the years.'

'Dr Wilson . . .' Savage moved into the centre of the hall. The stack of crates was a metre and a half high, Wilson towering above her like some circus stilt-walker. 'Peter. Calm down. We can work this out. Don't do anything stupid.'

'Anything stupid?' Wilson laughed. Wobbled. Reached up and held the rope with one hand to steady himself. 'I think it's a little too late for that. All I ever wanted was to settle the scores. Retribution, if you like, for sins committed.'

'Are you talking about adoption? Those women gave up their children because they had to. Because of the situation they found themselves in. Do you think anybody would willingly surrender a child they had carried inside them?'

'No one has to do anything, Charlotte. They neglected their offspring, handed them over to strangers, not knowing what would happen. You should have heard them trying to justify their actions. They were so self-obsessed, so full of self-pity. They made me sick.'

'But if anything the children were probably better off. They were placed with parents who were desperate for children, who loved and cared for them.'

'Really? You believe that?' Wilson pointed at Savage, at the envelope she held in her hand. 'Open it. Read it.'

'What's this?' Savage said, ripping open the letter and pulling out the pieces of paper inside. 'A confession? Some sort of attempt at absolving yourself from blame?'

'Read the fucking thing!' Wilson's legs juddered, the stack of crates shifting. 'It's all in there. The whole story. I wasn't to blame, it was the tart who lived at Tavy View Farm – Lara Bailey – my "mother".'

'Lara Bailey was your mother?'

'Yes, of course. But she gave me up as a baby. Better off was I? No. My new father beat me, he beat my new mother. Raped her. To me, of course she was my real mother. Mummy. The woman who loved me. I had no idea back then I was adopted. All I saw was her suffering, me too. Day after day,

326

week after week. And then Daddy cracks, goes even further, slices Mummy open with a knife. And do you know what day he did that on? Have a guess?'

'The solstice, the twenty-first of June,' Savage said. 'Which is why you abducted the victims on that day.'

'Not the solstice, you daft bitch. The twenty-first of June is my *birthday*. The longest fucking day of the year. All that daylight stops you sleeping. Plenty of time for me to remember what happened. To work out who was to blame.'

'For God's sake, Lara Bailey wasn't responsible, she was no more than a child when she had you.'

'But look what she turned into: a whore.'

'So you killed her.'

'Yes. And the others. They were as guilty as Lara.'

'Guilty?' Savage shook her head. 'It's over, Peter. You need to get down from there. We can help you.'

'Help me?' Wilson laughed. 'At one point I tried to stop the killing. I was scared by what I had done. I went away to the States, but when I returned the urges resumed. There was nothing I could do and last year I killed the Mallory girl. Then you found the bodies and with the twenty-first approaching I thought the only way would be to give you all the information you needed to catch me. I approached the Chief Constable and tried to help you find the killer, gave you clues, but you didn't succeed in time. Paula Rowland . . . I had to.'

'It's OK, you've done the right thing now.' Savage moved a step closer. 'As you said, there's no need for anyone to suffer anymore.'

'Year after year. Lying awake. Frightened.' Wilson sniffed, tears now flowing down his cheeks. Then he gulped. 'But you're right. No more suffering.'

Wilson held his arms out and then swallow-dived

forwards, screaming. As he swung towards her, Savage made a grab for his legs, but he smashed into her as he pendulumed across the space and then bounced off the wall, swinging back into the centre of the hall. Savage's fall was broken by a pillar at the bottom of the banisters and her head smashed against the hard oak. She tumbled onto her back and saw the rope snap taut. The chandelier shuddered and pieces of plaster fell from the ceiling. The wooden rail on the landing creaked as Wilson's full weight came on it.

'Heeelllppp!' Wilson's hands scrabbled to grasp the rope above his head and he tried to pull up to relieve the pressure on his neck.

Savage rolled over, moving her body out the way as his legs flailed in mid-air. She watched mesmerised as Wilson struggled, his face becoming redder, his eyes bulging.

'Urrrgggghhheeelllppp!'

Wilson was a serial murderer, Savage thought as he swung back again. Now he'd tried to kill himself but had chickened out at the very last moment.

'Ma'am!' A voice from somewhere, buzzing like an angry wasp. 'What's going on?'

'Puuurrrllleeeuuurrrgggheeelllppp!'

That was three times he'd swung back and forth. Savage touched her head, feeling blood on her scalp. She blinked, a woozy feeling, her head full of cotton wool. She tried to get up.

'We're on our way. Hang on!' Savage swatted at the annoying thing in her ear, pulled the creature out. She shook her head, spat. Saw Wilson pass through her centre of vision once again.

Four.

Her hand slipped away from under her. She didn't have the strength to get up.

'Bllluuurrr . . .'

328

Five.

Or was it the will?

'Uuurrr. . .'

Wilson's neck had extended and his feet just brushed the floor, slowing the swing.

'Ug-gug-gug . . . Gug. Gug. Gug.'

Six.

Outside a car's engine roared and stopped. Doors opened and closed. Feet ran across gravel.

Seven.

The body hung straight down now, hardly moving at all. The door opened a fraction, coming up against the safety chain.

'Ma'am!' Riley crashed through the door, wood splintering as the chain wrenched free, Enders bounding in just behind. The two of them rushed across to Wilson, Riley trying to hoist the comatose form to take the strain off the rope. Enders took the stairs two at a time and then went to work on the knot on the banister rail.

'Get a bloody move on, Patrick!' Riley said as he struggled to balance with the full weight of Wilson's body. 'Ma'am, help me!'

Savage pushed herself into a sitting position, tried to get up, but then Riley was collapsing under the weight of Wilson's body as Enders released the rope. The two of them came tumbling over, Riley doing his best to cushion Wilson's fall as the rope hissed down around them.

Wilson lay on his side facing Savage, his eyes half-popped out of his skull, the pupils dilating and contracting in minute little jumps, the dark black appearing to focus on her.

'You alright, ma'am?' Enders. Sitting on the bottom step and putting both arms out to help her sit up. 'You look like you got knocked out cold or something.'

'I guess I did,' Savage said, turning away from Wilson's body and shaking her head. 'But I'm fine now.'

'First bit of good news we've had in days, hey, Charlotte?' Hardin said as he climbed out of his car. He slammed the door, banged the roof with a fist and then looked over to Wilson's house. 'With the good doctor out the way the burden of proof just changed. We've solved the Corran murder and cleared up a notorious cold case in one.'

'But Wilson didn't kill Paula Rowland,' Savage said. 'Somebody else did.'

'I know you keep saying that, but Wilson *did* kill those other girls. His suicide proves it. There's something not right about the Manchester alibi. We need to come up with a theory which puts him in the frame.'

'In the frame? You mean stitch him up?' Savage shook her head. 'I don't see how.'

'This suicide note, as good as a confession from what I hear?'

It wasn't until after Wilson's body had been taken away, the paramedics giving up after half an hour of CPR, that Savage had found the envelope stuffed in her jacket pocket. Three pages summing up Wilson's life and his reason for carrying out the killings. He'd claimed he'd been adopted as a baby, his new father a wife-beater and in the end a murderer. Aged six when it happened, Wilson had then been placed with various foster families. It was only many years later that he discovered he'd been adopted in the first place and decided his birth mother was to blame for everything.

'And he killed her?' Hardin said. 'Lara Bailey?'

'So he said. At the time we thought she was just a tom getting on the wrong side of a client.'

'And then the next year he kills Mandy Glastone?'

'Yes. Wilson didn't bury her at the farm. Either because he hadn't thought of the idea or because Joanne Black was living in a caravan where the bungalow was. The following two years though he was able to do as he pleased.'

'So why the change from personal retribution against his mother to some sort of sick social engineering?'

'No idea. Maybe he got a taste for killing. The gap between the Heidi Luckmann and Katherine Mallory murders is easier to understand. Wilson was in the US. When he came back the killings resumed. But there's a problem: Paula Rowland. Wilson's confession doesn't wipe out his alibi.'

'Charlotte!' Hardin wagged a finger. 'We've got him. We just need to do the legwork to tie everything up.'

Hardin came round the car and approached the front door. A photographer was kneeling in one corner of the hall, trying to get the whole of the vertical fall of the rope in shot. The parquet flooring was a mess, the contents of the plastic boxes scattered across it. Hardin looked up at the rope, down at the rubbish and then across at Savage.

'You do realise this is the second time someone has died when you were supposed to be taking them into custody?'

'Sir, Wilson killed himself. I can hardly be blamed for his death.'

'Before I left the station I received an email from Professional Standards. Your old friend Assistant Chief Commissioner Maria Heldon. *Hatchet* Heldon.' Hardin paused. Let the words sink in. 'She's keen to get to the bottom of this. You're to have a report on my desk first thing.'

Savage opened her mouth to say something but Hardin strode inside the house, waving her protest away.

'First thing, Charlotte. And break the bloody Manchester alibi, OK?'

Savage turned and trudged back to her car, wondering if

the DSupt would like her to end world hunger while she was at it.

'Go home,' DCI Garrett said to Savage, when he found her slumped over a pad trying to write up the events of the afternoon. 'You look all-in.'

She was.

The rollercoaster ride of the last few days had taken it out of her; Wilson's dramatic suicide the final downward swoop.

Back home, Pete and Stefan sat in front of the TV in the living room. Not football though. Not tonight. The screen showed the continuing coverage of the case and there, cut in amongst a montage of images, was a picture of Savage standing in the driveway of Wilson's house as a body bag came out on a gurney.

Pete rose from the sofa and was hugging her even as she felt all the strength go from her legs.

'Well done,' he whispered to her as he placed his face in her hair. 'You did it.'

'Not just me,' Savage said. 'The whole team.'

'I'm off,' Stefan said, standing and making excuses about needing an early night.

Alone with her husband, Savage collapsed on the sofa. Pete flicked the TV off.

'All-in,' she said, repeating Garrett's words because they were the only ones which came to her. 'The last few days . . .'

'Shush,' Pete said. 'I'll run you a bath and then get something together for a late dinner. Jamie's asleep, but Samantha's still awake, she's only just gone to bed. Why don't you pop up and see her?'

Savage nodded, hugged Pete for a moment, and then struggled to her feet.

'Dad said you got him, Mum,' Samantha said, closing her

book and sitting up in bed as Savage entered her room. 'That he died resisting arrest.'

'Yes, he won't be hurting anyone ever again.'

'I'm glad he's dead, Mum. Is that wrong?'

'No, sweetheart. It's not wrong.' Savage went over and knelt by the bed. Put her hand out and touched her daughter on the cheek. 'Don't ever feel guilty for wanting to prevent someone from doing evil.'

'It's what you do, isn't it? Stop the bad guys from doing bad things?'

'Simply put, yes. But it doesn't always work that way.'

'It does, Mum, as long as you're out there.' Samantha handed Savage the book and wriggled down under the duvet. Then she smiled. 'And if you need a little help you can always ask Dad to open up with his cannons, right?'

Samantha reached for the little black and white dog she'd had since she was a baby and snuggled it under her chin. Savage leant across and kissed her and then pulled the duvet up a little. Samantha closed her eyes and Savage turned off the bedside light. At the door she stopped and looked back at her daughter. Security was something you took for granted when you were a child. No question in Samantha's mind that Mum and Dad would keep her safe. That Mummy would always manage to catch the bad guys.

Savage turned away. Hoped her daughter's faith in her was justified.

Chapter Thirty-Six

He's dead then. You saw it on the TV while you were in Currys checking out dishwashers. When they cut to his house the chill started to rise, washing up from your legs and engulfing your whole body. The reporter said his name and it was like your insides were being sucked out of you. Blind panic. You tried to walk away but Peter's face was on every television, a wall of hell stretching halfway down the shop.

All those wires. Peter in there somehow. Swirling around and mixed up with the dead girls.

'Off,' you shouted. 'Turn them bloody off!'

'Excuse me, sir,' a nearby sales assistant said. Spots, nylon shirt, hair sticky with gel. 'What size screen are you interested in?'

You punched the sales assistant in the face and ran.

Back at the farm and you're scared. You, singular. Before, 'you' always meant the two of you. You shared everything, shared the pain and misery. Shared the joyous moments too. The two of you thought the same, almost like telepathy or something magical. Maybe something demonic. If Peter felt hungry you did too. If he got a hard-on looking at a girl, you'd feel yourself stiffen as well. Duality. We think therefore we kill. But no longer.

You cast your mind back to the store.

Peter on the news. An old picture and then the shots of him talking to camera about the Candle Cake Killer. Footage of him after he'd been released from the arrest. On screen Peter looked grey, ill. It is hard to see him like that. And of course now he's even greyer.

Who's going to look after you now? Who is going to keep you on the straight and narrow? Peter always said everything would be alright, would turn out OK. It didn't for him, and it didn't for your mother and father. The Big Knife up to its handle for her, a length of electrical cord tied to the top bunk in his cell for him. Strange how Peter decided to re-enact your father's death.

You go to the window and stare out, hoping against hope the whole thing is a dream and Peter's car will come driving up the track. But no, there's just Mikey out there, kicking a ball around the yard. Black and white plastic from the pound shop. Rain or shine, he'll play out there until you tell him to come in. One quid goes a long way with Mikey.

Mikey can't help you though. In fact he'll only make matters worse, encouraging you, spurring you on. With Peter around the horror was restricted to just the one day a year and you always did as he instructed. Waited until he said. Waited for the Special Day. Even when Peter went away to the States you waited. All those years, Peter on the phone several times a week, that voice in your ear. The constant nagging – yes – but love too.

'Won't be long, Ronald. I'll be back soon. Until then you must promise me you'll be good. Can you do that?'

'Yes, Peter, I can.'

Mikey scores a goal between two upturned buckets and rushes to the corner of the yard, fist raised in triumph to the home fans. Wayne Rooney. With issues.

You and Mikey, could it work?

Peter was methodical, could weigh the options, make the

correct choices. You're a bit more spontaneous and Mikey . . .?
Mikey is fucking crazy. Still . . .

That last one. Paula. The way she squirmed and squealed
and bled. The more uncomfortable she became, the happier
you were. She made things better.

For a while.

Peter's pleasure was different from yours though. It came
from the anticipation, as much part of the fun as the actual
event. Deferring gratification gave him control, made him the
one in charge. Him, not the joker up above, not a butterfly
flapping its wings half a world away, not a piece of his brain
gone sour. Every day without a killing proved it. Which was
why he enjoyed the waiting. Even for the five years he was
away. But now Peter's killed himself to protect you and Mikey.
He's history, gone, dead. No longer telling you what to do. And
his death has fuelled the anger building inside. You don't want
to wait for release. And why should you?

Mikey's taking a break now. He's turned one of the buckets
the right way up. His trousers and Y-fronts are round his ankles
and he is pissing in the bucket, chuckling at some joke only he
would understand. Then you see the ball is in the bucket and
he is pissing on that, spray splashing out, Mikey howling with
laughter.

You should go out there and tell him off. Reinforce good
behaviour and punish bad. Otherwise actions can become
habits. And habits are hard to break.

Paula. Lovely. Nice. Fucking her felt good. Killing her, even
better.

There's a list with names on, addresses, phone numbers,
birth dates. Peter kept it locked in a drawer in the sideboard
beneath the Big Knife. Came out only when he said. A month
or so ago he showed you the sheet and pointed to Paula's name,
told you to memorise the information and then he put the

336

paper back in the drawer. Locked it. You're thinking you ought to go and crack the drawer open. Take a look at the list. Maybe have a word with Mikey and see what he thinks of your idea.

Then again, as you watch Mikey lift the ball from the bucket and give it first a sniff and then a lick, rational thinking has never been one of the boy's strong points.

Chapter Thirty-Seven

'I've got some good news and some bad news,' Davies said as he approached Riley in the canteen mid-morning Tuesday. 'Which do you want first?'

Riley took a swig of his coffee and considered his doughnut.

'Bad.'

'You're off the Corran case, back on Maynard's sheep-shagging investigation. Ding dong. *Cowbell.*'

'What!' Riley's raised voice caused a few people to turn in their direction. 'Don't wind me up, boss. Say it's not true.'

''fraid so. Maynard says he needs you. You've got all the background. Besides he reckons you've done so much hard work on the case it's only fair you should be there at the kill.'

'I don't *want* to be there at the kill. The thought of even one more hour out there in that bloody ditch . . .'

'Tough.' Davies eyed Riley's doughnut and chuckled. 'Personally I think Maynard appreciates your love of ornithology. I wouldn't be surprised if he lets you play with his scope.'

338

'What about Corran?' Riley ignored the joke. Right now he wasn't in the mood for laughing.

'Corran's going to be bundled up with the Wilson stuff. There's no rush now he's dead. Just a matter of squaring all the information for Corran's inquest. Everything's going to be coming under the auspices of *Radial*. We've just got to tidy our paperwork and hand the lot over to Hardin.'

'Fuck.' Riley tore a sachet of sugar open and stirred it into his coffee. 'What about the good news, you said you had some?'

'Yeah, that's right.' Davies reached for the doughnut and grinned. 'It's good news for you, for me . . . well it fucking stinks.'

'Go on.'

Davies bit down on the doughnut and mumbled through a trickle of jam. Wiped his mouth. Looked serious for a moment.

'Maynard's insisted on me coming back too.'

The report was on Hardin's desk first thing, the ink hardly dry before the DSupt was ringing through to tell her the document looked fine but there appeared to be some discrepancy with the timing. Wilson had only been swinging for seconds surely? No need to lie, he said, just make sure we get this right the first time. They could escape a full complaints commission inquiry if everything panned out.

Savage made the amendments, fired through a new version and then went to the crime suite.

Monday had not only seen Layton produce the bullet evidence, he'd also received two results from the lab. One, Paula Rowland had been in the boot of Wilson's SUV. Layton reckoned the girl had been wrapped in something but it hadn't been enough to prevent some droplets of blood staining the carpet on the left-hand side of the rear space. Two, they had a DNA match from semen obtained at the woman's post-mortem. The match was for Dr Wilson.

Which left the Manchester alibi. Cracking it was imperative.

'Sounds like some airport novel, ma'am,' Enders said as she briefed the team. 'Cheap thrills in the grim North. Talking of airports, a helicopter is the only way I can see he can have done the crime if the alibi holds.'

They batted ideas back and forth, one of the dafter ones being the psychologist conducting some sort of mass hypnosis on the people he'd met. Savage also dispatched two detectives to drive up to Manchester to double check the sort of journey times possible. Enders was on to UK air traffic control, checking flight plans for helicopters.

That done, the rest of the team began the difficult work of tying up the historical murders. Statements from half a dozen years ago needed to be checked, people re-interviewed, the new evidence evaluated alongside the old.

The new evidence included information provided that morning by an anonymous female caller to the incident hotline. Calter recounted the woman's story.

'It happened about eight years ago, ma'am,' the DC said. 'The woman says Dr Wilson stalked her. He became obsessed. They'd met at an event at the uni – a Christmas party – and subsequently gone on a date. She says she was flattered at first and bowled over by the psychologist's attentions. But then things turned darker, Wilson proposing marriage within days of their first night out.'

'Creepy,' Savage said. 'And it fits with the harassment claim made against Wilson. He certainly wouldn't take "no" for an answer when I was on the moor with him.'

'Yeah,' Calter said. 'The woman told me she hadn't liked

him that much. There was something not quite right about his eyes and his mannerisms. Besides there'd been someone else, so she spurned his affections. Five months later a chance encounter led to Wilson trying again and this time she flat-out rejected him. Apparently he got angry and flew into a rage. Professed undying love for the woman. There followed a string of abusive texts but eventually they stopped and he left her alone.'

'So if the first incident was around Christmas, five months would take us to May or June.' Savage looked across at the whiteboard where Gareth Collier was busy with a marker pen. Photographs of the victims had been incorporated into a timeline on one side of the board. 'Wilson had killed Lara Bailey – his birth mother – in the June of the previous year, now we find Mandy Glastone went missing the following June, not long after he'd been rejected.'

'So that was the trigger which caused him to start killing.' Calter followed Savage's gaze to photographs. 'She was to blame?'

'Of course not!' Savage shook her head. 'You know my philosophy: criminals make a choice when they commit a crime. In this case Wilson made his choice after being rejected again. Perhaps in his twisted mind he blamed his inadequacies where relationships were concerned on Lara Bailey, which led to his decision to enact some kind of vengeance on all women who'd given up children. Losing his new mother aged six must have been a shock, but no excuse.'

'Allegedly losing her.'

'Yes, for now we only have Wilson's suicide note as evidence. It could be complete fiction. His story is another part of the jigsaw we need to try to fit together.'

Collier, on cue, turned from the whiteboard. The office manager was in his element now. With the killer caught, he could concentrate on the painstaking work to bring the case to a close.

'You're right, ma'am,' he said. 'A jigsaw. We'll start by trying to validate Wilson's story about his birth mother and his new parents,' he said. 'The rest is nothing more than a giant equation. X plus Y equals Wilson. We'll get there in the end as long as the batteries in the calculator last.'

By calculator Collier meant the team. Shorn of the thrill of the chase, the monotonous work which the office manager enjoyed might well get the rest of them down. They'd be flagging in the summer heat as they trudged door to door, from witness to witness.

A couple of hours later and Collier was standing at the door to Savage's office, shaking his head, looking a little flustered himself.

'Got two problems,' he said. 'One minor, one off the bloody scale. Which do you want first?'

'Let's start small,' Savage said. 'And work up.'

'OK, first, we have the motive with the adoption thing, but we don't have any idea how Wilson was able to find these women. It's possible my equation can't be solved without the answer.'

'And nothing fresh has turned up at Wilson's house?'

'Not so far.'

'He wasn't into computers. Not like Glastone. I doubt he could have managed to access the information he needed online.'

'Some other way then. I'll leave that to you.'

'Sure. Number two?'

'Number two, yes.' Collier paused, bit his lip before continuing. 'I've been going over this Manchester trip with some of the team. I don't think we're going to crack it.'

'Not good, Gareth.'

'No. Nothing doing on the alibi, so I decided to check Wilson's movements for the killing a year ago and for the historical murders. It actually wasn't that difficult. He's attached to the university and there's a list of papers and conferences on the staff page about him going way back. For every one of the historical killings Wilson was away at a conference. For last year's – Katherine Mallory – he was in Rome. He didn't arrive back in the UK until the day after she went missing.'

'Shit,' Savage said.

'Yes.' Collier reached up and ran his hand across the top of his head. 'I don't care what the DSupt says, we ain't breaking that one.'

It was late Tuesday afternoon before Riley had a chance to head out on his own again. 'Over Okehampton way' Hegg had said. Tim Hamilton's place turned out to be about five miles south of the town and a mile off the A386. A narrow lane twisted through a dense copse and ended at a ramshackle house with a corrugated iron workshop to one side. A number of cars in various states of repair lay around a yard. From inside the workshop there was banging and the whine of an angle grinder. To Riley, Hamilton's business looked suspiciously like a cut and shut outfit. Cars which had been written off in front and rear end smashes would be bought cheaply and cobbled together to form a new vehicle.

Riley got out of his car and went across to the entrance to the workshop. Somebody was underneath a Ford Mondeo which stood over an inspection pit. A grinder showered sparks from beneath the car. Riley banged on the metal workshop door and the grinding ceased. A figure moved down in the pit and a face grubby with grease poked out from behind the rear wheel.

'Tim Hamilton?' Riley said, showing his warrant card. 'DS Riley.'

Hamilton shook his head and disappeared for a moment, reappearing at the front of the vehicle as he clambered from the pit. Hamilton wore a blue boiler suit, black in places with oil stains. He was thirty-something, but running to fat, the poppers on the suit open at the waist. He had a large wrench in his right hand.

'What now?' he said. 'I've got all the paperwork, everything's legal.'

'I'm sure it is, Mr Hamilton, but I'm not interested in your Build-A-Car workshop.'

'What then?' Hamilton wiped his hands on his boiler suit. 'Cos that's all I do.'

'Four years ago you repaired a blue Subaru Impreza. It would have had some minor damage to the nearside front. The damage could probably have been repaired without replacing the panel, but the owner would have been insistent. They wanted a complete new front wing.'

'Four years ago? Are you having a laugh? I can't remember repairs going back that long ago.'

'What about your records, invoices, bank statements, that kind of thing?'

'All cash in this business, mate. I tot the money up at the end of the week and give the lot to my missus.'

'Come on, Mr Hamilton. I know it was a while ago, but this was a rush job on a sporty car. Probably better than the usual jalopies you get in here. You remember – and if you don't, then I reckon I'm going to have to call a search team in here.'

Riley pulled his mobile out and made as if to walk back outside.

'Shit.' Hamilton tapped the wrench against his leg. 'You got me.'

344

'A name. That's all I'm after. No one's going to find out who told me.'

'No name, the lad didn't give one. Look, what's this guy done? Hit and run? Bank job? Some other shit?'

'You give me something,' Riley said. 'And then I walk away. No more questions.'

Hamilton turned and walked over to a bench at the side of the workshop. He clumped the wrench down.

'Yeah?' he said. Riley nodded. Hamilton sighed and then went over to the side of the workshop where a long beam supporting the wall held rows of battered number plates stacked several deep. 'Extensive front end damage. New grille, new front index too, so I made him one up. The old plate is here somewhere.'

'You kept it?'

'Sure.' Hamilton glanced across at Riley. 'Let's just say it was insurance.'

'And why would you need that?'

'Pays to be careful in this business.' Hamilton flicked a couple of plates forward. Replaced them. Moved along. 'Here.'

He pulled a plate out from behind several others and walked across to the bench. The plate clattered onto the surface next to a notepad and pen. Hamilton left it there and went back to the front of the car. He climbed down into the pit.

'I didn't *tell* you anything.' Hamilton's voice floated out from underneath the car. 'Never *said* a word. Understand?'

'Sure.'

Riley walked over to the bench and wrote down the letters and numbers. Ripped the sheet from the pad and walked out of the garage as the sound of the grinder started up again. Sparks flying, metal on metal, Riley thinking of the

345

damage the front of an Impreza would cause as it smashed into a child on a bike.

Lucy Hale didn't know much about cars. You pressed your foot down on the accelerator pedal and pointed one end where you wanted to go. At the other end was a hole you glugged petrol into once a week, giving up a sizeable proportion of your income so you could enjoy the freedom of the road. Assuming you weren't stuck in traffic.

Plymouth's convoluted road system functioned OK when the council weren't messing with its layout. Unfortunately that wasn't very often and the city always seemed to be choked with traffic. Right now though she'd be thankful to be stuck in a jam rather than sitting in her stationary car up here on Dartmoor. In front of her the tarmac curled to the horizon, not another vehicle or person to be seen. To the west the light faded behind a rocky ridge sending huge shadows creeping across the open moor. Night was coming and the cosy pub in Tavistock where earlier she'd dined with a friend seemed just a memory. Now she was beginning to regret having gone out that evening, beginning to regret having taken the route home across the moor.

Lucy got out and kicked the flat tyre. Wasn't sure why, just that's what people did. Somewhere in the boot the spare sat beneath layers of carpet. She supposed there'd be a toolkit and jack in there too.

Sod that.

She pulled out her phone and at the same time extracted a slim card from a pocket on her bag. She squinted at the card and thumbed in the number.

Thank God for breakdown cover.

Ten minutes later she wasn't feeling so pleased. 'Going to be a couple of hours at least' the man on the end of the line had said. Lucy had protested, saying she was a single woman, that it would be long dark by the time the tow truck arrived. 'It's where you are,' the voice said. 'Dartmoor. Not much cover. Plus we're very busy around Plymouth. I'll do my best.'

Typical. So much for the Knights of the bloody Road.

Lucy chucked the phone in through the open window of the car. Stared at where a bank of dark cloud tumbled in over the top of a tor. Nothing now but the hilltop and close by, a herd of ponies. Nothing but heather, rock and the road wending its way through inky shadows, just before the tor the road dividing and the left fork diving into a patch of glowing white which looked like snow.

Not snow, clay.

Lucy knew that the clay pits were on the edge of the moor so the road must be a shortcut towards the city. Half a mile to the fork, a couple of miles down off the moor, and she'd be in civilisation. The tyre might be shredded and the rim of the wheel ruined, but it was a small price to pay.

The car juddered along, a slight rocking motion the only sign something was amiss, until a mile or so later a clanging started up. A little after that came a bang and the steering wrenched to the left, pulling the car off the road.

Damn.

Lucy turned off the engine and got out, this time resisting the temptation to kick the wheel, now devoid of tyre and cracked across the middle. Leaning for a moment on the bonnet of the car she realised how dark it had become. The headlights sliced down the road, picking out a stone wall and a gated lane to some farm or other. In all other directions the night closed in, the shapes of nearby trees silhouetted against a blue-black sky, a few twinkling stars fighting the thickening cloud.

And then there was the wind.

A faint ticking came from under the bonnet as the engine cooled but the noise was all but drowned out by a shushing as gusts swept through the trees, their branches writhing in the air like demented arms on some giant demon. Throughout the day the wind had been building, a summer storm, the forecast promising gales and a deluge.

Pitter-patter, pitter-patter.

Oh great.

Lucy glanced up to where the stars had been only moments before. Nothing but black now. Black and water.

Sod it.

Lucy grabbed her bag and phone and slammed the door shut. What was the distance to the nearest village? A mile or two at the most? She set off, following the wall and every so often using her phone as a makeshift torch. At the gate to the farm she thought about seeing if anyone was in, but the lane led round a corner into some old quarry or pit and something about it felt a bit creepy. As if wind and rain and what seemed like almost total darkness wasn't bad enough.

Five minutes later and she could see lights down in the valley. Far in the distance, true, but comforting nevertheless. Then there were some other lights – headlights – a car coming towards her. The beams dazzled and she raised her arms to shield her eyes. The vehicle coasted to a stop a few car-lengths before it reached her. Not a car, rather a beat-up tow truck. A door opened and slammed, someone standing in the white glare.

'You got trouble, girl? Only we'd be only too pleased to help.'

We? Lucy could only see one person. But then the other door of the car opened and somebody else climbed down and slouched into the light too.

Lucy stepped backwards and slipped into the shadow at the side of the road, feeling her feet sink into mud. The two guys didn't seem right, didn't seem . . . *normal*. The second one had a head that lolled to one side, a mass of scraggy brown hair like wire atop a round face, nose all squashed up, the eyes an afterthought, mere dark slits painted on with a flick of a brush. The first one spoke again as she squelched away from them along the ditch.

'You want to be careful. It's not safe out here in the dark. All kinds of things can happen. Isn't that right, Mikey?'

'Guuurrll!' the other man said, jumping up and down in the light. 'Get guuurrlll!'

Lucy tried to pick up her feet to move faster, but the gloop sucked at her shoes. She smacked her foot into something and then she was falling over, sploshing down in the mud, her hands scrabbling for her phone as it sank into the water, the pale light from the screen glowing for a second before it went out.

'Now then,' the voice whispered close in the darkness, somewhere a few feet away. 'You don't need to mind Mikey, he only wants to be friends.'

Chapter Thirty-Eight

The girl is safe in the pumphouse round the back. She's been shouting her head off, but now she's quiet. Worked out there's nobody to hear her.

You've given Mikey some dinner and to calm him down you popped a couple of Molipaxins in there, mixed up with the sausage, beans and mash. The tablets haven't sent him to sleep but he's no longer pestering you about the girl. He's slouched on the sofa with a magazine. Junior sudoku. He's not clever, Mikey, but he recognises patterns, the way the numbers fit in the grid. Likes solving puzzles. Finding the answers. Like Peter. Only Peter never got any answers.

Mikey fills in a square and then bites the end of his pencil and chuckles.

Nothing much to laugh at you think, considering the seriousness of the situation. Peter wouldn't like this. Going against the usual way of things, getting all out of control. He always was a restraining influence. A hand on your shoulder, a friendly word of advice. You guess he kept you sane. Safe. Secure.

But where's Peter now?

Not here, is he? Not here to hold your hand or smack you down or make you look stupid. Not calling you up to tell you what to do. He's not watching now. The only person watching is Mikey, and the way he keeps looking up at you and grinning you reckon he's thinking along the same lines.

The girl.

It's only been a few days since the last one. Peter would say you should wait because there's no Special Day. No symmetry, no rhyme or reason to it. But hey, who came up with the idea of the Special Day anyway? Peter, wasn't it? And . . .

Fuck him! Who says you can only have one Special Day a year? Why not have one a month or even one a week?

Which is why you went into town looking for Hazel Tredfel – the next girl on the list. You located her house in Ernsettle, found she had two fat Staffies in the garden and a husband at least as fierce and twice as ugly.

'Discretion,' you said to Mikey, 'is the better part of valour.'

Mikey had looked at you, not understanding what you were talking about but reading the expression on your face. You'd driven off thinking you would need to get another name from Peter's little book.

'G . . . g . . . guuurrrlll!' Mikey pointed through the windscreen as you neared the turning to the farm.

For a second, your hand on the door handle, you wondered if you should just let the chance pass by. She was simply a woman by the side of the road. Probably done nothing wrong. Probably innocent.

Probably.

What the hell, you thought. Just this once.

She tried to run but there were two of you and the silly shoes she was wearing didn't help her much. You wondered why women insist on wearing such things. Might as well wear leg irons. You plucked her from where she lay in a ditch and shoved her in the pickup next to Mikey.

Scream, scream, scream. But with the wipers swishing and Mikey singing and the rattle from the old exhaust roaring out *it wasn't too bad. Anyway you were home in five, the girl locked away in the little stone pumphouse in ten, the sausages sizzling in the pan in fifteen.*

'Mikey,' you say, smiling at him as he fills in another square and looks up. 'We did it!'

And all without a smidgen of help from Peter, you think. Oh-so-clever Peter who right now is stuck in a drawer at the morgue, getting all cold and wondering what good a Ph fucking D is.

'Play, play, play!' Mikey has put the magazine down now. 'Play, play, play! Play with guuurrrlll!'

Outside the rain is teeming down, it's close to midnight, and you've done none of the usual preparation. Really you want to wait until tomorrow to get started. Mikey's got other ideas though.

'Guuurrrlll!'

Shit, you think, seems like the bloody pills must be wearing off already. You should have given him more than two. You ease yourself out of the chair and move towards the kitchen, wondering whether there might be a tin of apricots and some instant custard in the back of the pantry.

'Mikey?' you say, reaching in your pocket for the packet of Molis. 'Fancy a pudding?'

352

Chapter Thirty-Nine

Crownhill Police Station, Plymouth. Wednesday 2nd July.
8.55 a.m.

'DI Savage?' The voice came from behind as Savage got out of her car at Crownhill. A hint of familiarity about the accent. She turned round.

Dan Phillips. The *Herald*'s crime reporter.

'Dan. As always, a pleasure,' Savage said.

'How's the investigation going?'

'You were at the press conference, Dan. You know all there is. Dr Peter Wilson is dead and at this moment in time we're not looking for anybody else concerning the murders.'

'So you reckon you've nailed him, do you? Wrapped up the case?'

'Enquiries are continuing. Tying up the threads will be a long process.'

'No more missing persons then? Everyone's safe now and we can go back to having our barbecues outside?'

'I told you, enquiries are continuing. That's all I can say. Now I'm sorry to be rude but—'

Phillips held up his hand and Savage thought he was apologising. Then she noticed the white envelope held between his thumb and forefinger.

'Take a look,' Phillips said. 'Something for you to consider.'

'You're not trying to pull a fast one, are you?' Savage said, looking over Phillips's shoulder for one of the *Herald*'s lensmen. 'Get a shot of me acting dodgy accepting suspicious packages?'

'You know me better than that, Charlotte. Now, do you want to take a look or not?'

'The problem is I *do* know you better than that.' Savage paused for a moment and then closed the car door. 'Show me then.'

Phillips lifted the flap on the envelope and pulled out a photograph of a young woman. Late twenties, blonde hair in a bob like DC Calter's.

'What's this?' Savage said, cocking her head on one side. 'Some kind of prank?'

'Not from me, Charlotte. The girl in the picture has been missing since last night. The parents reported it but apparently now the killer's been caught mispers are back to their usual low priority. Nothing doing for twenty-four hours at least. Which was why the parents came to me.' Phillips tapped the picture with his free hand. 'Pretty, isn't she? We're putting her on the front page.'

'And what makes you think this could possibly have anything to do with the Candle Cake Killer?'

'Contacts.' Phillips moved his finger from the picture and brought it up to his nose. Tapped again. 'I hear there's a problem with some alibis concerning Dr Wilson.'

'If you print anything about—'

'Look, I want to help. That stunt I pulled the other day with Graham Bunce was childish. I'm trying to make amends.' Phillips smiled. 'Got to keep in your good books, haven't I?'

'OK, Dan. Thanks.' Savage took the photograph from Phillips. 'What's her name?'

'And?' Hardin said ten minutes later when Savage went to his office to brief him on the latest development.

Savage slid a printout across the desk to Hardin and then recited the details from memory.

'Lucy Hale. Twenty-nine. She lives in Ivybridge. Yesterday afternoon she drove to a pub in Tavistock to have a meal with a friend. According to the friend she left some time after nine p.m. She had an early start the next day and didn't want to be up late. She said she'd call in at her mum and dad's when she got back to Ivybridge.'

'So? She probably forgot.'

'No. She was calling in to collect her younger sister who lives at home. The sister was going to stay over at Lucy's place as the two of them were driving up to Bristol today to do some shopping. And then there's her car. I've just had a report that it's been discovered parked near Burrator Reservoir.'

'Suicide?' Hardin put his hands face up, expectant. 'Events would be no less tragic but it would be better for us if she'd topped herself. Maybe she took a handful of pills and went for a midnight swim in the lake. Worth thinking about.'

'I'll bear it in mind,' Savage said, wondering if it wasn't Hardin who'd taken some pills. 'I'm off up there now to see what Layton can come up with.'

She beat Layton to the scene. But only by seconds. As she pulled off the road and parked behind a patrol car at the south-east end of the reservoir, she saw the CSI's Volvo looming in her rear-view mirror.

'Had to happen sooner or later,' he shouted across to her as he got out. 'But think of it as the exception which proves the rule.'

The smart Golf lay off the road, parked in a mass of bracken. The offside front tyre had shredded, the alloy wheel all dented and split down the middle. Part of the bumper had been squished and the plastic had cracked.

'Boy racers?' Savage said as she stood back and let Layton get in close.

'Well they didn't race it here,' Layton said, pointing first at the front wheel and then the back. 'Look at the ground.'

Savage saw a deep rut caused by the rear wheel, but the front, which was more like the disc from a harrow, had made no impression.

'How then?'

'Towed.' Layton pointed to some more ruts which ran from the front of the car and curved back onto the road. 'The front of the vehicle must have been hoisted off the ground for the journey and then they dropped it off here.'

'You mean towed as in a recovery vehicle?'

'Yes, but not a pro job.' Layton was on his hands and knees now. He examined the front bumper. 'They simply attached a hook under the car and lifted it up. Didn't bother about what happened to the bodywork. You wouldn't do that if you were trying to recover the vehicle.'

'So she had some kind of accident and whoever bumped her brought the car here. A sort of hit and tow?'

'Nope.' Layton smiled. 'Where's the damage to the car? As far as I can see the only problem is the tyre. The damage at the front was caused by the tow chain or rope.'

'It doesn't make sense.'

'Unless all you want to do is get rid of the car.'

Layton stood and then moved to the side. He pressed his

face close to the driver's window and peered in. Then he moved to the rear of the car.

'No parcel shelf, so nothing concealed in the boot. No handbag or clothing. No sign of any blood. All windows intact.'

'So if she was attacked she either knew her attacker or she wasn't in the car.'

'That's it, Charlotte,' Layton said, moving back to the front wheel. 'She wasn't in the car because she got a puncture. She must have driven on with it deflated until the tyre destroyed itself and the wheel fractured. We'll never be able to tell if that's what actually happened though, not from the remains of the tyre.'

'But they will.' Savage pointed to an orange sticker in the front window. 'RAC. If she rang them then there'll be a record. Especially if when the recovery vehicle turned up she wasn't where she said she'd be.'

Savage called through to the station to get someone to chase the RAC while Layton examined the rest of the car externally. He explained that by not opening the doors they'd have a better chance of preserving anything important inside. Then he got on his own phone and Savage could hear him summoning officers for a fingertip search.

By the time Layton had finished his call Savage had confirmation from the RAC.

'They received a call at nine forty-seven last night from Lucy Hale,' Savage said. 'She'd got a puncture somewhere near Cadover Bridge. Whatever, from the state of the rim she didn't stay put.'

'So she was on the back road to Ivybridge then?'

'Yup. The patrolman came from Yelverton way around half past ten, he passed Cadover Bridge and drove on all the way to Cornwood. Another five miles. Then he doubled back for a second look. Nothing doing, so he called in and said he couldn't find the vehicle. Apparently that's pretty common. People solve their problem and don't bother to call back. The dispatcher tried to ring Lucy's phone but it was switched off.'

'I think we need to look at the RAC van,' Layton said.

'You don't think the mechanic could be involved?'

'Simply a matter of eliminating him. Anyway you'll need to get the exact route he drove, times and things.'

'And once he's eliminated?'

'Square one,' Layton said. 'Back to.'

By the time Hardin arrived at Burrator Reservoir a media scrum had assembled behind the cordon of blue and white tape. Savage ducked under the tape and went across to the DSupt intending to brief him on Layton's findings.

'Superintendent Hardin,' a BBC reporter asked as Hardin got out of his car. 'Do you believe the Candle Cake Killer is still at large?'

'No comment,' Hardin said as he began to stroll down the road alongside Savage.

'Can you assure the women of Devon they are safe?' ITN.

'No comment.'

'There's a girl missing, isn't there?' *The Times.*

'No comment.'

'The Candle Cake Killer has her, doesn't he?' CNN.

'No com—' Hardin stopped. Resisted the tug on his arm from Savage. Turned around to face the pack. 'No he bloody well doesn't! We have a missing person. Usually it's all we can do to get you lot even vaguely interested, but because you want the killings to continue you're sniffing around like the gutter rats you are. If you'd only behave like human beings and show some compassion to the family then perhaps we can bring this to a satisfactory conclusion.'

'Are you looking for a body?' Sky News.

'Jesus Christ!' Hardin turned to pick out the voice. Moved towards the man and raised a fist.

'Sir?' Savage said, gesturing towards the cordon.

Hardin seemed in two minds for a moment, but then he lifted the tape, ducked under and strode across to John Layton. Layton was watching as Lucy Hale's Golf was being winched onto the back of a flatbed truck. Nearby, CSIs continued to work on the soft verges, taking photographs and measuring impressions in the grass and mud.

'This,' Hardin said to Layton as he approached, 'had better be nothing to do with the Candle Cake Killer.'

'Promising nothing, sir,' Layton said. 'But I think the best we can hope for is a copycat.'

'Copycat.' Hardin looked at the car as it was secured to the bed of the truck. 'Completely different MO. Not at all like the others. Yes. Good. Excellent.'

Savage was about to say something about not being premature when her mobile rang. Calter. Round at Lucy Hale's flat in Ivybridge.

'Don't know what it's like with you, ma'am,' Calter said, 'but there's a bloody circus here. Reporters, TV crews, members of the public with nothing better to do than revel in someone else's misery.'

'And the flat?'

'Been a team in there for half an hour. So far there's no sign of anything amiss. They've not finished yet but one thing they are sure of is there's no cake. Something else too.'

'Go on.'

'Luke Farrell, the FLO, well, he's been with the parents for the past hour. I just spoke to him. No baby, ma'am. No way a pregnancy could have been concealed. They only live a few streets over from Lucy and see her at least once a week.

Never mind the TV soaps, in real life you can't hide the fact you're pregnant.'

Savage ended the call.

No cake, no baby, not the longest day and Wilson dead and out of the picture. For a moment the scene around her seemed to fade. Colour leached from the trees and the sky and a grey fuzz blurred her vision. The hubbub from the reporters vanished in a hiss of white noise. Savage had the sensation of falling. Not just her, but the whole world, everything tumbling down in some entropic dance, everything coming to a slow but inevitable end.

She shivered, blinked a couple of times and then reality snapped back. Vision, sound, a gruff voice.

'Well, Charlotte?' Hardin said. 'What the fuck's going on?'

'Peter Wilson could not have abducted Paula Rowland,' Savage said, pulling herself together. 'Nor could he have abducted any of the other victims. However he was involved it wasn't in the actual kidnappings. Wilson had an accomplice, someone who did the dirty work, and now he's operating on his own. He's gone rogue, if you like. Without Wilson there he's killing at random. Lucy Hale was just unlucky. This is no copycat. It's part of the sequence.'

'Oh my God.' Hardin breathed in hard. 'Please tell me you're joking?'

'No, sir.'

'Shit. Fuck.' The DSupt moved across to the fence at the side of the road and grasped a post as if for support, as if he was experiencing the same physical reaction Savage just had. He grunted and then stood up straight. Spoke. 'So where do we go from here?'

'Wilson's connections. Family, friends, acquaintances, people he's worked with. Somewhere in that group is the killer, but unless we act quick Lucy Hale won't be the last victim.'

'Not good.' Hardin shook his head, pulled his phone from its case, ran his fingers across the surface. Then he looked back at the camera crews for a moment. 'The problem is, what the hell are we going to tell that lot?'

Collier had already been working on Wilson's connections, but the material from the house search had produced no information about next-of-kin. No family photographs, nothing useful in his address book, no personal letters or emails.

Back in the crime suite Savage went through some of the other information they had. Outside of his work colleagues Wilson only had a couple of social contacts. Both were from the village of Crapstone, but according to the door-to-doors they were casual acquaintances. For all his talk of being best buddies with the Deputy Director of the FBI, it didn't look like he'd made many friends. Savage thought about the picture on the wall in Wilson's office at the surgery. Thought of the psychologist staring at it while somebody sat and poured out their innermost feelings.

You should have heard them trying to justify their actions. They were so self-obsessed, so full of self-pity. They made me sick.

'Of course!' Savage said to herself. 'The bloody patients. That's how he knew about the adoptions.'

She reached for the phone and in a few seconds was through to the exhibits officer on the case. Savage asked about Wilson's office. They'd removed Wilson's personal possessions from his office, yes? What about the Rolodex file, did they have it? A clatter of keys told her the officer was searching the computer and then he was telling her, yes, they had the Rolodex, did she want it?

Ten minutes later and Savage plonked the strange contraption down on a desk in the crime suite.

'It's like something from another age, ma'am,' Calter said, coming over to look.

'Wilson didn't like computers,' Savage said. 'He boasted to me that he helped the FBI capture a serial killer without any recourse to one. I guess that's why he used this to keep patient records.'

'But the health centre must have records on their system?'

'Sure, but Wilson wouldn't have trusted that.' Savage began to leaf through the file, stopping at 'M'. 'No Katherine Mallory, but here's another Mallory, her mother, Marion. Riverside Road, Dittisham. She must have been a patient of Wilson's. In therapy she would have told him all about her life. It's inconceivable she didn't mention her daughter's pregnancy and the subsequent giving up of the baby for adoption.'

'And the others?'

'One mo . . .' Savage flicked back and forth through the index cards. 'They're here too. Mandy Glastone, Sue Kendle, Heidi Luckmann and Paula Rowland. The first three were his patients before he left the UK. There was no breach of the database, no dodgy goings-on at the registrar's office. Wilson just sat in his big leather chair while the names were served to him on a plate.'

'You think people who gave up their babies were more likely to seek therapy?'

'I don't know, but it's probably irrelevant. Over the years he had hundreds of patients. Statistically, a number of them would have matched.'

'Why did nobody make the connection?'

'Before he went to the States Wilson worked alone. He would have been in charge of record keeping. The names on the card index may be the only records he kept.' Savage shook her head. 'And if you're in therapy it's not necessarily something you shout about either, is it?'

'Doesn't help us with Wilson's accomplice.'

'No,' Savage said, spinning the cards round once more. 'It doesn't.'

Chapter Forty

Riley was still in bed at seven when the doorbell rang. Once, twice and then continuously. He leapt out of bed and padded down the hallway to the entry phone. Davies' face filled the screen. Riley buzzed him up.

'Boss,' Riley said as he opened the door. 'This is too early.'

'Tell me about it. Maynard's called. Something's happening on the diesel case and he wants us up at the farm.'

'Fuck.'

'Put something on or you'll scare the neighbours. I'll be outside.'

Five minutes later, having brushed his teeth and squirted on some deodorant, Riley joined Davies in the car. As Davies started up and pulled away, Riley asked what was up.

'Intel.' Davies cut in front of a taxi and a horn blared out. 'You know all those fuel tanks round the back of McGann's place? Well, it appears as if he's started to dismantle them.'

'But they're full.'

'Exactly. He's going to have to shift a job lot of diesel and Maynard's got wind it's going to happen today.'

'About time. At least we can wrap this up and go back to proper detective work.'

'I wouldn't bank on it. Word is Maynard wants to form some sort of agricultural crime squad. He told me sheep rustling is the next project on the agenda. Seems like a load of swillyites have been going up on the moor and indulging in a bit of amateur butchery. In hard times, even your supermarket gristle brand isn't cheap enough.'

'You're joking, right?' Riley looked across at Davies. 'You're not, are you?'

Davies shook his head. Riley leant back in the seat. Nightmare. Fifteen minutes later and he woke with a start. They were outside Plymouth, Davies gunning the car off the main road and onto a lane to Bickleigh. Minutes later they passed the barracks and then the road wound round, climbing all the way to Wotter and Lee Moor. Either side of the road great heaps of white clay spoil transformed the countryside. When Riley had first moved from London he'd seen the pits from down on the coast. At the time he'd thought the white was snow. Seeing as it had been early September, Enders had never let him forget his mistake.

'That girl broke down somewhere along here,' Riley said.

'Be nice,' Davies said, chuckling, 'if we could do McGann for her as well. Maybe he's got her working the till in his DIY service station.'

To their right the countryside sloped down towards Plymouth and the sea sparkled in the distance. Lucy Hale had known she was somewhere on the road, but hadn't been able to orientate herself. At night, despite the lights from the city, the task would have been impossible.

'Here we go.' Davies took a turn and they bumped down a track towards a little wooden bungalow. The garden surrounding it bloomed with flowers and neat little gravel paths ran this way and that. The place faced away from the road and out back a deck spread from the property as the garden fell away.

'What's this?' Riley said. 'I thought we were going to McGann's place.'

'What – and sit in a mucky ditch all day long?' Davies stopped the car. 'No bloody way. I've pulled us a cushy little number.'

Before Riley could enquire further Davies was out of the car and had bounded up to and through a little wicket gate. A dog barked inside in response to his knocks and then the door opened to reveal an elderly woman, her hair the same colour as the fur of the white Westie which yapped around her feet.

Once they'd been shown through to the deck where chairs surrounded a plastic table, the woman offered them some tea. While she bustled around inside Davies explained that Mrs Kimberly had allowed them to use her property for the next few days since she was off to Bournemouth for the weekend. Davies gave an expansive wave of his hand and Riley could understand why. McGann's place lay around a mile and a half away somewhat to the right and below them. The track leading to his farm wound back up to the main road. Close obs and you were better down in the ditch, but up here you could see everything.

Mrs Kimberly served them tea and then Davies was away to the car, returning with a pair of binoculars and something in a padded bag.

'Spotting scope,' Davies said. 'Maynard's pride and joy. Says if anything happens to it we'll both be back in uniform.'

Davies unpacked the scope and set the instrument up on a small tripod.

'May I?' Riley said.

'Kid gloves, Sergeant. The thing is a Swarovski. Austrian

apparently, and according to Maynard worth the best part of two and a half thousand. And that's not including the carbon fibre tripod.'

'Shit,' Riley said, wiping his hands on his trousers before moving over to the scope. One hand went to the handle on the tripod and the other to the focusing knob. He bent to the eyepiece. 'Wow!'

'Good, eh?' Davies said.

Good was an understatement. Riley swivelled the scope and pointed the lens down towards the farm. In the garden out the back a woman stood next to a washing line. Riley could make out the lace edge to the piece of clothing as she pegged a pair of knickers to the line.

'What magnification is this?'

'Up to seventy. What you looking at?'

'There's a girl down at the farm doing something with her underwear. I'm so close it feels like I could touch her. This must be a perv's dream come true.'

Davies jostled in close and Riley moved aside. With his naked eye he could just about make out the farm. The woman was but a dot.

'Gorgeous,' Davies said. 'That must be the McGanns' daughter-in-law. She's going to be getting all lonely when her hubby goes inside.'

'Well, he won't be going anywhere if we spend our time bird watching.'

'There is that, Sergeant.' Davies looked up and patted the scope. 'But perhaps we can agree Maynard's hobby is not such a bad one after all.'

'Talking of which, can you see him?'

Davies bent to the scope again and panned back and forth. 'Got him! He's down in the ditch. Just taken his foil-wrapped sarnies out. Sad fucker.'

Riley pulled out a chair and sat down again, ignoring Davies' chuntering. He leant back, closed his eyes and enjoyed the warmth of the sun. Mrs Kimberly's place was an odd sort of house, but there was no denying the location was superb. Julie had been suggesting they get a place together, hinting she'd like to live out in the countryside. Riley wasn't sure. He was a city boy born and bred: five minutes to the corner shop and pub; ten minutes to the restaurants and clubs. Always hustle and bustle, noise and light. 'Not good for kids', Julie said. Perhaps she was right. There was space here. You could maybe put a pool in, certainly one of those tub things. A barbie in one corner, friends round, a couple of beers, he could almost forget city life. Riley smiled inwardly, aware that Davies was mumbling something else, letters and numbers.

'Did you hear me, Sergeant?' Davies said. 'Check the reg!'

'What?' Riley sat up and opened his eyes. Davies pointed to a scrap of paper on the table.

'Big tanker coming down the track to the McGann farm, no livery. Check it.'

Riley took out his phone and dialled through to the station. 'Index check,' he said and gave the details. After a couple of minutes he got confirmation and hung up.

'The Exeter mob?' Davies said. Riley nodded. 'Let's go then.'

It was Calter who came up with the goods. Mid-morning Thursday she knocked on the door to Savage's office. Entered without waiting for an answer.

'Lara Bailey,' she said. 'Took me a while, but I've tracked down her mother, Dr Wilson's grandmother. She'd moved to Spain to retire. Came back to the UK a few years ago on the death of her husband. In some old people's home now.'

'Where?' Savage said.

'Here, ma'am. Plymouth. Right under our noses.'

Now, with Calter still head down in a pile of documents seeking additional information, Savage and Enders drove to the care home.

Clovelly House sat on the eastern side of North Prospect Road. On the other side rows of graves stretched across acres of grass. Weston Mill Cemetery.

'Not what I'd call a great view,' Enders said as they pulled into the driveway. 'When you've finished dribbling into your tea and played yet another hand of whist all you can do is go for a stroll amongst your old friends.'

'I'd keep those thoughts to yourself, Patrick,' Savage said. 'Otherwise we might have a geriatric riot on our hands.'

Inside, a care assistant showed them into a large lounge.

'She's over there,' the assistant said. 'The one sitting on the chair. Rocking. I'll take you across.'

A high-backed armchair stood over by the window and Mrs Bailey sat perched on the edge of the seat. She was staring out through the glass across to the cemetery, her head nodding back and forwards.

'Jesus, ma'am,' Enders whispered. 'See what I mean?'

'Aline?' the assistant said. 'There's a couple of police officers to see you, love. I'll bring you all some tea and biscuits, OK?'

Aline Bailey glanced up for a moment and then resumed her rhythmical rocking.

The old woman was pushing ninety. Her frame had shrunk to almost nothing, the shawl she wore draped over her shoulders all angled by the bones beneath.

'Mrs Bailey?' Savage said. 'DI Charlotte Savage and DC Patrick Enders. We wanted to ask you some questions about Tavy View Farm and about your daughter too.'

'You're too late,' the woman said, still staring through the window. 'Lara died in two thousand and . . . two thousand and . . .'

'We know, Mrs Bailey, and I'm sorry for bringing the subject up again. It must be painful.'

'Time heals they say.' Mrs Bailey stopped rocking and turned her face towards Savage, a blue vein throbbing down the side her nose. 'Rubbish. Time makes things worse. I think of my little Lara every day. What happened to her. The life she led. She was our eldest child, you know?'

'And your husband?'

'Dead.' The woman's eyes flicked back to the window. 'A couple of years after he retired. Heart attack. I stayed in Spain for a while, but in the end I had to come back. Didn't want to die out there. Not right. Too hot. Too many bloody foreigners.'

'Lara, she had a child, didn't she?'

'Child? No, love. Not a child.'

'We . . .' Savage stopped. Had Calter got it wrong? 'We thought she got pregnant when you lived out in Bere Ferrers. Had a baby.'

'Yes, but not a baby.'

'Not a baby?' Savage said, not understanding. Was Aline about to tell her some horror story? Had the girl given birth to a dog, the devil, some kind of monster? 'If not a baby, what then?'

'Not *a* baby. Two children. Identical twins. Two bonny little boys.'

'*Twins*?'

'Yes. Gave them away she did. I said I'd look after them, but she didn't want that. She wanted to be rid of them. She was only fifteen, not thinking right, but those social workers were only too keen to grab the little ones. Of course, Lara regretted it later. That's why she went downhill. Broken-hearted, she was. Broken-hearted. Drink, drugs. Then selling herself. Prison. All sorts. Years later she was done in while working. Working, I ask you. Selling herself when she was in her fifties. She was murdered by some sicko. You lot, back then, didn't care much. One less prossie on the streets.'

'I'm sorry, Mrs Bailey.' Savage paused and then asked about Joanne's uncle. Was he the father of the twins?

'No. Gossip, all that. We moved into Plymouth to try and escape the tittle-tattle. The father was actually a young lad from the other side of Tavistock, no more than a boy really. Same age as Lara. No way the pair of them could keep the babies.'

'Attitudes have changed,' Savage said. 'I think now people would have tried to ensure they could. It's a tragic story.'

'Tragic. That's it. Now I'm just waiting here. Stuck with this lot.' The woman gestured around the room. 'Most of them don't know where they are. And they're the lucky ones.'

The care assistant returned with a tray. Three cups of tea, milk, sugar and a plate of Jammie Dodgers. She placed the tray on a table and left.

'Can I ask about the twins – do you know who adopted them? Did you ever have any contact?'

'No. They were taken a few days after they were born. I was told it would be best if I didn't know. At the time I could live with that, but many years later I wanted some contact. I tried to find out more but I was told I couldn't. I went to the registrar's to see if there was some information I could get from the amended birth certificate, but I couldn't get access. Something about the children being wards of court. Their identities had to be protected. I didn't understand, but couldn't get any further. My other daughter and my son all had children during that time and I guess the longing to see

371

Lara's children passed. I gave up my quest.' Mrs Bailey reached for a cup of tea and sipped the black liquid. 'If you discover anything, I'd like to know.' She stared out the window again. 'Only next time you come I could well be out there, so you'll have to shout.'

They left Aline Bailey with her biscuits and her memories and walked out to the car.

'Twins, ma'am,' Enders said. 'Are you thinking what I'm thinking?'

'Forensics,' Savage said. 'Identical twins share the same DNA. Which explains how Wilson could be in Manchester and yet the evidence pointed to him being at Paula Rowland's place. But he wasn't there. He didn't abduct Paula or any of the other women, it was his brother.'

'So now we know who we're looking for.' Enders stood by the car and gazed across the road at the cemetery. Rows of neat plots. Thousands of them. 'Question is, where is he?'

It was done and dusted by lunch time. A team over at Exeter entered a local hauliers and arrested the owner and the finance director. Down at the farm Maynard stood astride his Devon hedge and waved the troops on like he was going over the top from a trench in the Somme. A police van and a couple of car loads from Customs and Excise bumped down the track to the farm and officers piled out, blocking the road, securing buildings and rounding up the extended family. McGann and his two sons feigned innocence at first. Maynard went round the back and asked them what the complex arrangement of tanks, piping and delivery hoses was all about. The elder McGann came clean then, hoping for some sort of reward for good behaviour. 'Nothing doing,' Maynard said, a smile going from ear to ear as if he'd just taken down some arch-criminal.

Back at the station it was too early for the bar so Maynard put fifty quid in the canteen till. He managed a cup of tea with them and then he was away to complete some paperwork, leaving the rest of them to laugh at Davies doing birdsong imitations.

The whole exercise had, Riley thought as he sipped a cappuccino, been a total waste of resources. McGann would likely get a custodial sentence, as would the others. All would be out in a year or two. The operation would be dressed up as a success, saving the government millions in lost revenue. Would the police get any of that? No way.

The celebrations didn't last long and Riley returned to the crime suite to write up a report. Late in the afternoon, Riley still tapping away at his keyboard, Davies came over. He had a white look to his face, a carrier bag of tinnies dragging his right hand downward.

'In the shits,' he said. 'I've only just gone and realised I've left Maynard's spotting scope up at Mrs Kimberly's place. She's gone off on her mini-break and the bloody thing is sitting outside on the garden table.'

'Are you going back up there?'

'No.' Davies patted Riley on the back. 'Got a little meeting set up later. Can't miss it without raising suspicions. Thought you might do me a favour.'

'Boss! I was off home.' Riley glanced around. 'Can't you get one of the other lads to fetch it?'

'No can do. If that thing gets broken we're for the high jump. In the words of the DSupt, this job needs a quality officer. I can think of no one better.'

Riley began to protest again, but then gave up. Pointless. The scope was up at the bungalow and somebody had to get it. Riley pulled his jacket from the back of the chair.

'You owe me, Phil,' Riley said.

'Not anymore.' Davies grinned and raised the bag, eight cans of supermarket own-brand lager straining against the thin plastic. 'Don't drink them all at once.'

Riley took the bag, muttered a 'thanks' and left the room. He was tempted to leave the cans down at reception for the late shift to quaff after they'd finished but then thought he might as well take them home. He'd be able to offload them at a party.

Nearly an hour later, after having got lost twice, he arrived at the bungalow at Lee Moor. Davies had said Mrs Kimberly was away, but he tapped on the glass door, just to be sure. As expected there was no answer. He walked to the side of the bungalow and opened the low gate. The path wound round the edge through flowerbeds with not a weed in sight. The view hit him again, the countryside softer now the angle of the sun had lowered. With his naked eye he could see there was still a patrol car down at the farm. And there, on the table, was Maynard's scope.

Riley breathed a sigh of relief. He reached for the case, which sat on one of the chairs. Then he thought 'what the hell'. He'd driven all the way back up here, he may as well have another look through the scope. But not at McGann's farm, he'd had enough of that. He swivelled the scope away and to the left where the jumble of clay pits looked like they might provide something interesting to investigate. He knew nothing about clay mining and the pits resembled something from an alien landscape.

Riley focused in on one of the lakes. The opaque pale blue-green surface appeared as if painted on glass. He panned right and followed a track from the main road down to a farm nestled deep within the old clay workings. The track was white, like snow, and ended in a yard. A tractor with a trailer behind sat in the middle of the yard. To one side, a huge pile of white gravel. He was about to move on when he spotted another vehicle. The battered recovery truck had been parked round the back of a barn, out of sight from anyone visiting the property. The thing was rust brown with great splodges of blue paint.

Blue.

John Layton had found blue paint on the road where Corran had been knocked off his bike. He'd been unable to match the sample to any make of car. A re-spray, he'd reckoned. The CSI had also said a tow truck had been used to move Lucy Hale's car to Burrator Reservoir.

Riley stood up and with his naked eye traced the road to where it ran down into Plympton, a suburb on the outskirts of the city. The farm was on the route Lucy Hale could have taken. Although set back from the road, it surely would have been visited by officers. It was nothing to get excited about. But then again, there was the pickup truck.

Riley began to dismantle the scope and tripod. He placed them in their requisite bags and went back to his car. He had to get the scope back to Maynard, but first he'd call in.

The phone in the crime suite rang for ages until a probationer DC answered.

'Nobody here, sir,' the lad said. 'DI Savage is at Tavy View talking to Joanne Black. You could call her.'

Riley hung up and dialled the number and when DI Savage answered he put the information to her. Worth a gander, wasn't it?

Savage said it was and told Riley to meet her there. Just time, Riley thought, to take the scope back into Crownhill, put it on Maynard's desk and then return.

Chapter Forty-One

Joanne Black hadn't been able to add anything to Aline Bailey's story, but she'd poured Savage a glass of wine and they'd sat outside, Joanne reminiscing about her childhood. Another glass of wine and the conversation had turned to Savage's own children, family life, Pete and inevitably, Clarissa. A period of silence, Joanne's hand reaching across the table and touching Savage's, the moment interrupted by the trill of a mobile, DS Riley's voice on the end of the line. Something about blue paint, a pickup truck parked round the back of some farm.

Savage was up and away, thanking Joanne, and on a whim saying she must come over and meet Pete and the kids sometime.

She headed towards the village of Lee Moor and the area of abandoned pits Riley had mentioned in his call. The enquiry teams searching for Lucy Hale had been pretty thorough in investigating the whole area, but it wouldn't hurt to have a drive down to the junction of the farm track with the main road and have a look around. Just to be sure.

Ten minutes later and she'd found the spot. A board on

a fence post read 'Lower Lee Farm' and a track white with clay dust wound in amongst heaps of spoil. The entrance to the existing clay pits was a couple of miles farther on; this area had been worked out years ago. Savage remembered the clay which had been found in the mouths of the victims. An artist, Wilson had said. Now, of course, none of the psychologist's theories could be taken at face value because he'd played his part in the murders.

But only a part.

There was another one out there. Wilson's twin brother. He'd have some sort of connection to clay and had used a pickup truck to tow Lucy Hale's car. He likely lived somewhere remote because the killings would, in Nesbit's words, have involved 'a lot of mess and screaming'. Savage thought for a moment. Was it worth taking a closer look before she called the troops out? Apart from the probationer on duty everyone else would have gone home. Pointless to pull them all in on a wild goose chase.

Savage clunked the car back into gear and turned into the track. The rutted surface curled away to the right, spoil heaps rising on either side, sloping upwards at forty-five degrees. Savage wondered what sort of farm could exist in the sterile environment. As if in answer the land opened out, the track climbing through an almost lunar landscape to some sort of settlement. A large house sat to one side and a number of barns to the other. Arranged either side of the track were huge circular tanks, water splashing into each from pipes leading down from the hillside. There was a pond too, chicken wire round the edge, several ducks swimming amongst green weed.

What was this place? A sewage works? Then she saw a splash in one of the tanks, a flash of silver as something darted away into the depths.

A trout.

The place was a fish farm.

Now Savage could see water cascading down the moorland to the rear of the house, a stream leading to a collection tank from which pipes fed the water to various pools. The winding track ended at a gate, beyond a yard area, the ground coarse with silica residue. A tractor and trailer stood to one side of the yard, the trailer holding a large tank. The gate had a sign on with the words 'Keep out. Fish disease'.

Savage rolled the car up to the gate and stopped. She climbed out. She could see the shed which Riley had said hid the pickup from view, but there were no other vehicles aside from the tractor.

She placed one hand on the gate latch and with the other reached into her pocket for her phone. She was surprised to see a signal. Comforted too. The gate swung open and she crossed the yard towards the house. Brown pebbledash peeled away from one side of the unimposing post-war structure, while to the right-hand side of the house an extension looked like an afterthought. Curtains framed the windows of the downstairs front rooms, both sets drawn half across. Savage stepped closer. The room on the left was filled with shadows and dark oak furniture. On the back wall a display case hung above a table, but the glass reflected the light from the window and she couldn't make out what was within.

She moved across the front of the house to the porch and as she did so she heard a sound. She whirled round to see a large black shape shooting out from an open barn door, a chain rattling out from behind.

A dog!

The chain pulled the animal up with a jerk, wrenching it round. The thing was huge, some sort of Rottweiler crossed with a mammoth, and it snarled at Savage, drool spraying from foaming jaws. The chain led to a hook screwed into one side of the barn door and Savage could see the metal bending under the strain. Then there was a crack and the wood around the ring split, the hook catapulting out. For a second the dog stopped, as if unsure of what to do, but then it bolted forwards, the chain bouncing along behind.

Savage moved to the door, reached for the handle and pushed down. The door swung open and she stepped inside, slamming it shut. Outside, the dog snarled and then barked. There was a snuffling at the door, followed by a whining. Savage breathed out and then made sure the door had latched.

Inside, a hallway led to the rear of the house. A doorway at the end revealed a kitchen. To her left was the room she'd seen the display case in, some sort of dining room. She stepped in and pulled out her mobile. The room was dominated by a large oak table around which were several chairs, but the table had been covered with a plastic sheet. As Savage walked in the floor crackled and she looked down to see another sheet had been spread out there too.

She turned to the display case on the wall. Plastic plants and a mock riverbed along with a blue background suggested the case once held a stuffed fish. No longer. There was something else in there. Not a fish. A knife. The shiny steel blade was nine inches long with a handle stained darker than the oak furniture. The blade winked as she moved across and blocked the light for a moment and then flashed again. Almost like a warning.

Savage looked down at her phone. No signal now, not even for emergency calls. The walls of the house must be preventing reception. She crossed to the window. The dog was sniffing the ground near the gate, but should she open the door the animal would cover the space in a second.

She returned to the hall hoping to find a phone, but a little table against one wall was bare apart from a kid's puzzle magazine. She moved down the hall to the back of the house and entered the kitchen. Small windows above the sink and drainer looked onto an almost sheer face of spoil, the crystals of silica sparkling in the evening sun. The brightness outside made the room seem dark, gloom hanging in the air along with a taint of iron. To the right a wicker chair and a rocker stood either side of an ancient Aga, the stove from an age when such things were functional rather than trendy. Still no sign of a phone.

Savage crossed the kitchen to a door thick with faded white gloss. She lifted the latch and peered in. Some kind of pantry, light coming from a tiny grilled window. To either side jars, cans and dried foodstuffs stood on shelves, on the floor a large bag of potatoes, shoots sprouting from the tubers at the top. She bent to look closer at something in the shadows. Several Kilner jars. At the front a number of small ones, holding perhaps a couple of litres. Behind, some huge ones, almost bucket-sized. The liquid within each jar was murky, like a pickle fluid gone bad. Savage reached for one of the smaller jars and pulled it out. The contents floated in the liquid, indistinct, refusing to come close to the side. She turned the jar over in her hands until she could see what was within: pieces of meat, bits of flesh and gristle.

Savage felt her legs go weak and she dumped the jar back on the shelf. She bent farther down and reached for one of the larger jars. Filled with liquid, the container was heavy and she wrestled it bit by bit to the front of the shelf. Something moved inside, something the size of a football, strands of fibrous material floating. She squinted and put her face closer. The fibres weren't fibres at all, they were hair. Savage pulled her face back as eyes, a nose and a gaping mouth loomed through the strands of hair and rested against the glass.

Jesus!

The large jars contained the missing heads. The contents of the smaller ones had to be the genitals, hacked off in some mad frenzy.

From the kitchen came a ringing. Savage whirled round and left the pantry. There, on the dresser half-hidden behind a rusty microwave, was a phone on a charging unit. She moved towards the phone but the ringing stopped as she reached out her hand. An answer machine kicked in, a generic voice asking the caller to leave a message. Then a beep and somebody was speaking.

Mikey? You there? Wake up you lazy shit. I'm home in five minutes and twenty seconds.

The caller hung up. Savage waited for a moment and then reached for the phone again. A creak came from upstairs somewhere. Then footsteps padding across the ceiling. Savage looked at the phone, but didn't pick it up. She moved back to the pantry door, slipped through and pulled the handle shut. She scanned around for something she might use as a weapon. She selected a jumbo-sized tin of tomatoes from a low shelf.

Someone moved out in the kitchen, shoes on the quarry tile floor. There was a beep and the answerphone repeated the message.

Mikey? You there? Wake up you lazy shit. I'm home in five minutes and twenty seconds.

A sigh, and then the shoes tapping on the floor again. Savage heard the front door click open.

'Daaawwwggg!'

The door slammed and Savage paused for a moment. She lifted the latch and opened the pantry door. Nothing. Across the kitchen the hallway appeared dark. The front door was closed. She raced through the kitchen and down the hall. At the front door a glance showed a big bolt placed in the centre. She drew the bolt across and then ran back to the kitchen and picked up the phone.

One ring. Two rings. Three rings. Come on, answer!

'Major Crimes?'

Savage blurted out her name and the address of the farm. Told the surprised young detective to call Response and send a TAG team out immediately. She chucked the phone on the side and rushed back to the front of the house and looked through the dining room window. The man outside was some kind of freak of nature. Hair like crumpled-up brown paper sat above a round face, nose like a mushroom. He was huge and lumbering, stooping slightly as he walked across the yard and back to the house. Savage moved forwards to peer round the edge of the curtain. The man pushed against the front door and then stepped back, puzzled. He tried again and then glanced to his left. He caught Savage's eye and then exploded with rage. He bent and picked up something just to one side of the front porch: a pogo stick. Then he swung the metal pole at the window. The glass shattered and the guy swung the pogo stick again to clear the remaining glass from the window. He began to clamber through the frame.

Savage turned and ran from the room, sprinting back down the hall to the kitchen. To the right of the pantry was a door to the backyard. She rushed across and tried it. Deadlocked. No key. Down the hallway something was moving, dragging itself along the corridor. Savage moved to the pantry, clicked open the latch, stepped inside and closed the door.

Out in the kitchen, nothing. Not a sound. Savage put her

ear to the door. Silence. A minute passed, then another, and another. She waited, wanting to be sure. Where had he gone? Was he hiding out there, ready to surprise her? Maybe he'd retrieved the knife from the display cabinet and even now was standing behind the door. After a couple more minutes she moved to lift the latch. As she did so something scraped on the tiles in the kitchen. A chair being moved. She stepped back and reached for one of the large Kilners. The head inside bobbed as she heaved the huge jar from the shelf. The latch on the door rattled, lifted, and then the door swung open, Savage behind it. A swathe of light painted the floor, a long shadow in the centre. The shadow grew in size. Savage tensed, raised the jar above her head, ready to bring it down.

'Ma'am?' a voice said.

Riley!

Riley stepped into the pantry, putting his hands up when he saw Savage with the jar.

'What the hell is that?' he said, his mouth hanging open as his eyes rose to the contents of the jar. 'My God.'

'Out. Before I drop this thing.' Savage lowered the jar and followed Riley into the kitchen where she clumped the jar down on the table. The head bobbed and rotated inside. 'Where's the nutter?'

'Didn't see anyone. I parked behind your car. Could hear sirens coming up the track so I didn't bother waiting. I got in through the broken window.'

'Dog?'

'Uh-uh. Didn't see a dog either.' Riley shook his head and then moved forwards to the table. 'Bloody hell. Is that one of the victims?'

'You should be a detective,' Savage said and then nodded back into the pantry. 'There's more in there. Body parts too.

Genitals. John Layton was spot on. He told me the killer would have kept them as trophies.'

'Armed police!' The shout floated down the hallway.

'DI Savage and DS Riley,' Savage said. 'In here!'

A TAG team member, all in black and holding a pistol, ran into the room, whirled left and right and then lowered his weapon.

'Check upstairs,' Savage said. 'And then we need dogs. He's probably gone off out the back somewhere.'

The officer left and Riley moved to the table.

'Have you found Lucy Hale?' he said.

'No, but there are other jars in the pantry.' Savage pointed at the head inside the jar on the table. Long brown hair. 'This one's Paula Rowland.'

'Jesus, poor kid.' Riley bent to peer closer. 'I was going to say I hope she didn't suffer, but she did, didn't she?'

'From the looks of the cuts on the body, yes.' Savage gestured to the door. 'Come on, let's get out of here and leave all this to Layton. It's just his idea of fun.'

An hour later, and the TAG team had declared the property secure. John Layton and members of his team arrived, keen to pick the house and outbuildings to pieces. The hum of a generator floated in the air as the CSIs began to set up several sets of floodlights to illuminate the yard as it grew dark.

Calter, Enders and numerous other detectives from the team had sauntered along as well. Faces tinged with a hint of guilt as there was no real reason for them to be here, yet no one wanted to miss out on being a little part of history.

Of Lucy Hale, there was no sign.

'Butchered,' Hardin said when he turned up. He gestured around at the spoil heaps, the white clay beginning to turn to grey in the dusk. 'Body somewhere out there for the crows to pick at.'

'Well if she's around here the dogs will find her.'

Three dog handlers had arrived with specialist search dogs. Two would try to pick up the trail of the man who'd attacked Savage while the third would work the area near the farm. While the two tracker dogs would need a bit of luck to catch up with the suspect, the handler looking for Lucy Hale was confident that if she was on the farm – alive or dead – the dog would find her.

Hardin, thankfully, was wrong. Lucy Hale hadn't been butchered. Twenty minutes after the dog team's arrival an excited yapping announced the discovery of the woman cowering in the recesses of an old pumphouse halfway round the back of one of the spoil heaps. She was frightened and hungry, but otherwise unharmed.

'They never touched her,' Savage said to Hardin once she'd talked to the woman. 'They locked her up Tuesday night and left her. Never came back.'

'Huh?' Hardin raised his eyebrows. 'Doesn't make sense.'

'Who cares if it doesn't make sense?' Savage said. 'She's alive and she wasn't raped or assaulted. I'd call that good news.'

'Yes, of course.' Something else was confusing Hardin. 'Hang on, you said "they"?'

'She said there were two men, yes.'

'Charlotte, I hope you're joking. *Three* of them in all?'

'It makes sense. The man who attacked me wasn't Wilson's twin brother and he was . . . how can I say this in a politically correct manner? He was subnormal. A loony.'

'Well he'd have to be to go chopping people up.'

'No. I mean he was mentally and physically ill.' Savage pointed down at the trout pools where moonlit water swirled.

'There's no way he'd be able to look after all this on his own. Plus, while I was inside somebody rang. I heard them leave a message on the phone for the guy, called him Mikey. They said they'd be back in five minutes. Obviously they turned up and found the place swarming with us lot.'

'Possibly picked up this Mikey?'

'Since the truck is still here then either he got a lift from someone or he's out on the moor.' Savage looked around. The spoil heaps of clay and silica reflected the light from a rising moon, their surfaces almost glowing, something demonic about them. 'Whatever, he's long gone.'

End of play the next day – Friday – and Savage sat alone in her office working on a report. A few minutes earlier DI Maynard had been in to collect some of his files.

'Credit goes to Operation *Cowbell*,' he said. 'Bit of luck we were there, hey? And that DS Riley. Not a bad lad for a city boy.'

Maynard picked up his papers and left with a chuckle and a shake of his head.

Luck? Or was it, to use Hardin's well-worn phrase, bloody good policing? Whatever, it was going to take a little good fortune to catch Wilson's brother and the man known as Mikey. A force-wide manhunt had been initiated but so far they had nothing. The *Radial* team had worked through the day trying to get more information on the brothers and the full story didn't differ markedly from the one Wilson had told Savage before he killed himself. The murder of his wife by Wilson's adopted father, had taken place up country, London way. Not such a big event up there, not surprising nobody remembered about the adopted twins. Especially as the case was several decades ago.

Peter and his twin, who they now knew was called Ronald,

had been given new surnames and identities to protect them from press intrusion and fostered out to various families. Coming of age, the twins had left the care of the state and went about their lives. Peter went to university and having graduated built himself a career as a psychologist, indulged in some private practice. Ronald, however, found life more difficult. Petty crime and casual violence in his early twenties led in the end to a conviction for a string of vicious sexual attacks on prostitutes in towns and cities along the M4/M5 corridor. He served fifteen years, much of the time spent at Full Sutton in a unit dealing with severe personality disorders.

When Ronald was released he returned to Plymouth and he and Peter were reunited. What happened then was conjecture, but Lara Bailey had been killed on the longest day of the year, the date coinciding with the twins' birthday. There was no direct evidence to link either brother to the murder and yet that one or both of them had killed her seemed self-evident.

Revenge taken, demons exorcised; that should have been that. Ronald ended up in the clay pit, trout farming an unlikely choice of profession. Peter continued in private practice but may well have been the one to instigate the Candle Cake killings, the woman who rejected him being all the excuse he needed. He never took part in the actual murders – they knew that from the alibis – but he as good as signed the victims' death warrants when he provided Ronald with a name each year. Likely as not after the torture and killings he helped Ronald bury the bodies on the farm, the sight of each woman being entombed on the spot where his life began bringing some sort of catharsis.

Savage shook her head as she read through the report on the screen once more. Then she closed the document, switched off her computer and gathered together her things.

He found the love of a good woman.

As she left the office and went down to her car she recalled Wilson's words to her about a serial killer in the States who stopped killing when he got married. Wilson hadn't found the love of a woman though. What the hell was wrong with some men, Savage thought, that if they didn't get what they wanted, they took it anyway?

Chapter Forty-Two

Basically, she's ruined everything. She killed Peter. Turfed you and Mikey from your home, left you with nothing. And thanks to you giving Mikey a few too many Moxis he slept for thirty-six hours solid, so you didn't even get to have some fun with the new girl.

Which means the bitch has got to pay.

But it won't be so easy. Not with her being a police officer. Finding her place wasn't difficult. Bit out of the way. Off the beaten track. But you like that. Quiet. You won't be disturbed. You move down the footpath which skirts the property. A thick hedge conceals you from the family larking about in the garden, but you doubt they'd notice you anyway. They're too busy having fun.

Fun. It's what's been lacking from your life, you think. Apart from those moments of sublime transcendence when your victims squirm beneath the knife. Then again, it's not really fun. Except for Mikey. But then, one of his hobbies is chopping up earthworms.

You nestle down behind a bush, the pair of binoculars heavy round your neck. If anyone should come along the coast path you'll just seem like a crazy birdwatcher. You don't need them to see what's going on in the garden though. Two kids. An older girl and a boy. He's probably around six years old. The sort of age you were when Daddy slipped the Big Knife into Mummy's stomach. The laughter stops now and there's only the occasional noise from the garden. You see the mummy has brought some ice creams out and everyone is sitting on the grass eating.

Yummy, yummy, yummy. Sweet. Not like the cake which went bad.

You raise the binoculars and pull the focus. The image blurs and then the woman snaps sharp. Red hair. Red-handed. The woman's guilty. Killed Peter. End of story. End of her story, anyway.

You lower the binoculars and pull yourself up from the brambles. This is going to be fun after all, you decide.

Now you just need a plan.

An hour later and you've got one.

'Mobile phone data eliminated him from the inquiry.' You snigger to yourself, remembering a newspaper report about Glastone, the guy over in Salcombe they fingered for the killings a week ago. He got off. Thanks to a phone. Which gave you an idea. 'Hear that, Mikey? A mobile phone.'

'Ha, ha, ha!' Mikey laughs. Grins. Dribbles. 'Apple?'

'No idea,' you say. And to be honest you don't care. Apple, Samsung, Nokia. Once you've seen one slim biscuit packed with those incy-wincy bits of circuit board, you've seen them all.

You stare down at the thing in your hand. It's not a phone, although the device looks awfully like one. The wording on the box says 'GPS tracker' and that's what it does. You're in the big Go Outdoors store, the assistant demonstrating what the unit can do. He starts talking about satellites and text messages, WGS-84 and IPX7. You begin to move back, almost knocking over a display of aluminium water bottles.

'Tracking,' you say, 'does it do tracking?'

'Oh, yes. Updates on a map. Sends your location to Facebook or Twitter or by text to a phone. All sorts. You'll need a service plan.'

Jesus, you think. Facebook. Twitter. This thing is evil. All those bits of information flying through the air. Still, you need to side with the devil. Just this once.

'Battery life?' you hear yourself say, as if you knew what the fuck you were talking about.

'You should get several days' continuous use from one set. But you can always carry spares.'

You're sold. You reach into your coat pocket, pull out a bundle of notes and thrust them into the man's hands. There's a couple of hundred pounds at least. A twenty breaks free and flutters down to the floor.

'Is this enough? For everything?'

The assistant looks at you and then bends and picks up the twenty. 'Sure,' he says.

You buy the thing and not long afterwards you're at her place again, Mikey keeping watch in the lane. They're out now, all of them, but you have no idea when they might return. The sports car is on the front drive. The husband washed it earlier and the paintwork gleams in the sunlight. The car's an old one, nothing fancy and certainly no electronics. Not yet.

You approach the car and examine the front wheel arch. You run your hand underneath. All clean thanks to the wash. You take the GPS tracker from one coat pocket, a roll of gaffer tape from the other. You pull off a strip of tape and use it to attach the tracker under the wheel arch. The thing won't have a clear view of the sky, but you've read the instruction booklet several times and you think it will work well enough.

You peer up at the heavens for a moment, thinking on the kind of madness needed to keep those infernal satellites hanging up there.

Beep.

You reach into your pocket and bring out the phone. It's an ancient model, but it works. You peer down. There's a text message. A load of numbers. Latitude longitude. To most people they'd be meaningless without a map but you can visualise a picture in your head. The contours, the spot heights, the terrain. Those roads, all different colours, connecting towns and villages and houses together. The text message means the tracker is working, sending coordinates into the sky where a satellite beams the data back to earth and the mobile network sends the numbers to you. All you need to do is wait until the woman goes somewhere quiet and then you'll have her.

'Whoooarrrhhh!'

A noise like a gorilla comes from near the front gate and you see Mikey waving his arms. You sprint to the gate and take his arm.

'Walk, Mikey. This way. Slowly.' You wheel Mikey round and begin to stroll down the lane. There's an engine noise and then a red van is turning into the driveway. A man jumping out, slipping letters through the door as you and Mikey begin to hum the tune to Postman Pat.

Chapter Forty-Three

Bovisand, Plymouth. Saturday 5th July. 6.30 p.m.

The call Savage had almost given up waiting for came as she was sitting at home alone late Saturday afternoon. Pete, Stefan and the kids were out on the boat and were then going for a pizza. She'd cried off, wanting simply to relax for a few hours, not have to think about anything.

'Charlotte?' The voice was coarse. 'Been a while, but we're getting there.'

Fallon. Kenny Fallon. Plymouth's high-flying, down-in-the-dirt crime boss.

'Jesus, Kenny. It's been months.'

'Yes, love. Sorry. Took time. Time and help.'

There was a pause, Savage feeling Fallon was going to say something else. Nothing came.

'So?'

'So, we meet. You free today? Now?'

'Of course,' she heard herself say, only half listening as Fallon told her where and when. She felt her heart begin to race. All these years and now, in just an hour or two, she'd know who'd killed Clarissa.

Fallon hung up and Savage tidied away her simple dinner. She wrote a note for Pete, locked the house and then went and backed the MG out into the lane. Fallon wanted to meet on the moor, near to the spot where Clarissa had been hit by the car. Over the top, she thought, but then again, perhaps hearing the name out there would bring the events full circle.

An hour's drive took her deep into the wilderness of Dartmoor, tors closing in all around as the route twisted into a valley. She pulled the car off the road and onto a patch of gravel, just enough room for two cars to park. A few hundred metres down the lane was the place where she'd picnicked with the kids, where Clarissa had been knocked off her bike by the hit and run driver. Savage clenched her fists and then released them. She breathed in and tried to stay calm as she waited. July had seen the weather return to more changeable conditions and low swirling cloud enveloped the moor around her, bringing a persistent drizzle which hung in the air. Earlier she'd driven past walkers, but the rain had sent them scurrying for the pubs or back to their campsites.

Fifteen minutes later, there was still no sign of Fallon. Savage pulled out her mobile, unsurprised when she saw there was no signal. A small tor rose from behind the car park and the top would offer a three hundred and sixty-degree panorama. If there wasn't a signal up there then at least she'd be able to spot Fallon coming into the valley. Savage climbed out of the car. She didn't have the right footwear but she'd brought along a waterproof. She set off for the top of the tor, following an easy path up through clumps of bracken and before long she was looking down at her car, looking down at her mobile too, cursing as there was still no signal.

Across the other side of the valley she could see somebody atop a similar tor. He or she was prostrate on a large rock, almost as if they were sunbathing in the rain. Then there was a ping from close to Savage's feet, a piece of granite flying up, somehow dislodged from the rock. She glanced down and saw dust drift away from a small hole next to her right foot. She began to bend down and it was as she did so she heard the retort. A crack, like a whip. She looked again towards the figure on the rock. He had a beard and scraggy hair, but there was something familiar about him. The spindly limbs, a strange angular head . . .

Dr Wilson! How the hell . . .? No, of course not Savage thought. The man must be Wilson's twin brother, Ronald. Then the ground exploded a metre to her left and she understood what the dust at her feet had meant: a gunshot.

The crack from the second shot came as she dived off the top of the tor and rolled down a slab. She slammed against a boulder, bruising her leg and elbow, and couldn't stop herself letting out a gasp when she saw her bloodied knee poking from beneath the ripped material of her trousers. She moved her leg, flinching at the pain.

Ronald Wilson. He had a high-powered rifle. The gun was probably the rifle which had belonged to his brother. Savage moved a metre to her left, where a line of sky showed in a fissure between two boulders. She peered through. Ronald lay atop the tor, the rifle visible, the barrel on some kind of mini-tripod. The weapon would be difficult to aim without some sort of support, Savage thought, impossible to do so while the shooter was moving or standing on rough ground. She just had to wait because unless Ronald had a night-vision scope she'd be able to slip away come dark.

She took out her mobile. Eight o'clock. With the cloud dusk would fall in an hour or so. If Ronald moved she could make a run for the car, otherwise she'd stay put. She sighed, breathed out, tried to relax. Easy to say when a sniper was on a ridge a hundred and fifty metres away. She squinted through the crack again. Ronald was still there, but now he was waving at something or someone. Savage tried to follow his line of sight down the valley. There seemed to be nothing down there but bracken and sheep. And then she saw him. A man lumbering across the boulder field, hunched over, arms swinging, mouth set in a grimace. Even from a couple of hundred metres Savage could see the round face and the nose like a button mushroom.

Savage felt a wave of panic. It was the nutter from the farm. Mikey, Ronald had called him. Not right in the head. She looked again and saw the light glint off something in his right hand. A knife! She weighed her options. Run and risk getting shot by the one man. Wait and get gutted by the other one. Some choice.

She turned her back to the rock and scanned the landscape. Nothing but empty moor. To her right was another tor, higher than the one she was on. Could she find a mobile signal there? She peered through the crack again. Mikey was climbing her side of the valley, every now and then looking up, still with a demented grin on his face. A few more minutes and he'd be at the top and Savage would be forced to move anyway.

Mind made up, she jumped out from behind the rock and began to run at an angle down the valley. She was shortening the distance between herself and Mikey, but hopefully he'd not notice for a minute or two.

'Miiikeeey!' The shout from Ronnie echoed off the rocks. Mikey looked back over his shoulder. Ronald was on his feet, gesturing. Mikey turned, saw Savage and then let out a howl. He began to run again.

Savage cursed and went faster. Downhill, going fast wasn't a problem. Tripping over and twisting an ankle was. She bounced from boulder to boulder, slipping on a patch of scree, but regaining her balance. At the bottom of the valley was a small stream. She jumped the water, squelched across a patch of mossy bog and then was climbing to the next tor.

At any second she expected to hear another shot, but none came. Perhaps Ronald wasn't so stupid. Hitting a moving target with a long-range rifle was almost impossible. The climb sapped her energy and halfway up the tor she ducked behind a rock. Mikey was still coming, but for a moment she was protected from Ronald by several tonnes of granite. Savage looked farther away, back towards her car. With every step she was moving away from her means of escape. Then she saw something coming down the lane. Fallon's Range Rover. Thank God!

The vehicle slowed at the entrance to the car park and pulled in. Fallon got out of the Range Rover, paused next to Savage's car and then took something from his pocket.

Mikey was only a hundred metres away now, but Savage stood out from the rock and shouted at Fallon. She put her arms above her head and waved. Fallon turned, as if he'd heard her, and then he was slumping onto the bonnet of the MG, sliding down to the ground. A second later came the retort of the rifle.

That was why Ronald hadn't been shooting at her. He'd seen Fallon's car approaching and lined up his shot.

Mikey was just thirty metres away now. Savage could hear the grunts he was making as he sucked air in and out. She turned away and continued to climb to the next tor.

'Guuurrrlll!' came the cry from Mikey. 'You killed Peter!'

Strictly speaking, Savage thought, that wasn't true, but she didn't want to stop and argue the point. She reached the top of the tor and clambered round to one side, making sure to keep plenty of rock between herself and Ronald. She took out her phone again. Yes! Three bars on the signal indicator.

She touched the screen to bring up the number pad. Nothing. She tapped again. Still the phone didn't respond, the display frozen. She turned the phone over in her hand. The back plate had a long scourge down one side. It must have been damaged when she fell over.

'Fuck!' Savage said the word aloud and then stumbled away, wondering what lay to the north, other than miles of open moorland.

She almost tripped over the walker sitting in the lee of the tor. He'd spread a mat out to sit on and was eating the last of his sandwiches leaning against his rucksack.

'Hey?' The man pushed himself to his feet. He stared at Savage and then looked at her knee. 'Are you OK?'

'Police.' Savage fumbled in her coat and pulled out her warrant card. The man looked bemused. 'Have you got a phone?'

'What? I don't—' He stared past Savage, mouth dropping open.

'Guuurrrlll!' Mikey lumbered into view, the knife held forwards. 'You killed Peter!'

'Jesus!' The man was on his feet now and he grabbed his hiking pole and thrust it towards Mikey. 'Get away, you awful man, get away.'

The action was ineffectual and Mikey's free hand shot forwards and snatched the pole. For a second the walker held on and the two of them were engaged in a mad comedy tug of war. Then the pole buckled and snapped and the man was left holding a short piece of aluminium about twenty centimetres long.

'Come on!' Savage grabbed the man's arm to pull him away. 'Run!'

The man stared down at the useless piece of metal in his hand and then Mikey was lunging in at the man's neck with the knife. The man clutched at the weapon, hands shredding on the blade. Next he was falling backwards, Mikey on top of him, twisting the knife in at the man's throat, blood splashing out onto the ancient granite.

Savage stepped back and stumbled on the man's rucksack. Mikey was sitting astride the man now, sweeping the knife up and down, slicing through the poor guy's clothing. Swish, swish, swish. The knife moved in a definite rhythm, as if Mikey was repeating some sort of pattern. For a moment he seemed to have forgotten about Savage and was absorbed in his new task. Beneath him the man's chest was now a mess of ripped clothing and blood. Then Mikey stopped cutting and looked up.

'Arrrggghhh!' He leapt to his feet. 'You killed Peter!'

Savage turned and began to run away from the tor and into the depths of the moor where the light was disappearing fast, the mist and rain adding to the gloom. She came to a small grassy col and then descended to a stretch of terrain with nothing but tall bracken and rock. Behind her she could hear Mikey roaring in anger.

Savage ran on, following a little sheep track through the dense bracken, the fronds reaching to neck height. Then she was slipping over, grasping at the bracken stems as her feet fell away from under her, some sort of chasm opening up beneath. She stuck out a foot and braced on the edge of the hole, felt the bracken cut her hands, but hung on.

Black gaped beneath her feet, the darkness below absolute. A mineshaft.

She scrambled back up the side and rolled away, crawling into the undergrowth and lying still. From down the sheep path came the sound of voices. Mikey and Ronald. Savage groped around in the dead bracken and moss and uncovered a fist-sized lump of rock.

'Where gurl?' Mikey said, lumbering into view. 'She killed Peter.'

'I know, Mikey, I know. We'll get her, don't worry.' Ronald followed a few paces behind, the rifle slung over his shoulder. He stopped alongside Mikey at the hole. 'There, look. She's gone down the bloody mineshaft!'

Savage peeked from behind a frond. Ronald pointed down at the mess her feet had made at the edge of the hole.

'Haaalooo!' Ronald cupped his hands and shouted down, leaning over to peer into the dark.

'Guuurrrlll!' Mikey roared.

'Careful, Mikey. Not too close. You know how dangerous mines can be.'

'Gurl down there?' Mikey said.

'I wonder . . .' Ronald turned half away from the shaft, his eyes scanning the bracken.

Savage leapt up and at the same time threw the rock. It arced through the air and struck Ronald on the cheek. He thrust an arm up and flailed, knocking Mikey. The giant staggered for a moment and then lost his footing, slipping over the edge of the hole and sliding from view.

'You bitch!' Ronald turned, unhitched the rifle from his shoulder. 'You're going to pay for that!'

'Ronnie!' A hand scrabbled at the top of the hole, fingers clawing at the loose rock and earth. 'Help me!'

Ronald turned back, for a moment unsure. Then he was kneeling, lowering the rifle so Mikey could grab hold of it. Mikey's fingers grasped the barrel and Ronald pulled back, both hands on the stock, straining with the weight, all his will concentrated on the task in hand.

Savage crept forward just as Mikey's head popped over the edge, black eyes meeting Savage's.

'Behind you!' Mikey screamed. 'Guuurrrlll!'

Ronald began to turn and as he did so he lost his balance, the weight of Mikey pulling him over. He toppled sideways and down, Mikey slipping away too, the sound of the pair of them crashing into the side of the shaft some way down. Then silence for a moment, before a thud and a long, low wail of a roar from Mikey. Nothing from Ronald, but the shouting from Mikey going on and on, his voice echoing into the still Dartmoor air.

'Guuurrrlll! You killed Peter! You killed Ronnie! You killed my brothers!'

Savage backed away from the hole, heart beating. She was aware in the now near-dark of torchlight sweeping back and forth, people shouting, figures approaching. Emerging from the gloom came a tall, handsome man, his voice floating out, the Scottish accent one of the most beautiful sounds she'd ever heard.

'DI Charlotte Savage,' Callum Campbell said, pointing down at her flats as he approached. 'What have I told you lot about wearing proper footwear?'

Epilogue

Two weeks later

Riley's call had come on a Sunday morning, cryptic, but when he'd mentioned Kenny Fallon she'd known what it was all about. Now she waited for Riley by the ruined building at the top of Burgh Island. There were tourists everywhere on the little lump of green, hundreds of them, but their presence didn't detract from the panoramic view. To seaward a blue-green canvas dotted with white sails; in the other direction the stretch of sand separating the island from the coast; beyond the sand Bigbury-on-Sea, the car park there rammed with cars, the beaches packed.

Savage turned back to the sea and the yachts. A few weeks ago she and Pete had been out there, gliding east towards Salcombe with the wind and tide in their favour. Many tides had come and gone since then, Savage thought. Much water.

Radial was drawing to a conclusion, just a stack of paperwork to finish now, the remaining loose ends all wrapped up.

Devlyn Corran, the team surmised, had met Ronald Wilson up at Full Sutton prison and when he transferred to Devon he'd encountered Peter Wilson over at HMP Channings Wood. Wilson was a common surname – which was the reason the twins were given it as part of their new identity – but of course Peter and Ronald were identical twins. True, Ronald wore a full beard, his hair loose and unkempt whereas Peter had short hair and was clean-shaven. Nevertheless, Corran would have been alerted by the name to underlying similarities in the two men's appearances and guessed that they were related. He must have wondered why Peter Wilson made no mention of his brother. Corran had probably trailed Peter to the clay pits and discovered Ronald was living there. The team believed that at first Corran might not have known the brothers were the Candle Cake Killers – the blackmail was simply about Corran threatening to reveal Ronald, a serial rapist, as Wilson's brother: *I know who you are*. Maybe later, when Corran did some detective work of his own, he'd got an inkling of who he was dealing with.

Mikey, the man with learning difficulties – or as Savage had labelled him 'the nutter' – was now in a secure mental hospital where the doctors said he was claiming to be the twins' younger brother. A DNA test disproved that, but who he was or where he came from was a mystery. As far as anyone could tell the man had been living rough on the streets of Plymouth and the twins had taken him in and cared for him. As an act of compassion it was a strange twist which didn't fit with the brothers' cruelty and callousness towards their victims.

'Charlotte?'

Savage turned to see Riley standing a couple of paces behind her, his breathing quickened by the walk to the top of the island. Riley gestured away from the building and the throng of tourists and they strolled off the path and towards the cliffs. There was no fence, just a sheer drop, dozens of metres, the sea crashing into rocks below, white foam surging back and forth.

'Why here, Darius?' Savage said. 'Bit off the beaten track for you, isn't it?'

'Julie, ma'am. Wanted a trip out. I came here with Patrick the other week and thought the Pilchard Inn would be a nice spot for a bite to eat. She's down there now, nursing a beer. I told her I'd be fifteen minutes, no more.'

'I see.' Savage noted the way Riley had first used 'Charlotte' and then 'ma'am'; felt a tinge of regret he wasn't alone. 'Well?'

Riley nodded and took something from his pocket. He stared at the piece of folded paper sitting between his thumb and forefinger, the edges fluttering in the breeze. Savage felt her heart rate rise. If Riley opened his fingers the paper would be blown away, carried on the wind over the cliffs and out to sea.

'Down to me, ma'am,' he said. 'Kenny Fallon being incapacitated.'

Fallon was still in hospital. He'd taken the bullet from Ronald in the shoulder. Painful, but he'd been able to use his mobile to summon help. Fallon had called her from his bed a few days after it was all over. He'd suggested she speak to Riley.

Time and help, Fallon had told her. Now Savage knew what he meant by the help at least.

'You didn't have to, Darius. Help me, I mean.'

'I know, ma'am. Fallon was going to give you the registration number of the Impreza up on the moor, you to do the work from there. In the end I looked it up myself. Thought I might as well finish the job. The car's changed owners a couple of times since of course, but the name you need is on here. As for helping . . . Well it seemed the right thing to do.'

'Yes. Thank you.' Savage paused. The right thing to do. 'Give it to me, Darius.'

'Is that an order, ma'am?'

'No. Off-duty. It's a request from one friend to another.'

'Thing is, ma'am, I don't know if you want to know. I can't see the information helping much.' Riley closed his hand around the paper. 'Could be torture.'

'Torture is what I've been feeling for the past four years. My little girl taken from me. Someone out there, guilty, but enjoying their life scot-free. Absolved of having to face up to their responsibilities, while my family suffers.'

'But you can't just take the law into your own hands.'

'That's for me to decide.' Savage moved closer to Riley. Lowered her voice. 'Look, your Julie. Are you telling me if somebody hurt her you'd trust the system to get her justice? Come on, Darius. We see it every week. Lives ruined on the one side and some scrote getting off with a laughable sentence on the other. No way you'd stand by on the sidelines.'

'No, you're right, ma'am,' Riley said, eyes narrowing. 'I'd want to avenge whatever wrong had been done.'

'So what's the problem? Just give me the name.'

'But I'm part of this now, aren't I? I tracked down the guy. The name didn't come to me by accident.'

'You should've thought of that before you got involved.' Savage shrugged. 'But by all means refuse to give me the name if that's the way you feel. Now I know it can be done I'll work out who the person is for myself. I'll ask Fallon.'

'Like I said, Fallon doesn't know. Doesn't *want* to know either.'

'Fine. Report the matter in the usual way if you feel obliged to. Whatever happens, I'm going to get justice for Clarissa.'

Riley sighed. Looked down at his fist. Then he passed the scrap of paper across.

Savage took the paper and held it for a moment. Could see her hand shaking. Was Riley correct? Did she really want to know?

405

Yes, of course she did.

She walked away from Riley, putting a few paces between them, and then turned her back. She unfolded the paper and read the scrawl of biro.

Owen

The name meant nothing to her. She half turned towards Riley and gave him a stare. Opened her mouth to speak but, still puzzled by the name, said nothing.

'Told you, ma'am,' Riley said. 'Better not to have known.'

'I don't understand,' Savage said. 'Is Owen a first name or surname? I don't know anyone called that.'

'No?' Riley walked over to Savage and took the piece of paper from her hand. He held the paper up in the air and released it. For a second the paper hung there before being taken by the up-draught. It spiralled into the air and was then sucked out seaward, disappearing against the bright sky.

'No. I don't get it. Tell me what on earth's going on.'

'Owen is the lad's first name,' Riley said. 'You might not know him directly but you sure as hell know his dad.'

'Darius, please don't mess me around.' Savage shook her head, feeling angry with Riley for playing silly games, angry with herself for getting worked up too. 'Just tell me who he bloody well is.'

'Full name of Owen Fox,' Riley said, placing a hand on Savage's arm, 'and his dad is Simon Fox, the Chief Constable.'

Read more in the DI Charlotte Savage series . . .

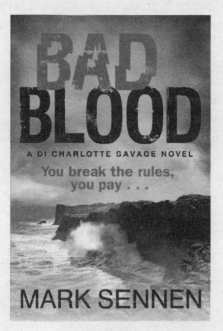

DI Charlotte Savage is back, chasing a killer with a very personal grudge.

BAD BLOOD is available now in all good book shops.